RESISTING MR. KANE

The London Mister Series (#2)

Rosa Lucas

AUTHOR NOTE

The following story contains mature themes, strong language and explicit scenes, and is intended for mature readers.

Content warning: there is a scene that involves hospitalisation.

The vocabulary, grammar, and spelling of Resisting Mr. Kane is written in British English.

1

Elly

"What's he saying?" Megan whispers as our five-foot Greek boss berates us in half English, half Greek. "Is he going to fire us, or what?"

I listen intently. I'm not fluent but I know enough to hold a decent conversation.

"θα σου χέσω το γάιδαρο!"

"The literal translation is '*I will shit your donkey*,'" I explain through gritted teeth. "Greek people say it when they're pissed." That's the thing about Greek and English: never use a translator app on an angry Greek person. Their classic one-liners are ripe for confusion.

"You two are big headache." He spits on me a little when he's talking, and I take it. Dimitris has *connections*. I don't mean mafia; I mean he owns all the businesses on the island paying backpackers cash in hand. We can't piss him off.

Megan and I are spending the summer on a working holiday in idyllic Mykonos, aka the number one party island in the Greek islands. We were convinced that we'd make hundreds in tips.

The reality is that everyone wants a piece of paradise, and the island is saturated with swarms of hardened backpackers from Australia and New Zealand, and those guys know how to hustle. *Never* try to compete with an Aussie backpacker. Most of them have been globetrotting since they were in the womb. They have acquaintances in every coffee shop, hostel and bar on the island, allowing them to nab the lucrative gigs, leaving us sunburnt British backpackers with scraps.

The only option we had was working for Dimitris, earning a measly two euros' commission per boat ticket sold. Today we haven't drummed up enough to buy a bag of potatoes.

"So, you wanna clean the shit pipes of the yachts instead?" he yells, gesticulating wildly. I assume his question is rhetorical. "You break my heart. Watch!"

Dimitris snatches the placard from me. My role is to hold the placard and lure tourists onto the mediocre, overpriced boat trip. I've mastered the holding part but flunk at anything beyond that. He aggressively launches himself on the many groups of people strolling the boardwalk of the Mediterranean Sea.

Then he spots them.

The perfect prey.

They are in their fifties, maybe sixties, the innocent-looking couple dragging wheeled luggage walking straight into his trap. They don't stand a chance.

He waves the placard at them like a weapon. Then comes the hard sell. Caves? No problem. Nudist beaches? No problem. Lost cities found under the sea? No problem. It's a cross between a wildlife extravaganza and a luxury cruise line.

They are swept along the gangway, protesting in vain, with Dimitris stalking after them. He flings their luggage onto the boat, sealing their fate.

"They actually looked like they were on their way to the airport." I grimace as the man looks back at us. "I can't do that. No chance."

"I guess that's our sales careers over."

We don't know what the plan is for the next few decades. I've just finished a Law and Criminology degree at Swansea University in Wales and Megan is a stylist in a salon. If I've done enough to earn first-class honours, I'll apply for a trainee contract at one of London's elite law firms. Results are out in twelve days. Eek.

For now, we are taking it one boat sale at a time.

"This job tonight, it's not solely commission-based, right?" I eye Megan suspiciously. She's apparently landed us *the* backpackers' dream job from a guy she met on the beach. "An upmarket cocktail bar, you say?"

"Uh-huh." She smiles unconvincingly. "*Very* exclusive."

"I've never made cocktails before."

"Don't worry, you'll pick it up. You just need to learn on the job and smile at the customers."

"If someone else tells me to fucking smile, I'm

going to smack them." I wave a brochure feebly at a family who ignores me. "What should I wear? I've nothing suitable for working at a high-end cocktail bar."

Megan steps in the path of a couple, forcing them to break their hand-holding. Tutting, they flow around her. "Don't worry, we get uniforms. Oh my God!" She punches me. "That couple is coming over."

We shift into position, holding up a display of brochures.

"It's your turn," she points out.

"Fine," I mutter, launching into a lacklustre sales pitch to the couple. I'm a few unsold boat tickets away from getting us fired. I couldn't sell whiskey to an alcoholic.

***

Megan is eating her words five hours later.

"Bounce?" I stare at the neon sign above the bar. "Are you sure *this* is the place?"

In front, two guys lie on the pavement. One is heaving beside a discarded kebab and his friend is attempting to light the wrong end of a cigarette. It's only 7:30, for Christ's sake.

"It's probably much better on the inside." Megan laughs but looks less sure of herself.

I observe the outside clientele engaged in drunken mating rituals and can guarantee that it's not. There's not a local in sight. I've passed loads of elegant up-market bars on the island, and this is most certainly not one of them.

"Nice tits, love!" the guy smoking shouts at Megan, and she shows him the middle finger.

"No way. I'd prefer to spend my night sitting in a public toilet." I turn on my heel, but she catches my arm.

"Ah, come on! The guy said we'd be raking in the cash," she coaxes me. "We can work one night and if we don't like it, we never come back."

"That's what they all say." I groan. "Dimitris practically sold it to us that we would be millionaires."

She uses the pouty expression she knows works on me. "Let's just see what it's like on the inside."

Begrudgingly, I trail after her as she approaches the bouncer.

"Yiasoo." She beams, and he doesn't return the smile. "I was told to ask for Jonas."

Grunting, he nods toward the door. "Inside. Left hand corner."

We squeeze into the neon-lit bar, where dozens of inebriated teenage lads compete for the prize of biggest wanker on the island.

"Not a chance," I hiss, but she can't hear me over the banging house music.

We weave through the drunken crowd to the other side of the bar.

A Greek guy wearing a white top with a deep V exposing most of his chest beckons us over. He must be Jonas. "Are you the girls Nikos sent?"

"Yiasoo." It's the only word Megan knows. "I'm

Megan, and this is Elly."

He grunts and sizes up our assets. "Tonight's a trial. You do okay, you have the job." He nods towards a door. "Go in there to get changed. Uniforms are hanging up. Come back, and I'll explain the rules."

I do a double take as I clock the bartenders' dress code. "I think there's been a mistake," I explain firmly to him. "I am *not* wearing a bikini." This guy is on another planet if he thinks he can get me into those red shorts and yellow bikini top. Hell will freeze over sooner.

A well-endowed female bartender walks past us. She gets in the path of the strobe lights and I see the full outline of her nipples through her bikini. I haven't even been this exposed at the beach.

Jonas laughs in my face. "You want to work here then you wear the bikini, lady. No negotiation."

"I don't have a price for wearing a bikini," I retort indignantly. The nerve of this guy. "No, thank you."

He laughs again. "Everyone has a price, lady. Up to you, I don't have all night. Trial. Two hours. If you want to earn 150 euros a night, then hurry up and get changed."

Say what? How much? We've been earning twenty euros a day *max* at the boat tour stall.

Maybe I do have a price. If we work here for a week, we have enough to go island hopping. How bad can it be? I eye him suspiciously. "What do you have to do for 150 euros?"

He smirks at how quickly I abandon my morals.

"Serve the drinks, talk to the punters. You've worked in a bar before, yes?"

Last summer I worked in the village local, The Wee Donkey. The closest I got to making cocktails was a Jack and Coke. Does that count?

Behind the bar, a bartender slams down eight shot glasses at lightning speed. He fires two bottles in the air then simultaneously pours all eight shots and sets them on fire.

I'm not sure the skills I gained at The Wee Donkey are transferable.

"You know how to smile, sweetheart?"

I bare my teeth, curling my lips upwards. 'Smile for salary' is the name of the game here.

He looks us up and down. "You." He points to Megan, asset number one. "You start behind the bar."

"You," he mutters something that sounds suspiciously like lips and legs under his breath in Greek. "Let's try you out front, pulling in the crowd."

He wants to put *me* outside to pull in the crowd? Megan should be showcased outside first. Flirting is her forte. I've watched her hone her skills for a decade and she is top of her game. She's the dick whisperer.

"What does that entail?" I ask. "Do I have a promotion sign or something?"

"Yes." He points between my breasts. "These are your promotion signs. Do whatever it takes to get them into the bar. Then it's up to the bar staff to keep them here. Be back here in five minutes changed otherwise stop wasting my time. The trial has started so you're losing money by the minute."

***

"It's humiliating, Megan," I wail.

We're standing in front of a half-length mirror. Unfortunately, I can't see my bottom half, but I can feel a draft around my bum where a half-moon has formed in my Lycra shorts. I pull the shorts down for a fuller coverage but give myself a plumber's crack at the top. It's a trade-off. "Nudists wear more clothing than this."

Megan turns to me, looking like a whore. They didn't have any red shorts left in her size so her slight muffin top hangs over the Lycra, two sizes too small. "No one's wearing any clothes here—we fit in. Stop being a granny."

Side by side, no one would mistake us for sisters. I'm all gangly legs and arms, more akin to an ostrich than a Victoria's Secret model, whereas Megan is short with sexy curves and fiery red hair. With my dark hair and high cheekbones inherited from my Croatian mother, I'm sometimes mistaken on the island as a native.

The bikini bra covers more of my modesty than Megan's. I'm a decent B cup but next to Megan I look flat-chested. A bloke once had the audacity to compare me to two Tic Tacs on an ironing board, and that was with my clothes *on*.

"Ready?" Megan asks in the mirror.

"As ready as I'll ever be."

She takes my hand and forces me out of the changing room.

While walking back to Jonas, I notice that attention to us has multiplied by a billion percent since the outfit change. No one looks above the neck. Now I'm just a headless body with bright yellow tits.

Jonas nods his approval, gives us instructions, then hands me a tray of green shots. Together with my breasts, the shots are bait.

"See you later," I whisper to Megan, feeling needy. "Good luck."

She squeezes my hand and I head out to brave it on the street.

Up and down the pedestrianized street, hustlers just like me compete to lure drunk tourists into bars. It's the red-light district for bar hustlers. An Oscar-winning performance is needed here.

My bait tray narrowly escapes being tossed by two brawling boys. "Watch it, dipshits," I hiss at them as one knocks into me.

Beside me there's a deep grunt; I turn in horror to see I've spilled sticky alcohol all over a guy's T-shirt. He's tall and broad-shouldered, wearing a white T-shirt that moulds nicely over muscle in all the right areas. In fact, I can see the definition *through* the T-shirt. To my dismay his thick chest is now splattered in neon green. The baseball cap hides his face. I can't help but wonder what he would feel like on top of me as he attempts to remove the mess I've caused.

"I'm so sorry, sir!"

My eyes travel up from his chest to see piercing

blue-grey eyes fixated on me. Annoyed.

Oh. Wow. My breath catches in my throat.

So, *this* is what drop-dead gorgeous looks like. He's older than me, maybe late thirties, forty max. Broad but with a natural bulky physique, not a gym bunny. But it's his face that winds me—an angular jaw, strong Roman nose, high cheekbones, heavyset chin. Not to mention the most beautiful dark eyebrows framing his striking eyes.

Fuck me.

A modern day Adonis. Thank you, Greek gods.

"I really am sorry," I stammer, taken completely aback.

"Forget it." He speaks in a deep baritone that is laced with frustration. Like *really* deep. One hundred per cent sexy British gravel. It's an English accent, but I can't pick up on the region.

Jonas watches us from the door. "The trial's over if you don't get someone in the bar within ten minutes," he shouts in Greek at me.

Laughing hysterically like Jonas just cracked a joke, I turn back to the hot grump who is observing me like I'm contagious. "Please don't complain to him that I spilled a drink over you, it's my first night working here," I babble, being my own cock block. "My friend and I are on trial and we really need this job."

"It's fine, excuse me," he says dryly as he sidesteps me.

I silently curse myself for bumping into the most handsome man I have ever seen in my life in such a humiliating situation. "Wait!" I grab his forearm to stop him from escaping. It's warm, slightly hairy and solid with muscle. A pair of forearms that could lift you up and throw you over a shoulder with little effort. "Don't go. Come into the bar," I plead.

With a tight grip on Adonis's arm, I shout in Greek to Jonas, "It's fine. You don't need to watch me. This guy is coming in to buy loads of drinks."

Adonis regards me, bemused. "What did you say to him?"

I blurt out a milder version of the truth. "I said you expressed an interest in coming inside."

"I haven't," he grates, prising my hand from his muscular forearm.

Mission not accomplished.

I hit him with my best sales smile. "It's the most exclusive bar in town! *Amazing* cocktails. Very friendly atmosphere."

He looks at the two guys who are 'ladding it up' beside us, then back at me, raising one of his beautiful thick brows. "Sorry, I'm not in the mood," he replies gruffly, moving away.

Jonas is still watching, with a gleam in his eye that tells me I'm close to getting the chop. Desperate, I step forward to block Adonis, pushing against a wall of hard muscle.

"Please, please, please?" I beg, in a last attempt since I'm one Adonis away from being fired. "Could you please walk into the bar? You can just leave after two minutes . . . If I get people over the line, I've done my job. Maybe you need to use the loo? You could go here!"

He stares at me, unimpressed. "You're begging me to come into this bar?" His voice is deep and icy and makes me feel like I'm being told off. I like it.

I shrug. I'm wearing a bikini in the middle of a street full of bar hustlers. What did he expect?

The buzz of his phone in his pocket diverts his attention downwards.

Damn.

A gang of young blokes stagger up the street. *This* is the clientele I should be targeting, not older self-assured, devastatingly handsome guys who have a million better alternatives.

"I don't understand," Adonis shouts into the phone, his face creasing into a frown. "Speak slower."

Ooh, he sounds angry. That voice is giving me a serious dose of the horn.

Adonis stands a few metres away from me and repeats himself on the phone. Speaking louder and slower, he repeats the same words but in different ways. He appears to be throwing out random Greek words in the hope that something will stick. Some of the words seem made up or . . . French? Yes, that's definitely French.

As a result, the guy on the other end raises his voice as well, becoming more animated until the conversation is just a futile exchange of noise.

It gives me the chance to subtly ogle him. I wonder if he's military or Marines. A fitness instructor maybe? His watch suggests he's rich. The only reason I know it's a Cartier is because Dimitris is selling knock-offs next to his boat stall. I assume Adonis's watch is the real deal rather than a Dimitris sale special.

I see my opportunity and step forward into his space. "Do you need someone to translate?"

His nostrils flare. "No." Then he pauses and observes me warily. "Are you fluent in Greek?"

"Amongst other languages," I reply, deadpan. I know he's judging me based on my yellow bikini and red shorts ensemble. Hell, I would too. I smile sweetly back at him, thinking *fuck you* in four different languages.

I watch his mind ticking over.

Those eyes. The law should force him to wear dark glasses so womankind can continue functioning.

"Okay." He gives a curt nod. "Thank you, that's very kind." Adonis puts the phone on speaker, and I hear someone on the other end babbling in Greek.

"Excuse me, sir," I cut in, in Greek. "One moment."

I put the phone on mute and look at him expectantly. "Does your boat need fixing?"

A ghost of a smile flickers on his perfect lips. "I'm impressed."

I shrug. "What do you need me to ask him?"

"Tell him he needs to send someone asap to look at the cooling system. The engine is overheating, and I need to sail back to Athens tomorrow."

I translate to the guy on the phone, then listen. "He says he can't get someone out until Wednesday afternoon."

Two days from now.

Adonis curses under his breath. "Tell him I'll pay him whatever it takes."

I inform the guy that Adonis has an open chequebook. A sharp intake of air can be heard through the phone.

My brows crease as I listen intently. I'm not used to technical boating terms in English, never mind Greek. "He needs a part to come from Athens. I don't know what the name of the part is in English. I can only repeat it in Greek."

"Seriously?" Adonis rakes a hand through his dark, slightly wavy hair. "Tell him he needs to expedite it, or I'll use another company." Every word comes out in a gruff authoritative tone. Maybe he is military.

I feel like I'm being told off just as much as the boat guy. I wonder how long I can string out this phone call.

"He'll try," I translate as the man on the receiving end becomes panicked.

Adonis mutters something unintelligible under his breath and takes the phone. He disconnects the call before I can say goodbye. So, the guy doesn't do goodbyes. I make a mental note to research personality disorders with that trait.

"Thank you." For a moment his eyes hang on me. "I wasn't expecting a Welsh accent. Are you part Greek?"

I shake my head, ecstatic for the conversation opener. "Nope. My mum's Croatian but she spent quite a bit of time in Greece when she was younger. I learned Croatian and Greek from her. I don't really have anyone to speak Greek to in Wales so I'm not fluent. This trip has really improved it though."

His eyebrows jump up. "Three languages, impressive."

"Four." I smile innocently. "We learn Welsh in school. I helped you. Now will you help me in return?"

I watch him stare at the neon sign, grimace, then turn back to me. "I'd prefer to stick forks in my eyes."

I nod, shuffling away from him. I gave it my all.

"But I'm a gentleman and it would be rude of me not to help a lady who's done me a favour." He exhales in defeat as I whip my head around, shocked. "One drink. Just because you helped. I'm assuming it doesn't serve my brand of Scotch."

"Doubtful." I beam, bouncing back to him. "But for £1.50 a shot, you can get so drunk you forget how rubbish the place is."

Like the Aphrodite that's got the Adonis, I beckon him to follow me.

"Fuck me," he says as I lead him into the bar, our eyes adjusting to the intense strobe lights. *Don't mind if I do.* "It's actually worse on the inside than I imagined. This place is going to give me a headache."

He's not wrong. I was just in it forty minutes ago, and it's even worse than I remember.

When I turn to head back out, he stops on the spot, frowning. "Are you staying outside?"

"For the next fifteen minutes." I smile. "Then we

rotate. Have fun."

With me, I plead silently.

2

Elly

I count down the minutes until it's my turn inside. I've been watching the door like a hawk for thirteen minutes to make sure Adonis hasn't escaped. I'm not sure what I'm expecting to happen, but I don't want this guy to disappear just yet.

"Rotation time." Megan comes up behind me with a fresh tray of shots. "How did you do?"

"Terrible." I grimace. "Let's just say I'm not the Pied Piper of bar crawlers."

Mischief dances in her eyes. "That stallion you managed to pull in is sitting at the bar scowling like we've given him a jail sentence."

I grin. "But he's still here, though."

"Every ovary in the bar is quivering." She grins back. "I never thought I'd see the day. A triple whammy. Body, face, voice."

"Oh, were you talking to him?" I huff. Which is ridiculous because I've got no claim over him.

"I asked him what he would like to drink. He told me he wanted a beer and whiskey chaser and I swear

I felt it in my gut."

I roll my eyes but I know *exactly* what she's talking about.

As I enter, I see him propped against the bar, sipping a beer and looking at his phone. Megan wasn't wrong. Around him, women perform human mating strategies, such as standing unnecessarily close to him, accidentally bumping into him while dancing, laughing and talking loudly beside him to attract his attention.

His rigid posture tells me he's not impressed with the venue. I laugh to myself; he really does stick out like a sore thumb here.

I resist the urge to approach him directly. Priorities first. I need to secure this job.

"It's my turn to rotate," I shout to the guy yelling orders behind the bar.

"Hurry up," he barks, snapping his fingers.

I scurry under the counter behind the bar, where the guy in charge is flanked by three others, all backpackers by the looks of things. "This is your scanner. Each drink has a barcode above the optic, see? Swipe the barcode, then open the till and swipe it here. Soft drinks added are a flat one euro. Keep to the left section of the bar."

That sounds easy-ish.

I scan a sea of impatient raucous faces shouting orders. I don't know where to start.

The intense blue eyes at the end of the bar are the ones that draw me. He shakes his head, grimacing. I smile back, flustered, mouthing "I'm sorry."

I take the order from the guy who shouted the loudest, asking for ten shots of tequila. He's the same guy that was sick outside. Flustered, I search the spirits, looking for tequila. Another bartender whizzes by carrying five drinks like she has octopus limbs. How are they working at the speed of light? Oh God, this really is an art form.

"Get a move on, love," the tequila guy yells, leaning across the bar. He is part of a group of lads banging their hands on the bar like drums.

Fumbling, I move bottles out of the way until I find tequila. My elbow knocks a shot glass to the ground. I'm *so* not cut out for this. I clumsily pour the tequila, spilling more on the bar than in the shot glasses.

Meanwhile, the group of lads discuss my breasts like I have no eyes or ears. Yet somehow I feel ten times more naked when I lock eyes with the hot grump at the corner of the bar. Tequila guy grunts, hands me the cash, and takes the tray of shots.

I look over to see Adonis studying his phone, bored. Shit, he looks ready to escape.

My face heats as I walk towards him. "How's the drink?"

"Like piss." He exhales heavily. "I thought a beer would be a safe choice. Nope."

A giggle accidentally escapes me. *Act cool, woman!* "Thanks for braving it. What's your name?"

"Tristan," he says after a beat.

I glance at his ring finger. No ring and no tan line either. Girlfriend perhaps? How could a guy like him not be attached?

"And yours?" he returns in his gravelly voice.

"Elena."

His expression softens. "Nice name. It suits you."

"Thank you." I blush. "Would you like another drink?" Of course, he doesn't.

He stiffens, drumming a beermat on the bar. "I was just about to leave."

"I don't blame you." I smile to hide my disappointment.

A long moment passes as he stares at me with those arresting ice-blue eyes, his lips pressing together in a slight grimace. "Oh, fuck it," he says, his voice gruff. "Give me a beer and chaser."

"Coming right up!" I respond, suppressing the urge to whoop. "Bad day?"

"Something like that."

I grasp the top of the pump and pull down. The beer flows out in spurts, vomiting from the nozzle. That's not right. His eyes widen in dismay as I pump harder and more frantically.

He sucks in a breath.

"Uh . . . it's not the best delivery." I inspect the thick layer of foam on top of the beer and flinch. "I can start again if you like." I resist the urge to tell him that this is not a reflection on how well my hands can do other activities.

His eyes crinkle slightly at the corners. "Don't bother. I'm not sure the next one would be any better. No offence."

"That's true." I let out a nervous laugh and hand

over the beer that looks more like a cappuccino. "I've been on the island for three weeks with my friend Megan, and I've already gone through three jobs. I'm not cut out for hospitality. I worked in a bookshop back home."

"A bookshop?" He smiles slightly. "I would never have guessed." His gaze travels down my body, lingering on my breasts, then back up again. "Sorry. Your outfit is . . . distracting."

I roll my eyes. "I think that's the intention."

"Maybe I need to visit more bookshops."

Was that . . . an expression of interest? Speaking of books, he's hard to read.

"I don't want to work in a bookstore forever though. It was just to get me through university," I explain, leaning in close to hear him.

His eyes flicker with a hint of interest. "What are you studying?"

"I've just finished. Law with Criminology. Waiting on results now and then graduation."

"Huh." His forearm brushes mine as he lifts the whiskey chaser. It was only a slight touch but it made my breath trip. "I guess you shouldn't judge a book by its cover. You're a multilingual law student who works in a bookshop but masquerades as a provocative bartender at night."

I've never heard a sexier way to describe myself. "Only in Greece, where I have the luxury of anonymity. It's either this or kidnap tourists onto boats."

"Ah yes, anonymity." He takes a sip of the beer

and fails to hide a grimace. “So why did you choose law for your degree?”

He actually looks interested in my answer.

“When I was younger, I witnessed a hit-and-run. I ended up going to court to testify and it was the most thrilling ten days of my life. After that, I always wanted to be a criminal lawyer and work on exciting court cases, but I guess that's what everyone says.” I laugh, feeling like I’m a babbling idiot. “I’m not gonna deny the prestige and money sounds nice too. Stupid reasons.”

He scans my face as if trying to figure something out.

“It’s so hard to know what degree to pick,” I continue babbling. “I mean, how can you tell what you want to do for the next few decades or whether you’ll be any good at it if you haven’t done it before? But I enjoyed the law degree for the most part. Right now, I’d do anything just to get a foot in the door at one of the top law firms.”

Still, he gives me a funny look. “What do you do, Tristan?” I ask, ignoring the angry drinkers desperate for attention.

“I own a few businesses and invest in property,” he says after a beat. “You can pour me another or you’ll get in trouble for talking to me too long.”

“Oh.” I have no idea what questions to ask a property investor. Ungracefully I lift the bottle down off the shelf. “What type of property?”

“Hotels and apartment blocks mostly,” he replies, a hint of weariness in his voice that makes me wonder if he's worried about me being a gold-digger.

"Where do you live?" I probe.

His eyes drop to my chest and a muscle in his jaw jumps. When he meets my gaze, it's less apologetic this time. My stomach tightens.

"London."

His voice makes me want to have sex. It's a good thing he's not a newsreader. "Do people say you have a really nice voice? It's so posh. Are you from London?"

"Thanks, I'll take that as a compliment." His eyes crinkle with the hint of a smile. "I'm from the Midlands originally but my parents are Irish so I had a mix of accents growing up. Apparently, I've lost any identifiable regional dialect. It's not deliberate."

I grin. "How very British."

He reaches for the Scotch as I hand it to him, brushing his fingers against mine. "It's got nothing on your beautiful Welsh lilt. It's very endearing. My name sounds good when you say it."

Fuck.

"I'm hoping to live in London soon," I explain with a dry mouth. "It's just so damn expensive. Megan and I are going to look for a house-share. That's Megan over there." I point to her for no reason.

He nods like a man who hasn't understood what expensive means for years and hands me over twenty euros without asking how much the drinks cost. "What are you, twenty-three? You have your whole life to make money."

"Twenty-four. Nearly twenty-five," I add quickly. "I worked for a few years before starting uni. Why are you in Mykonos, *Tristan*?"

"I've been asking myself that since I arrived," he replies darkly.

I frown but don't probe anymore. The guy is a closed book.

Someone heckles me further down the bar. "I better serve the other customers."

I move about the bar serving customers. Every now and then, I glance over at Tristan. Most of the time he is reading something on his phone, scowling. But sometimes, his gaze is fixed firmly on me. I never took myself for an exhibitionist, but there's something highly sexual about Tristan watching me in little more than underwear. Like a private show I'm doing just for him. It's distracting, which isn't good when you're as bad a bartender as I am.

Megan comes up behind me as I'm pouring shots of sambuca. "Are you going to have sex with him?"

"Shush, Megan!" I hiss at her and look over to see if he heard. If he has, he pretends not to. "Of course not. Talk about going from A straight to Z."

"Why, *of course not*? He's hot. No-strings-attached sex. You need to loosen up. You've had one dick in three years and before that it was limp pickings."

Barely even that, I think to myself. "I can't have sex with some random guy just because he's hot. Besides, think about logistics. I can hardly take him back to our cockroach-infested studio, can I?"

She purses her lips. "The beach then. Loads of people do it on the beach."

I laugh loudly. "No, Megan."

She grabs my shoulders and gives me a little shake. "Elly! This is what this summer is about. We have years to be reserved and boring. Take your chance."

I open my mouth and close it.

"Come on," I say in a lowered voice as I set the sambuca on the bar. "The guy must have women falling at his feet. Look at him. He's just being polite because I helped him."

She rolls her eyes dramatically. "Oh please, you don't believe that for a second. Everyone is looking at him and he's looking at *you*. If you don't make a move, don't complain to me for the rest of the trip. There's a gorgeous man, by far the hottest bloke in this bar, no scrap that, the hottest bloke on the *Greek islands* who is expressing an interest in you and the best you can do is give him doe eyes?"

I bite my lip suppressing a smile. I should be used to Megan's no-nonsense attitude to men by now. She's right. Would it really be so bad to enjoy myself tonight? To just offer myself up to a gorgeous stranger for no-strings-attached sex? I've never actually had a one-night stand before. Not because I'm averse to them, I just haven't met anyone I wanted so badly that I needed to rip their clothes off within twenty-four hours.

My last relationship was a three-year thing with John, a guy I met at university. Sex with John was rigid and a bit tense. He seemed to have learned sex from a rulebook, then would mix it up between chapters. His signature move, where he spread my legs, dived his head in and performed something akin to a motorboat on my vagina, was more ticklish than sensual.

It took me a long time to realise we had floated into the friend zone and I'd stayed with him way longer than either of us deserved.

So, I wholeheartedly agreed with Megan that I had to make up for lost time. I just wasn't sure if I had the guts. In my head, I'm a siren with a love life worthy of a porn channel. However, the reality is that I had a love life as limp as a dick in a fridge.

The bar gets busy, and I spend the next hour serving shots so I don't have time to debate my intentions with Tristan. Every so often, I gravitate back to him. Shockingly he doesn't leave. I even manage to pull a few more laughs from him. Whatever has happened to Tristan, it's been a bad day.

At midnight, the crowd empties out to go to the local nightclub. Jonas puts me on floor-mopping duty as punishment for pouring more alcohol on the floor than in the glasses. I'm just about hanging on to the job.

My eyes flit from the floor to Tristan as I mop up the spillage. He puts his phone and wallet in his pocket ready to leave. Do something, fool! Talk to him. *Give him your number*.

Then he looks up, catches my gaze, and smiles.

I rush over like an eager beaver.

"I gotta go. It was nice to meet you, Elena."

I telepathically beg him to ask me out. "You, too, Tristan. I'm sorry your day was so bad."

"It brightened up at the end."

Ask me out, ask me out, ask me out.

He opens his mouth, then closes it and raps his fingers on the bar where a napkin with cash is peeking out. "Don't forget your tip."

Before I can thank him, he turns and walks out of the bar. I look under the napkin. Five twenty-euro notes shine up at me.

And he didn't touch a drop of the beer.

Damn, guy.

3

Elly

"Do you have any ID?" I size up the teenager across the bar. A gold necklace complements his tracksuit and baseball cap, and his lip is adorned with a light patchy moustache that is very distracting.

"Yeah," he replies sullenly, handing over a UK driver's licence. The laminated edge of the licence curls upwards where it has been tampered with and a new photo inserted over the original.

I calculate his age. There's no way this guy is twenty-nine. "This is a falsified ID. Is this your twenty-nine-year-old brother's licence?"

He shifts nervously. "What are you on about? It's mine. Gimme a vodka and coke."

"Watch your mouth, kid," a gravel-infused voice demands from the corner of the bar.

I glance up and stare into the eyes of Tristan.

Huh, so this is what it feels like when your heart stops. Like a sexy angina attack.

He came back.

Tristan breaks our gaze to glare at the young

bloke. The guy sizes up Tristan's hulky stature, glances over at his mates, and decides it's not worth the effort. He walks to the other side of the bar to repeat his pathetic attempt at getting served.

"You're back," I say in a high pitch. The goofy smile sweeps across my face before I can restrain it.

"Elena."

My stomach flutters. The way he says my name, it's so *intimate*. I imagine his breathy moan against my ear, repeating my name over and over in a litany as he climaxes.

A smirk builds across his face as if he can read my dirty mind.

I lean across the bar full of giggles. "So, you decided this place isn't so bad after all?"

"No, it's even worse than I remembered." He shudders. "I'm staying in a hotel nearby . . . it's convenient."

"Uh-huh," I say, my throat tight. "What did you do today?"

He props himself on a stool. He looks tired. "I had business back home to deal with. Then I went for dinner at Botrini's."

"The Michelin-star restaurant?" I've been dying to go there.

"That's the one." He shrugs, clearly not as excited as me. Probably because he can afford to dine there every night of the week. "Have you been?"

"No." I laugh. "We've been eating gyros from a beach stand most days. Even sometimes for breakfast," I admit.

He shudders. "Food from the street?"

"You make it sound like I'm rummaging in dustbins . . . You can't only eat high-end food everywhere you go. Trying street food is part of the local experience."

"I can only eat high-end wherever I go."

Asshole.

"I eat anything," I announce, wondering where I'm going with this.

His eyes crinkle at the corners. "Glad to hear you are so adventurous with what you put in your mouth."

Embarrassment spreads from my face down to my neck. I'm not on my A game here. "Did you have company at dinner?" I ask casually.

"No, just me." It's all he offers.

I open my mouth to say something, then stop. What's his deal? He's clearly not here with a wife or girlfriend. He doesn't *appear* to be having a good time by himself.

A crowd sweeps in from the street, and I reluctantly move along the bar, trying to keep up with the shouting of orders. Bartending is not my forte. Doubled up with his presence, I'm extra jittery.

He came back. He'd rather stick knives in his eyes, but he came back!

With the grace of a baboon, I move around the bar, knocking over glasses and serving shit cocktails. I'm hanging on to this job by a bikini thread but how can I focus on anything other than the visual and auditory delight in the corner?

Calm down, Elly. Pull yourself together.

Jonas puts me on floor mopping duty when the crowd begins to thin out. Out of my peripheral vision, I see Tristan putting his wallet in his jeans pocket.

Shit. He's escaping again. This is my last chance.

I decide that his corner of the bar has a particularly dirty floor and needs extra attention.

"I'm leaving now," he says when I'm in earshot.

"Sure, it's late," I reply. *Don't go. Stay. Ask me out. Do something. Anything!*

He rises from the bar stool, and I flash him my brightest smile. "Good night, Tristan. It was lovely to meet you." As much as I want to barricade him with the mop, I restrain myself.

He nods, walks a few steps, and then stops. "Are you walking home by yourself?" His brow furrows. "I see your friend isn't here tonight."

"Megan has a hangover," I explain, my heart thumping at the thought of where his line of questioning is leading. I had to convince Jonas she had something contagious so she wouldn't get fired on day two. "I'm sure I'll be fine."

"Can I walk you home?" he asks. "I'm not trying to come on to you," he adds quickly. "You can't walk home by yourself dressed like that."

I give him a twisted smile. "I change before I walk home."

"Still." He raises his eyebrows. "Well?"

"Yes, Tristan." I laugh nervously even though it's not funny. "You can walk me home."

Forty minutes later, I change into my jeans and a T-shirt and examine my underwear. I'm wearing a soft cotton bra and underwear set designed for comfort, not sex, damn it. What am I even saying? I'm not having a one-night stand with this strange Adonis of a man, no matter how much I'm craving it. Besides, logistics will force the situation. Megan and I share a bedsit with two single beds, and the last thing I saw when I left was Megan sprawled over her bed whimpering about becoming teetotal.

As Megan said, no one is getting nooky on this working holiday unless it's on a beach.

When I head outside, Tristan is leaning against the wall across the street. In a few steps, he closes the gap between us. He's been out here waiting for twenty minutes while I finished up.

His eyes blaze as he takes in my new outfit. "Better."

I'm in a world of trouble here. I look at this guy and want hot-ass sex.

"You're stunning, Elena."

"Hardly." I snort. "But it's better than the uniform."

The streets are littered with drunken teens taking inconvenient naps on the pavement and impatient moped riders trying to swerve around them. It's like *Night of the Living Dead.*

To me, it's the most romantic stroll of my life.

I feel his hand slide down my lower back as we amble through the streets. Heat spreads up my spine. It's distracting.

"Where are you staying?" I look up at him.

"The Athena."

Of course, he is staying in the five hundred quid a night five-star resort. "I thought you were staying on a boat?"

"I'm between the hotel and the yacht."

One half of the world doesn't know how the other half is living. Some people are living between houses. This guy? He's living between a five-star hotel and a yacht. I shake my head in disbelief.

"Do you usually walk home with your friend?" He frowns as we pass a few dubious characters lying on the curb. "These streets aren't safe this late at night. This isn't the best part of town."

"Yes. She usually walks back with me to our *place of residence*." I groan. "Only the cockroaches call it home."

"Here we are," I say.

He stares gobsmacked at the decaying apartment block with rubbish littering the doorways and dirty blankets dangling from the windows. "Now I understand why people prefer to sleep on the pavement."

I'm mortified but also amused. "It's cheap. We pay fifty euros a week for a studio."

"You *sleep* here?"

I roll my eyes. "I'm backpacking, Tristan. It's fine. Don't you remember backpacking?"

"Not in this decade," he says dryly. "I'm nearly forty."

"Okay, don't you remember being young then?" I tease.

"Cheeky."

"Do you want to come up?" I ask tentatively, wondering if I can persuade the cockroaches to give me some privacy . . . or Megan to stop moaning.

"Absolutely not." He makes a face. "But I'm not leaving you here either. Can I pay for a hotel for you?"

"No!" I shriek indignantly.

We shuffle awkwardly as we dance around what will happen next. This is it. He either says goodnight or he makes a move. Our eyes lock, and I angle my body towards him.

He steps back.

"Wait." I grab his arm and smash my body into his wall of hard muscle.

His brow furrows and he actually *shudders.*

My cheeks burn with rejection.

Just as I'm about to step back, his face presses down to touch my forehead, and his open mouth comes down onto mine.

I open my mouth, too desperate and eager, and like I've opened a floodgate, his mouth takes hungry possession of mine. I press my body flush against Tristan, thrilled to find a growing hardness pushing against my stomach.

His hand grips the back of my head as his tongue invades my mouth with urgency now.

My thighs part and I wrap my arms around his muscular waist so I can press his bulge closer against me. *Oh*, that feels like something I want.

In response, he groans into my mouth, kissing me like he hasn't kissed a woman in years. Then as quickly as it starts, he breaks away, looking at me for so long I think he's going to say goodnight and leave me here.

I stare back at him with unashamed begging in my eyes.

"Would you like to come back to my hotel?" he asks quietly. "There's a private beach. We can go for a walk on it. I can get you back safely here afterwards."

"Sure," I choke out. "Walking is fun." My head warns me not to follow a strange guy to his hotel, but my body is ready to mount him like a jockey.

He takes my hand and leads me through the streets towards the posh side of town. The Athena is about twenty minutes away and, as we walk, his thumb draws teasing circles on my palm. It is a delicate movement that sends shockwaves directly between my thighs. By the time we reach the Athena, I'm at boiling point. I'm barely able to focus on what he is saying.

The Athena is perched high on a hill overlooking secluded beaches, blending in seamlessly with the landscape of whitewashed houses dotted along the Mediterranean coastline. Golden streetlights bounce off the water and the buildings in the darkness, creating shades of orange.

I gasp. "I wish I had my camera with me."

"I doubt you'd get a good shot in this poor light though."

"I invested in a good lens for night photography," I explain. "I did an evening photography course last year at uni and I've been chasing the perfect night photo ever since. It's one of the reasons we decided on the Greek islands, it's such a beautiful landscape."

"I would love to see some of your photos sometime." *Sometime* hangs in the air. "Translator, trainee lawyer, photographer; a woman of many talents." His eyes crinkle. "Maybe not bartending."

I slap him on the chest. "You haven't seen *all* my talents yet," I return, winking. *Christ,* Megan would be proud of that one.

Caught off guard, his brows rise. "Come on, trouble, I'll show you the best beach on the island."

"Holy shit!" I say too loudly as he leads me through the hotel lobby. A few hotel staff look on, disapprovingly. "This place . . . I can't imagine staying here."

We walk out the exit door to the secluded beach where dark waves are crashing in the moonlight. I make a mental note to tell Megan I've found the perfect beach for nooky.

"I prefer the sea at night," I muse. "Megan and I did a night kayak when we first arrived. It was amazing. You must spend all your time in the water here."

He shrugs. "I haven't been in yet."

"What?" I shriek in horror. "Are you crazy? If I had this on my doorstep, I would be swimming morning, noon and night." In fact . . . "We have to go for a midnight swim!"

"What?" He snorts, crossing his arms over his wide chest. "Absolutely not."

My heart hammers and I don't know if it's the darkness of the night or the tequila shots I had earlier, but I decide to be brave. "Fine," I reply, shimmying out of my jeans.

"What are you doing?" he demands, as I pull my T-shirt over my head.

"I'm going in," I say before I can chicken out.

"Those waves are rough tonight," he growls. "You are *not* doing this."

My brows shoot up. Is that an order?

He stares down at my cotton bra and panties.

I race towards the sea until I'm submerged waist-deep, acclimatising. It's not freezing but it's cold enough for my nipples to peak. Turning back to the beach, I see him glaring at me, his arms still folded.

"It's warmer than it looks," I shout to the shore, my voice drowning in the sea sounds.

Waves crash over my shoulders, pulling me under. Unfazed, I dive under the current. Growing up twenty miles from a beach and despite the Welsh weather, I've been swimming for years. The mistake many people make is freaking out, opening their mouths, and swallowing gallons of water.

As I glide along the seabed, strong arms pull me out of the water.

"What the fuck, Elena?" He pulls me to standing and glowers at me as the waves crash around our waists. He has stripped down to his boxers. His chest heaves up and down, his dark hair wet and clinging to his forehead.

Goosebumps break out along my skin and I'm not sure if it's the water temperature or the growing heat between my thighs, or maybe both. *Damn, he's sexy when he's angry.*

"I thought you were in trouble," he mutters. "You could have told me you swim like a mermaid. I nearly had a heart attack."

"At least it got you in the water." I bite my lip.

His eyes darken as he fixes them on my chest with Clark Kent heat vision and a low grumble escapes his throat. I'm starting to worry I'll burst into flames.

I glance down, shivering. My cotton bra has turned transparent in the water. My nipples protrude like bullets. I might as well be topless.

My gaze follows the treasure trail of hair down his delicious V-tapered body. The water moulds his boxers around his growing hardness like a wrapped present just for me.

Time stands still as we brazenly devour each other's bodies with our eyes.

Yes, please.

"I'm so turned on just looking at you," he whispers hoarsely, eyes meeting mine. He swallows hard, his Adam's apple bobbing up and down. "It's embarrassing."

Stepping forward, I run my fingers over the wet sculpted muscles on his broad chest.

Delicious.

"Now you have me in the water," he murmurs.

"What are you going to do with me?"

My fingers trace down his chest to his stomach, dancing above his boxers. He gives me an arrogant smirk while he gauges whether I have the guts to go lower. His eyes urge me further and all my remaining inhibitions drown in the water as my hand slides down his lower stomach into his boxers.

Wrapping my hand around his hard length, I let out a delighted gasp at what I find.

He's massive. And so ready.

As my grip tightens around him, he groans, and I begin to stroke up and down his swollen hardness. Hell, yeah, this feels good.

I need to see him. *All of him*. I lower his boxers, and his erection springs free.

I stare down, half terrified, half in awe.

"It's okay," Tristan says softly, reading my face. "We don't need to do anything you don't feel comfortable with."

"That thing looks like something NASA should launch into space." I continue my slow and steady motion, sliding my hand up and down him.

He lets out a loud laugh. "You're the only girl who has made me burst out laughing while I'm hard." His hands curl around my buttocks, and he presses me hard against his bare erection.

I feel it through my flimsy cotton panties and whimper, grinding against it. Like we are fucking with our clothes on.

His mouth crashes down on mine. As one hand remains on my butt, the other hand moves around to my lower stomach, playing with the hem of my pants. He pauses, giving me the opportunity to stop him. Instead, I squirm impatiently; I need his fingers lower. *Now*.

I widen my legs.

He looks into my eyes and slides his large hand into my wet underwear. Then I spread my thighs apart for easier access, writhing against his fingers to push them to where I need them to be.

"Horny little thing, aren't you?" He chuckles as his fingers rim my entrance. "I'm going to enjoy making you come."

"Yes," I say in a choked voice into his shoulder, not sure what I'm saying yes to. Just *yes.*

His entire palm is now massaging my opening. Spreading me open with two fingers, he thrusts his middle finger into me, first slowly, then deeper, faster.

"This feels . . . good." I groan, gasping as he pushes deeper.

"Good?" he grunts, sliding a second finger in.

I whimper as he *really* starts working me down there. Then his thumb finds my clit.

"Ahhhh!" I tighten around his fingers as his thumb circles. The pressure is too much. Tingly shivers erupt over my entire body. This is it. The real deal. I've never had the big O with a bloke, I'm ashamed to say, it's only ever been self-administered. My ex, John, never managed to get the job done. He rubbed so hard that I felt like I had carpet burns.

Tristan's other hand tilts my jaw, forcing me to look up at him. "Look at me when you come."

I let out a strangled sound that would be embarrassing if I wasn't so close to climax. Something about doing this in the ocean makes it doubly arousing. Anyone who looks out their hotel room window will see me naked in the sea grinding against a man I met twenty-four hours ago, and it's the biggest fucking turn-on ever. Pleasure bubbles up inside me as he touches me like no one else ever has.

I claw at his biceps as my muscles contract around his fingers again and again, desperate for release.

"You feel unbelievable."

"Tristan . . ." I moan, my body spasming as he strokes my clit furiously. I spent all last night in bed fantasising about that deep voice talking dirty to me. It's even better than I imagined "I'm going to . . . I'm coming."

It's too much; my entire body shakes as the most explosive orgasm of my life erupts.

A low growl reverberates from his chest as he watches. My legs buck, and his other hand catches me, pulling me to him.

I stare at him, my mouth hanging open, trying to find my breath. I need more. "Take me to your room," I say hoarsely.

His eyes darken as he studies me. "Are you sure?"

I nod. My hands curl around his length, hard and ready for me. I've never been more sure of anything in my life.

He growls against my ear and bundles me up in his arms like I weigh nothing.

I cling to him with a goofy smile as he strides through the water to the beach. Tonight, I have no inhibitions. I'm going to have the best sex of my life with this man.

I'm going to try *everything*.

4

Elly

I skulk through the hotel lobby self-consciously trailing behind Tristan. Two growing mounds of dampness cling to my T-shirt from my soaked bra, the same at my crotch. A passing hotel guest looks at us suspiciously before dropping her jaw when she notices the massive tent in my companion's jeans. He strides towards the elevator bay like a man on a mission.

Adrenaline courses through me. In minutes I'm going to have Tristan in a private room.

He jabs at the elevator button impatiently. The doors slide open, and he wastes no time pulling me into the steel box. Before they can fully close, he has me pinned against the back wall, thrusting his large thighs against mine. For a second, I wonder if he's going to try to fuck me here in the elevator. His mouth crashes down on mine, and my mouth and hips both respond at the same time, craving closeness. I swing my leg around his hip, tilting my hips up, so his erection is right in my apex. Let's hope there aren't any cameras in here.

The door springs open, and we stumble down the hall, grunting and moaning as my greedy hands ravage his body. With ragged breathing, he fumbles in his pockets to find the door card.

The door flashes red. He curses, flustered, and tries again, slamming the door open when it flashes green. We fall into the room, panting, hands clawing clothes and flesh.

His fingers find the hem of my T-shirt, pulling it up over my head and onto the floor. One hand expertly unfastens my bra from behind, grunting as my breasts come free.

He needs no invitation. His lips drop to my breasts and he sucks each nipple in turn, sending a message straight to my clit.

I fumble with the hem of his T-shirt, clumsily trying to pull it up over his chest. I need skin on skin; I need my breasts naked against his chest. He releases my nipple from his mouth to pull the T-shirt off, exposing his ripped, muscular chest.

Grunting, he undoes his jean buttons and pulls them down, taking out each thick muscular leg in turn.

My breath comes out in jerky moans.

"If you keep whimpering like that, I'm not going to last." Fixing a slow sexy smile on me, he pushes his boxers down to stand naked in front of me. His cock stands thick and powerful, pointing upwards, waiting for me.

I'm dickmatized.

"Take your jeans off."

I swallow, my throat dry. I do as he demands until I'm standing naked before him.

For a moment, Tristan stands and watches me with a feral gaze that tells me *exactly* what he plans to do to me, and I wonder if I have bitten off more than I can chew. He lunges and sweeps me up by my thighs, so my wet core grinds against his stomach. Every step he takes causes hot friction as he gracefully walks me to the bed.

Then I'm dropped on the mattress. My arms fall over my head.

Climbing on top of me, he pushes my legs apart and stares down at my freshly shaved opening. His knees force my legs wider, and his hand travels downward. I gasp sharply as his fingers spread my lips apart.

"Do you know how beautiful you are, Elena?" His voice is thick. "Lie back and let me take care of you tonight."

I feel two fingers enter me and I shudder. My legs tighten against his knees like a vice as he starts to plunge his fingers in and out of me, groaning at the sound of my arousal.

It's not enough. His mouth travels down my stomach planting soft kisses then bypasses my core and finds the skin of my inner thighs. Slowly, sensually, like he has all the time in the world.

I don't. I can't wait. "Please . . ." I moan, my legs bucking at his mouth trails my inner thighs. His stubble on the side of his jaw tickles my entrance with a delicious friction.

"Please, Tristan!" I say, more urgently.

I let out a loud moan as his tongue dips deeply into me, his fingers holding me wide open. That's the spot. I'm so exposed, so spread open. I writhe on the bed, but he has *me* in a vice now, merciless, fucking me with his tongue, his eyes on mine the whole time.

My back arches like a woman possessed and my hands fist the sheets.

"Wait," I rasp, struggling for air. "I want you inside me when I come again . . . please."

He looks up through hooded eyes, then his expression is laced with irritation. "Damn. I wasn't expecting to have sex. Do you have condoms?"

"In my purse." I flap a hand towards my bag on the table.

Tristan jumps off the bed and strides towards the bag, pulling it open roughly. The contents spill all over the floor. "Sorry," he mutters. "I'll put them back later." Finding the condom, he tears open the foil and gives himself a few long strokes before rolling it onto his length.

Good God, this guy is packing. That thing should have its own passport.

Then he is back on the bed like he means business, his knees pushing my legs apart and his hands wrapping them around his waist. Caging me with his body, his cock juts upwards between my thighs, nudging my opening, teasing me, *torturing* me.

"*Please . . .*" I moan, surprised at how much I am begging. I dig the heels of my feet into his buttocks impatiently.

"Are you trying to give my butt a sports massage with your feet?" He chuckles.

I dig my heels in deeper.

Mischief dances in his eyes as he runs his tip along my slit a few more times. "Is this what you want? Say my name."

"Yes, Tristan." I groan. "Hurry up."

His mouth comes close to my ear. "What would you like? Fast and hard or slow and deep?"

I don't usually get a menu. "All," I croak. "I'll take it all."

He chuckles then he slides in deep, and he's fucking me, fucking me so hard, I'm seeing stars.

"You're so tight," he says, grunting in my ear. He stops for a second, deep inside me, watching me. "You okay?"

I nod because no words can do justice. My hands palm over his thick chest as he thrusts into me, deeper and faster.

He's stopped trying to be gentle now; he's too close.

I moan as another orgasm swells inside me, stronger than before. "Don't stop, don't stop," I pant over and over again.

I drape my hands around his shoulders for support, fingernails digging into him. I come hard on his cock, and a muffled groan escapes him as he releases into me with heavy, furious pulses.

So, *this* is how it should feel.

When he finally catches his breath, he trails a finger down my cheek, smiling softly.

"Απίθανο," I stutter in Greek.

Amazing indeed.

A few hours later and I'm spent. I think he is too if he would admit it. We lie in bed facing each other, my face so close I feel his hot and minty breath on my cheek.

"I don't usually do this." I slide my bottom lip between my teeth. Something makes me want him to believe me. "This is my first one-night stand." I laugh. "Said every girl after every one night-stand. Ever. But honestly, it's true."

"One-night stand?" Tristan smiles. "You make it sound so sordid." He leans forward and lightly kisses my nose. "You don't need to justify yourself to me, Elena."

"It's not that I've never *wanted* to," I continue in case he thinks I'm building this into something bigger than it is. "It's just rare that I meet guys I want to jump into the sack with right away."

"Or the sea." His blue eyes sparkle. "I'm honoured you chose me in that case."

This close, I can see every blade of dark stubble on his square jaw. I trace a finger lazily down his arrogant, masculine nose, his lips and his jawline. "I think this jaw is sculpted out of marble. Sorry, cliché but it's true."

"You flatter me," he murmurs lazily. "You know,

you're very witty." His eyes hold mine. "Since we are telling the truth, I'm quite taken with you."

My heartbeat quickens. Are you supposed to talk like this on a one-night stand? "You're very direct, Tristan," is all I can manage.

He reaches out to brush a strand of hair off my face. "Are you not used to it? Yes, I'm direct. I'm a man, not a young guy."

A man? I stare back at him in silence.

I'm starting to think you're a god.

***

For the first time since I arrived on the island, I slept through the night. Most nights, there's something keeping me awake: mopeds, drunks, lack of air conditioning, and cockroaches having a nocturnal party. They thrive in the drainage pipes and our shack has shit drainage.

I awoke this morning to silence, hotel quality sheets, a comfortable room temperature and a gorgeous man lying beside me. Last night was indescribable. I'm done with college slobs. *This* is a real man. This is the type of man I want. I don't want to settle for less.

He lies on his back, mouth slightly open, sound asleep. It gives me the opportunity to stare at every curve, every ripple of muscle, every line, every hair on his perfectly moulded body.

The sheets bunch around the defined V of his lower stomach, daring me to push them down. I can tell he's hard under the covers.

I stifle a laugh. I could study his face for a lifetime. That square jaw, those dark eyebrows, defined cheekbones. He told me his parents were Irish. I might need to pay Dublin a visit if this is what they are mass-producing in the Emerald Isle.

What time is it?

I didn't have a cockroach alarm this morning.

My watch says 7:40. I have exactly twenty minutes to get dressed, run a mile to the dock and meet Megan to start our cleaning shift. I've no time to change, I'll have to go as I am.

As promised, Dimitris demoted us from sales to cleaning crew. We're receiving this week's pay in two days, after that we can tell him to shove his placard up his ass, but we can't risk it beforehand. Talk circulates amongst backpackers about not getting paid after quitting early.

I sneak out of bed and tiptoe over to where my jeans are discarded on the floor. There is a clothes trail of destruction from when we fired everything off us in a lust haze. I dress as quietly as possible and gather up the contents of my bag.

The tip he left on the bar two nights ago slips out. I place four of the notes, making up eighty Euros, on the bedside table beside him. Twenty euros was more than enough for a generous tip.

"Goodbye, my handsome Adonis," I whisper, stealing one final stare. He told me he was leaving for Athens this morning. With his ship sailing, so too is ours. Ours sailed the moment I let a guy I met

twenty-four hours before finger me on a beach. You do that and you lose any hope of something more meaningful.

If I sneak out now, it won't be awkward.

I creep into the bathroom to wash my face. In daylight I see just how lavish this hotel is. An extensive selection of expensive toiletries is arranged across the sink and a remote control sits on top of the bath. I spot more knobs and levers on the bath than a plane. *Can* that thing fly?

Pity I don't get to enjoy the five-star treatment.

Scanning the room, I do what any normal backpacker would do. I open my bag and sneak in a few mini shampoo and shower gels. He's leaving today, he'll never notice. It would be a shame to waste them.

Then I tip toe towards the main door and close it behind me. Who knew I was so good at being a hussy *and* a thief?

5

Elly

"I didn't think you had it in you," Megan sniggers as she hands me an apron. "Although I'm mad at you for not texting me to say where you were."

I take it, irritated. I'm exhausted, and the last thing I want to do is clean yacht toilets. "I'm sorry, I'm a terrible friend. I didn't mean to make you worry." I tie the apron at the back. "Tell me how these aprons help? They don't cover our clothes."

She shrugs. "Dimitris wants us to look like professional cleaners."

I roll my eyes. "He didn't exactly look at our cleaning credentials. At least we don't have to sell anything," I muse. "Cleaning toilets might actually be better than trying to coax people onto boats."

Boy, was I wrong.

One hour later, I'm stuck cleaning a massive pretentious yacht owned by the biggest pain in the ass on the Greek islands. That title is fact.

It's obvious she expects me to clean the yacht without being present as she entertains a small group of equally irritating friends. I try to clean around them as they get progressively drunker. They opened a bottle of champagne, forgot, then opened another one. Meanwhile, a nanny is entertaining the annoying lady's child in the bedroom. The kid seems to spend most of his time on his phone, a phone way more expensive than mine. He must be no older than six or seven.

The woman is exquisite, I'm not sure I've ever seen such a beautiful creature in the flesh. The kind of woman who looks incapable of farting and is annoyingly dainty and willowy. I imagine her to be a rich ballerina who does lots of fund raising. Despite the island heat, her long blond hair isn't frizzy, her sweat glands don't seem to function, and her face is sculpted and contoured to perfection. It's like she's applied a real-life Instagram filter.

I spotted her husband on my way in. He must have a tiny dick to need a boat this big.

"Excuse me, sweetie," she says loudly and slowly, looking at me like I've got the IQ of a scarecrow. She beckons me, showcasing the most obnoxious engagement ring I've ever seen. The ring looks like a weapon. Maybe she's mafia?

"Yes?"

"I need you"—she points at herself then me for the avoidance of doubt—"to pair the underwear and socks. Do you understand?" She rolls her eyes at her friends. "The dry cleaners are appalling."

"No." She wants me to match up her underwear? I'm a cleaner, not her mother.

Exhaling heavily, as though talking to me was draining her, she snaps open the dry-cleaning bag. Taking out a racy red lingerie set, she turns to me, "This," she says loudly, enunciating every syllable and pointing to the bra. "And this." She points to the thong. "Do you see? In these drawers."

If she complains, I might not get this week's pay. I'm not exactly part of a trade union so the risk is high. I remove my jaw from the floor and smile as sweetly as possible at the waif-like beauty. "I'd be honoured to match your underwear."

Her eyes narrow, and she glances at me suspiciously, then nods, flicking her hair over her shoulder, and returns to her friends.

I get down to the critical business of matching the underwear and the socks from the dry-cleaning bag. I'm tempted to fluff her pants with the toilet brush, but I resist, being the bigger woman. Metaphorically and physically.

Not even five minutes later, she emerges. "Hi sweetie. I need you to pop out to the shop." She's talking very slowly to get me to understand.

"I'm Welsh," I explain for the umpteenth time. Surely she can detect English is my mother tongue?

"We've ran out of bottled water. Oh, and we need limes. Key limes." She thinks. "Also some more pomegranate and mint. So that's bottled water, key limes, pomegranate, mint," she repeats slowly. "Cash is on the table. I can make a list if it's easier for you?" she says kindly as if she's doing me a favour.

Does this woman understand the job description

of a cleaner? I don't think it extends into personal assistance.

"Sorry, I don't have time. My shift is ending now."

My pushback leaves her affronted. We are interrupted by her son, with the nanny trailing. I suspect she's been told to keep him away from the party.

"Daniel, Mummy is entertaining her guests. Is everything okay?"

"When are we going home?" He sounds bored.

"We'll sail when Daddy's ready."

Good riddance to you all, I say.

***

"That's twelve euros," I tell the guy communicating with my tits. He doesn't answer. "Did you hear me?"

He hands me a twenty euro note. "Take one for yourself, sexy."

"Thanks." Does this guy even realise I have a face with two big fucking eyes glaring at him? I take a generous one for myself.

"Ass," a man yells at me across the bar. "I need ass."

"What did you say?" I bark back. How dare he! Just because I'm wearing provocative clothing as part of my uniform, does this man think that he can objectify and sexualise me? That he can talk to me as if I'm lacking mental capacity just because I'm wearing a bikini?

"He wants *ice*." Megan bumps me out of the way

to get to the ice dispenser.

Oh.

Perhaps I'm extra ratty tonight because I know the man of my dreams has departed the island. How is it that in the space of forty-eight hours you can meet your dream guy, have mind-blowing chemistry with him, then poof! That's it, your time's up.

I regret not leaving my number. I thought I was keeping my dignity intact by creeping out before we had the awkward morning after the one-night stand. Instead, I should have stayed, waited until he woke up and begged to have his babies.

Megan shoves me to the side as she leans over to get the sambuca.

"Watch it, Megan," I snap as sticky liquid hits my arms.

"Stop being so grouchy, or you'll get us fired." She tuts as she pours the sambuca into shots. "You've got a face like a slapped ass tonight. I'm already walking a fine line after the suspicious, contagious, twenty-four hour bug bullshit you made up."

She's right. I didn't know I could experience both ecstasy and pain at the same time. The pain part is winning right now.

"What you need to do is get back on the horse."

"The horse has bolted," I mutter.

"Not that horse. A different horse. There's a whole flock of horses on this island waiting to be straddled, ridden, and fed."

"A stud," I correct her. "Not a flock."

I move out of the way as she passes over a tray of shots to some teenagers. She still manages to spray me with sambuca. It's irrelevant. By the end of the night, it'll be stuck to me like Teflon.

She takes the money then turns to me. "Now saddle up, girl, and get ready to rodeo."

"Are you done? You must have exhausted your horse innuendos by now. Although kudos for not using the stallion cliché."

She is about to laugh when her jaw falls open slightly. "Not quite done. A horse walks into a bar. What does the bartender say?"

"Oh, Jesus." I slap my forehead. "*Hay*."

"Say hay to your horse, Elly." She twirls me around, and I look right into the eyes of Tristan.

He's here. He's here, in the flesh, in front of me.

My heart somersaults in my chest.

His lips twitch as he registers my shock.

"You stayed?" I approach him and try to calm the adrenaline pumping through my veins. "I thought you had . . ." I'm too excited and nervous to think straight. "Did the boat not get fixed?"

"It's fixed," he says, looking me directly in the eye. "I wanted to see you again. You left without saying goodbye." His smile slips slightly.

"Oh!" A ridiculous squeal escapes me. "You stayed because of *me*?"

"You left eighty euros on the bedside table. Did you think I'd let you get away with that? I felt like a prostitute."

I lean across the bar, trying to hold it together.

"But I thought you had important business back in London?"

"I do," he says, deadpan. "But I realised I have very important unfinished business in Mykonos. There's a lady who has been eating street gyros for weeks and hasn't been for dinner at Botrini's yet. It's a crime."

"Uh, I . . ." Christ, I can't speak.

Damn. "I can't go for dinner tonight," I say, dismayed. "I'm working until midnight."

"I guess my important business back in London will have to wait even longer then."

Oh.

"I didn't mean to make you feel like a prostitute." I laugh. "I kept twenty euros for a tip, four euros for each hour you spent at the bar."

"Very precise. And under-charged if you ask me." He grins, pulling out his wallet and places a number of twenty euro notes on the bar. "Since I'm going to have to tolerate this shithole for another night just to be in your company, here's my tip in advance. That's for five hours. Then hopefully you'll let me show you how much I enjoyed last night by reliving it all over again."

I choke a little as I swallow too much air.

Play it cool, woman.

"What makes you so sure it's a done deal?" I ask defiantly.

He raises his eyebrows.

He was right. I'm all talk. The deal was done the minute he set foot in the bar tonight.

"Well, if we are playing this game," Tristan starts with a smirk. "Last night I discovered there is nothing hotter than watching you come while you moan my name in your lovely accent. So tonight, what I want is to make you come so loudly that every room in the hotel hears your little pants and screams. That's worth sitting in this sweaty bar watching a load of lads half my age throw up on each other for five hours. Does that sound like a good plan?"

Oh my God. This is fifty shades of fuck.

"You seem like a thorough planner," I squeak.

"I'm direct, I say what I want," he continues with unwavering eye contact.

That, he does.

"And I get what I want."

I let out a laugh but he's not joking. This man is going to ravage me tonight.

God help me.

And he does get what he wants. I'm a bag of nerves as he opens the hotel room door with one hand while the other rests on my lower back. The outline of his hardness is visible through his trousers, and I wonder if my ravaged body can handle round two so quickly after last night.

And just like that, we are attacking each other again, hands, tongues, thighs everywhere, trying to cover as much body surface as possible, like we both know this might be the last time. Taking off our clothes like they are on fire until I'm wearing nothing but my mascara.

He pushes me up against the wall, so I've got nowhere to go, no way to escape his demanding erection pushing up into my apex. Half kissing me, half panting into my mouth, he unbuttons his jeans.

He's not waiting around tonight.

God, he smells fantastic. It's a man-musk I want to take back to Wales. I yank his jeans down over his thick thighs, his cock springing free, curving upward, and I drop to my knees. He was so attentive to me last night. It was all about me; I want to show Tristan that I can give as good as I take.

Looking up at him with big eyes, I wrap both hands around his shaft and take his cock in my mouth.

He lets out a shudder that sounds almost painful. "It's been a long time."

My hands tighten further around his straining shaft. I pulse gently first, then more aggressively as his low husky grunts become louder and his grip around my hair tightens.

He groans my name as I speed up, and I wrap my hands around his buttocks so I can take him as deep as I can. Pushing himself deeper into me, he hisses as he hits the back of my throat each time. No one has ever fucked my mouth like this before, and it feels so damn good to be in control of this man's pleasure.

"Elena." He groans. "I'm coming. I'm going to come in your mouth if you don't let me pull out," he warns, his breathing ragged.

I tilt my head up to look him dead in the eyes. It's so sexy to watch him losing control. I pull him out of my mouth just in time. His eyes, hooded with arousal, meet mine and his face contorts into a mix of pain and pleasure as warm liquid sprays over my breasts.

"I couldn't," I whisper.

"I don't expect you to."

As he picks me up from the floor, he grabs my thighs and pulls me up, so I'm straddling him in mid-air. He walks us slowly over to the large armchair beside the mirror. Holding me in his arms, he lowers himself into the chair. He makes it look easy, like I'm weightless. I straddle his thighs, running my hand over his pectorals; I can feel his heart hammering in his chest.

He exhales a deep breath and gives himself long strokes up and down to refuel. His thick cock springs to life again, nudging my inner thigh.

"I thought older men took longer to recover."

"Older men?" he mutters, slapping my ass. "Cheeky mare."

Megan's horse jokes flood my head.

"Condom, cabinet," he says, pointing in the direction of the cabinet drawer.

I'd be pissed at the demanding tone if I wasn't so horny. I leap off his lap and run over to the drawer, pulling it open.

He's been shopping. Two packets of unopened condoms shine up at me. I rip open one of the packets and take out a silver ring.

"XL," I read on the packet. "No wonder I can feel you all the way up to my ribs. Two packets of twelve?"

He gives me a smile, half tender, half predatory. "I'm a thorough planner, remember? When a man meets someone as enchanting as you, they want to be inside you all the time."

I roll my eyes. "I can't believe you just referred to yourself in the third person."

"I'm talking on behalf of all men on earth. Now get back here and sit on me."

I swallow a lump in my throat as I walk towards the beautiful man, his masculine thighs spread wide and waiting for me. Climbing on top of him, I take his wrists and hold them above his head.

He smiles wickedly back at me and lets me hold them in a lock, although we both know he could easily break free. "You're in control," he murmurs. "Do what you want with me."

With one hand still holding his wrists, I take his length in the other and run it up and down my entrance, circling its tip around my clit.

"Do you like that?" he whispers. "I love feeling you on top of me."

I give a curt nod. If I keep massaging myself, I'm going to come. Forcing myself to stop before I'm past the point of no return, I position my opening directly over his cock. I lower down onto him, first the tip, then letting his entire length in.

A low growl rumbles in his throat and his hands clench, but he doesn't break them free.

I spread my legs further, so I swallow him whole then start hitching up and down.

Damn. This man is the best chair ever.

His face contorts as I thrust aggressively in an optimal position to stimulate my clit.

"Too fast," he says in a stuttered breath, watching me jut up and down. "I won't last."

I ignore him. *I* control the pace, the depth, the pleasure. He'll come when I want him to, and right now, I'm speeding towards climaxing so fast I feel dizzy.

"Elena" he groans, "I can't stop it."

I clamp down tightly on him, owning him. With a final choked groan, his whole body goes rigid, and his seed pumps into me, tipping me over the edge. I shudder over him, and I moan so loudly I'm sure the reception staff heard me ten floors below. "Oh. My. GOD."

His hands flop down, and he falls back into the armchair as I ease him out of me. Sweat glistens on his forehead.

He runs a finger down my nose. "Careful," he murmurs. "You've reeled me in now."

I swallow hard, taking in his words and meeting the eye of a man who I know always gets his own way.

I've reeled *him* in? He's got me. Hook, line, and sinker.

6

Elly

"I don't have any posh restaurant-appropriate outfits," I whine to Megan. We have laid out all my clothes in the suitcase as well as the bits and bobs I bought here on the island, like sarongs.

The situation is dire. When I was leaving this morning, Tristan asked if he could take me to Botrini's.

A real date.

I'm a bundle of nerves and excitement, not just for seeing Tristan again but also for eating something other than a street gyro.

Megan shrugs. "I dunno why you're so worried, he seems to prefer you with your clothes off anyway." She holds a colourful beach sarong against my chest. "Maybe we could make a top out of this?"

"Do you have a sewing machine lying around here you're not telling me about? I've got twenty minutes. I can't make a nice top out of a bloody sarong." I rummage through the tops and hold up a white vest top. "Blue jeans, white top. It'll have to do."

She nods. "At least it's nice and tight. It'll make him think about you naked. That's the aim, right?"

I tug on the jeans, fraying at the ankles and knees, and pull the white top over my head. I've overcompensated with makeup, opting for a bold power pout with deep red lips and a sultry feline eye flick.

I'd have preferred more time and resources for this date considering the most heart-stopping man I've ever met, with a body that won't quit, has only seen me in a gaudy yellow bikini and jeans.

I'm well aware that my days are numbered. A man like that isn't going to hang around this island all summer for a fling with a backpacker. This will be my last night with him.

"He's on the street." Megan is perched at the window. "Oh, he looks scrumptious. You are in for a *treat* tonight."

My heart goes from resting to racing, just knowing he's in the vicinity.

She lets out a low wolf-whistle.

"Megan, the window is open." I fix my hair over my shoulders one last time and blow her a kiss. "Wish me luck!"

"You don't need luck. He's a done deal."

I strap my ankles into the only dressy heels I have with me and trot down the stairs.

"Bring me back some leftovers please!" she shouts after me.

Outside, Tristan is leaning against the railing,

having what seems to be an animated, angry conversation on the phone. His expression is thunderous. When he spots me, it softens, and he puts his finger up to signal he'll be off the phone soon.

His forehead wrinkles into a deep scowl as he tries to keep his tone controlled. What is going on with this man? I'm not stupid, I know there's stuff he's not disclosing to me, but I can't exactly ask him to bare it all after two days.

"Sorry." Tristan strides towards me. He looks delicious. He's in jeans and a crisp white shirt that sculpts nicely over his superheroic body parts.

I'm going to enjoy this meal this evening.

"You're tall tonight." He wraps his hands around my waist and pulls me in for a kiss, tongues and all.

I swoon a little. I'm five foot seven without heels. He still towers over me; he must be at least six foot three. "Sorry I'm so casually dressed. My packing itinerary didn't cater to five-star restaurants." I don't admit to him I have no fancy clothes, period.

"You're perfect just the way you are. It doesn't matter what you wear." He takes my hand. "Shall we? I've arranged a car for us."

***

"So, you eat everything." His eyes crinkle across the small table adorned with candles. "I'll hold you to that."

That was a complete lie. I have Crohn's disease, a type of irritable bowel disease, but it doesn't feel like a first-date disclosure. Most of the time I can manage it if I'm careful with my diet. But it's always at the back of my mind. When a restaurant host asks me if I want a window seat, I always say, "No, I'd like one beside the toilet, please." It's the same with planes and trains. One eye is always watching the bathroom queue.

I can't do that tonight.

I wasn't expecting Botrini's to be so quaint. I study their menu, salivating. I'm regretting wearing these tight jeans.

Wait, what if we're splitting the bill? I shouldn't assume he is paying, should I?

"What type of wine do you like?" Tristan asks.

What type of wine *do* I like? I've only had a few solid years of wine drinking. Megan and I have been choosing our wine by the alcohol percentage, so I think that makes me more of a wine ignoramus rather than a wine connoisseur. My knowledge ends at red, white, rose, and orange. Although I've never tasted orange. "You decide," I say.

"I'm going to order a bottle of the Chateau Mouton Rothschild 1989." He closes his menu decisively. "You'll love it."

I scan the list of wines trying to find it. "How much is it?" I ask tentatively. Wine older than me sounds *very* expensive.

He looks affronted. "I'm paying, Elena. I asked you here."

I let out a breath. Fantastic. I won't be sticking to the house wine in that case. "Why do I have a feeling that you always like to be in control, Tristan?"

His eyes darken, and he leans back in his chair. "Happy for you to take full control this evening."

I smile sweetly back. "Happy to."

The waiter approaches us, greeting us in English. Tristan begins to speak but I place a hand over his, and address the waiter in Greek, ordering the wine.

"So, I'm in control, huh? Does that mean you trust me to order food for us?"

"Be my guest."

I launch into a full-scale conversation with the waiter, stretching my Greek vocabulary to its limit.

Tristan watches my face intensely, like I'm the most important person in the restaurant—no, scrap that—*in the Greek islands*. As the waiter leaves, he leans forward with a hungry glint in his eyes. "There is something insanely sexy about a woman being in control. Particularly a multilingual one."

Mission accomplished.

My eyes widen. "Shit! I never asked if you have any allergies?"

"No allergies. Just addictions." He winks. "To breath-taking Welsh Croatian multilingual women."

I roll my eyes as the waiter comes back with our middle-aged wine. "Too cheesy."

"Sorry." He shrugs as the waiter pours. "It's still true." Brow creasing into a serious line, he takes the wine glass by its stem and tilts it to study it in the light. Satisfied, he swirls it and sniffs before taking a sip.

I think of the supermarket wine in a box I had been drinking that you don't want to see, smell *or* taste; you just let it flow through you.

I follow suit, attempting to drink the wine like a grown-up. I tilt the glass and pretend to study the wine. I've no clue what I'm looking for so I skip to the next stage and take a large sip. It slides down my throat smoother than the supermarket wine. Test passed.

Tristan leans forward, resting his strong forearms on the table. "If you like that wine, we could go on a wine tasting tour tomorrow. There's a lovely one on the other side of the island."

My eyes widen. There's a tomorrow for us?

"I can't," I say, disappointed but happy that he also looks disappointed. "I promised Megan I would go to Delis Island. To see the ruins? She wants to paint them."

"The photographer and the painter." He smiles. "It makes me mildly surprised you want to be a lawyer."

"We have this romantic vision of travelling all over the world painting and taking pictures, then we'll open an art gallery and sell our work. For millions, naturally." I roll my eyes. "But I'm not that good, it's just a hobby. Megan is really talented though. She has painted some beautiful works in Mykonos."

"I'm sure you'll find a balance of the best of both worlds. Corporate and creative."

"We'll see. Right now, I'm just trying to bag a trainee law contract." I take a sip of wine. "So, tell me your story, Tristan. You said you work in property?"

His jaw flexes. "I buy and sell property with two mates of mine. One's a full-time developer."

"Are you here in Greece to buy some?" I ask.

He shifts in his seat. "No. Although some of the architecture is truly stunning."

I wait for him to elaborate, but he doesn't. It's like drawing blood from a stone. "Are you always such a closed book?"

He blows out a strained breath, then his large hand encloses mine. "I'm sorry, I know I'm being evasive. There are parts of my life that are . . . complicated right now. I didn't mean to meet someone on this trip. So, I haven't thought this through at all. I wasn't prepared to answer questions."

Unease rolls around my stomach. Is he married?

He squeezes my hands tighter when he sees my face fall.

"But I'd like to see you back in the UK when you get home. Then we can get to know each other better."

My feet do a jig under the table.

"I understand if you don't want to see me after this," he adds. "I'm older than you and, believe me, pursuing a hot grad makes me feel like a cliché, but . . . let's just say I'm not sure I'd be able to give you up that easily."

"I don't get it." I shake my head. "Are you saying

you want to . . . date me?"

He frowns. "Yes, why not?"

I shake my head. "You're clearly a successful, well-established guy. I just thought you would be more interested in someone that's got their shit together."

His gaze roams my face. "You're more impressive than you give yourself credit for. And it's been a long time since I met someone who could make me laugh as much as you."

My face heats. "Says the guy who owns a yacht to the girl with cockroach squatters."

"Cockroaches and an uncanny ability to deflect every compliment." He strokes my hair. "You're my little stress ball."

I scrunch up my face. "I remind you of a squidgy ball? That doesn't sound very sexy."

"It's very sexy. And exactly what I need right now." He looks at me impatiently. "Now will you give me your number?"

An excited squawk erupts from my throat. "I only have a Greek number right now," I explain, pushing my phone across the table. "I lost my UK phone two days before I arrived in Greece."

What's the opposite of a smartphone? That's what mine is. He takes out his latest edition phone and copies my number from the dumb phone.

"You know, I have contacts that are senior partners at a few law firms in London. Dawson Law? I could line you up an interview for when you get home."

My eyes double in size. "Seriously? Oh my God, that would be amazing." Dawson Law is one of the top law firms in the UK. Not *the* top. That's Madison Legal, where I eventually want to end up. But I'd gladly take an *in* at Dawson Law. This guy is the gift that keeps on giving . . . Michelin-star food, my best orgasm, now this?

We laugh and talk for hours through the 11-course tasting menu I order for us. *Yes,* I wanted this meal to last and I'm making up for three weeks of gyros.

The conversation is just so easy. At one point, I laugh so hard at something he says, I snort wine up my nose. I thought he'd be the type of guy to only go after sexy women at the top of their career, who have it together, live by themselves and know how many degrees to tilt their wine glass. Not *me.* Perhaps that's why I introduced myself using my full name and not just Elly.

Slowly I gnaw away at him, picking up snippets of his life. The picture is forming, but there are still large parts of the puzzle I can't piece together. Whatever's the cause of his anguish these past few days, he's not giving anything away.

Good things come to those who wait.

Me? I'm an open book. His eyes brim with interest as I chat about my degree, life as a student, my hopes and fears, our island-hopping plans.

A few hours later, it's a hat-trick. Three glorious nights of award-winning sex followed by the sweetest pillow talk ever. More than I've had in my lifetime. Thank you, Greek gods.

***

I happily plunge the brush down the toilet then flush. Not even the rich ballerina and her passive aggressive demands can wipe the smile from my face today.

He wants to see me again.

Humming to myself, I move to the bath and pull her hair out of the drain.

After Dimitris pays us today, we can politely tell him to stick his placard *and* his toilet brush up his ass. We can save enough money working at the bar to take the few weeks off we wanted at the end of the trip to go island-hopping.

"Bathrooms done!" I call out merrily.

"I'll be upstairs on deck." She smiles at me and scoops up a pair of sunglasses from the table and puts them on her head. In shorts and a bikini, she shows off a figure that can't be ignored. I make a mental note to start doing squats every day.

I get to work in the kitchen. Crumbs paint the breakfast bar surface like she deliberately threw food around to give me work. Whatever, it's fine. I run the hot water tap to fill the sink. Behind me, two animated voices, hers and a man's, get louder as they descend the stairs to the lower deck.

When I turn to see who is with her, my heart vacates its cavity.

It's not the guy I saw onboard the other day.

Tristan.

My Tristan.

His jaw drops when he recognises me, just as mine does. We stand frozen, staring at each other.

He's holding hands with her son.

His son?

His face turns white. "Elena."

But that means . . .

"You're married," I choke out. The scene couldn't be clearer if someone drew a picket fence and a dog around them.

He blinks rapidly. "It's not how it looks."

I stand stiff, not moving, not breathing.

This isn't happening.

The ballerina looks between us, narrowing her eyes. "You cannot be serious. You fucked the *cleaner*? The cleaner?"

Tristan turns abruptly to her. "Not here, Gemina, not in front of Daniel."

"Damn you, asshole" she roars at Tristan, triggering the son to start bawling his eyes out. Ballerina rushes forward and pushes against Tristan's hard chest. "You think you can humiliate me? No!"

With a swift swipe of her arm across the breakfast bar, she sends two plates hurtling to the ground, smashing into tiny pieces.

I jump about two feet in the air.

Tristan steps back, stunned, then recovers. "Don't do this in front of Daniel," he pleads. "Sara!" he roars in the direction of the stairs. "Can you take

Daniel and go for a walk? Daniel, go upstairs to Sara. Everything's okay, Mummy and Daddy just need to talk. Mummy's a little upset."

Daniel stands still, eyes closed, mouth contorted, letting out a wail that could rip through your bones.

I feel like doing the same.

Just get out of here. Process it later. With shaking hands, I gather up my belongings and put my rucksack on my shoulders.

Unleashing a slew of expletives, the wife picks up a third plate and hurls it at Tristan, missing him by an inch. It smashes hard against the wall behind him.

"Gemina!" he hisses through clenched teeth. "Daniel, go upstairs."

What the fuck? I didn't ask for front-row seats at the theatre production of *The Exorcist.* This woman is taking the Greek tradition of plate smashing too far.

I scuttle past, getting out of the angry woman's line of fire.

She turns her wrath on me as I escape. "You're nobody, girl! Just another fling," she screams as I stumble up the steps. "He's just trying to make me jealous!"

Sara, the nanny, passes me on the stairs, giving me a fleeting panicked look.

I reach the deck and feel a strong hand pull me back.

"Wait," Tristan begs, holding me in his grip. "It's not how it looks. You need to let me explain."

I refuse to let the tears fall. I shrink back from his touch and slap him hard across the face. So hard, it sounds like a whip. "Fuck off, Tristan!" My voice has an uncontrollable tremor in it. "Don't come near me again!"

I climb off that boat faster than an Olympian runner and sprint down the dock, ignoring his shouts of my name behind me.

When I turn the corner, the dam opens, and I blubber uncontrollably on the street, ignoring the stares of random vacationers. My dumb phone pings. With trembling hands, I unlock the phone.

"Where are you? Let me explain. Please."

Wiping snot from my face, I click on his contact details and hit block. What a gamut of emotions I've gone through in a single day.

How could he? And how could I be so easily fooled? I hung onto every word he was saying. I thought I was smarter than this.

Nope. I'm just a naive girl who mistook a holiday romp for a fairytale.

If this is what island-hopping is about, I'm ready to bungee jump off this place.

One thing he didn't lie about: he *is* a cliché. And now, he's made me one too. The dopey younger woman who falls for the older playboy leading a double life.

He made me a mistress at twenty-four.

7

Elly

Seven months later

My ears are assaulted by the creaking bed and a headboard slapping against the wall upstairs. The rhythm quickens, followed by two loud moans, one male, one female.

Does this guy ever stop? It's midweek, not even the weekend.

That's Frank the Shagger, one of my housemates, upstairs. We don't talk too much but I know intimate details about his love life, like some sick Peeping Tom. It's the closest thing I have to a love life. That and listening to the foxes mating in the garden. There's been a drought since *him*.

My phone says six a.m.

I feel dazed like I went to sleep ten minutes ago. Am I awake? I'm not sure. It's so hard to get up when it's dark outside.

Megan's first alarm goes off next door. She won't wake up; she never does. Her snooze button is banged more times than a hooker. The alarms will go off every ten minutes until I wake her. I, on the other hand, wake up with her first alarm.

Megan and I live in a house-share in Tooting, South London, with six random strangers. We moved from Wales a few weeks back and it's been a culture shock. The only rule you're taught is to 'mind the gap' in the underground. Megan and I had to pick up the others the hard way such as standing on the RIGHT side of the escalator. Standing on the left will earn you a scolding. Also, always have your ticket ready at the barrier and don't dither. In fact, any dithering inside the London zones is not permitted.

And the one that nearly got me wiped out—some cyclists are colour-blind and cannot see red lights.

The house is a three-story Victorian built for a large family, not eight separate lodgers living separate lives. Ironic, given our setup is like the college house-share, except now we pay three times the rent. How can eight strangers know such intimate details about each other? I know Frank the Shagger's orgasm moan, four people in the house form a nightly snore choir, and *everyone* knows I have irritable bowel disease. We barely talk but walk to the shower in our towels. Rafal, the Polish guy living on the floor below, doesn't even bother covering his butt cheeks.

I force myself out of bed, bang on Megan's wall to wake her up and gather my toiletries. That's the thing about house-shares, you have to keep everything in your bedroom, or they disappear.

Tiptoeing out into the hall, I try the bathroom door on our floor. *Damn*. Someone is even earlier than me. I venture downstairs, avoiding the creaky floorboard to check the other bathroom. Bingo, it's free.

Except for the surprise in the toilet staring up at me. I'm entirely bemused. Rafal's got hands; I've seen him use them to steal my food from the fridge. Can he not learn how to use them to flush a toilet?

The joys of communal living are that no one can have a shower simultaneously. Someone is hogging all the water in the bathroom upstairs, so I rotate myself like a chicken roasting on a spit in an attempt to wash myself with my allocated dribble.

I'm nervous as hell. This is the first day of my two-year trainee contract at Madison Legal. *The* Madison Legal, the most prestigious law firm in the UK! Also notoriously competitive, so I'm damn proud of myself. Madison Legal doesn't just expect you to have a first-class honours degree. No, you must be an excellent, well-rounded human being. Hence my extensive charity work last year.

Of course, I didn't follow-up on the lying, cheating asshole's offer of a referral. I'll never work for Dawson Law if I know *he's* got friends there.

I roll my tights up my legs and inspect the finished product in the mirror. The advice online for lawyers was '*keep it simple with a neutral tailored suit or a timeless sheath dress.*' I'm in a black shift dress with a fake designer leather bag.

Will they spot I'm a fraud?

The house starts to creak as people wake up. I

bang on Megan's door one last time before heading downstairs. She started in a North London hair salon two weeks ago, promoted to a senior stylist. The commute is killing her. It's only fifteen miles, but it takes an hour and a half door to door.

That's London for you.

I open my bread bin, ignoring the droppings of last night's dinner on the kitchen counter. There's no time to get annoyed with the farmyard this morning.

The expensive gluten-free bread I bought yesterday is gone. Thieving bastards! From now on, I'm going to lick every single slice of bread front and back.

I take a cup out of the top cupboard.

What the . . .?

It's so dirty I'm better off pouring the coffee straight into my face.

Breakfast aborted.

By the time I reach the Tooting underground station, it is 7:20. My belly is full of butterflies. Can I do this every day until retirement? It was a mission just to iron the dress.

The average walking speed per hour is two to four miles; Londoners accelerate to 1000 horsepower minimum in rush hour so either you keep up or you'll end up trampled on the ground.

I join the fight to board the train. How can the Northern Line be so busy already? It's incredible what we subject ourselves to in rush hour. In any other circumstance, I wouldn't allow myself to be spit-roasted between two strangers. On the underground, we are just one big angry mass of germs, saliva, sweat and much worse.

My phone buzzes as I'm nearing the stop for the Madison Legal headquarters. Surely Mum has remembered this is my first day at work? Nope, it's Megan wishing me good luck.

Emerging victorious through the sea of London commuters, I stride down Fleet Street, the heartbeat of London's elite law firms.

Then I'm standing in front of it.

Madison Legal London headquarters. Sex on bricks. That's not me exaggerating; it won 'London's sexiest office space' last year. Even if you don't work in law, you'll know the building, thanks to its sexy architecture.

The imposing twenty-storey building with the sleek logo stares down at me defiantly.

I follow the crowd through the revolving doors into the elegant lobby with its double-height ceilings and am swept along to the large reception area at the far corner.

"Hi," I squeak to the brunette behind the desk. "I'm meeting HR at 8:30."

Behind her is a fish tank that stretches from floor to ceiling. She flashes me a bright smile. I wonder if Madison Legal is paying to get her teeth whitened. "Name please?"

"Elly . . . Elena." I show my ID as instructed in the email.

Her eyes flit to the screen then back to me. "Okay, Elena. Take the elevator to your right to the tenth floor." She smiles kindly at me and hands over the pass.

After a few swipes of the pass at the barriers, I am in an elevator with the swarms of Madison staff. With each floor, my anxiety levels rise.

These people could write the manual on the lawyer dress code.

The elevator dings open, and I'm on the tenth floor. I'm greeted by a view of St Paul's Cathedral through floor-to-ceiling windows. Holy shit . . . this is my office? People pay good money for this view.

A well-dressed man is waiting at the lifts.

"Hi, I'm Elena Andric."

He holds out his hand, which I reluctantly take, weary of my sweat glands working overtime. "I'm Jeremy, one of the HR leads."

We exchange niceties in such a manner that tells me Jeremy is tired of greeting the new recruits. I follow him into a room where about twenty people are milling around, some looking as nervous as I am.

I'm not good at networking. I can't work a room the way Megan can. I need to warm up and focus my energy on a small number of people until I feel safe in numbers. So I stand awkwardly in the corner, smoothing down my dress. There's another girl with the same tactic taking refuge beside the coffee stand. We play the shy game, smiling at each other and looking away until I have the guts to walk over.

"Hi, I'm Elly."

"I'm Amy." She looks relieved.

"Are you on the trainee programme too?" I ask. Stupid question, of course, she is.

She nods. "Everyone in this room is. Are you nervous?"

"Terrified," I admit.

"Me too," she whispers. "But we have lots of presentations today as part of the employee induction programme, all the admin stuff, office tour, welcome to the company, et cetera. I think it will be a gentle start."

Her words make me relax a little.

There's a dull roar around the room as we wait for something to happen. The same conversation echoes through every huddle. *What's your name? Oh, that's nice. What university did you go to? Oh, that's nice.*

Jeremy clears his throat loudly. "We'll be heading into boardroom five now to kick off the induction programme, 9 a.m. will be the Madison Legal introduction, 10 a.m., mission and corporate values, 11 a.m., our CEO and Managing Partner, Mr. Kane, will be saying a few words to welcome you to the firm."

It sounds like Amy's right, today will be easy. Just relax, listen and take notes.

"Count yourselves lucky," Jeremy continues. "Mr. Kane rarely has the time to do this. We are extremely honoured today."

"Oh." Amy digs me in the ribs with her elbow. "Tristan Kane is talking to us!"

Ugh. I hate that name. Still, I can't hold one man's mistake against them all.

Two hours, and a corporate vision presentation later, my attention is waning. We have two full days of people talking to us to get through. Amy and I bagged seats in the front row. I take a large sip of coffee to perk up as I have to appear extra attentive for the CEO up next. We've been waiting fifteen minutes for him so far.

There's a knock and a woman pops her head around the door. "He's ready now."

Jeremy beams at us. Every head turns to the back of the room to get a good look at the man entering behind the woman. I can't see his face from the front row. As I strain my neck, I catch sight of stubble shaped around a chiselled jaw. It's not until he is halfway up the aisle that my blood runs cold.

Oh. My. GOD.

It can't be.

It's him.

He can't be . . .

"Our managing partner and founder of Madison Legal, Mr. Tristan Kane." Jeremy claps his hands earnestly, and the room follows suit.

I move my hands together, but no sound comes out.

This makes no sense. He told me he worked in property.

But he was a liar.

Fear seeps into every pore of my being. Are my

eyes playing tricks on me? Something like eight million people live in London, one of them is bound to look like him.

He's closer now.

No, it's definitely fucking *him.*

The source of my three-day production line of orgasms that sent my oxytocin levels off the charts. My natural Viagra. The guy I thought was a fling, then thought was a love interest then realised was a lying cheating bastard.

The guy that fucked me hard then fucked me over.

My fight-or-flight response kicks in for the second time around Tristan, who I now know as Tristan Kane, CEO. And for the second time, flight wants to win. I need to escape, hide, combust, fast-forward time, pull a fake fire alarm, bomb scare. Something. *Anything.*

Instead, I sink into my chair, but in the front row I will be right in his line of vision. What's he going to do when he realises it's me?

Terminate my trainee contract?

This is so messed up.

I clutch my notepad to my chest like armour. I wonder if I could put it in front of my face and pretend to take notes. By the time the owner of this 8000-employee strong global company arrives at the front of the room, I'm feeling full tremors in my hands and legs. *Breathe, Elly. Breathe.* He might not even recognise or remember me. He's probably had a million one-night stands since then.

Gone are the jeans and T-shirt and in their place, is an expensive tailored dark blue suit. It moulds perfectly around his athletic physique. I imagine my fingers running across it and mentally slap myself. I wasn't building him up in my head. He is drop-dead gorgeous. Sometimes, I think I imagine him differently, better.

When those intense blue-grey eyes that haunted my dreams collide with mine, my heart stops.

Oh. He recognises me all right.

It's as if we're caught in a vortex, our eyes pulling towards each other.

His eyebrows rise, a slow smile spreading across his face.

I look down at my feet, unable to keep eye contact. A deep blush soaks into my cheeks spreading outwards until my ears feel impossibly hot. Maybe I am going to combust after all.

"Hello. I'm Tristan Kane, managing partner and founder of Madison." There's that low dry voice. The voice that makes my breathing rushed. How many nights have I dreamed of a new happy ending to our story, where that voice said exactly what I wanted it to?

Now he's here, in the flesh, in my worst possible nightmare.

If my presence has fazed him, he doesn't show it. Rather than standing behind the podium, he just leans in front of it, a few metres away.

Looking right at me.

Stupid nerd, Elly. Sitting in the front row. Too

close. He'll be able to hear my pulse from there.

I'm too wound up to focus on what he says. All I can see is the wide-open stance of those thick thighs, the relaxed posture, and his easy breathing as he delivers an unhurried speech and I wonder how he can be in this ridiculous state of calm when I need a fucking ambulance?

I fixate on my notebook, taking a few useless notes on the company vision.

"This is an intensive two-year trainee contract . . ." He leans against the podium, his hands in his pockets.

People around me lean forward in their seats so far, they're at risk of falling. Except for me, I'm rolling my head into my neck, personifying a tortoise.

I was expecting an old codger. Why didn't I research Madison Legal's owner? I was too busy searching forums for information on how to get into Madison Legal and what their interview questions were. Though I checked the website and would've remembered if that face graced it.

"You'll get a broad range of experience and get to shadow some of the most competent lawyers in the world," he says. His fingers drum lightly against the podium.

I'm going to stalk the shit out of this bastard online when I get home.

He keeps talking but I can't hear him. Maybe I'll start applying for other trainee contracts too. Dawson Law also offered me one.

"If you want to be a behind-the-desk, paper-shuffling lawyer, then you should walk out the door now."

I'm in eyeline with his dick. I stare at his crotch, getting flashbacks. To my horror I drop my pen and it rolls along the floor stopping near his feet. What if he thinks I'm trying to get his attention?

He continues talking without missing a beat but bends to retrieve the offending item and steps towards me. Those intense blue eyes focus on me, the same eyes that looked up at me as he devoured me.

I suck in sharply. One half of my body is in full panic mode and the other half is dying to get laid.

With an eyebrow raised, he stands right in front of me and offers me the pen. As I reach out to take it with a shaky hand, his fingers touch mine.

Beside me, Amy gives me a funny look.

"So enough about Madison." Tristan paces slowly across the room, putting his hands back in his pockets.

Smug, arrogant bastard, swaggering around like he owns the place. Because the motherfucker does.

"I want each of you to give a brief intro, so I can get to know you a bit better."

Just when I thought it couldn't get any worse. I chew hard on my pen.

He starts at the back of the room, meaning I'll be one of the last, giving me plenty of time to stew into a frenzy. In turn, everyone says their name, where they're from, and what university they've come from. Like it's the easiest task in the world. Soon it's Amy's turn. I hear her voice beside me as if I'm underwater.

I can't do this.

I take slow deep breaths from the pit of my stomach as advised in my public speaking classes.

It's my turn. Don't they realise I can't talk?

"Um," I start in a pitch too high. "Uh, hi, I'm Elena Andric. Elly for short. I moved from Wales to London two weeks ago to join Madison. I studied Law and Criminology at Swansea." I don't breathe through the entire speech.

But you already know all that, Mr. Kane.

"Elly," he repeats slowly, stopping in front of me. "Nice to have you at Madison."

I'm on fire now, the heat from my cheeks enough to sizzle sausages on.

As cool as a CEO, he moves to the next trainee.

For the next forty-five minutes, I sit stiff as the room laps up every word that comes out of that lying, cheating heart-breaking bastard boss's luscious mouth.

Only when he leaves the room, striding off for another meeting, can I breathe properly.

Amy turns to me, both hands flying to her mouth. "Oh no, Elly! You have ink *all* over your mouth."

Same disastrous day, just later.

I'm a quivering wreck. After the inductions, I am

shown to my desk and introduced to Sophie, the lawyer Amy and I will be shadowing. She explains everything to us at a snail's pace without being patronising so I instantly warm to her. I log in to my email for the first time and proudly set my signature.

Elena Andric, Madison Legal.

An email appears in the inbox that makes me bolt upright in my chair.

Elena (or Elly?)

I hope you are settling in well. I need to discuss a matter with you.

I'll be expecting you at my office at 5 today.

Please treat this as confidential. My PA will let you through.

Tristan Kane
CEO
Madison Legal

I read the email over and over again. No hint of tone. Should I pack my bags now? For so long, I fantasised about bumping into him, about our encounter being different. In some fantasies I knee him in the bollocks, in others it's a scene akin to Jack and Rose on the bow of the Titanic, except he's taking me from behind.

But not like this, not threatening the career that I spent thousands in student loans over.

Of all the law firms in all of London, my dirty summer fling had to own this one?

8

Tristan

"Mr. Kane, your son's school is on line two for you," Ed announces over the intercom. My PA is militant, detached, and sparse with chat, just how I like my PAs.

"Connect me." For a second, I think the worst, as I always do, even though it's more likely related to a school trip or a scrap Daniel's got in.

"Mr. Kane?" says Daniel's teacher.

I wince at her tone; I'm in for a scolding.

"Mrs. Maguire, so lovely to hear from you." I use my most winning voice. "How can I help?"

"There's been a situation in the after-school club." She launches straight in with a Northern Irish tone of brisk authority. Pleasantries are done. Mrs. Maguire sets the rules in our relationship. She reminds me of my Irish mother. "We can't get hold of Daniel's mother. Unfortunately, Daniel will be losing his privilege of attending the school trip tomorrow to London Zoo."

Damn, Daniel, what have you done this time?

"Surely that's not necessary. What's the issue?"

"The *issue* was that he called Miss Hargrove, our teaching assistant, a '*son of a bitch.*'"

I suck in sharply. I feel like I'm the one who's been naughty. Where did my seven-year-old son even learn that? No one uses the phrase 'son of a bitch' in England.

"I'm so sorry, Mrs. Maguire." I'm seven again and back at confession with Father Murphy. "Gemina and I will ensure Daniel is reprimanded accordingly. Please pass on my apologies to Miss Hargrove."

I hear her lips smack over the phone. "This behaviour is becoming more frequent, Mr. Kane. We will need to get to the bottom of this."

"I know," I say heavily. "I'll speak to Daniel tonight. We'll sort this out. I'm happy to come into the school to discuss it."

"Please see that you do. Make alternative arrangements for Daniel tomorrow."

The phone goes dead.

The scrap with his best mate, firing the lunch across the canteen floor, making the Menzes girl cry, now this. I should have named him Damien not Daniel. These past few months he's acting like the kid out of the fucking *Omen* movie. I stare out at the London skyline with its sharp edges and growing skyscrapers.

It's no surprise. I'm a terrible father.

"Mr. Kane, Elena Andric is here to see you," Ed interrupts my thoughts for the second time. This time it's welcome.

"Tell her to come through," I respond, running a hand through my hair.

She enters, her eyes awkwardly darting around the room, like making eye contact with me is excruciatingly painful.

She's even more stunning than I remembered. She's wearing a tight dress that accentuates her curves without revealing too much skin. Dark glasses frame her blue-green eyes, and her dark hair is pulled into a tight ponytail. She can try to hide her sexiness, but it's not working.

I'm not a man that gets flustered easily but that look she gives me with her big eyes and parted pout makes me weak in the knees.

I'm done for.

My lips curve into a smile. "Hello, Elena." I lean forward in my chair and gesture to the seat in front of the desk. "Close the door and take a seat."

She bites down on her bottom lip but nods and closes the door. "Hi," she replies, taking a seat and adjusting her view downward. Her skirt rides up revealing a hint of toned thighs.

"This is a pleasant surprise," I say softly, examining her face.

"Yes, it's a surprise alright." Her voice is strangled.

My eyes flit down to where her knuckles grip the side of the seat. Today, she's not the confident, sassy woman I met in Greece. "So, you really didn't know who I was?"

She finally looks up from the floor to meet my gaze. "Of course not." She purses her lips. "You don't have a photo on the company website."

"I don't," I agree. "Believe it or not, I don't court the media."

"You told me you worked in property," she says in a clipped tone.

"I buy and sell property. I wasn't lying about that."

Her eyes flash with resentment. "You weren't telling the truth either. I told you I had finished law school. Didn't you think that was a good opening to tell me you owned the most successful law firm in the UK?"

My gaze drifts down to her breasts, rising up and down with her laboured breathing. An image fills my head of her in the sea, wet and so aroused. I snap my eyes back to hers.

A deep flush runs up her neck and face. Not surprising, really, since she knows when I'm turned on. She's just as embarrassed now as she was when I was talking at the induction.

Huh. Maybe she really didn't know who I was in Mykonos.

"I'm sorry I wasn't forthright about owning Madison, Elena. *Elly.*" I try her nickname. "It's not something I advertise when I meet someone in a bar. Especially a bar like that. I wasn't sure whether it was going to be a fling or something more serious. Given my position, sometimes I need to be . . ." I pause looking for the right word ". . . cautious."

She gives me a withering glare then recovers. "It's fine. It doesn't matter. I'm assuming that we can keep our indiscretion a secret. Is that why you wanted to see me?"

I frown. "Not quite."

"I won't tell anyone," she says, her voice panicked. "Mr. Kane, I need this job."

So, I'm *Mr. Kane* now.

"I tried so hard to get into Madison Legal. I even took up new hobbies to show how well-rounded I was. Because you need to be the perfect human to be accepted. I've done a year's volunteering at a cat's rescue just to add it to my CV." She laughs dryly. "I don't even like cats."

My lips twitch. "I've read your CV. It's impressive for a graduate. I'm more of a dog person, unfortunately."

"Please don't fire me, Mr. Kane," she says, her eyes wild with worry. For a moment, I think she might cry.

I frown, shifting in my seat. Where the hell did she get this idea from? "I've no intention of firing you, Elly."

She straightens her dress with long, nervous strokes. "Oh, so what did you want?"

To rip that dress off, push you down onto my desk, spread your legs and bury my throbbing cock hiding under this desk, deep into you. Is it too early to disclose that? She *does* want me to be honest, after all.

"Have dinner with me," I blurt out. "Tonight. I can get a table anywhere you want."

She gapes at me like I've demanded she stick

pins in her eyes. What the fuck is wrong with her? "Why?"

My jaw tightens. This isn't going how I planned. "I want to take you out."

"Is this a condition of not firing me?"

"What? No," I reply, irritated. "I want to resume what we had in Mykonos. For us to get to know each other."

Her face distorts with disgust. "No. I don't sleep with married men. At least not willingly."

"I'm divorced, Elly. You can check it online."

"Of course I won't, it's irrelevant to me." Her face tells me she's already checked. She tucks a strand of hair behind her ear that isn't loose. She's nervous. I recognise her mannerisms from the first night outside the hellhole she was staying in.

"You weren't divorced then," she snaps. "Frankly, I find it hard to trust you. I don't agree with you as a man." She raises her chin. "Regardless, you're the best in the business, and I want to learn everything I can from your company so we can put the incident behind us. You have my discretion and professionalism."

My hackles rise. She disagrees with me *as a man*? I let out a frustrated breath. "I'm sorry for what happened on the yacht. I never meant to put you in that situation. But you didn't exactly give me opportunity to explain it."

"Do you know how humiliating that was?" she whispers bitterly. "For your wife to treat me like a servant then to find out I'm a bit on the side? I've slept with a married man."

"Ex-wife," I correct her. "And you weren't a bit on the side."

"She was your wife at the time." She snorts. "You made me a mistress before I turned twenty-five."

"Legally, yes," I admit. "But she was my ex-wife on all but paper. We were already separated when I met you. I was a free man."

She lets out a humourless laugh, her anger with me *as a man* winning over her fear of me *as a boss.* "You were on *holiday* with your *family*," she spits out. "Do you think I'm stupid? That's disgusting."

I raise an eyebrow, unimpressed. She's overstepping. "I'm not the big bad wolf you think I am, Elly. My situation was, *still is*, complicated. On the trip, I had already started divorce proceedings. The holiday was just for the sake of my son."

She stares at me. "She was wearing her obnoxious engagement and wedding rings," she bites out.

Obnoxious? That engagement ring is worth fifty grand. "That was my ex-wife's choice."

Her nostrils flare. "I guess that's why you're a successful lawyer, with your ability to stretch the truth and evade questioning."

I bite my tongue to refrain from reprimanding her. She might be the woman I've fantasized about every night for months, but she's still a newly graduated junior lawyer in my company.

We stare at each other in tense silence.

"Couldn't you have waited until the divorce papers were dry?" she asks in a low voice.

I let out a heavy sigh. "I didn't plan it. I met a woman. She intrigued me, more than anyone has in years. I didn't want to let her go. Sue me. I tried to find you. If only just to explain. I didn't know I was looking for an *Elly*."

Imagine my delight when HR showed me the new recruitment intake last week, and I saw Welsh Elly from Swansea coming to join us.

Her eyes hold mine, guarded.

"Do you have a boyfriend?" I ask softly.

She looks away. "No."

"Then come to dinner with me."

"I'm not your type," she replies flatly.

"You are exactly my type. Everything about you is my type." Damn, is she going to make me get on my knees and beg?

Her lips curl in disgust. "I met your type, remember? I cleaned her bloody toilet. Beautiful. Demanding. Passive aggressive."

That was close to the bone. "I'm not discussing my ex-wife with you," I reply through gritted teeth. Was she this hot-headed in Greece?

Her lips tilt into a dismissive smile. "No, thank you, Mr. Kane. I decline your offer of dinner. I'd prefer our relationship to stay professional."

"I don't believe you."

Her eyes narrow into thin slits. "Because I don't want to go to dinner with you? Do all your other employees say yes?"

"Don't be crass, Elly," I growl. "I haven't asked an employee out before." I clench my jaw to keep my cool.

"I don't believe you, and I don't trust you," she chokes out, fumbling with her bag on the ground. "Are we done here? I'm leaving." She jerks to her feet.

"No, we are not done," I seethe, pushing back my chair to stand up. I close the distance between us in quick strides.

Turning away from me, she grabs the door handle.

"Wait, Elly." My fingers tighten over hers on the door handle. Her skin is soft and warm. "Let me win back your trust."

"No. And trust isn't all you took from me, Tristan," she mutters, snapping my hand away so she can turn the handle and fling the door open.

What the hell did that mean?

"It meant more to me than a fling," she whispers, not looking back.

"It meant more to me too," I call after her, but she's already out the door.

Elly

I'm physically shaking when I get on the underground train after work. I expected my first day to be tough, but not this shit-show. My emotions are all over the place.

I'm disgusted with how much I've obsessed over him. Not a day goes past without him possessing at least some of my thoughts. Every night, to the sounds of Frank the Shagger's real love life, I devise new scenarios in my head revolving around Tristan. It's my guilty pleasure.

Pathetic.

How could I let myself get so wrapped up in a three-day fling? I'm ashamed to say it was a fairy tale for me. Except in my imagination, the fairy tale has a happy ending, the one where we meet in Greece and he *isn't* married with a family.

He claims he issued divorce papers even though he was on holiday with his family. Then why did his ex-wife start a war with the cutlery? She wasn't acting like a woman who had agreed to a separation. And she was wearing her rings.

I want to believe him. If only so that I can remember our time together as something meaningful rather than just evidence of me being a gullible fool.

I take out my phone and enter the code. Of course, I was lying when I said I wouldn't look him up online. I could only scan the basics in work today. Looking for dirt on the CEO of your new company doesn't feel like a productive first day activity. Like an itch aching to be scratched, my next few hours will be consumed with cyberstalking Tristan Kane.

My ultimate goal since I decided to study law was to end up at Madison Legal. Now, this changes everything. I knew the owner was one of the top lawyers in the world. How the hell had I not bothered to check what he looked like? I was so buried in case studies, interviews questions,

Glassdoor reviews and articles on how to bag a trainee contract. I ignorantly assumed Tristan Kane, CEO was a stuffy old bloke to have amassed such a CV.

Not *him*.

I type in his name, and immediately a number of predictive search suggestions pop up.

Tristan Kane net worth
Tristan Kane age
Tristan Kane Gemina Kane
Tristan Kane Madison Legal
Tristan Kane Reid case
Tristan Kane Danny Walker

Which one do I start with?

I select *Tristan Kane Gemina Kane* and click on images. A plethora of photos invade my eyes. Most of them are of Tristan and Gemina at posh events around the globe. Some of the photos are of him outside London's supreme court or on podiums speaking at events. There are a few videos of him being interviewed by the BBC that send tingles up my legs and between my thighs. Hearing that man's voice broadcast across the British nation is very erotic.

The bastard is sexy as hell. On and off paper.

I click on an image of Gemina Kane. She's wearing a dark purple gown and is clearly singing on a stage. Oh my God, is that the Royal Opera house in London? Is she famous? Famous in theatre circles it would seem from the number of pictures of her. She really is devastatingly attractive. It makes me wonder why he chose me to have a fling if this is his standard.

The next photo is one of both of them standing outside a theatre. Gemina is smiling for the camera whereas Tristan is looking at her.

It winds me how he looks at her. Every woman wants a man to look at her like that. The article is dated the start of last year.

Rebound springs to mind.

I click out of the search. This isn't good for my mindset.

There are lots of photos of him with Danny Walker, the Scottish tech tycoon who owns the Nexus Group. Interesting. They must be friends. There's another guy in all the pictures. Jack Knight, I read. It would appear handsome attracts handsome.

I click into info about Jack Knight. Owner of The Lexington Property Group. It takes me a minute to register where I know them from—the chain of hotels and apartments in every major city in the world. So, this is his friend with whom he owns property.

This is Tristan Kane's world.

The divorce must have gone through after Greece. I type *Tristan Kane girlfriend* and click search.

Now photos of Gemina are replaced with photos of Tristan with other beautiful women. I can't find two photos with the same girl. My thoughts float back to what happened that day and Gemina's voice echoes through my head, '*You're nobody.*'

I didn't blame her for hating me. What woman wouldn't?

One of the images takes me into an article called 'London's sexiest lawyers.' Who knew that was a thing? As I scroll through the article I laugh bitterly, causing the people next to me to stiffen. No one expresses emotion on the underground.

Tristan Kane was voted number one.

Guiltily, I try one last search. It was the first suggestion that came up, so it would be rude not to. My eyes bulge when the numbers render on screen: 500 million pounds?? This guy is worth 500 *million* pounds?

I shut my phone. Why am I torturing myself? No good can come of creeping on Tristan Kane online. Seeing photos of his glamorous life is just heart-breaking. None of those women in the pictures look like they live in a house-share with seven other people and stock toilet rolls in their bedroom.

No, I've learned my lesson. I'll focus on my work, keep my head down and get everything I can out of this trainee contract, then move on. Sophie is a good mentor; I can learn a lot from her.

He can sleep with other trainees, not me. Greece wasn't me; it was a temporary lapse of judgement. And it's never the subordinate that comes off well in these situations, is it? I can't jeopardise my career before it's even started. For all I know he's looking for a quick fumble then I'll be ghosted or worse, fired. I need to protect myself. While I've been in a no-sex bubble for months, he's been schmoozing all over London, by the looks of things.

I'm almost convinced except for one niggling thing. I can't stop thinking of the way he looked at me.

The look told me Tristan Kane is a man who gets what he wants.

9

Elly

"I'm never drinking again" is a mantra Megan and I adopt weekly, usually on a Sunday. Megan's the instigator. If it weren't for her, I'd be in bed by 10 every Saturday night with a book.

It's Saturday night and we are super excited. Sophie has landed me two last-minute spots on the guest list for Liquid Venus, the newly opened exclusive nightclub in the city. She says it's teeming with seriously hot men, fire-eaters and burlesque dancers. Madison Legal HQ is just around the corner, so I hope I don't run into any Madison lawyers.

Except our buzz is waning slightly. The nightclub queue is a good forty people deep, hasn't moved in thirty minutes, and it's starting to rain. In an attempt to revive my love life, I'm wearing a top with a slash down the side and rocking the side boob look, but it's creating a draft.

Megan is dissecting the Tristan situation with me. She thinks I'm overthinking everything.

"So he was separated in Mykonos . . . and he's

now divorced," she muses. "It's not as bad as you thought."

I roll my eyes, shivering as spits of rain fall. "Whose side are you on? He lied. And yes, okay, if I'm going easy on him, he withheld vital information rather than lying. As a lawyer he should have known it would have a negative impact on his case," I add sarcastically. "He was treating me like a one-night stand."

"*We* thought you were a one-night stand," she points out. "One-night stands don't bare their souls and recite their CVs to each other."

"We turned into a three-night stand with copious spooning. What's that called?"

"Greedy."

"I still think '*I have a family*' is a fact you disclose up front," I grumble. "I broke bread with the man."

"It's a big debate for online daters. How much do you disclose upfront? You don't know if you're going to see them again. What if they end up being psychos?" She offers me the wine-filled water bottle. "He's asking for another chance. And you clearly like him despite your protests. Would it really be that bad to just go for it and see what happens?"

"Yes, it would be that bad."

We inch up the queue.

"There are pictures of him all over the internet with actual *supermodels*, Megan. Supermodels don't just have hot bodies, they have *professionally* hot bodies." I take a mouthful of wine. If Tristan could see me drinking budget wine from a water bottle, he'd be appalled. "And do you know how sad I am? I tried counting to see if I could figure out how many women he's been with since Greece. All he wants is a quick fling and the stakes are too high for me."

"So cynical," she says. "You don't know that for sure. Besides, standing in photos with hot women doesn't necessarily mean he had sex with them."

"Remember what his wife said? *Just another fling*," I remind her, handing back the bottle. We need to finish the wine before we get to the front of the queue. "I don't know what he's capable of. I don't know anything about him, really."

"Ummm," she says, thinking. "But you said she seemed mean so you don't know that's the truth. With everyone you meet, you take a chance. What are you so afraid of?"

"In Mykonos we were two strangers who had chemistry. Here, it's too entangled with my life. I mean he could ruin my career. These things never end well. The trainee and the CEO? *Come on*. If I give in, I leave myself wide open." I take another deep slug of wine.

"You do. Wide open." She smirks. "Here's the important question." Her expression turns serious. "Do you think about him in the bath?"

I spit out some of the wine. "You think I'm brave enough to have a *bath* in our house? Hell, no."

She puts her hand on her hip, waiting.

"Okay," I admit. "I do think about him. Too much."

She folds her arms. "And that's exactly why I'm

creating an online dating profile for you. If you're not going to take Tristan Kane up on his offer, then we need to get you back in the dating game. Starting tonight. You're twenty-five, not eighty-five."

I nod hesitantly. "Fine. Speaking of online dating, did Aaron reply to you?"

"Damo," she corrects.

"That's the guy from Bumble?"

"No, you're thinking of the estate agent. Damo is the fitness instructor from Tinder."

"There are so many dating sites." I try to keep up with Megan's dates, but she switches them up a lot. Most guys get one date, max.

"Tell me about it." She groans. "It's an admin nightmare. If I make updates to my profile like adding a new picture, I have to push it out to all my dating apps. I need version control."

"So Damo is the new one." I need to start tracking these in a spreadsheet so I can keep up. "Didn't you see Aaron, the estate agent, on Wednesday?"

She nods. "We went to the cinema. Such a nice guy. So considerate, kind—a true gentleman. And he wants to commit to me."

I smile. "Aaron sounds lovely!"

"Oh, he is," she agrees. "But I've never been so bloody bored in all my life."

I give her a blank look. "Then why are you still sleeping with him?"

She shrugs. "He's so courteous, I feel it would be rude not to. I can't tell him I don't want to see him because he's too *nice*."

"A pity shag. But Damo is the one you're interested in?"

Her mouth twists into a grin. "Yeah. We're meeting tomorrow night. God, Elly, we haven't even had sex but he's so full of testosterone I worry I'm going to get pregnant just looking at him. If it goes well, I guess I'll have to tell Aaron it's over."

I chuckle. I've only seen pictures of Damo but he looked like a hottie. "Just remember I can hear everything in the next room and I need a good night's sleep before work on Monday."

The queue moves forward until we reach the top, where four bouncers and a glamorous hostess check IDs.

"Hey." I smile confidently, showing my driver's licence. "The names are Elena and Megan. We're on the list."

The hostess doesn't return my smile but looks down at her clipboard. Then she smiles brightly, a genuine smile.

I beam, and start to walk in.

Her arm blocks the way like a parking lot barrier. "You aren't on the list."

"Excuse me?" I ask. She must have made a mistake.

"You're not on the guest list. Either pay thirty pounds for entry or leave."

"But my friend got us on the list. Let me see, we should be on it." I lean over to look, but she snaps it away.

"Honey," she says, bored. "Read my lips. You're not

on the guest list."

"Hurry up!" someone shouts from down the line. "Go in or get out of the bloody line!"

I don't have time to call Sophie with everyone complaining behind me; that would mean leaving the queue, back to square one.

When I look at the hostess's face, I see my attempts are like arguing with a calculator. Pointless. "'Fine," I mutter. "We'll pay."

She turns to someone farther up the stairs. "Excuse me, Arnie?" Now she is yelling. "I have two non-VIPs here coming through paying full price. Non-VIPs."

I feel the entire queue of eyeballs boring into the back of our non-VIP heads. Crying inside, I claw my card out of my bag. Thirty quid, and we haven't even bought a drink yet. There'd better be a hot male burlesque dancer eating fire in here for us.

We are inside but penniless because of it. It's pink, plush, and posh. I scan the bar quickly, looking for somebody famous. So far, the search is unsuccessful. We spot a few D-class celebrities from reality TV in the corner pretending to be bored and above all this.

Hitting the bar, we wait so long I feel like I'm queueing for my pension. I holler "Four Pornstar vodka martinis" at the barman, making an executive decision to double up on our drinks. I've spent too many hours in queues tonight, and I'm not doing it again.

He presents them in teeny glasses with long stems and large lumps of passionfruit. I'm bemused by the passionfruit versus alcohol ratio in the glass.

"That's £79.20, please."

"Excuse me?" I feel faint. I thought vodka was a communist drink. "Can I see the bill, please?"

"Certainly." The bill is presented like a crown on a little gold dish. I check to see what extra services I'm paying for. A foot rub? Down payment on a flat? Sex with a fire-eater? But no, a single Pornstar martini costs £16.50, *and* there's a 20% service charge added on top! Whimpering, I present my card.

A banging tune comes on, and Megan sways against the bar, spilling sloshes out of her cocktail.

"Megan! You're spilling a pound a minute there! Careful." I bring the glass to my lips and sip. It burns my throat.

She looks at me with a dangerous glint in her eyes. Her first martini has nearly disappeared. "Tonight, we are hitting this town *hard*, Elly. Hard."

Uh-oh.

3 a.m.

As I down another Pornstar martini, I know Megan and I will be chanting our mantra tomorrow. Teetotal from this day forward. Still, my Fitbit says I've burned 500 calories dancing. Very productive night!

A guy is talking to me. I *think* he's handsome, but I suspect my vision is impaired. He shouts something over the music, and I nod. I've no idea what he said.

Megan teeters over to me on her ten-inch heels.

"I'm going to request some tunes," she bellows. "That DJ is a *snack*. Look at him!"

I laugh, turning to check out the DJ. Typical Megan, she has a thing for DJs and bouncers.

"Watch this." She winks at me, and I watch her shimmy over to the DJ booth. This DJ is putty. Men just seem to fall at Megan's feet. She leans over the booth flashing her biggest come-fuck-me smile. He frowns and says something short to her, turning back to the decks. Oh, this one isn't biting. Perhaps he's not allowed to chat up women on the job.

She's not deterred. Megan is a determined woman. A man playing hard to get is just a minor obstacle that will make victory all the sweeter.

She switches tactics and leans against the door on the side of the booth, pushing her breasts over the top of it.

My mouth falls open. She doesn't realise the door isn't shut properly. "Megan!" I shout. "No!"

It's too late.

It swings open ninety degrees, and she falls through, face-planting into the DJ booth.

From where I'm standing on the dance floor, I can't make out the commotion, but it involves an angry DJ, an irate bouncer, and a hysterical Megan.

"Excuse me," I slur at the guy whose name I don't know. As I squeeze through a crowd of drunken dancers, I catch up with Megan halfway to the exit as she is being dragged by a bouncer.

"That's my friend!" I cry.

"Oh really?" he says gruffly. "Then you're out too."

"So, he wasn't interested, huh?" I mutter to Megan as we are marched out.

She pouts. "I can't be expected to be on my A game *all* the time."

Moments before we reach the exit, I feel a cold sharp sensation running down my front, making me gasp.

"Sorry." The owner of the sticky strawberry cocktail hiccups in my face, not looking sorry at all.

It's syrupy, stinky, and seeping through my dress, past the point of recovery.

We arrived as two VIPs, were demoted to non-VIPs and now we exit as convicts. The cool air hits me as we are escorted outside.

I look up and down the street, teeming with partygoers. "Let's check out the night buses," I say, propping up Megan with my arm. I'm teetering on the brink, but Megan is off her tits sloshed. Perhaps the bouncer was doing us a favour.

A motorbike comes up close beside me. Too close. Is he trying to park here? I step back. Before my brain can register what's happening, the motorbike guy snatches my bag from my arm and speeds off.

"What the hell?" I cry, watching him disappear. "He can't do that!"

A guy smoking a cigarette against the wall next to us shrugs. "Robberies by motorbike are rife around here. You should hold on to your bag tighter."

That's not helpful.

"Megan, I had all our things in that bag!" I wail. "Yours too! Now we've got no bank cards, phones or house keys! How the hell are we gonna get home?"

She squints at me, expelling a small burp. "Another club?"

"And pay how?" I moan. "Besides, everywhere is closing soon. How many miles is it to Tooting?"

She wrinkles her nose. "Seven? It's fine!" She giggles, launching into song.

"Quiet!" I groan, suddenly feeling sober. It's too far in running shoes never mind stilettos.

We're screwed.

So, we've got no money or phones to get home. The underground is closed for maintenance, meaning we can't jump the barriers and get home that way. Not that I would have the guts to try it and considering Megan just face-planted into a DJ box, I don't think we can risk more gymnastics tonight. Perhaps we could beg a bus driver? No, Megan has tried that before, and they told her to get lost. They'll be worse when they see the state we're in. I could try to find a payphone and call Frank the Shagger, reversing the charges, but do payphones still exist? Besides, I don't know his number off by heart.

Our only option is to find a free internet cafe and contact Frank over social media asking him to come into town to give us cash. We'll never find one at night, though.

Megan leans against the wall in a daze. She can't be consulted.

I stare up at The Rosemont Hotel, and an idea starts to form. It's ridiculous, but it's either that or walk all night in the cold.

"Follow me, Megan," I instruct. "Keep your head down. We're going to find a spot in that hotel to sleep for a few hours until we can contact Frank or someone in the morning to come and get us."

"A hotel room?" She hiccups.

"No," I grimace. "A hallway or something." With that, I straighten my back, cover my cocktail-stained dress with my flimsy jacket, and swing open the doors of the five-star Rosemont Hotel.

"Walk like you own it," I mutter to Megan as we stride towards the elevators. It is essential to keep the pace of a person who belongs here. Too fast or too slow will arouse suspicion. Our noise level has to be just right too. "Like you've stayed here every day since *birth*."

We reach the lifts without being stopped.

Megan looks confused. "What now?"

I exhale heavily. "This is a long shot," I say in a low voice, jabbing the elevator button. "Paul Sharpe from uni told me that he was so drunk one night that he couldn't remember which hotel room he was in, so he slept in the hallway next to the gym. The plan is to take refuge somewhere for a few hours."

As soon as the elevator opens, I pull her in. From the control panel, the gym and spa are on the lower ground floor.

We exit the elevator into a dark hallway.

I breathe a sigh of relief. There are no bedrooms on this floor.

"Come on." I walk down the hall, keeping Megan upright. "Let's just find a corner to nap for a few hours. No one will be using the gym until at least 6 a.m."

There's one nondescript door without a key card lock, I decide to try it. Maybe it's a spa with lounge beds? To my surprise, the door swings open to reveal a linen closet with rows of wooden shelves filled with bed linen.

Like bunk beds.

Dare we? The shelves look sturdy enough to take our weight. We would even have bed linen. I can't imagine the cleaners starting before 6.

I make an executive decision. "This'll do."

"Is this allowed?" Megan peers in.

"It's not *illegal*," I say to convince myself more than Megan. "I think. Just frowned upon. Up to you. Do you want to sit outside on the floor or lie horizontal for a few hours with some sheets over you?"

She walks inside and plops herself on the bottom shelf.

"Just lie down, then we'll leave really early, okay?"

She fires her shoes off like she's at home and lies down then rolls the linen sheets over her until she's buried in them. "Good night." She smiles up at me.

"Don't get *too* comfortable," I warn, slipping off my strappy sandals. "We'll have to make a quick exit. We need to be out before the cleaning shift starts." I climb up to the shelf above her and lie horizontal, gently covering myself with a sheet. The last thing I need is to be liable for damage to hotel property.

That feels good. I'll just take a brief nap . . .

***

Something's wrong. My head feels like it's been fracked overnight for precious fuels. Memories and thoughts are foggy.

Am I dreaming?

Two female voices talk animatedly. Not in English, Spanish perhaps? The pounding in my head won't let me focus. I shift in my hard wooden bed. Oh God, that feels bad. A shudder throttles my spine as my back spasms. With a huge effort, I force my eyes open and tilt my head towards the noise.

Shit!

We fell asleep.

Three hotel cleaners are standing in the doorway, limbs flapping and talking in a highly animated tone. It's too fast for me to decipher what they're saying, but I get the gist. They are furious.

I abruptly incline and hit my head on the shelf above. "Megan," I bark as I rip the linen off me. "Get up. NOW."

She moans softly below me, but I don't hear movement.

The cleaner that appears to be in charge jerks a thumb in our direction and gets out her radio phone.

"I'm so sorry," I say. I scramble to get down from the shelf but get caught up in bed linen. "We're leaving! Right now."

She says something in Spanish over the radio.

I make out two words and catapult myself off the shelf. *'Gerente del hotel.'* Hotel Manager.

"Hop it, Megan!" I shrill, fumbling with my stilettos. She's lifted herself off the bed but is moving too slowly given the situation.

"You stay here until our manager arrives!" the head cleaner snaps at me.

"I'm so sorry," I repeat as I push past her. What else can I say? It's not like we can redeem ourselves. "Megan! Hurry the fuck up!" How bad is this situation? Can we get arrested? We haven't technically damaged property unless they count the fake tan on the sheets.

We leg it out of the linen closet and down the hall with the cleaners in a high-speed pursuit. My heel abruptly decides to snap off, and I go down on my ankle. My ankle twinges, but I don't falter; I keep going with my heel hanging off.

"Not the lift!" I shout to Megan when I see her shuffling towards it. "The stairs."

We sprint up the stairs gasping for breath with the Spanish inquisition ascending behind us. There's lots of noise coming from their radio. It sounds like an angry hotel manager.

In reception, a manager-looking bloke and two others are waiting for us. Every face in the check-in queue turns to see what the commotion is. Behind us, angry cleaners close in.

We are surrounded.

"Ladies, can you explain what you were doing in one of our linen closets?" The manager stares at us, aghast. "Are you guests in this hotel? Did you take a wrong turn?"

"No," I say meekly. "We ran into a few unfortunate events last night and we needed to . . . ah . . ." I search for an appropriate word. ". . . *borrow* one of the linen closets."

"So, you thought it appropriate to sleep in one of our linen closets?" His mouth slackens in disbelief. "This is not a hotel that permits unrespectable nocturnal activities."

My brain misfires. Wait, what?

My cheeks heat. "We're not prostitutes," I announce loudly to clear up any misconceptions. It's difficult when I'm wearing a drink-soaked dress and hovering on one heel. Last night I prided myself on such a well-thought-out executed plan.

The crowd hushes as they listen.

"Elly?"

I whip my head around.

Tristan.

I don't know who is more shocked, him or me.

His eyebrows shoot to his hairline as he takes in the ambush. "What the hell is going on?"

"These *ladies* were found sleeping in one of our linen closets, sir," the hotel manager reports. "We apologise deeply for the ruckus. We're dealing with it. So sorry to disturb you, Mr. Kane."

The blood drains from my head and pools in my ankles as Tristan stares at me like I have two heads. What the hell is he doing here? Of all the hotels in all the towns, in all the world, he has to walk into mine? I thought I would have to avoid him at work, not all seven London zones. I haven't seen him since the awkward meeting on my first day.

His gaze drops to my feet, where I'm balancing on one shoe, then back up past my stained dress to my guilty face. Shocked is not a strong enough word for how Tristan looks at me. No word is. His expression needs its own entry in the Oxford dictionary. "Elly? What the hell is going on?"

I fidget with the breast lift tape which seems to have come loose under my arm. "My bag was stolen last night," I say in a small voice, mortified. "We had no way to get home, so we . . . ah . . ." I can't find a better way to describe it. ". . . *borrowed* one of the linen closets."

"Christ," he splutters. "Sir, charge a hotel room to my card for your inconvenience. Will that appease the situation?"

I shout "No" as the manager says "Yes."

"Do you know these ladies, Mr. Kane?" the hotel manager asks in disbelief.

"Yes," Tristan grits out, handing his bank card to the manager. "I'll take it from here. Are we good?"

"Yes, sir," the manager replies, recognising his cue to leave.

Tristan eyes me, like he is seeing me in a new light. No hairbrush, no toothbrush, no dignity. This is *not* how I wanted to meet Tristan Kane. Not when I look like the Joker.

"I'll pay you back," I swallow. "What are you doing here?"

"I'm a member here," he says dryly. "It's convenient, being close to the office. I've taken my family and friends out for breakfast."

Oh.

I glance over his shoulder to where a table of people are watching us. There's an older lady, dear Lord, is that his mum? I don't have my glasses on so she's a blur. Tristan's son is sitting on her lap. I recognise Danny Walker, the tech tycoon, and a girl about my age. It must be his sister. The other bloke from the photos, Jack someone, is sitting beside a younger girl.

"My two sisters and my mum," Tristan explains. "It's Mum's birthday."

"That's nice," I choke out. I smile and wave meekly.

Most of them smile back in amusement. The mum looks appalled.

"Lovely to see you again, Tristan," Megan jumps in.

He smiles at her then turns back to me. "Are you okay? Were you hurt?"

"I'm fine, I can replace my keys and phone. It's annoying but I'll live. The only thing that's hurt is my pride. It seemed like a good idea at the time." I can't think of a better explanation.

He rubs his chin. "You could have gone into a police station. They would have driven you home."

Damn. Do they do that? "I thought it needed to be more serious before the police would help."

"You could have called me. I would have collected

you." His jaw flexes. "That's if you haven't blocked my number."

"Thanks, but I don't think that's in the scope of the CEO's role."

Tristan's not amused.

"Plus, no phone, remember?"

He pinches the bridge of his nose like he has an incoming headache. "You need to go home, Elly," he says in an accusing tone. "You reek of alcohol, and you only have one functioning shoe. You're an employee of Madison Legal, this is hardly appropriate behaviour."

I open my mouth with a comeback, then close it. I'm in no position to take the moral high ground.

He sighs heavily. "I'll get my driver to take you home."

"No, it's fine," I protest meekly. Actually, that sounds like heaven.

His eyes narrow, daring me to argue.

"That sounds great, thank you." Faced with his disapproving gaze, I look down in remorse.

He calls his driver, who appears to be outside at his beck and call, as the guy comes through the door at the speed of Superman. "George, take the ladies home, please."

George looks at us like he's seen it all before.

"I need to get back to the others," Tristan says. A ghost of a smile flickers on his face. "Try to behave yourself in whatever quarter-life crisis you seem to be having."

I cringe. "I'll try."

"A fucking linen closet," he mutters, shaking his head as he walks away.

"You might have solved your problem. He probably won't want to date you after this," Megan adds unhelpfully.

10

Tristan

"Mr. Kane?"

I snap my eyes up from Elly Andric's social media profile on my phone. Why did she introduce herself as Elena if all her goddamn social media is under Elly? Her social media seems tame enough, but Sunday morning's surprise encounter has left me thoroughly confused.

"We have secured the McKenzie case," Sam says. "They signed the papers today."

"Good." I nod. Sam is one of my London managing partners. The McKenzie lawsuit is projected to pull us in £2.5 million this quarter. "I'll personally oversee this one," I say to the boardroom. "Mark McKenzie and I go back years."

I turn to Liz, head of operations. "What's the headcount we need on it?"

She squints at her laptop. "Ten senior lawyers, roughly fifteen juniors, a few paralegals supporting for circa six months."

"We're at capacity," Rebecca cuts in. She's worked

for me for fifteen years and she's the only one who has the guts to question my judgement, on the rare occasion. "Tristan, we need more staff. Right now, the ratio is about one senior lawyer to thirty-two cases. Maybe we should relax our recruitment criteria. Giving one in every forty people we interview a position isn't efficient."

"We are not compromising on quality," I bark back at her. "We are *Madison.*"

Her lip curls in displeasure. "Then we have to start turning high-profile cases away."

I exhale heavily. "Can't Hong Kong take on some of the international ones?" I look to my Hong Kong managing partner across the video link.

"Sir, the Hong Kong office is already on overtime," she says over the link. "We're executing an aggressive recruitment campaign but getting bums in seats is difficult."

"The right bums," I correct. "What's the current headcount?"

"Globally 8,060, give or take," Simon, head of recruitment, responds. "We need an uplift of ten per cent this year alone in Asia and Europe."

I rap my knuckles on the desk. "Let's look at the recruitment budget again. Send me the numbers, Simon."

"Yes, sir." He nods.

I turn to Paula, our secretary. "Any more items on the agenda?"

She scrolls down her laptop, brow furrowed. "Rebecca wants to discuss one of the cases under contract negotiation—the Garcia case."

"That's right," Rebecca addresses me. "Tristan, we have to turn it down. We don't have the headcount. It's too high-profile without the right people on it."

My eyebrows crease together. "Remind me what it is?"

"Maria Garcia, wife of Rocco Garcia?" she prompts. "She's seeking asylum in the UK. She claims that she killed Rocco in self-defence by stabbing him with a knife when he attacked her."

"What's so special about this one?" I ask. I recall snippets of the case.

"Rocco was a famous hotelier across Central and South America," Liz reads from her laptop. "Maria fled to the UK before the trial claiming she was in danger with the Colombian mafia. She says that Rocco was part of a ring of sex traffickers, and they will kill her because she knows too much. The Colombian government want to extradite her back to Colombia to stand trial for murder."

The name is familiar. Rocco Garcia . . . Jack bought two hotels from him a few years back.

"Media coverage is swelling," Rebecca adds. "But we have to turn it down. Such a pity because these types of cases are perfect for our junior lawyers to shadow on. They don't come up often."

My spine straightens. "No, let's not turn it down. I'll do it."

The entire boardroom looks at me, confused.

"*You* will do it, sir?" Sam asks.

"That's right."

"Why, Tristan?" Rebecca probes. "If you really want us to do it, we'll give it to the East London office."

"No need," I say, irritated with my senior staff for questioning me. "I'm still a lawyer, last time I checked. I'll do it."

"But sir . . ." Sam starts.

I stare at him.

"Nothing," he stammers.

I dare them to question me further. Even Rebecca stops when she sees the look on my face. I know it's ridiculous for me to take the case.

"Anyone specifically you want on the team, Mr. Kane?" Simon queries.

A brief smile spreads across my face.

Elly

It's midnight on Thursday night, and I can't sleep.

Thank God it's Friday tomorrow so I can complete my first full week of professional employment. Twenty percent of the work is interesting, and the other eighty percent is shit I don't want to do. Movies only show court scenes and lawyers having important conversations as they walk quickly down corridors. Doing exciting lawyerly stuff.

They don't show the lawyers working their way up by photocopying, proofreading and taking minutes, do they? In fact, I've come to the conclusion that ninety percent of every job, whether you are a lawyer, brain surgeon or priest, is reading emails.

Over forty hours is a *long* time to be sitting down, and I have to repeat it for the next forty years. I've sat in eighteen meetings this week. That's thirty-four thousand meetings I will attend throughout my career. Please, someone pass me a brown bag to breathe into.

Still, I can be thankful that Tristan Kane hasn't approached me all week. I haven't seen him since the shame of getting kicked out of the Rosemont on Sunday morning. Maybe Megan was right, #linenclosetgate was the nail in the coffin to make him realise I'm not worth the hassle. Or he has simply moved on to his next conquest. Perhaps it *will* be easy to avoid him for the next two years. If he stays in his ivory tower on the top floor and I stay on the tenth floor, buried in photocopies, I'll be safe.

What a roller coaster week.

I hear another thud upstairs. Frank has been wrecking around bumping into shit for an hour. What the hell is he doing?

This is officially the house-share from hell. Chances are, at least one of us will leave in a body bag, and one of us will be charged with murder. Right now, I don't mind which one I am.

This thud sounds like he's fallen over. Argh.

My thoughts drift back to Tristan Kane.

As I do every night, I shut my eyes and try to drown out Frank's commotion so I can focus on visions of Tristan's ripped, naked body. My guilty pleasure. I need to stop this. I need to move on.

The door upstairs slams open, and I hear Frank stumble down the stairs followed by a loud bang where he must have missed a step.

My bedroom doorknob rattles suddenly. What the hell? The door is slammed open against the wall with such force that small flakes of paint chip off the wall.

I jolt up in bed to see a dazed Frank standing in the doorway. "Frank," I bark, but he doesn't seem to hear me. "What the hell are you doing?"

He doesn't respond. I'm not sure he knows I'm here. He's sleepwalking or really drunk, maybe both, I can't tell. "Frank," I repeat louder. "Frank, you idiot!"

Nothing. He just stares at the wall with glazed eyes. Don't they say never to wake sleepwalkers? Maybe he'll leave on his own accord.

Instead, he walks over to my dirty clothes basket and lifts the lid up against the wall. I'm irked but mildly curious. What's he doing? Unsteady on his feet and muttering under his breath, he fumbles with his jean buttons.

Realisation dawns on me. He thinks this is the bathroom.

No. No. NO.

"No, Frank! No!" I shriek, clawing on the floor for a T-shirt I can grab to cover myself.

It's too late. Before I can react, he yanks out his dick and pees in my clothes basket.

"It's not a fucking toilet, Frank!" I bellow. "It's my clothes basket! Wake up!" I might as well be a ghost. I pull the T-shirt over my head and jump out of bed.

He shakes his dick and allows me to shove him out of the room. It's too late, the damage has been done. He doesn't look for the sink, so now I have proof he doesn't wash his hands. I'll never accept toast from him again.

I can't cope with this. I'll have to start barricading my room at night.

Trainee lawyers don't get paid as much as people think. I'm up to my eyes in student debt and helping my mum with her rent. It will be at least a year until I've saved enough so Megan and I can move into our own place. As for Megan, she had to get a loan from her sister just to move to London.

I pick up my wash basket and creep downstairs to put my clothes in the washing machine. Of course, it's full of wet clothes that someone forgot to take out, meaning no one else can use it.

Something soft runs over my foot in the dark, and I yelp. Maybe I won't make it to the end of my first workweek after all.

***

Sophie touches my arm in concern. "You look tired."

That's an understatement. I look like a panda caught in headlights, I'm so tired.

I'm grabbing a coffee in the canteen with Amy and Sophie. Calling it a canteen is an insult;

Madison Legal canteen could rival a Michelin-star restaurant. This is no school dinner selection, these guys are professional chefs and baristas trained to make world-class coffee. The baristas are coffee connoisseurs imported from New Zealand, which explains a lot.

It's a constant reminder of Tristan Kane and his particular tastes. Sophie says he has final approval on all the lunch menus and the sourcing of the coffee beans. Control freak.

"Did I work you too hard this week?" she asks. "You've been staying late every night."

"No, Sophie. It's my flatmates. I didn't sleep very well last night." I sigh. "Again." It's not just me that's exhausted. Yesterday, Megan said she was so tired at the salon that she nearly cut someone's ear off.

"Frank at it again?" Amy giggles.

I nod, regaling the disaster of last night.

Sophie shudders. "Can't you get him evicted? Christ, I'm glad my days of renting by the room are over."

I laugh dryly. "Frank's not the worst of them. Anyway, better the devil you know than the devil you don't. Statistically, living with seven other people, I reckon you'll get at least one nutcase in the house." I take a giant slug of my coffee. "It never stops. It's a production line of noisy human movements throughout the night. Someone is up at the toilet every hour or coming in late from pubs or getting up early for shift work."

"Can't you and your friend move somewhere

else?" Amy asks as we walk to the elevator.

"Not anytime soon." I shake my head as we wait for the next elevator. "It's cheap, and we can't afford a two-bed yet. Although I'm spending any extra savings on takeaways because the kitchen is *always* occupied, and I swear I'm buying toilet paper for the entire house. The couple in the basement leaves us little 'presents' in the kitchen like half-eaten toast. It's just all getting on my nerves."

A man clears his throat behind us, and we turn, and I look straight into the eyes of Tristan Kane. He and another man are standing in the elevator waiting for us to get in.

"Mr. Kane," Sophie says in a breathy tone.

He arches a brow, smiling, and beckons us into the lift. "There's room."

I step tentatively into the elevator and turn to the front to avoid his gaze. The elevator doors close, trapping me inside with him. It's too cramped now. The box isn't big enough for his presence. What is it about elevators that just intensify everything by 100 percent? Holding my breath, I watch the buttons light up on the elevator control panel as we ascend. I feel like hitting the emergency alarm button.

"Maybe you could look at a neighbourhood further out? It's cheaper at the end of the Northern line," Amy whispers loudly.

What's she on about? *Oh*, the conversation we were having.

"We looked through ads last week," I say in a low

voice. "The only one in our budget was advertised as 'looking for a female to share with one mature male, free of charge.'"

Amy and Sophie chuckle. Easy for them to laugh, Sophie can afford a mortgage, and Amy's secured a flat from the bank of Mum & Dad Ltd.

As the elevator pings open on the tenth floor, I rush out, taking in a deep breath.

"Have a good day, ladies," the deep voice calls after us.

Sophie and Amy swoon and respond, but I'm halfway down the aisle, sprinting to my desk.

"What do you think of the first proper week?" Amy asks me in a hushed tone when Sophie excuses herself to take a call.

I check if Sophie is close enough to hear us. "I'm finding the financial services cases a bit boring. Particularly the documents I need to review. Four years of debt, twenty different student flatmates, three infestations of mice, and gallons of bad cider. Sometimes you wonder if it's worth it."

She shrugs. "Apparently ninety percent of law is admin. Even the most exciting cases require you to read the same document five times. I think we'll have to get used to it."

"I know, and I sound ungrateful when it's been my dream to get a position here. I'm just so cranky after no sleep."

She claps her hands together. "Oh, there are drinks tonight! That'll wake you up. I can't wait to see the bar upstairs."

"Are the drinks in the building?" I ask, surprised. "There's a bar here?"

She looks at me like a moron. "Top floor."

"It's just the trainees, right?" I ask cautiously. Any possibility of Tristan Kane in the vicinity makes my anxiety levels hit the roof.

"Apparently the HR team will be there to babysit us. To make sure that the new grads don't go buck mad and wreck the place." She laughs. "Or buck one another, I guess."

I nod. "Makes sense."

Sophie comes back into earshot.

"Sophie, none of the partners will be at the drinks tonight, right?" I ask. "Any chance of Rebecca Milford and . . . eh . . . Tristan Kane joining?"

She snorts. "No chance. You probably won't talk to them for the next two years except nods in hallways. Your induction talk was an exception. You can have fun at the drinks without worrying about behaving yourself in front of management."

Good. I can relax now. There's no reason why Tristan Kane and I would cross paths. I can take the stairs from now on, it's only ten floors.

11

Elly

At 5:30 that afternoon, Jeremy from HR rounds us up and herds us into the elevators, destined for the top floor. He doesn't look thrilled to be babysitting.

"Why are you going, Soph?" I ask as six of us squash into the next available elevator.

"They request some of the qualified lawyers and HR mingle with the new trainees. So we can tell you more about Madison," she explains.

I nod.

"Really it's so you behave yourselves and don't wreck the bar," she adds cynically.

"Lucky you." I smirk. My ears pop as we ascend to the twentieth floor. We get off the elevator into a lounge area with panoramic windows overlooking the London skyline.

"Whoa," I roar without an ounce of composure.

"I told you!" Amy squeals.

Sophie grins. "That's the typical reaction. Nice, isn't it? The Lexington Group architected it. Friends of Tristan Kane apparently."

The hot guy, Jack, from the pictures all over the internet.

"Champagne, girls?" she asks, laughing at the shock on our faces. "It's a free bar."

"No," I say firmly. "I'll have a beer. Champagne gives me a hangover and brings out the fear in me." The last time I had champagne was in *his* hotel. I can't look at a champagne flute now without feeling tricked.

"I thought the Welsh could drink as well as the Irish." Amy grins.

"I'm a lightweight." I gawk around as we make our way to the bar. Waiters flit between groups of thrilled trainees, serving food and drinks. It's more decadent than the last wedding I was at.

"Canapé?" a waiter asks, holding out the tray to us.

"What are they?" Amy asks suspiciously as Sophie orders our drinks. "I'm a pescetarian."

He points to the first dish. "This is smoked eel, golden beet, and elderflower jelly."

"Can pescatarians eat eels?" I ask, confused.

She wrinkles her nose. "I don't think so. Although it's not something I've been offered before."

"This one"—the waiter points to the next dish—"is the cured salmon caviar with violet flower and red beet. Finally, we have the salmon tartare cornets."

I give him a blank stare.

"It's a running joke." Sophie laughs and hands me a beer. "Tristan Kane has *very* exquisite eating habits. He controls the restaurant and bar menus, to the annoyance of the chefs."

"Sounds like a psycho." Amy stares at the tray as the waiter waits patiently. "And he *chose* eel?"

"I'll have all three." I hold out my plate and take the bizarre little canapés. "It's my right as a new trainee to accept all free food and drink." Even if it does flare up my Crohn's. Just like Amy, I've never needed to research the effects of eel on a dodgy bowel.

"Brave," Amy says. They watch me put the elderflower jellied eel in my mouth.

It's surprisingly refreshing.

"Gross." Sophie screws up her face and changes the subject. "Did you hear we are taking on the Maria Garcia case? It's all over the news. Have you been following it?"

I nod, picking apart the violet flower. I'm not sure if it's edible. "The Garcias were a bit of a celebrity couple in South America."

"It'll be an interesting case," Sophie says.

More interesting than the cases I'm working on in the Financial Services sector, but I can't say that out loud or I'll sound ungrateful. Helping banks with regulatory demands and public policy wasn't the thing that I imagined myself doing four years in university for. But my foot is in the door . . . even if I can't stay at Madison Legal for longer than the trainee term.

"Oh my God." Sophie gasps, flapping her hand and nearly flipping my plate. "I can't believe he's here."

My heart stops for a beat as I absorb her words. I already know who *he* is because there's only one person in the company who makes everyone's voice go up a notch.

He's by himself. Spines throughout the room gain a few inches as everyone attempts to be noticed by him.

My hand curls tightly around the beer glass.

The atmosphere immediately changes, like the Prime Minister has just walked in. Even HR and the senior lawyer babysitters seem excited. He looks like he's walked straight out of Savile Row in a suit so sexy he should be gracing GQ magazine.

The three of us watch from the sidelines as junior and senior lawyers cluster around him.

I step behind Amy, trying to make myself inconspicuous.

"Does he use this bar often?" Amy asks, watching the scene.

"He does," Sophie confirms. "Just rarely with the employees, only with management, and he *never* attends trainee drinks. In fact, this is a first as far as I've heard. How exciting! Airtime with Tristan Kane."

"He's easy on the eye, isn't he?" Amy murmurs.

I stiffen. "Hadn't noticed."

Sophie's eyes widen. "You *must* be tired."

"Or blind," Amy adds. She's right, it's clear as day that the man is heartbreakingly handsome.

I watch people hover around him with a tightness in my chest. Some of the women are blatantly flirting. If I succumb to his advances, I'll just be another girl unable to resist Tristan Kane. *Do you realise that, you fool?*

He works the room starting in the opposite corner. I don't know whether to feel relieved or disappointed. I let my eyes briefly skirt over to his to find I already have his attention. When our eyes meet across the crowd, he gives me a slow sexy smile like a private acknowledgement passing between us. As if he knows the power his gaze has over me.

My breath catches in my throat, and I look away, flustered.

"Let's get more drinks," Sophie suggests.

We nod at that fantastic idea and gravitate back towards the bar.

Out of the corner of my eye, I see Tristan cosying up to one of the senior lawyers. The striking redhead stands out across the room. Mara, I think her name is. She's tall and sexy beside him, a perfect match. He says something, and she laughs loudly, tilting her head back to reveal her neck. Flirting 101. A pang of jealousy shoots through me.

I swallow the lump in my throat. I've got no claim on him. Of course he's going to flirt with gorgeous women. How many women in this company has he *really* propositioned?

I turn my back to him. Out of sight, out of mind.

"I've changed my mind. I'll have champagne," I announce to Sophie when she starts to order our next round at the bar.

"Champagne's a good option for you." Amy grins.

"You'll be able to sleep through Frank the Shagger's bedtime antics."

"Or maybe you'll sleep *with* Frank the shagger." Sophie hands me the champagne.

"God, no." I laugh loudly. The champagne slips down too quickly. "I won't be sleeping with Frank the Shagger."

The girls' eyes widen like saucers as a deep voice behind me chimes in, "Unusual surname."

How the hell did he manage to cross the room so quickly without me noticing?

"Mr. Kane," Sophie says in a high-pitched squeal. "We weren't expecting you. Don't you have the Law Society annual ceremony this evening? You usually speak at it."

I grimace and force myself to turn around. Standing with your back to the company owner isn't the most strategic move, even if I am trying to hide from him.

"I sent one of the partners," he answers Sophie, but his eyes hold mine. "I wanted to welcome our new recruits. I interrupted your conversation." His lips curl into an amused smirk. "Don't stop on my behalf." He takes a step into the circle.

For Fuck's sake. I stink of salmon and eel. I take another deep sip of my champagne.

His eyes fall to my lips as they part around the champagne glass, watching the liquid pass down my throat. The bubbles come out too quickly and I choke, spilling drops down my chin. Can't he look at the others?

"What were you talking about?"

Our eyes dart between us. Do we make something up?

"This is outside of work hours. You don't need to talk about work, ladies."

"Eh," says Amy, "Elly was just telling us the funniest stories about her house-share." She grins at me as Sophie grimaces. "You should start a blog."

"I'm pretty sure most graduates can resonate with my issues," I reply dryly.

Amy looks guilty. With her flat fully paid for by her parents, she's the exception.

"Who do you live with, Elly?" His voice is deep and husky. I wonder if Charlie and Sophie notice how seductive it sounds.

"Just a bunch of lunatics," I mutter.

"Last night, one of them mistook her bedroom for the bathroom when he was sleepwalking," Amy discloses, and this time Sophie's look is filthy. I guess we're wasting valuable airtime. "Can you imagine!"

Tristan looks appalled. "How do you know this guy?"

I shrug. "From the Internet. Eight of us have been thrown together by fate/misfortune/the devil's work . . . however you would like to view it."

"Eight of you?" He scowls, turning towards me. I wonder if the others notice. "It sounds like a commune. You're telling me you don't know any of them?"

"Oh, I know things about them that I should *never* know," I say. "I know their eating habits, sleeping patterns, work schedule, exercise regime . . . I could go on."

He stares aghast. "Why don't you find somewhere by yourself to live?"

What a ridiculous question to ask someone under thirty in London. Does he know how expensive even renting a studio is?

"I can't afford it," I say in a clipped tone. "*Yet*."

He rakes a hand through his thick dark hair. "How many are men?"

"Most of them," I reply haughtily. "Have you always lived by yourself, Mr. Kane?"

He stiffens.

Sophie's eyes widen.

"No," he says after a beat. "But I'm alone now."

Silence envelopes us. That was quite the conversation killer.

"What are your weekend plans, Mr. Kane?" Sophie asks with a dazzling smile.

He smiles warmly. "I'm spending the day with my son tomorrow. We've got tickets to rugby at Twickenham then we're going to the Harry Potter theatre production. He's getting to meet the cast."

"Sounds lovely," Sophie croons.

"Does he look like you?" I ask, feigning innocence. I already know the kid is the spitting image of his willowy ex-wife.

A muscle in his jaw jumps. My question has hit a deeper nerve than I expected. I just wanted to get a rise out of him. "No, he doesn't look like me." He changes the subject. "What are you ladies doing for this weekend?"

Sophie and Amy explain their weekend plans.

Now, it's my turn.

His eyes brim with interest.

Me? What am I doing? Should I lie? Oh, what's the point? "I'll wake up early so I can be first in the queue for the washing machine. Then I'll supervise the wash because if I don't, someone else will take it out, and I'll lose half my socks."

Masculine laughter rings in my ears. The girls laugh too, like I've made a joke, but I'm deadly serious.

"That doesn't sound very relaxing," he says softly. "Perhaps you need to do something fun after it." His eyes gleam. "Like swimming."

I swallow too much air.

"I personally love swimming," he continues in his low voice with a hint of humour in his eyes. "Really gets the blood pumping. Helps release tension. Especially if you have a great swimming partner."

He slowly and deliberately runs his tongue over his bottom lip, smirking at me. I feel my face match the shade of the salmon tartare on the plate and I glance at the others. They look like smitten dogs.

"I love swimming too," Amy chimes in.

"I would go swimming," I reply, my throat dry, "if there weren't so many arrogant swimmers in the water these days. It's not worth it."

He chuckles. The girls laugh loudly, overcompensating for their confusion. I don't blame them; this conversation makes no sense. I'm wasting our precious moments with the CEO talking about arrogant swimmers?

"You should give it a chance again." His lips twitch. "You might remember what you enjoyed about it. It can't have been all bad."

Sophie scrunches up her nose, *very* confused.

What's he playing at?

"Maybe," I squeak. Before he can respond, I down the last of my champagne. I'm going to have the final word here. "I have to run. I'm late. Enjoy your night."

His smile vanishes as I slam the flute down on the bar, harder than I meant to.

Sophie flashes me a warning look.

Waving at the group, I turn on my heels, not looking back.

It's a small victory. No one walks away from Tristan Kane.

Tristan

As I lift the velvet rope guarding the doorway, I see my best mates, Danny and Jack, already seated at the table. It's sectioned off from the main restaurant because we like our dinners to be discrete, especially Danny, who finds random pictures of himself eating on the internet.

"Always late." Danny rolls his eyes as I stride towards the table.

"Always busy," I reply, smiling at the beautiful hostess who takes my coat. "Why did we choose this place?" I ask in a low voice when she's out of earshot. "The reviews aren't amazing. Their steak tartare is barely *supermarket*-worthy."

Jack snorts. "Then don't order the tartare, simple."

Danny shakes his head. "I don't know where it's come from. Your parents are Irish, for Christ's sake, you grew up eating potatoes as a staple. How are you such a food snob?"

"I'm making up for lost time." I nod to the Scotch without an owner. "Is that mine?"

"We pre-ordered one for you." Danny smirks. "We didn't want to keep you waiting without a drink."

They toast me, and I take a sip.

Jack leans in. "Why did you bail on the law society dinner? You go every year religiously."

I take a larger sip of my Scotch. "I'm not in the mood. I went to the welcome drinks for the new interns instead."

"How saintly of you." Danny cocks a brow. "I'm assuming for Tristan Kane to grace his presence at a lowly *intern* event, a certain gorgeous young Greek Goddess was there?"

"She's not Greek. I just met her in the Greek islands. And she's not a damn intern either, she's a junior lawyer."

"You didn't answer the question," Danny fires back.

Jack scrunches up his nose. "Remind me how you managed to orchestrate it so that she works for Madison?"

"I didn't need to. Elly did." I shrug. "She studied law, and I own Madison Legal. It's a no-brainer. Where else would she want to work? Lucky for me, she's clever enough to make the cut." I undo another button on my shirt. "I asked her to go to dinner with me. I couldn't tell you guys at breakfast with Mum listening like a hawk."

"She's a bit of a live wire." Jack chuckles. "Sneaking into hotels and staying the night there? Aren't you paying your staff enough?"

"Don't start. I'm hoping that was out-of-character behaviour."

"Jack's right." Danny frowns. "She's a junior at your firm. Is this wise?"

My face tightens. "It's unfortunate but I'm not willing to give her up." I run my hands through my hair. "It's tortuous knowing she's a few floors down. I can't look at her without remembering her with her clothes off. I'm walking around with a permanent semi."

Danny grins. "That must make work very . . . hard. So, when is this dinner date happening?"

I clench my teeth. "Actually, she said no."

Jack presses his hands together in a slow, loud clap and looks at Danny. "This is a momentous occasion. The first lady in history to resist Mr. Kane."

"It's a setback," I mutter. "I'll talk her around. Although Rebecca will have my nuts for pursing a junior lawyer."

Jack cocks a brow. "Then what? Once you've dipped your pen in your own company ink, then what?"

"Stop making it sound so sordid."

"A junior and the boss?" Danny rolls his eyes. "This reeks of a mid-life crisis."

"Speak for yourself." I snort. "How's my sister?" Last summer, Danny's tech company, Nexus, acquired the firm that my younger sister, Charlie, worked for. They started an affair behind my back. It was a turbulent time, and our friendship hit the rocks for the first time in two decades. Needless to say, I wasn't happy when I found out, but Danny seems to be serious about Charlie. Although it's very early days.

"She's great, we're heading to Scotland next weekend." He smiles. "Besides, you can't compare. I'll marry Charlie. Are you going to marry a twenty-five-year-old trainee lawyer that sleeps in linen closets and make her a stepmum? Can't you just buy another sports car and get this crisis out of your system that way?"

All valid points.

"So why this woman?" Jack tilts his head studying me. "I've seen her, she's gorgeous but you've been out with women just as beautiful. Can't you just sleep with someone else who doesn't work at Madison?"

I let out a heavy sigh. "It's not just sex. I liked *being* with her. She's funny. When I was with her I felt less stressed. Not to mention she's intelligent. And being multilingual is sexy as fuck. I made her moan in Croatian."

They exchange glances.

"Just fuck a language teacher in that case." Jack laughs. "I think it's because she's resisting you. This could all end in tears. Likely hers."

"The odds are stacked against us," I admit. "Besides, what twenty-five-year-old wants to carry my baggage?"

Danny's brows furrow. "On that," he starts carefully. "Are you going to talk about it?"

"No."

Danny darts a glance at Jack for backup.

Jack clears his throat. "We're worried about you, man. This isn't something you get over easily."

It. This.

Danny lowers his voice. "Tristan, you've barely talked about it since you found out. You're bottling it up. This isn't healthy."

My chest tightens. "Leave it. I processed what happened a long time ago. Let's enjoy the evening."

Danny eyes simmer with frustration. "You processed half the story."

Like I don't know that.

"How is Daniel?" Jack asks, shaking his head subtly at Danny.

I slump into my chair. "He's acting up a lot, not surprisingly. He's not listening to the teachers in school, he's sulking when he's at home. We're taking him to a child counsellor to process the split but I don't know if it's helping." I release a breathy groan. "What do I do, ask my child to stop being a dick? The guilt I feel every day from breaking up his family . . . It's soul-destroying."

Danny leans in. “Can’t your mother help with advice?”

“No chance.” I groan. “She’ll march him down to the priest if she knows what he called the teacher assistant.”

“Don’t look at me for advice.” Jack chuckles. “Although I’ll admit I'm slightly jealous. I would like a mini-me. Think how handsome he would be.”

His face falls. “Sorry, man.”

“No need.”

I had come to terms with the fact I wasn’t Daniel's paternal father. Bloodline or not, you can’t switch off feelings.

I drunk a whole bottle of Scotch the day my DNA test came back. Then I did the same the next day, and the next day. But eventually I processed it and found a way to move forward.

But Danny was right, that was half of the story.

12

Elly

Monday morning and I'm ready for another week of contract reviewing and minute-taking.

Sophie wheels her chair over to my desk. "I've got news for you. I don't want you to get too excited because you're there just to shadow, but do you remember the Maria Garcia case we talked about?"

"Of course." I bob my head in agreement. "It's gaining more publicity by the day." I slap a hand over my mouth as realisation dawns. "No way!" I squeak.

"You're on a part-time loan to the case team, a few meetings here and there, that's all," she warns. "But it will be good exposure. You get to watch senior lawyers in action on a delicate case."

I bounce in my chair. "I can't wait!"

"Good," she replies. "Because there's a meeting in two hours. The retainer has just been signed. Look for the instructions in your emails."

***

I step out of the lift on the nineteenth floor.

Why is the meeting room so close to the senior management floors? Suddenly I have a bad feeling about this.

I smooth down my blue shift dress so it stretches past my knees. When I walk too fast, the hem rides up, showing too much leg. I've bought a few of them in different colours in the sales. It screams low-end high street fashion, but it's passable. I can't afford to shop where Sophie and Amy shop. Not yet anyway.

Room 111, 112, this is it, 113. Three other people, two men, and a woman, are in the room talking when I nervously peer around the corner. "Is this the meeting for the Garcia case?"

The woman looks at me and smiles. "Yes. And you are?"

"Elly Andric." My eyes dart between them when there's no recognition. Has there been a mistake?

After a moment, one of the guys snaps his fingers and turns to the others. "The junior shadowing."

He beckons me to take a seat. "I'm Adi, this is Jacob and Lisa. Welcome, Elly."

I take a seat opposite Adi and say hello to the team. They acknowledge me politely then return their focus to their laptops. With everyone studying their screens, I'm at a loss as to what to do with my hands, or eyes, for that matter. Do I pretend I have important business on my laptop too?

I focus on my hands. "I'm so excited to be supporting this case," I say. "Who is the lead lawyer on it?"

"I am," comes a smooth deep voice behind me.

Seriously?

Lisa looks up, startled. "Mr. Kane."

The same emotions flit across their faces like dominos—apprehension, fear, excitement. A chance to impress the CEO first-hand.

He takes the only available seat beside me. So close, too close.

I stare straight ahead at Adi and try to steady my breathing.

Adi folds his laptop shut, sitting up straight. "What a surprise and an honour. So you are leading this case, sir?"

Please say no.

My heart plummets. It's too much of a coincidence, yet would the CEO of Madison really go out of his way to handpick trainees?

I was nervous walking into this room, I'm so anxious to make a good impression at Madison and not look stupid at one of the world's most elite firms. Now *this* added into the mix? I'm going to need a pacemaker to survive this assignment.

Tristan lets out a low chuckle. "Everyone seems shocked by this fact." He leans back in his chair, the only person relaxed in the room. "It's an interesting case that's got the media's attention."

I smell his aftershave, the same aftershave he wore in Greece. It hits my nose, and the memories flood back; we're in the restaurant, walking on the beach holding hands, in the bed with him between my legs. How many nights have I wanted that man musk as a candle in the bath whilst I'm pleasuring myself Down Under?

"Mr. Kane, have you met everyone?" Adi asks.

Blood rushes in my ears as he looks right at me.

"I have." Tristan scans the room. "You'll be my starting team for the case." He checks his watch. "I have ten minutes. You've been granted permission to the case files on the system. There are fifteen charges filed against Maria Garcia. I expect you to be familiar with all of them by Wednesday. Last week, Colombia made an extradition request to the UK. The Secretary of State has already sent the case to the courts so an arrest will likely be issued imminently for Maria. Also on the system are the notes collated regarding Maria's appeal for asylum, which has been declined."

He launches into our strategy and approach in such a fast-paced delivery I struggle to keep up. It's just another day in the office for him; for me it's the highlight of my short career.

Such a waste. I could learn so much from this experience. His name is one of the most recognised and respected lawyers globally. Getting this opportunity, even just to shadow on one of his cases, isn't something that comes up often in a lawyer's career. Even if it is via suspicious circumstances.

Instead, I'm a quivering wreck.

The team leans in on high alert as he discusses the approach they will take and their roles.

One thing I know now for sure. Every person in this company is crushing on Tristan Kane.

Including me.

***

Tristan ordered two cars for four of us to travel to where Maria is staying, just off Kensington. To my relief, I was told to travel with Adi, although annoyingly I felt a pathetic pang of jealousy when he insisted Lisa travel with him.

I use the car journey to scrutinise the case's contents one last time. Last night, I stayed late in the office to review each detail of all fifteen charges against Maria Garcia.

We pull up outside a four-storey white stucco villa in Holland Park, an affluent part of London filled with embassies and old money. It's beside the Uzbekistan Embassy and almost the same size. Adi said Maria was living here alone. She must be the richest asylum seeker in the country.

Outside there are three burly security men. We show our passports to gain entry onto the grounds.

As adrenaline surges through my system, I forget about the tall, muscular figure in the perfectly fitted suit leading the way in front of me. Cases like these are the reason I wanted to become a lawyer. A case interesting enough to consume your every thought. I don't want my thoughts consumed with regulatory body act number 42 and trading act 1977.

We are led by one of the security men up the wide steps and into the hallway, which has high ceilings and walls adorned with paintings and art installations.

"Apparently it used to be an embassy," Adi whispers. "The entire street is embassies or former embassies."

Maria is waiting for us in a lavish library, the perfect space for entertaining if she were allowed to have guests other than lawyers. I recognise her immediately, although she's gaunt now compared to the glitzy media pictures. The story of the handsome hotelier and his young model wife. It was a fairy tale in Colombia for many years until it turned into a horror story.

My heels catch in the frays of the impractically thick carpet, and I trip into the room, cursing.

"Careful," Adi mutters, narrowing his eyes.

"Maria?" Tristan asks with a professional smile.

She glides forward offering her own dazzling smile and takes his hand, shaking it how I imagine royalty would. To my surprise, she's just as impeccably dressed as the media presents her. I was expecting someone about to get arrested to be in loungewear with no make-up.

Her eyes flash with interest, as every woman's eyes do when they meet Tristan Kane.

I stand behind the others as Maria offers us seats. I know my place, my lack of experience automatically ranks me as the inferior in the room and I should do as I'm told.

Adi beckons to a chair beside him, and I take it.

It's easy to see why Maria Garcia would capture the interest of one of the richest men in South

America. Before she killed him, that is. A natural brunette, her flawless features and icy blue eyes make her look almost doll-like. Her long legs stretch out under the coffee table, and I wonder how she manages to maintain her hair at salon quality while hiding out. She's exquisite, and it doesn't go unnoticed by the males in the room.

At least I know Tristan can't sleep with his client. I hope.

Tristan reclines in the leather armchair closest to Maria. He takes up more space in the room than anyone else, and I don’t just mean physically. Taking control of the niceties he introduces the team and our roles. His words are drawn out and low with pregnant pauses, perhaps to relax Maria. He asks pleasantries about the house and the neighbourhood, which he seems to know a lot about.

She anchors her attention on Tristan. She doesn’t look like a woman pleading for help or concerned about impending jail or death. More like a predator who has found her next meal.

If Tristan notices, he doesn't react. The darling of Colombia's fashion shows sits across from him, mirroring his body language, smiling and dazzling at the right moments.

Maria signs the consent form and I start recording the meeting.

I listen in awe as Tristan explains the intricate details about her extradition request and what will happen once an arrest warrant is issued. He rolls his sleeves up to his elbows showing his muscular forearms. I try not to let my gaze drop down to his naked skin.

"How long can I expect to be in prison until the preliminary hearing?" Maria asks. I look around the library which is more luxurious than most hotels I've stayed in. Maria seems tough but transitioning from a luxury house in Kensington to prison seems like it would be a shock to the system.

"Two to three weeks," Tristan confirms. "We will be working on your asylum case in the meantime. Your initial asylum interview will be this week. One of our team will be with you in the meeting."

My teeth latch on to my bottom lip as I watch Tristan in action. This is why my heart couldn't handle only a quick fling with him. There's nothing sexier than a guy who is top of his field. Ironically, I'm not sure if I'm more aroused hearing his low husky voice groaning my name as he climaxes or discussing the intricacies of the asylum-seeking process.

As if feeling my eyes on him, he tilts his head in my direction and gives me an intimate smile. It's enough for Maria to also turn her attention to me. I smile back politely then look away flustered.

Over the next ninety minutes, I make a conscious effort to focus on his words rather than him. With a slow calm dominance that isn't forced, he teases what we need out of Maria.

In those ninety minutes, I get a very confusing picture of Maria. The media Maria is different from the real-world Maria. This one is just as charming, but I see flashes of something darker. When she focuses her unnerving, beautiful gaze on me, a chill bolts up my spine. Intense, unblinking eye contact makes me feel like someone has walked over my grave.

By the time we are done I walk out of my first client meeting, hot, flustered and ready to submerge myself in an ice-cold bath.

13

Elly

"The cars will take you home," Tristan informs us as we walk out of Maria's house onto the street where the two Aston Martins we came in sit parked.

"That's not necessary for me," I respond politely. "I'll take the underground."

The drivers are waiting outside the cars. Panic sets in as I lock eyes with the driver of the car I hadn't arrived in. It's George, Tristan's driver who I did the drive of shame with from the Rosemont Hotel. His brow furrows as he tries to remember how I'm familiar to him. I return a strangled smile.

"I insist." It's not open for negotiation. "Lisa, Adi, take the first car. Elly, get in the second car. George is going southbound."

The others shrug and get in the first black Aston Martin.

I give in, deciding it's not worth the fight, and climb into the back seat of the second car. This is going to be a long drive.

George climbs into the driver's seat. "Are we

heading to Tooting, Elly?"

Before I can open my mouth to speak, the opposite door opens and Tristan climbs in.

"You can have this car," I stammer, my hand latching on the door handle. "The underground is fine for me."

"Stay," he growls with such ferocity I freeze. He makes himself comfortable by spreading his thighs wide. His trouser-covered knee brushes against my bare knee and I flinch.

"Most people would appreciate airtime with the owner of the company," he mutters.

I bite my lip to stop what is in my head from shooting out my mouth. I need to be careful here. He's still the boss. He could make or break my legal career.

I focus on a spot above George's ear.

"Where do you live?" Tristan asks.

"Tooting," I reply, trying to sound natural. "But you already knew I was travelling south."

He leans forward. "George, we'll drop Elly first in Tooting, then you can drop me off."

George twists around in the seat to face his boss. "Sir, can I get a second car for Elly? That would be much more convenient for you."

"One car is fine," Tristan responds, his tone laced with irritation. "South London first."

George looks confused but quickly turns in his seat and revs up the engine.

"Water?" Tristan offers me a closed glass bottle.

"Thanks." My voice comes out breathy.

As he hands it to me, his fingers brush against mine.

I stare out the window at the roadworks trying to calculate how long the journey to Tooting will take.

"I would prefer not to have a conversation with the side of your face."

I force my gaze from the window.

"That's better."

"Mr. Kane," I start briskly, deciding to use this airtime with the CEO to my advantage. "Do you have advice for me starting out? Is there anything I should focus on in my first year? Or areas I should research? I know data protection and GDPR are boring topics, but they seem so important these days no matter what sector you're—"

"Elly," he cuts me off softly. "If you want mentoring, I'll give you all the mentoring you need. That's not what I'd like to talk to you about now." He presses a button to his right, and a divider starts rising, separating us from George.

"What are you doing?" I ask in a shrill voice as the divider closes at the roof of the car.

"It's soundproof."

I shoot him a look. "And that's not at all creepy?"

He shrugs. "It's for confidential calls and conversations, that's all. George is used to it." He drapes his arm across the back seat so that his hand is dangerously close to my neck. "Do you want me to put it down again? I will if that's what you want."

I shake my head.

"You seem to have gotten the wrong impression of me. I want to rectify that."

"Oh really?" I raise a brow. "So, seeing you play happy family the same day as we had sex in the morning gave me the wrong impression?" Heat floods my face at the memory of that morning. He made me come twice. I take a large sip of cold water.

His eyes fill with frustration. "Yes, actually it did."

I fold my arms across my chest. "Why did you and Gemina split up?"

He sighs softly. "So, it's still about my marriage." His jaw tightens like I've hit a massive nerve.

He doesn't speak for a long moment.

"She cheated on me with some rich old fuck."

"A richer older fucker than you?"

"Ouch." He chuckles. "Always the smartass. That hurt. I tried to search for you. I thought you'd be easy to find. Not having a second name didn't help. They wouldn't disclose your contact details at Swansea University because of data protection."

"I thought you didn't want to talk about data protection," I say dryly. "Contacting my university could be considered romantic or stalkerish depending on your point of view. What would a court say?"

"It was a risk I was willing to take. Would you have preferred I forgot about you and moved on?"

I don't respond.

His fingers lightly touch the base of my neck sending a shiver coursing through me. I shift in my seat. He's only touching my neck but with the way I'm breathing you'd think he's giving me a tantric massage.

"Elly." His quiet voice broke the silence. "What's stopping you from giving me a chance?"

I ignore my common sense and lean into his touch sending a trail of goose bumps down my body.

His eyes fix on mine telling me he knows *exactly* the effect he's having on me.

"I'm not risking my first job on a fling," I say, my voice shaky. "It's not the boss that loses out in these situations. What's going to happen to you, you get a warning? You get fired?" I let out a humourless laugh. "Me? I'll be the office gossip until the next poor sod sleeps with the wrong person or sleeps with *you*."

"I haven't dated an employee before you," he states simply. "We don't know that this will just be a fling."

I eye him sceptically.

"Am I so far off the mark?" he asks when I don't respond. "If I recall correctly, you came on to me." He winks. "There was even some *begging* involved."

I narrow my eyes and open my mouth then snap it closed again. Actually, I couldn't deny that.

"You could ruin my career," I whisper. "You have the power to."

"I could," he agrees. "But I've no intention of doing that. I keep my personal life separate from my professional life. I expect you to be able to also. If we date and it doesn't work out or if you cheat on me, that's not a reflection on your professional ability. Your reputation won't be impacted."

I stare at him, deadpan. If *I* cheat on *him*?

"Why are you on this case, Tristan?" I ask. "And more importantly, why am *I* on this case?"

"You're a junior lawyer. We always have the juniors shadow cases like this. You told me in Mykonos you wanted to experience criminal law. Aren't you an obvious fit?"

My eyes narrow. What bullshit.

"Do you want to be taken off the case? If that's what you really want, it's done."

"No."

"Good." He smiles at me. "Do you think about me, Elly?"

I don't answer him.

"Have you thought about our nights together?"

"No," I whisper, turning towards the window. I won't disclose that my vibrator is named after him.

"Your face says otherwise."

I roll my eyes. "There are pictures of you all over the internet with different women. Don't tell me you've been pining for me. Is this how you woo women?"

His lips twitch. "So, you did some research on me. Don't believe everything you read. Stories are exaggerated. I'm often photographed at events. And it's not a line. I think about you all the time."

I rub my hands down my dress and stare back at him. "Oh, really? What do you think about?"

My traitorous eyes travel down his broad

shoulders and wide chest ogling every muscle along the way until they land on his thighs. They are clothed in an expensive tailored suit that did nothing to stop the memories flooding back. I loved his naked thighs. They made me feel small and feminine.

He waits until I meet his gaze before he talks. "I haven't seen you in months but I can still remember your body like it was yesterday. I think about that first night, in the water. Your underwear was soaked through, showing me every curve, every line of your beautiful body. I was so turned on, I wanted you there and then." His lips twitch at the corners. "Should I go on?"

No, throw me out the fucking window. It's been months since I had sex. If he were to invite himself up my dress right now, I'm not sure I would have the willpower to resist.

I keep my eyes trained on his, afraid to breathe.

"You took my goddamn breath away. Then you let me, no, *invited* me to touch you. You were so wet, so ready for me. Those little breathy moans you made ruined me."

My heart slams in my throat as I hang on every word.

"In the hotel room, you came over and over again, clenching on me like you couldn't get enough. I can picture it so vividly."

My eyes widen. This man should be a narrator for an erotic novel. I try to steady myself. If I attempt to talk, I'm not sure what will come out.

"I've thought about you every night since. I need to taste you again, Elly." It sounds like a demand more than a request.

"What?" I squawk. How can he be so comfortable while I'm the opposite? I jabber at the window switch to put the window down. I need to let out some of this sexual tension. It's too hot in this big black car. My bare legs feel taut and sweaty against the leather upholstery. I need fresh air fast.

He doesn't take his eyes off me. "If I had my way, I would take you back to mine and spend the entire night reminding you how good I can make you feel. But first, I would make you beg. Tease you until you can't take it anymore. Then I would spend hours making you come so hard that everyone in London hears you screaming."

My treacherous legs part. I can't think past the carnal urge to act out his story.

One of his brows rise. "You want that too, Elly, don't you?"

Fuck yeah, I want that. My body is craving, *aching* for him to touch me there. I put the bottle to my lips hoping he doesn't notice my shaky hand and resist the urge to pour the cold water over my head.

"It's just sex," I say in a hard tone.

He looks at me as if he's considering the statement. "No." His mouth quirks. "My little stress ball. Let me take you to dinner. The date we had in Mykonos . . . I can't forget it easily. I want that again. So do you, Elly. It's written all over your face."

I take a deep breath. "I can't," I whisper. "How

many women have you had sex with since me?"

He runs his tongue over his teeth. "Why does that matter? I'm single."

It matters to me.

"You expected me to stay celibate waiting to find you, Elly?" His voice softens. "Look, I won't be pursuing anyone else when I'm with you. It's *you* I imagine lying on top of me every night. It's you that I can't get out of my head."

I swallow hard.

"Give me one chance," he says finally. "If you tell me you aren't interested, then I'll leave you alone."

The car slows to a halt outside my house. I hadn't even realised we were on my street.

"Where do you live?" I ask curiously.

He looks sheepish. "Holland Park."

"Holland Park?" I stare at him as my brain misfires. "But we've just come from there."

"I took the scenic route home," he admits. "Seems I enjoy the scenery in Tooting. So, Elly?" He asks like a boss instructing a subordinate, not a man asking a woman on a date. "Shall I pick you up at eight for dinner?"

I summon every ounce of willpower I have left.

"It's not a good idea," I say under my breath, fumbling with the door handle. I need to get out of this car before doing something I regret. "Goodbye, Tristan."

I yank the door open, jump out of the car, and shut the door.

14

Elly

"Holy God, I'm hot just *listening* to that story," Megan shrieks as she takes a strand of my hair and wraps it in the curling iron. For years I've been Megan's guinea pig. "I've never had a man talk that dirty to me. Scrap that, I've never had a man *be* that dirty to me."

"That was the PG version," I mutter, flinching as she scalds my ear. "The unedited version is a lot raunchier. No wonder he invested in an isolation partition in his car."

She wrinkles her nose. "Like how passengers are separated from drivers in taxis?"

"Exactly like that," I say. "Except this one is soundproof."

She stops mid curl. "It sounds like it's built for murder. You know he basically had you in a cage?"

"A woman starved of sex caged in with a guy she wants sex from." I grimace. "I'm extremely proud of my restraint."

I yelp as she pulls my hair back.

"There." She places a mirror in front of me.

"Sexy. Mr. Fuck-me Kane doesn't stand a chance."

It's not bad. The curls bounce loosely over my shoulder. I nod approvingly.

Her lips twitch. "You have to admit, it's pretty hot that he's your boss."

"No." I frown. "This could ruin my career before it's even started."

She waves the curlers dismissively. "Stop being so serious, Elly. Enjoy the attention! Besides, it might actually help your career."

I snort. "I'm not climbing Mr. Fuck-me Kane to climb the ladder."

She rests the hot tong on my shoulder.

"Ouch!"

"Sorry. But you want to sleep with him, don't you?"

"That's irrelevant." I shrug. "That's the issue, I'm not programmed to handle just sleeping with him. I can't just be a fling then see him in the office and pretend everything is okay."

"He'll move on if you don't act," she warns me, fixing some final breakaway strands. "Guys like that don't hang around."

My chin tilts in defiance. "Well then he didn't like me that much."

"What if it's been so long it's closed over downstairs?"

I give her a withering look. "It's not a *wound*. It's a dry patch," I reply defensively. "I went on a date with that chef a few months back. And the sexy cyclist before that."

"Yeah, but you didn't get past first base with either," Megan points out.

"I have no solution. I want Mr. Fuck-me Kane but I can't sleep with him. And I can't sleep with anyone else because I want him." I sigh. "Any word from Damo?" Damo had gone silent on Megan the past few days.

"No." She tuts. "A week ago, his responses were real-time. Now? Tumbleweed. I've got texting anxiety. I'm doing irrational things like restarting my phone and Wi-Fi. Just in case it's the phone. I stalk when he is last online. Then when he *is* online, I start typing in case he sees that I'm online and thinks that I'm stalking him. Which I am."

"Forget him, Megan," I say firmly.

Her eyes go wide. "But I need to know *why.* Why, why, why? Ghosting is a form of torture they should use on inmates."

I bite my lip. "You'll never know why. Let's look at some new profiles tonight. You once told me to get back in the saddle, remember? The stud farm in London is *huge.*"

She giggles. "Enough bucking bronco innuendos. I get the point."

"Let's focus on your exhibition," I say excitedly. "This is amazing. I'm so proud of you."

Tooting council is putting on an exhibition for local artists and Megan has managed to get a small stand at it.

"It's in a library," she scoffs. "It's not exactly the Tate Modern or MoMA."

"So? It's still your first ever exhibition!"

She can't contain a smile. "Yeah, it's cool."

Downstairs the fire alarm goes off.

She looks at me in the mirror. "Takeaway again?"

"I think we'll have to eat it in our bedrooms." I groan. "Let's order something then look at some house porn of where we *could* be eating dinner."

***

Tristan doesn't talk to me for the rest of the week, even during the second meeting with Maria Garcia. The woman still makes me uneasy. What with Maria Garcia giving me the chills and Tristan Kane giving me hot flushes, I'm starting to wonder if this is what menopause will be like.

In fact, he was so professional on the second trip that I suspected the previous car journey was a dirty dream I had mistaken for reality. Instead, I'm treated with the polite detachment that a junior lawyer would receive from a partner.

Perhaps he realised he had made a mistake. Did he regret propositioning me? Or had he already moved on to the next conquest, like Megan said? Has the cat found a new mouse?

The guy is a mind-fuck.

So tonight, in an attempt to revive my dire love life, I have joined millions of lonely and/or horny Londoners in the online dating minefield. Megan said that there was no need to spread myself across all the dating apps; eighty percent of entries are the same.

This evening is a date with Chris, twenty-eight, from Yorkshire. According to his profile he spent two years teaching English in China before moving into coding and is now a senior developer at Nexus.

Yes, the same Nexus Group that Tristan Kane's friend Danny Walker owns, but that's irrelevant.

We've arranged to meet in the top bar at the Regency Hotel, an exclusive restaurant in London Bridge near the Nexus HQ. Apparently, the Nexus staff get discounts. It better be ninety per cent off. I checked the drink prices before I came out, and they are freaking hideous.

London Bridge is bustling with Thursday night drinkers already in weekend mode. I wrestle my way through the crowds until I'm inside the hotel.

Fortunately, Chris resembles his profile picture. I meet him at the entrance, and we travel up in the elevator, exchanging nervous niceties.

In the mirror, I catch him checking out my butt. I'm wearing a blue top that Megan says makes my eyes pop. It cuts too low at the back, and I'm starting to feel self-conscious.

"Thanks for meeting me here, Elly," he says as we are seated at a table by the host. Chris seems nice but I already have zero sexual interest. "My work project means I'm leaving the office really late these days. But you'll like it. It's got great cocktails."

"It's lovely." I look around the plush bar. Oh, there's a button Press for Bubbles on the table! "That's cool that you get a discount."

He nods. “It's because the Nexus CEO Danny Walker is friends with the owner of the Lexington Group. They own this place.”

I flinch. Jack Knight, another guy who witnessed #linenclosetgate.

Chris runs a hand through his hair. "I have to admit, Elly, I'm rusty at this. I split up with someone, and this is my first online date.”

A sense of relief floods me. “Me too!”

He nods. “Have you just been through a break-up?”

“Uh, no.” I falter, feeling stupid. “I'm just . . . rusty.”

We order cocktails, discussing in unnecessary depth the ingredients of each in an attempt to drum up chat. The conversation is pleasant, if a little stilted. I find myself subtly looking at my phone to check the time.

Chris tells me he is into cricket. I tell him I watched it once and gave up when I realised it would be going for another five hours.

He laughs. “That's what my ex-girlfriend used to say. She couldn't stand it when I sat indoors until a cricket game was over.” It's the only time his eyes light up.

We both look down at our drinks as the conversation dries again.

“Your profile said you work for Madison Legal?” he asks.

I nod proudly. “I just started about a month ago at their headquarters on Fleet Street. I'm on their two-year trainee contract."

"Fleet Street," he repeats like it's the only thing he heard in the sentence. "I used to go out around there after work. My ex worked there."

"Really?" I ask, my smile faltering. That's a few times he has mentioned his ex-girlfriend.

"Do you know Fleet Street gets its name from an underground river—the River Fleet?" he explains. "She told me that."

"Who did?" I ask, confused.

"My ex-girlfriend, Mai," he replies.

Ah, we are still on the subject of the ex. "Were you together long?"

He looks distant for a moment. "Six years."

"Quite a while." I gulp. "When did you split up?"

"Three months ago."

"Oh, that's a pity," I reply, wondering where I'm going with this. Where are these cocktails?

He shrugs. "These things happen. In the end, we found we just weren't compatible. She wanted to get married, and I didn't. Don't get me wrong—she was lovely. I'm just not ready for the next step."

"Plenty of time for all that," I offer, wondering how I managed to turn my first date in ages into a counselling session.

I'd prefer to talk to myself. What's the polite minimum number of drinks these days? He bought the first round so it would be rude not to buy him one back . . . two should be enough, right?

Chris's eyes flicker with interest at something behind me. "Bossman is here," he murmurs.

"What?" I turn and am hit by smouldering blue-grey eyes, unapologetically hungry with lust and maybe something close to anger, blazing at mine.

Tristan

Her eyes nearly pop out of her head. I stare back at her then my gaze drops to roam up and down her body.

Who is this idiot with her?

The idiot waves in our direction.

"Is this guy trying to antagonise me?" I bark at Jack and Danny. "Why the fuck is he waving at me? Is this Elly's idea of a wind-up?"

Danny chuckles. "He's not waving at you. He's a developer at Nexus. He's waving at me."

Danny gives a salute back, and the guy beams.

Elly looks distraught, like a deer in headlights.

Serves you right for dating someone else, I think bitterly.

"She's stunning," Danny murmurs. "He's a lucky guy."

I glare at him as my temperature rises. "He's not fucking lucky."

"I don't think she's wearing a bra," Jack observes.

My hands tighten around the glass. "I can see that, Jack," I snap. "Keep your lecherous eyes off her."

"My hotels have the best linen closets, you know," he says. "Maybe Elly and her date could try them out."

My jaw tightens. I'm not in the mood for their banter.

"Do you know his name?" I ask Danny in a steely voice.

Danny thinks for a second. "Nope. And by the look on your face, I'm not sure I'd tell you if I did. I don't want to be an accessory to murder."

I jerk to my feet, lifting my coat and Scotch. "Get up. It's time for you to become acquainted with your employee."

"What?" Danny looks at me dubiously. "You want me to crash their date?"

I stand over them impatiently. "That's exactly what I want you to do."

Jack laughs loudly. "Oh, man, I'm definitely coming along to see this."

Danny cocks a brow but makes no attempt to get up. "And what exactly is your plan here? Do I tell him it's against company policy to date Elly?"

"He's waving over here like a simpleton. He's gagging for your attention. The friendly CEO of Nexus is going to take an interest in the welfare of his employees. Get up," I bark.

Jack jumps to his feet. "I'm game!"

Danny sighs heavily but hoists himself to his feet. "You owe me big time for this, Kane."

Her date watches us approach like all his Christmases have come at once. "Mr. Walker?" he calls out disbelievingly as if Danny might be an apparition.

"Hi," Danny says in his smooth baritone. "Tim,

isn't it?"

"Chris!" he says. Chris looks apologetically at Danny for not being Tim.

My eyes lock with a shocked Elly. Chris's and Elly's cheeks glow a similar shade of red.

"Chris, of course, it is. How stupid of me." Danny clears his throat.

Chris puffs his chest out.

"Mind if we join you?" Danny asks.

"We'd love that!" Chris leaps a foot in his chair. "Please, Mr. Walker, sit." He makes exaggerated hand gestures to the empty seat beside him. "Elly, you don't mind, do you? Just for a drink?" he asks as an afterthought.

Her mouth falls open. "Actually, I . . ." Her soft voice trails off as I lift a chair from the nearby table and plant it down right beside her.

We take a seat. Danny beside Chris, to Chris's delight, and me beside Elly, to her dismay. Jack is sandwiched between us.

"Isn't this cosy?" Danny comments dryly as five people squeeze into a table for two.

"We're on a date," Elly chokes out in a hoarse voice, giving Chris a dark look.

"Sorry, Elly," Chris says excitedly. "I'll make it up to you on the second date."

Second date? Elly and I both narrow our eyes on him.

"Hello, Elly," I say softly, my leg brushing against hers under the table. She jolts like a current of electricity has flown from me to her. "Meet Danny and Jack."

"Hi, Danny and Jack," she says in a strangled voice.

Jack's eyes dance. "Lovely to meet you, Elly."

Chris looks between Elly and me and frowns. "Do you two know each other?"

"He's the owner of Madison Legal," Elly rasps as my leg touches her bare leg again. This time she doesn't move it away and her warm skin stays firmly pressed against mine.

"Oh my God." It's my turn for Chris to fawn over me. "You own Madison Legal? Oh my, what a privilege to meet you, Mr. Kane."

"That's right." I grunt. Now fuck off, Chris.

"Well, isn't this fun!" Jack roars. "Both of you on a date, and your bosses join. It's a small world, isn't it?"

"Tiny," Elly says. "London is starting to feel like a Welsh village."

"Can I just say, you two make a lovely couple." Jack has a permanent grin plastered over his face.

I glare at him. "They don't know each other."

"They'll get to know each other," Jack counters, trying to contain himself. "Elly, you look beautiful. Doesn't she, Chris? You're the luckiest guy in the room."

A sound erupts from my throat.

Beside me, I feel Elly shift in her seat. She jabs the champagne button repeatedly. "This thing isn't working," she mutters. "I need express delivery."

"Every time you press it, you're ordering another

glass." I chuckle, leaning closer to her. "That's the tenth you've ordered."

Her eyes widen in panic. "Are you serious?"

"No." I give her a private grin. "I'm kidding."

She exhales hard.

Danny throws me a lifeline and launches into a conversation with Chris about his current project. Jack leans in, pretending to be interested in Chris's project when really, I know he's eavesdropping on mine.

"Your date is an idiot," I say in a low voice, although I don't care if the idiot hears. "If I were on a date with you, you would have my undivided attention."

She lets out a little snort.

The champagne arrives, and Elly takes a large gulp.

My arm rests on the top of her chair. If she leans back my arm will be around her shoulders. At this angle, the others can't see it. Her idiot date is too invested in lapping up every word Danny says.

"You look breathtaking, Elly," I murmur. My fingers lightly stroke her shoulder. She tenses but doesn't move away. "Are you happy to see me?"

"You're unbelievable," she whispers, angrily. "You actually have the audacity to gate-crash my *date*? What exactly is Paddy Irishman's, Paddy Scotsman's and Paddy Englishman's plan here?

My grin widens and for a minute I'm speechless. The woman can put me in my place. "Come on, you have to admire my persistence. My plan is for you to ditch this guy and spend the evening with me. Are you hungry?" My fingers run lazy circles on her exposed neck.

"Stop it!" She glowers at me. "Chris will see."

I cut her a serious look. "I don't give a fuck who sees. Well?" I ask impatiently. "Are you coming with me?"

"No!" she snaps. "Can you choose someone else for your mid-life crisis please?"

Christ, this woman is going for the jugular this evening. My cock twitches under the table.

She turns her attention to the other three, leaving me staring at her with a slack jaw.

"Chris?" she asks, her voice stilted. "Perhaps you could tell me more about cricket."

Chris looks gutted at the interruption of his verbal sucking of Danny's cock.

"Chris, you're neglecting your date. It's all our fault," Danny chides while giving me a wicked smile. I preferred him when he wasn't going out with my sister. He was grumpy and had no banter then.

Chris apologises and starts a mindless conversation that I don't bother listening to.

My eyes fixate on the brunette beauty sitting agonisingly close to me. Her entire back is exposed and at this angle, I have the perfect view of the curve of her breasts in the silk top. Exactly how I know she wants me to.

"So, this is your hotel, Jack?" I hear her ask.

He grins. "Sure is. If you ever want a complimentary stay, be sure to tell Tristan. Or do you prefer to call him Mr. Kane?" He winks at me.

"That would be amazing!" Chris jumps in, misreading the room for the fiftieth time this evening.

Elly fidgets awkwardly with her champagne flute. "Excuse me," she mutters. "I'm going to the ladies'." She leaps out of her seat and speeds off.

I drain my glass and follow her with zero hints of subtlety. Danny must hire some gormless developers because Chris turns back to Danny and starts a new conversation.

The inside of the unisex bathroom is all dim lights and mirrors. At first, she doesn't notice me standing at the door watching her as she fixes her hair in the mirror.

I clear my throat.

Her mouth briefly opens, then closes again as I take measured steps toward her until I'm standing behind her and staring at her in the mirror.

She freezes. The hand that was halfway to her hair falls limp onto her chest as she watches me with big eyes.

A long moment passes, our eyes locked.

I take a further step forward, pulling her between my open legs until her backside is firm against my cock.

Her lips part as she wordlessly stares at me. In the dark sexy shadows of the bathroom, we are just Elly and Tristan. Nothing else matters except the need to be in her presence, to feel her body against mine.

My hands tighten around her hips as my arousal

grows harder against her warm body. All because of her. And all hers.

I slip my fingers ever so gently under the hem of her top at the small of her back. It's a bold look for her, a plunging top that drops to her lower back. She lets out a ragged breath but doesn't protest, so I tease my hand further under the hem and slide my hand around her waist until I find her bare stomach.

"I'm glad you're on a date." I breathe against her ear. "So you can see how much better it would be with me."

I press my palm against her stomach, pushing her body flush against mine. Her stomach contracts in shuddery movements.

I smile wickedly at her in the mirror stroking her stomach with my fingers. "Do you want me to go up or down?"

She takes small shallow breaths not reaching the pit of her belly.

My hand slowly travels up just below her breasts. I'm not in a hurry.

She sucks in sharply as my fingers tickle the under curve of her breast, not quite reaching the nipple.

"Down it is, then." I smirk as I trail a line down her stomach to the hemline of her underwear.

Her eyes tell me she wants my hand to travel south and, hell, I want to, but instead I gently move her hair to one side, exposing her neck. I'm not going to fuck her in this toilet. When I fuck her, it will be slow, hard, and somewhere private where she can moan my name in her beautiful lilt. My lips dip to her neck, and I lick and kiss her soft skin from the top of her jaw all the way down to her shoulder.

She closes her eyes, rolling her head back to settle on my chest. As my mouth devours her neck, she presses herself against my cock.

"Give me a chance." My eyes lock with hers again in the mirror. "Let me show you how good it could be between us."

She closes her eyes, pained.

"It doesn't have to be one or the other. Your career or me," I continue, almost pleading as I stroke her stomach. "You can have both."

The bathroom door flies open, making both of us jump. Two girls stop in their tracks when they see us. "Somebody needs to get a room!" the one says loudly to the other.

Elly stiffens and whips my hand out of her top, her face like beetroot. "I have to go," she stammers.

I call after her hoarsely, "Elly, wait!" but she ignores me, running from the bathroom, leaving me with a throb the size of Mount Everest.

15

Tristan

"I have fifteen minutes, folks," I explain as I enter the meeting room.

All four look nervous, even Adi, my senior lawyer. It's his first time working directly with me. Yesterday the judge issued a warrant for Maria's arrest. Our next visit will be in Bronzefield prison, just outside London. I take a seat at the front of the room and make myself comfortable.

Adi clears his throat. "We're pursuing the claims that Maria was acting in self-defence. Maria wasn't subject to a complete medical examination after informing the police that her husband applied physical violence with intent to kill. She was taken immediately to the police station, and a doctor wasn't called until forty-eight hours later. We've been granted access to her hospital records. They clearly establish that Maria suffered deep bruising to the chest and, neck and a broken wrist."

"So we've got a case for police misconduct?" I ask.

"We have the transcripts for the twenty-four

hours following her arrest and the official police report. It's evasive regarding why a full medical wasn't established immediately. There was little attempt to ascertain whether there were signs of a struggle, either within the property or on Maria's person," Jacob explains.

I nod. "Sloppy or deliberate police work?"

Jacob shakes his head. "The evidence doesn't tell us yet. Maria knew the officer in charge. She claims he has been taking bribes from her husband for years. If Maria is telling the truth, then it's intentional police misconduct."

My attention focuses on the captivating brunette in the corner. It's been a week since I ambushed her date. Unless I make a concerted effort there is no reason our paths will cross, and I know she won't instigate it.

I force my eyes away from her and back to the dossier Adi has set down in front of me.

"Do we have any evidence of bribery?" I ask, turning back to the team. "I'm assuming we have no police officers willing to testify."

"Absolutely not," Jacob confirms.

I flick through the brief until I find what I'm looking for. Maria told us she secretly recorded her husband discussing one of the girls, known as girl D. "What about Maria's claims of the recording?"

"I'm pursuing that," Lisa says. "We've expedited the request with the phone carrier to get the back-ups. The Colombian police won't turn over Maria's phone."

"Okay." I nod, scanning the brief. They've made good progress. "We have four weeks until the extradition hearing. Ed will email the date once it's known. Keep looking until you find something we can pin Article 3 on."

We need to prove that there is a real threat to life if Maria is extradited. So far, we don't have enough.

"Anything else?" I ask, moving to the final pages of the dossier. "What are these notes?"

Adi leans over to see what I'm reading. "Ah, Elly was studying the transcripts and recommended we probe more into girl D with Maria."

I look at her. "Why?"

She swallows nervously and pushes her glasses up her nose. "Maria said she never met girl D or any of the girls," she explains, fidgeting with her hands. "She made a joke about her husband liking the girls feeble and petite so he could feel important. Photos of girl D have never been publicised and the police never questioned Maria about her. So it strikes me as strange that Maria knew she fit the description. I didn't pick up on it until I listened to the transcripts a second time."

She looks at me with bated breath, like I might laugh or shout her out of the room.

"Agreed, delve into it," I confirm, and her shoulders relax. "We cannot have her withholding information."

I do a final scan then close it. "Good report."

Adi smiles at Elly. "Actually, Elly did the report. I only had to make minimal changes."

She blushes. I remember she's not good at accepting compliments or praise.

"Very good, well done, Elly. How are you settling in?"

"Good, Mr. Kane." She shifts in her chair, clearly unappreciative of my attention before the team. "I'm supporting three cases including this one. Sophie is a good mentor."

"Glad to hear it." I turn to Adi. "Are we done for now?"

"Yes, sir," Adi replies.

I nod, standing up. "Let's meet again in two days. I'll review the full brief by tomorrow."

They expect me to stride out of the room. I have places I need to be, and Ed has my meetings lined up like dominos.

Instead, I linger as they pack up their laptops.

Still, she avoids eye contact although the deep blush on her cheeks tells me she feels the full weight of my gaze. She studies her laptop like it's the most fascinating thing she's ever seen.

They follow me into the hall, Elly trailing behind. My senior lawyers have the good sense to address me on the way out.

Elly gives me a brief nod, making eye contact with my chin. She walks towards the back elevator at top speed while the others walk in the opposite direction.

"Elly, wait," I call as she stabs the down button in rapid succession. The elevator opens and she disappears instead. What the fuck? I don't expect my staff to ignore me.

I jam my foot in the elevator before the door can close. “Did you hear me?”

She looks up, startled.

“Mr. Kane.” Ed reaches the elevator bank, slightly out of breath. “You have a meeting in Canary Wharf in thirteen minutes, and it’s a twenty-minute car ride. George is waiting outside.”

For fuck’s sake, who is chasing who here? Why does he have to be so good at his job all the time?

“In a minute, Ed,” I grind out, stepping into the lift. “I’ll be back up to get my stuff.” I jab the close button on the panel before he can respond.

The door slides back open but not because of Ed.

“It’s full,” I growl at the poor paralegal in the wrong place at the wrong time.

“Sorry, sir,” he stammers, scuttling backwards.

I hit the button again and we descend in the steel box filled with the sound of our ragged breaths. Elly stands as far away from me as any human possibly could in an elevator, pressing her body flat against the opposite chrome wall. She inspects the panel of buttons with meticulous detail.

“Look at me,” I say sharply. I have roughly twenty seconds for this elevator to descend twenty floors.

Her eyes slam into mine.

“You want me as much as I want you,” I say, my voice thick with months of pent-up sexual frustration. “I’ll make sure our relationship doesn’t reflect badly on you at Madison. Let me give you what you want.”

"There's nothing between us."

"Bullshit." I slam my hand against the red button making the elevator jerk to a halt.

"What are you doing?" she stutters, blinking rapidly.

I take a step forward, closing the gap between us. I take another step into her personal space, cautiously, allowing her time to push me away.

I'm close enough to touch her now. Another step, and I'll be close enough to lift up her dress, pull her underwear to the side and bury myself deep inside her. My cock strains in my trousers.

"I need you so damn badly," I say hoarsely.

"Why?" she asks, eyes wide.

"You're everything I could ever want in a woman."

My truthful answer seems to shock her.

"I'm not, Tristan," she says almost sadly. "You don't know everything about me."

"Let me learn everything about you."

She bites her lip as if my answer troubles her. "I can't be just a fling." She narrows her eyes. "I can't handle that. It's all or nothing."

"I'll take all," I say without a second's thought.

For a moment we just stare at each other. Then I'm on her, caging her with my arms as I push her against the wall of the elevator, thrusting my erection hard against her stomach. I lower myself slightly until my cock is centred into the apex of her legs. *That's the spot.*

A small whimper escapes her lips as she throws

her arms around my neck. Surrendering to her own lust.

Christ, I don't know if I can handle this now it might finally be mine.

My open mouth comes down on hers and her lips open to let my tongue in. I explore her mouth hungrily, desperately, like a teenage boy having his first kiss. My hand finds the thick mass of her hair in the ponytail and frees it so it spills down her back.

Her hand slides down my thighs finding my thick swollen cock. She moans softly as she feels how hard I am for her. Her fingers curl around me from the outside of my trousers and I jerk. There's too much fabric between us. I slam my hips into her, grunting into her mouth.

Her thighs part and she curls a toned leg around my waist, her dress riding up her thighs. I grab her thigh, yanking it tight around my waist so that I can line my hardness up directly with her pussy underneath the panties. I can feel she's wet through the underwear. My dick pushes painfully against it. Too much fucking fabric.

She grinds against my hardness bringing herself close, little jerky moans echoing in the elevator.

I stare down, my forehead pressed tight against hers.

Elly's lips part and she lets out a moan that makes me drop to my knees. I want to please this woman more than I've ever wanted to in my life.

Hoisting up her tailored dress, I roll the flimsy black lace knickers down her thighs. Her fingers curl into the roots of my hair and pull hard as I gently separate her thighs and find her clit with my tongue.

"Ah!" Her legs buck in my grasp, and I hold her steady. She releases another desperate moan that makes me wild.

Just as I think I'm going to get her there, Elly stiffens, staring down at me.

"I shouldn't be doing this here," she rasps, pushing me away.

I get to my feet, dazed as she yanks up her underwear and pulls down her dress.

"I'm late for a meeting," she stutters, pushing past me to jab the panel. The elevator jerks to life again and she repeatedly presses the button for the next floor.

The doors slide open and I come to, realising I'm in the elevator of my company building trying to make my junior lawyer come. "Sorry," I manage hoarsely. "I forgot where we were."

She evacuates the elevator in a rush.

I draw in a frustrated breath and slam the button for the twentieth floor. I have twenty floors to steady both my throbbing cock and my hammering chest.

I need to get my belongings and work out how to make the twenty-minute journey to Canary Wharf in five minutes.

And more importantly, I need to figure out how to convince Elly Andric to put both of us out of our misery and give me a chance.

***

"How much do you want, Gemina?" I sigh heavily into the phone.

After the disaster of trying to get across London in traffic jams I don't need this shit. I stare at the view of St. Pauls from my office and try to steady my breathing.

"Twenty should be fine," she says quietly. Like she's doing me a favour asking for only twenty thousand pounds.

My knuckles grip the side of the desk as I feel my temperature rise.

"You know he's going through a hard time. Please, Tristan."

I don't know that. What I know is that Danny said *he* rented a private box at the Formula1 last week. My hands fly to my hair. I don't want to talk about *him*.

God knows what they are doing with all this money. She's had her healthy divorce settlement and receives excessive child maintenance for Daniel. The woman seems to haemorrhage money and has nothing to show for it. However, money is the only language we speak these days, so that's how we communicate.

"The car will pick Daniel up at 9 a.m., Saturday." I strain to keep my voice level. "Agreed?"

"Fine, Tristan. See you then."

I hang up the phone, staring out at the London skyline. I spent years working to get this view. It means nothing now. If I lost it, I would recover eventually. But I won't recover if I lose my son. That, I can be sure of.

I breathe through the tightness in my chest, suppressing the ball of stress rising from my stomach. I need to soothe my temper before Elly arrives. My stress ball. She doesn't know how much I need this.

I knew she wouldn't decline my meeting request for two reasons: one, rejecting a meeting with the CEO is career suicide and two, as much as she protests, Elly Andric can't bring herself to stay away from me. Now, I've found a solution that she can't refuse. It's the only option I have other than selling the damn company so I'm no longer her boss.

I'll talk in a language Elly is comfortable with. Not money talk. Law talk.

There's a knock on the door that kicks my heart rate up a notch. I knew she would be punctual even if she wanted to play hard to get.

"Elly." I smile at the intoxicating brunette closing the door. "Take a seat." I resist the temptation to surge towards her and kiss her.

She sits down, clutching her laptop bag to her chest like a shield.

"Drink?" I offer, walking to my cabinet.

"No." She scowls. "It's 4:30."

I pour two Scotches and set one down in front of her.

She glares at me and pushes it away. "Sophie wants me to be back at my desk in twenty minutes to finish something."

She's guarded again. It was only hours ago that we were dry humping each other in a lift and she was opening her thighs so I could eat her out.

Instead of taking a seat behind my desk, I lean against it directly in front of her, spreading my feet wide.

She squirms, crossing and uncrossing her legs. It makes her dress ride up, revealing more of the shapely thighs underneath. My hands tighten around the edge of the desk.

She looks at me, aghast.

"What?" I frown.

"There's a stain on your shirt."

I look down at my collarbone. There's a small patch of evidence from when I was on my knees. It's barely visible. "I don't think anyone will be able to figure out you caused that." I smile but she looks dismayed.

Her forehead creases and I sense she is fretting about earlier.

"It's okay," I assure her. "What happens between us stays between us."

"I didn't mean for things to go so far. I got carried away."

"I can't say I regret what happened, far from it, but I don't want you to feel uncomfortable."

When she stays silent, I hand her the white paperwork on the desk. "I'm hoping this will allow you to rethink your decision."

She frowns. "What is it?"

"It's a non-disclosure agreement," I state simply.

"Between us, me and you."

She stares up at me in disbelief. "Why am I signing an NDA?"

"It's a mutual NDA. We'll both sign," I explain. "I already have. You've made it clear your objection to dating me is based on my position in the company and the threat to your reputation."

Her eyes narrow. "And the fact I'm not sure I trust you."

"We can work on the trust issue."

She anchors her gaze on the paperwork, skim-reading the pages.

"This will give you the protection you need," I say confidently. "Page ten has my obligations. You'll want to ingest the details yourself, but I'll summarise for you. In the scenario that an employee of Madison Legal obtains information about our relationship causing your reputation to come into question, I'm liable to pay damages to you of a sum of up to 150 thousand pounds."

Her jaw hits the floor.

"To cover professional reputation damage," I add. "That's your trainee contract salary covered and a bit more if you choose to leave. Does that appease you, Elly?"

"Let me get this straight," she starts slowly, looking at me like I've grown an extra head. "If I go on a date with you and someone from Madison finds out, you will give me 150k in compensation?"

"Up to 150k. If it's one of the cleaners at Madison, there might be a negotiation," I say dryly. 150k is just enough to give her a security blanket and not enough to make her a fool not to take it.

She gapes at me. "*Why*?"

"Why?" I repeat, amused. "Because of this. The fact that you're considering it."

She shakes her head in disbelief. "Our three-day fling was worth 150 thousand pounds?"

I chuckle. "I think I've spent more than that in all the minutes I've thought about you."

She opens her mouth and closes it. It seems I've blindsided her with this one.

Her brows form a deep frown as she studies the wording on page ten. "I feel like a hooker." She snorts.

"That's not the intention."

"Has this NDA been developed by Madison Legal lawyers?" She gasps. "Oh my God, lawyers in the company know?"

"No. My personal lawyer produced it. The same one I used for my divorce. I don't put personal matters through the company. For the same reason as you, Elly, I need discretion. I don't need my staff to know my personal business." I tap my fingers on the table, waiting.

She studies my face.

"Have you heard of the new restaurant, Asha's?" I ask, watching her fight fade away.

"You are fucking nuts," she says under her breath.

It's not a no.

"As an apology for what happened with my ex-wife," I coax. "You don't even have to talk to me. You can sit at another table and the only person you need to talk to is the waiter."

She's wavering. Apprehension flickers in her eyes followed by something else, excitement perhaps. "I can't be one of many."

"I'm not asking you to be one of many."

"Fine," she whispers. "One date."

"Tonight, Elly," I murmur, excitement swelling in my stomach and lower down. "I'll collect you at eight."

16

Elly

It's just dinner, right?

Hell, who am I kidding?

My last date barely split the bill; Tristan Kane wants to date me so badly he's drawing up NDAs. It might not be the most romantic gesture, but it is enough to convince me to take a leap of faith. That, and I'm so sexually frustrated, I might start humping his leg like a dog in the next Garcia meeting.

"It only looks good if I don't move my head." I study my face dubiously in the mirror. "When I tilt my head, it looks streaky."

Megan is trying to contour my face based on instructions from a YouTube video. So far, she has used half of my sixty available minutes to get ready.

"I'm slightly regretting going straight into the advanced sculpting technique with multiple hues," she murmurs as she adds yet *another* shade of grey powder to my cheeks. "It'll look great in the end though."

I disagree. I look like a freaking Picasso painting.

She tilts my face from side to side.

"What now?" I ask suspiciously.

"I need to add more layers."

"You just keep adding layers?" I say doubtfully. "When do I have enough layers? I'm starting to resemble a stale layer cake."

"Shall I give you bigger eyebrows as well?" she asks, taking my jaw in her hand and rolling my head around. I've never seen her look so serious.

"He only saw me a few hours ago." I pull back from her grasp. "Won't he notice if my eyebrows grow in size?"

"No chance." Megan scoffs. "Men don't notice these things. The guy I dated last year, Seanie, didn't notice when I got my eyebrows tattooed."

I shake my head. "No, I won't mess with the formula. He seems okay with my existing eyebrows."

"I'm so glad you finally decided to give him a chance," she says.

I sigh. "I just can't believe I let it get so far in the elevator. I'm mortified. But no other guy has gone to this much effort to win me over."

She flicks a brush up and down the middle of my nose to make it slimmer. Apparently.

"Maybe contouring only looks good in photos?" I frown.

She studies me for a long moment, tilting my head in all different directions to inspect cheeks, nose, forehead, and chin with meticulous detail. "You're right," she says solemnly. "Take it off. Take it all off. I think we need to start again."

"Take it all off?" I glare at her. "Bloody hell, Megan, I don't have time to do my whole face again." I grab wet wipes from the dressing table and rub them on my cheeks. Thick grey powder deposits onto the wipes.

"Maybe we'll stick to the natural look," she suggests. "He liked you in Greece, and you barely put a brush through your hair there."

"Fine. Just make me look less like the undead, please. Remove all the grey lines from my cheeks."

"You're very on edge." She chuckles, massaging my cheek with makeup remover. "Admit it. You've been pining after this man since Greece."

I exhale heavily. I can't deny it.

"Who cares about your face? More importantly, are you ready down *there*?" She makes eyes at my crotch.

I roll my eyes, but I am *so* ready. Landing strip prepared for landing. Of course, I'm not *planning* to sleep with him. It's just in case.

"It's just dinner." I brush her comment off. "He only wants me because I'm resisting him. He'll get bored."

"Are you sure about that?" She applies a tinted moisturiser to my face.

I hope I'm wrong.

"That's better." She nods at her handiwork then pushes my dress down past my right shoulder. It's an oversized jumper.

"Why did you do that?" I frown.

"I read in an article that bare shoulders remind men of bare breasts," she muses. "It must be to do with the shape."

I'm not convinced. "Couldn't you say that argument about knees then?" I ask sceptically. "You are seriously saying I show him a bit of shoulder socket rolling, and he's putty in my hands?"

"Fine, don't take my expert dating advice." She tuts. "But you need to hone your flirting skills. At Venus Envy you were like a viper with fangs out anytime a bloke came near you."

I narrow my eyes. We said we wouldn't talk about that night again. "I'm not sure I'm capable of flirting. My Crohn's disease is playing up like it always does when I'm nervous." I chew my lips. "I hope I don't spend the whole date in the bathroom." How many dates do you wait until you tell someone you have a dodgy bowel?

There's a knock on the bedroom door and Frank the Shagger pops his head in.

I glare at him. I still haven't forgiven him for mistaking my bedroom for the bathroom.

"Ah, come on, don't look at me like that," he says. "You're still huffing with me over a little mistake? I said I would do your cleaning slot for four weeks."

"That's only useful if you actually clean," I reply dryly. "Hiding things in cupboards is *not* cleaning."

"Says who? Anyway, I came to tell you, there's a bloke here to see you. He looks fancy."

I turn to Megan in horror. "He's twenty minutes early!"

Frank shrugs. "He's in the living room."

My spine jerks upright. "You let him into the living room?"

He gives me a blank stare. "Yeah, why not?"

"No, no, no!" I leap up, trying to locate my shoes.

Locating the second shoe under the bed, I barge past Frank and race down the stairs with Megan hot on my heels. I fire open the living room door.

"Tristan!" I greet him, flustered. "I –" I stop talking.

Oh.

He looks devastatingly handsome. I can't even put my finger on why. He is leaning against the wall, looking completely out of place and too big for the room. He's wearing jeans and a shirt that strains against his wide chest. He looks completely different than he did this afternoon. More like the Tristan I met in Mykonos.

One of his eyebrows rise as he takes a slow step forward. "Elly, you look beautiful."

"Thanks," I say breathily.

His gaze falls to the cut of my breasts in my dress, trailing a line down my stomach to my bare legs so slowly and purposefully, I have to look down to check I'm wearing underwear.

Someone clears their throat from the sofa. I turn to see my army of housemates watching us.

Did they all have to make their presence known at this particular moment? Three of Frank's friends are sprawled out across the sofa and the floor, watching what appears to be bear attacks streaming from

YouTube. The kitchen-hogging couple have formed a brass band with pots and pans, as they do every night. Their washing is drying all over the living room. Isn't there some sort of etiquette about not drying your underwear in a house-share communal area?

I eye Rafal's friend, Martina, suspiciously. She doesn't live here, yet I see her here every night. Has she moved in on the sly?

Well done flashes in her eyes at me as she gives Tristan a greedy once-over.

"Let's get out of here," I mumble awkwardly, trying to ignore the gawking eyeballs. What I mean is, get the hell out of here before any of my housemates say anything to show me up.

Megan hands me my coat and bag, giving me a conspicuous wink, and I shepherd him out the front door.

Nerves clutch my stomach as he walks me to the Aston Martin where George is waiting in the driver's seat.

George gives me a polite nod.

"Interesting bunch of tenants," Tristan observes, arching a brow. "It was like separate groups of people taking up space in the living room but ignoring each other."

"Welcome to living in the real London."

He opens the car door to let me in, then pauses to take my jaw in his hand.

My breath hitches as I wait to be kissed.

He inches closer, his breath hot on my face.

God, the suspense.

He tilts my face to the side. "You have a few smudges on your cheek. Are they pencil marks?"

Damn you, Megan, and your epic contour fail. "Must be pencil marks, yup," I mutter, stepping out of his hold to rub my cheek violently.

***

As we approach Clapham, I start to get excited. *Really* excited. A reservation to this place is gold dust. I would have said yes to the devil himself if he offered me dinner at Asha's, the most coveted restaurant in London. It recently snagged the third Michelin star and was the driving force behind the rush of celebrity sightings south of the Thames.

The fluttery feeling swirls in my stomach. Never a good thing for a bowel disease sufferer visiting a lavish restaurant with the casting member of their raunchy dreams.

What if I'm not dressed fancy enough for this place? I'm wearing a flowing dress and dressy sneakers. Sneakers are acceptable now so long as you don't actually do sports in them, right?

Tristan leans over and takes my hand. "Elly, tonight I want you to forget I own Madison. I'm just the guy you met on holidays. A guy that has given you no reason not to trust him. Can you do that?"

I look back into those intense eyes and read a hint of vulnerability there. "Yes," I answer and I mean it.

We pull up outside the unassuming grey doorway

on a quiet side street just off Clapham High Street. You would be forgiven for mistaking it for a warehouse rather than an exclusive and hideously expensive high-toned French restaurant.

As we get out of the car, a hostess appears from out of nowhere. She flashes a predatory smile at Tristan and puts her hand on his lower back, ignoring me. "Mr. Kane," she purrs. "Right this way."

My hackles rise.

Taking my hand in his, he leads me down the stairs lit only by candlelight to the restaurant in the basement.

It's not often a restaurant makes me horny, but this is the sexiest damn restaurant I've ever set foot in.

I enter first, his hand on the small of my back as he follows behind me. It's hard to miss the heads turning at each table as we walk through the dimly lit basement. Whether they recognise him or are just blown away by the broad-shouldered, ridiculously handsome bloke, it's hard to tell. If he notices the attention, he doesn't let on.

I scan the sea of heads and see some vaguely familiar faces. Is that guy from *The Apprentice*? More importantly, I make a mental note of where the toilets are.

We stop at dark red velvet curtains.

"This way, sir." Eye-fucking Tristan, the hostess pulls up the curtains to reveal a door underneath and pushes it open. We walk into a room that is all darkness, mirrors and candles with a single table for two in the middle.

I look around, bewildered. "Are we the only ones in here?"

“The private room is by request,” Tristan explains casually as we are led to the table.

He pulls out a chair for me, and I sit down.

“Let me take your coat, sir,” the hostess says in her phone-sex voice. In the process of pushing his coat down and off his shoulders, she gives him an unnecessary rubdown that airport security staff would be proud of.

He pulls out the chair opposite, inches it closer to mine, then sits down.

“How did you get a table here last minute?” I ask as three waiters fuss over us, pouring water and fluffing napkins. "Isn’t it notorious for being booked up months in advance?”

He leans back in his seat, his legs spreading so that our knees touch under the table.

“I own the restaurant with Danny.”

I pinch my eyes shut in confusion. “You own . . . this place?”

“Yup.”

I’m rendered speechless for a moment. I look around the room lit entirely by candlelight. “The building insurance must be astronomical.”

He lets out a loud laugh.

“Christ, Tristan, we are worlds apart.” I look at him doubtfully. “I don’t even own my own car yet. The only thing Megan and I can afford to buy together is a bottle of wine. We aren’t on an even keel here."

"It's okay." He winks. "Next time you can cook me dinner."

"Champagne, miss?" Two glasses of champagne materialise in front of us.

"Yes, thank you." I smile politely. The wall-to-ceiling mirror lit with candles creates the illusion that there is an army of servers serving us. Will they be here the whole time, watching and listening to us? The room is so echoey with just the two of us.

Tristan raises his glass, and I clink mine with his. I take a sip, and it's delicious. It tastes expensive.

"Lovely, isn't it?" Tristan comments. "Clean, crisp . . . you can really taste the honey, can't you?"

That's nice. My only requirement with champagne is that it doesn't leave me bent over with trapped wind. I make a mental note to learn some swanky phrases about champagne.

I nod, making a deep hmmm sound.

"The French chef is known for his creative style of cooking." He grins as he follows my gaze to the menu. "It's why we chose him. Some of the dishes aren't for the faint-hearted."

Escargots. They're quite nice, I can handle those.

Sauteed frog legs. Mmm, guess I could give one a go.

Tagine of Goat! I could pretend it's chicken.

"Tartare de Cheval?" I say loudly. "Is that . . ."

Holy Mary, Mother of—

"Horse tartare," he finishes, giving me a wicked smile.

I swallow hard. I'll have to subtly check my phone to see if these things trigger irritable bowel symptoms.

"Anything can taste amazing if it's cooked right." His eyes twinkle. "I'm very adventurous. You were warned."

Are we still talking about food?

"I ordered last time," I say, feeling brave. I close the menu. "You have carte blanche to order whatever you want for both of us. Except for the horse. Anything but horse."

He grins and beckons the waiter over. "We'll start with a selection of all the starters and bring us a bottle of the 2009 Pauillac," he informs the waiter. "Except the Tartare de Cheval," he adds as an afterthought.

"I said carte blanche for us two, not the whole restaurant," I hiss as the waiter walks away. "How will we eat ten starters between us? Are you some type of feeder?"

He chuckles. "I want you to have the chance to experience everything."

"That's so wasteful."

His eyes flash. I guess he's a man who's not used to being chastised.

I take a gulp of champagne to calm my nerves.

He leans forward tenting his fingers together on the tabletop. "You're nervous."

I bite my lip. How could I not be? I'm trapped in a sexy fire hazard with no windows and the hottest, most intimidating male I've ever clapped eyes on, about to be served frogs' legs. Which isn't exactly the sexiest food, is it?

What would have happened if Edward Lewis had ordered frogs' legs for Vivian in Pretty Woman instead of the strawberries?

"A little," I admit. Having dinner with him in Mykonos was fun and carefree, now knowing who he was . . . this feels weighted. "This is so normal to you, private dining at an exclusive restaurant. Not to me."

His brows rise. "Eating with you isn't normal to me. I've been looking forward to this since I stood up in front of you and welcomed the new trainees."

I swirl the champagne in my flute, stumped for words. *Why*? I want to ask him.

His hand disappears under the table and finds its way onto my bare thigh. "Tell me about growing up in Wales. You didn't talk much about it in Mykonos."

"There's not much to know," I say as the waiter approaches with our wine. "My mum came over from Croatia when she was twenty. She worked in London, met my dad, followed him to Wales, and never left. She's a bit of a hippy."

"They still live in Wales?" he asks after thanking the waiter.

"Mum does." I clear my throat. "My dad . . . I don't know where he is. I've never met him."

His expression softens and he takes my smaller hand in his large one. "I'm sorry. Was it just you and your mum growing up?"

I nod, swallowing. "Although there were always

people in and out of the house, friends of hers who would come and go."

"Was that good?" he asks, concerned.

"Sometimes. Other times . . . no." Christ, this date is going to end up as a counselling session too.

"What does she do?" he asks, lifting the wine glass to his lips.

"Sometimes she works in a friend's restaurant. Every now and then she helps a friend with a cleaning job. She's . . . a bit flaky." My cheeks heat. "That's why I need this job. I can't mess it up."

He squeezes my hand gently. "Your contract is safe," he says in a low voice as our starters arrive. He ordered so much food that it had to be wheeled out on a trolley because the table wasn't big enough. If I ever treat him to dinner, I'm putting a cap on the number of dishes he orders. "And from what I can see you're a very intelligent, conscientious lawyer. You'll do well. Stop worrying about what others think. Now, let's feed you some fine French cuisine."

My cheeks heat at the compliment. "Do you care what others think, Tristan?"

The waitstaff leave us alone in the room.

I stare at the frogs' legs swimming in garlic butter.

His eyes flicker to my lips as he watches me drink the last of the champagne. "Only people who are worth it. Like my family. My son." He chuckles. "Although these days I think he sees me as an embarrassing father. I'm kissing him in front of his friends too much outside the school gate, he said."

"What age is he?" I ask as I grasp a snail in my tongs. This could go very badly. Butter drips out but I catch it just in time with a napkin.

"Seven," he replies, his eyes twinkling in amusement as I fumble with the slippery fucker. "He's growing up so quickly. I do a double take on some of the questions he asks me. The other day he was a bit naughty at school so I threatened I would tell Santa. Then he started asking loads of questions on exactly how I would ask Santa. He asked me if I would contact him on Instagram."

Finally, I extract the snail meat with the tiny two-pronged fork. "Is he on Instagram? Your son I mean, not Santa, obviously."

A warm garlic rubbery sensation explodes in my mouth and oh my God, damn. "This is amazing!" I reach for another one and pick it out of its shell. "Bloody hell, I never knew snails could taste so good. What is happening in my mouth?"

Tristan watches me, laughing. "Easy there, don't eat too many, they're quite rich. No. He knows of all the social media sites, but he's not allowed his own account yet." He shudders. "He's way too young. He said his classmate told him Santa wasn't real. He can smell bullshit. He asked so many questions that eventually I had to break the news that I was Santa."

"How did he take it?"

"I think I was more upset than he was."

"I just realised I don't even know your son's name."

"Daniel." A smile sweeps across his face. "He's

named after Danny Walker. Danny's his godfather.

"That's sweet, you and Danny must be very close." I hesitate. "Is it hard not living with him permanently?"

His expression darkens. "Yes. It kills me every day."

I sip my wine. There are so many questions I want to ask. "Do you and your ex-wife get along? When she is not trying to kill you with dinnerware."

He lets out a strangled laugh. "I forgot you witnessed that."

I haven't.

His dark brows knit and something that looks a lot like pain flashes across his face. Perhaps I'm not competing with all the women in the online pictures. Perhaps I'm competing with just one.

"She burnt me pretty badly."

"Do you want to talk about it?"

His jaw hardens. "No. Let's enjoy the evening."

That's annoying. It's niggling me. Did he split up with her because he stopped loving her or because she hurt him?

The hand that rests on my thigh starts tracing circles. Tingly shivers course through me.

"Do you feel that? he asks hoarsely. "There's so much chemistry between us. You drive me wild, Elly."

He finds my hand under the table and places it on his thigh. My fingers graze his bulge as he leans forward and pulls my mouth against his.

Garlic alert, garlic alert! I've eaten too much garlic

with the snails.

But this is nice. Fuck the trainee contract. Fuck the fancy restaurant and the overly attentive waitstaff. I *need* this. I need *him*.

"Tristan," I rasp. "We're in a restaurant."

"My restaurant," he grunts. "No one can see us here."

I spread my hand over his dick. It's warm and hard and exactly what I've been craving. He groans into my mouth then deepens the kiss. His hand finds my thigh again and slowly traces a line up my leg until it's under the hem of my dress. I cling to him, my fingers digging into his biceps.

His fingers dance around the same spot just inches below my core.

Damn tease.

My core pulses with months' worth of sexual frustration. I need this so badly.

I catch a glimpse of my wide eyes and flushed cheeks in the mirror. "This better not be a two-way mirror into the kitchen," I mutter.

He lets out a deep throaty laugh. "No, sweetheart, it's just us."

His fingers continue to skirt over my inner thigh, and I feel myself getting damp. I'm so wound up already, this is embarrassing.

"Tonight, Elly, I'll give you everything you want. I'll finish what I started in the elevator. I've missed hearing your little moans," he whispers against my ear.

I stare at him as his words make their way from

my brain to other areas of my body.

God help me.

***

We find the restraint to calm down and finish every drop of the bottle of champagne and the bottle of 2009 something wine.

Thank God it's not a school night.

My defences have fallen so low I don't care if there's a slot at next week's all-staff call to explain how the CEO got me all hot and bothered in a French restaurant.

"Will you accompany me back to my house, Elly?" He raises his eyebrows in question.

"Actually, I can't," I say reluctantly. "I have to be up at 5 in the morning for a train to Wales. I haven't even packed yet."

He frowns. "Can you book a later train?"

"No." I sigh. "It's my mum's birthday. I've got a surprise booked. I have to get that train to make it on time."

"I'll get you a car to Wales." He goes to pick up his phone. "If that's too slow, I can arrange a chopper."

My eyebrows shoot up. *A chopper?*

"No." I grab his arm. "Don't be ridiculous!" I tug his hand away from the phone, interlacing my fingers with his. "I'm leaving from my house tomorrow," I say firmly, more out of principle than desire. He can't get his way every time, and I need to keep some self-respect. "Maybe we can do this . . .

another time," I suggest.

He gives me an exasperated look. "Let me get this straight—the only way I can continue seeing you tonight is if I go back to your hippy commune?"

I stifle a giggle at the thought. "I don't remember dishing out an invite," I reply cockily.

He won't do it. There's no way Tristan Kane is going to spend a night in my house-share. It's his way or the highway.

"Elly." He exhales hard, a defeated look crossing his face. "Can I come back to yours, please?"

I bite my lip to stop a goofy smile from taking over my face. "I suppose."

"I'll get the bill and call George," he says, beckoning to the waiter.

"It's a few stops on the underground, Princess." I scoff. "That will be quicker."

Trying it Megan's way, I pop a shoulder out. That'll show him who's boss.

17

Elly

"Are you stockpiling toilet paper in case there's another pandemic?" He stares at the pile of rolls under my dresser.

"I didn't think you'd be back here tonight," I huff. "Or I would have hidden those." I have to hide them in my room because nobody replaces them but me. I'm sick of bankrolling their ass wipes.

I coax him away from the dresser to the centre of the room. If he looks closely, he'll spot the premium bamboo rolls stolen from Madison Legal.

"The perils of a London house-share." I shrug and let out a pathetic giggle. Standing here with Tristan Kane in my bedroom is turning me into a hot nervous mess.

When he draws himself up to his full six-foot-four height he knocks into the light fixture.

"And this isn't *your* bed?" He hovers above it like it's been dispatched from a nuclear power plant.

"No, the room came furnished," I explain. "Only the armchair and the dresser are mine. Why?"

"Do you know how many people have had sex on this bed?"

I give him a withering look. "Sorry, I didn't think to ask the estate agent."

"No wonder you sleep in linen closets," he mutters. "We don't know how many people have used this bed. It's like having sex in a brothel."

"Hey!" I whack him against the chest. "I've got a mattress topper. That's what renters do, we buy mattress toppers and don't think about all the renters that came before us." I roll my eyes. "Try to search within yourself to find a modicum of reality, will you? Have you forgotten how normal non-CEO people live?"

"Can we have sex standing up?"

"You are acting like the princess and the pea." I glower, putting both hands on my hips. "*And* you are being very presumptuous. Who said I want to have sex with you, anyway?"

He smirks down at me. "Of course you do. I'll get you so steamed up you'll be begging for me to fuck you."

That arrogant, infuriating, handsome face. He's so confident in himself, so certain I'm a sure bet. It turns me on and annoys me in the same instant. I don't want to give him the satisfaction of joining the million girls that beg Tristan Kane to fuck them.

"*As if.* I don't beg men."

His eyes blaze as he steps into my personal space. Wrapping his hands around my waist, he pulls me in and presses me against his groin, his hardness jutting against my stomach.

My core flutters with excitement. I was bluffing before.

Of course, I'm going to let him fuck me.

I reach up on my tiptoes, and he comes down to meet me, pressing his lips against mine.

"I'm making a big mistake," I whisper into his mouth.

"Boss's orders. I guess you have to do as you're told."

He reaches behind my back and unzips my dress so that it hangs loosely around my shoulders, then pushes it down past my waist, exposing my black lace bra. I step out of it, standing before him in only underwear.

He responds with a growl and unclips my bra, sliding the silk straps down my arms. "That's much better," he says gruffly.

His massive hands cup my breasts possessively and he dips his head down to pinch a nipple with his teeth.

I make a desperate little mewling sound and fumble with the top of his jeans.

"Not yet," he growls. Before I know what he's doing, he lifts me off the floor and walks us both to the bed.

My whole body trembles in anticipation as he lays me down on the bed. I'm so ready, it's embarrassing.

Glancing around the room, he walks to the dresser and lifts two satin scarfs I bought to dress up my work outfits.

"You're fully clothed," I pant as he approaches the bed again.

"I'm the boss. My rules." His eyes roam over my body from above.

I spread my legs, willing him to come on top of me.

A grunt falls from his lips in response. He gently takes my wrists, pinning them above my head, and ties each one to the bedpost with a scarf. Then, he pulls down my underwear and climbs on top of me, his large thighs inching open my legs.

I'm naked, exposed, and his for the taking.

Heat flares in his eyes. "Beautiful," he breathes. He leans down, caging my body with his biceps as his mouth trails hot kisses down my collarbone.

I arch my back and push up my breasts.

He's taking his sweet time. He kisses the top of my breasts then travels down at a tortuous pace to just above my nipple. My nipples are so hard it hurts.

His tongue circles one, and I moan impatiently.

"Please," I whisper, my heels digging into the bed.

Heat pools between my legs as his mouth finally engulfs my nipple. He goes from nipple to nipple, pinching and sucking. Then he's on the move again. Slowly his mouth trails down past my belly button to my lower stomach. His mouth hovers just above my apex.

My core muscles clench.

Using his thumbs, he gently pulls apart my sensitive folds of flesh. A feral sound rumbles from his throat as his eyes devour my most intimate parts.

I'm a mix of aroused and embarrassed. He can see *everything.* I wriggle, trying to set my hands free but he has them tightly fastened. He's in control. His tongue pushes deep into my entrance.

I arch my hips into his face, crying out.

As his tongue thrusts in and out relentlessly, his thumb circles around my clit, teasing me faster and faster.

My toes curl, and my legs shake; the pressure is too much.

"Oh God, oh God, oh God," I chant as he holds me in a firm grip, feasting on me. My head arches back towards the headboard.

"Elly," he murmurs from between my legs. "I want you to watch."

I look down and meet his eyes as his tongue flicks in and out of me. "There." It comes out as a croak. "*Yes*. Exactly like that." My legs thrash as the pleasure rips through me in violent shudders.

He looks up at me with a satisfied smirk.

He moves off the bed before I can recover and rips his clothes off then stands in front of me, naked.

It's even better than I remember.

My hands stay tied to the bedpost. Tristan climbs back on top of me and pushes his knees between my legs so that I am spread wide apart.

"Damn," he hisses. "Condom."

"I'm on the pill."

"Can I come inside you? I'm clean."

I nod, thrusting my hips. I need skin on skin.

He slams his thick length into my opening. A low groan erupts from him, and it's the sexiest damn sound I've ever heard.

I clench around his cock, my hands tightening around the bedposts, desperate for freedom so I can maul every inch of his body. "N-not f-fair," I stutter.

A low chuckle is the only response I get. He thrusts in and out, holding my hips in place, my breasts jiggling with every thrust. "Elly." He draws in a stuttered breath. "You feel so good."

The slapping of our bodies gets louder, faster. Tristan's face contorts in pleasure, and I know he's close. Just watching him come to pieces is breaking me. Our moans mix together, his low and throaty, mine high-pitched and frantic.

With a final deep thrust, he lets out a shuddery breath, and he comes so hard I'm scared he's never going to stop.

I cry out, feeling the warm liquid pulsing into me.

Trying to steady his breathing, he hovers on top of me, his elbows holding the weight of his broad chest.

I'm wet all down my inner thighs. We are sticky and sweaty, and I've never cared less.

"I guess hoarding toilet paper in your room does come in handy." He grins, untying my hands from the silk handcuffs.

His inner thighs glisten as he climbs off the bed. I can't keep my eyes off him.

"I was wondering . . . our first meeting in my office, you said that's not all I took from you. What did you mean?" he asks as he gently wipes my legs.

"Nothing," I say, brushing it off.

He frowns. "I want to know. Tell me."

My cheeks begin to flame hotter. "I meant . . . I meant you were . . . *are* the only man to ever make me come," I whisper.

He stops wiping and stares at me, alert. "Were you a virgin, Elly?"

"No. But I'm not exactly a sexpert, either. I've had a few sexual partners and one long-term boyfriend, and it just never happened," I say, feeling self-conscious.

"What about after Greece?"

"I haven't actually . . ." I fiddle with my fingers. "I mean, I haven't . . ."

"You haven't had sex since us?" he asks quietly.

"Not deliberately," I say quickly. "Truth is, I haven't met anyone these past few months that I wanted to have sex with."

He looks at me for a long minute, discarding the tissue in the wastebasket. "I'd be lying if I said I wasn't delighted."

"I wasn't saving myself for you," I snap defensively. "It's just that the nun-hood seemed better than some of the buffoons I've met."

"Shush." He trails a palm across my collarbone. "It's too early to define this," he says seriously. "I don't want to hurt you, and we're in different stages of our lives. I'm divorced, and my priority has to be my kid."

I nod, pain twisting in my chest. I'm getting the

brush-off.

"But I'd like to keep seeing you, Elly. To explore this."

I bite my lip to contain the grin.

"If we see each other, we can't see anyone else," I say in a small, firm voice.

"As if I would want to." He rolls the blankets down. "Come on, I don't want you to be tired for your mum's birthday. Is this a single bed?"

"No!" I say crossly. "It's a double. Stop complaining, or you can sleep on the floor."

"I suppose the smaller it is, the harder it is for you to escape," he grumbles, climbing into the bed behind me. "What is this made from? Bamboo sticks?"

I hit his chest.

He wraps his body around mine, his strong arms pulling me flush against him. This man could win awards for his spooning.

***

"Who the fuck are you?" says Tristan in a low growl beside me.

I rub my eyes and peer out into the darkness.

What's going on? Is it 5 a.m. already?

Feeling my way in the dark, I find the bedside lamp and switch it on.

I squint my eyes, adjusting to the light. There's a girl hovering at the bottom of the bed. She claws at the duvet in an attempt to get under the covers.

"Someone has escaped from the looney bin," Tristan yells, his voice thick with sleep. Both of us sit up topless in bed. "Is this one of your housemates?"

She sees us then releases a half giggle, half burp. Beer gas assaults me.

"This isn't . . ." she slurs, swaying to imaginary music.

"He's called *Frank*," I say in a groggy voice, covering my bare breasts with the duvet.

Her glazed eyes give Tristan the once-over. "*Oh*."

I'm momentarily distracted by Tristan's naked muscular chest. "Not him," I hiss. "The guy you went home with is *Frank*. Frank's room is *upstairs*."

"Get out of here," Tristan snaps, catapulting out of bed.

Despite being saturated with alcohol up to her eyeballs, her jaw hangs slack as she takes in the well-endowed naked man. She stumbles backwards a few times. Finally, she gets the message that three is a crowd and zigzags towards the door. With the last of her motor skills, she yanks the door open and staggers out.

Tristan strides forward, closing the door.

"No way to lock it." He pinches his eyes in confusion and moves a chest of drawers towards the door.

"It's fine." I wave my hand in the air, too tired to react further. "She won't come back."

"It's not fine," he barks. "I'll get you a new rental tomorrow, Elly. This isn't safe."

"Stop being ridiculous." I suppress a grin as he barricades us into the room. "If anything, you're the one not safe from her, not me. Is that why you're barricading us in?"

He ignores me. "I hope there's a fire escape in this building. There should be, with this many bedrooms. Now we're going to burn to a crisp because of some mad lady."

"Where, Tristan? Did you see a slide or a pole?" I snort. I fling myself back down onto the bed, refusing to engage in this conversation. My phone says 3:30. My alarm will be going off in 1.5 hours.

"Having flatmates is worse than having children," he mutters, climbing back into bed. "Coming into your room at all hours demanding attention."

I shake my head. He may be a hotshot CEO, but he wouldn't last a minute in a hostel.

He lies flat on his back taking up most of the bed. I climb on top of him. It's either this position or curling into a small ball in the corner. His strong arms envelop me and he lets out a long sleepy sigh. I bury my face in his chest, listening to the rhythm of his heartbeat. Our bodies mesh together, warmth flowing from his body into mine. There is nothing more sexy or intimate than lying on top of a sleeping Tristan Kane and feeling every inch of his skin touch mine.

When his hand loosens from where it is intertwined in my hair and his breathing slows, I know he is asleep. And then I lie there, my breasts rising and falling on his chest, breathing in his musk and I wonder how I'm ever going to sleep bursting with this much happiness.

Somehow, after many minutes (maybe hours), I close my eyes and drift off to sleep, smiling.

18

Elly

An obnoxious buzzing sound pierces my ears. I lie rigid, willing it to stop. It *can't* be time to get up. I'm so disoriented I'm not sure if I slept at all. I hear a grunt, and the noise stops.

"Elly," Tristan says in a gruff voice in the darkness. He gently shakes my shoulders.

"Yes?" I say sorrowfully, my eyes closed. What I mean is *fuck off and let me sleep!*

"You need to get up." His voice is sterner this time. In an unwelcome embrace, he shakes me a bit harder.

My eyes flit open and I fix on Tristan's shadow rummaging through the room.

"Tristan?" I bolt upright and turn on the bedside lamp, squinting as the light floods the room.

"There's no toothpaste in your bathroom," he says with a grunt. "And you had two bodies in your living room when I went to get a glass of water."

Only two? A quiet Friday night, then.

"Did you sleep?" I ask, knowing the answer from

his murderous expression.

“Not enough.” He perches on the edge of the bed and nudges me. “I was too busy protecting you from the mad woman, remember? Anyway, it's 5. You need to get a move on.”

I let out a long drawn-out sigh. “Yes, Daddy.” I groan. *Interesting.* I’m vaguely turned on by his new nickname. Perhaps I have disappearing-daddy issues. “Sorry for waking you. Feel free to sleep in.”

“Not a fucking chance.” He grimaces. “I’ve called a car. It will drop you at Paddington station on the way.”

With a moan I throw back the duvet and dramatically fling my legs off the bed. It’s pitch-black outside. This is an inhumane time to get up on a Saturday. Why didn’t I just say yes to a lift in a helicopter? Goddamn stupid pride. Next time someone offers me a chopper, I’ll say “That sounds lovely, thank you.”

***

The last thing I want to do this morning is the four-hour trek to Wales after two hours of sleep.

Besides the fact we spent a large proportion of the night shagging, when we finally laid our heads down, Tristan proved to be a very distracting presence.

Not only because I was on high alert after the gas-inducing dinner but because his body is so large, he takes up the majority of the bed.

And he snores.

My train journey is a clusterfuck of emotions as I process last night's events. I have a two-hour train to Swansea then I have to change onto the slowest train in the world to get to my village. Torture.

My inner harlot revels in the fulfilment of a fantasy I've had since I boarded the flight from Athens—to be shagged senseless by an unattached Tristan. My inner nun is freaking out over the fact I'm a dirty gullible grad who slept with the CEO.

Oh, who cares? Right now I'm too tired to give a shit.

The issue is that despite his asshole behaviour in Mykonos, I placed Tristan on a pedestal that no other bloke could reach. He left me in limbo. Megan says I don't give blokes a chance, but no matter how attractive, funny or kind the guy is, I always come to the same conclusion.

They're not him.

My stomach is a tangled mess of nerves and garlic butter snails. I regret my show of bravado. Now I'm lurking beside the smelly train toilets instead of the lovely window seat I booked.

The snails were worth it.

Finally, I reach the concrete building that I call home. Built in the 1950s, our social housing flat is grey and ugly; there's no way to dress it up. I wonder what Tristan would think if I took him home.

"Mum?" I call out, turning the key in the door.

Nothing. She didn't answer her phone when I called from the train.

I scan the drab brown kitchen. It seems to deteriorate a little more with every visit. There are three empty wine bottles on the kitchen table, the rubbish bin is overflowing, and the dishes in the sink look days old. I hit redial on my mum's number for the seventh time this morning.

"Elly, sweetie," comes her breathy voice down the phone. I put her on loudspeaker.

"Mum, where are you?" I try not to sound tense since it's her birthday. "I'm home."

"Oh, sweetie, I forgot you were coming so early. I'm having brunch with Barry."

"Barry?" I repeat in a clipped tone. "Barry who? Did you have a party here last night?"

"Don't be silly," she says breezily. "Just Barry and me."

"You got through one and a half bottles of wine each?" I ask.

"It's my birthday!" she huffs. "I can't believe you'd begrudge me a little fun on my *birthday*."

"Remember the spa treatment I booked for your birthday?" My voice rises. "It starts in forty-five minutes."

There's silence.

"Oh dear, I thought it was tomorrow. Can we do it tomorrow?"

"I doubt it," I say sharply. "I booked it months ago. I'll lose my money."

"Sorry, sweetie." She doesn't sound sorry; she

sounds drunk. "You should have reminded me."

"I did," I snap, my blood boiling. "Last week. Yesterday. *And* this morning." Deep breaths, Elly. "So?" I demand. "Are you coming home so we can go?"

More silence.

"I can't leave in the middle of brunch. I'm so sorry, I must have read the date wrong."

My hands ball into tight fists. Why did I bother coming home? She doesn't care if I'm here.

She says something to Barry about ordering more olive oil and bread.

"Hello?" I snap. "I'm still here."

"I'll see you in a few hours, okay?" she says. "Then we'll have a nice catch-up."

I end the call before I say something I regret then call the spa and beg them to rearrange it. The angel on the phone takes pity on me.

What a waste. I could have spent extra glorious hours in bed with God's gift to women.

My eyes sweep the dirty kitchen in dismay. I'll never relax in this mess. Finishing the dregs of my coffee, I lift the evidence of last night's party and put them in a fresh recycling bag. Instead of getting pampered in a spa, I'm spending the next hour cleaning.

I take my anger out on the plates, scrubbing them with ferocity. What I really want to do is smash her dishes on the floor, Gemina style, but instead, I open the cupboard to stack them away. In the back corner, there are pill bottles instead of plates.

"What the hell is Diazepam?" I say out loud, examining the bottle. A search of the name online tells me it's Valium. Why does Mum need Valium? She never told me she was prescribed these.

Sometime later, I open the front door to find a two-seater red convertible sports car in the driveway. To complete the cliché, a bald man in his sixties, maybe seventies, sits in the driver's seat.

"Elly, darling!" Mum spills out of the car and staggers through the door, giving me an eyeful of cleavage.

Barry locks up his late-life crisis and follows behind her.

"So good to see you. I've missed you so much," she says excitedly, alternating between Croatian and English. Her Croatian accent only comes out when she's drunk. She flings her arms around me, suffocating me with alcohol fumes. "Meet Barry. Barry, this is my daughter, Elly. She's a lawyer!"

"I'm just in training," I correct her.

Barry and I study each other warily in the doorway, neither of us wanting the other one in the house. "Nice to meet you, Barry." I narrow my eyes. I'm at least a foot taller.

Mum sweeps into the kitchen, oblivious to the fact that the house now gleams, and begins banging open cupboards in search of something. "Go into the living room, Barry, relax." She waves her hand at him and he scuttles off.

"How are you, Elly?" She pulls me in for a massive

hug. "I can't *wait* to hear all about the new job! Tell me everything!" She doesn't mean it, not in this state. I could tell her I'm running for Prime Minister, and she'd say, "Oh, that's lovely!" I give her a half-arsed recollection of my first month at Madison Legal, enough to make her feel like she's a caring inquisitive mother.

She dances around the kitchen opening cupboards and drawers.

"Looking for something?" I shake the bottle of pills.

She snatches the bottle. I watch her put two pills in her mouth and swallow without water.

"Why are you taking those?" I ask. "Did the doctor prescribe them for you? I'm sure they'd have said not to drink with them."

"They're for my anxiety," she says airily, flinging open the fridge. "Can you fix the three of us some cheese, sweetie?"

"Why are you anxious?"

"It's hard being a single parent, living all alone." She moans. "Supporting myself."

I give her a cynical look. "I pay all your bills, Mum."

In her heyday, Mum was mildly successful. She had a clothing shop that kept us afloat, but her excessive spending eventually ran it into the ground. I've paid her rent and bills for these past six months and, while I want to help my mum, it's a dependency I need to break. I hope Barry is rich and senile enough to marry her.

"Sometimes you don't appreciate what I went through for you, Elly." She pulls a bottle of white wine from the fridge.

"You've told me a million times," I say through clenched teeth. "Loose skin and a weak bladder."

I need to rein it in, I don't want to fight with her on her birthday. It's just that. . . it rubs me the wrong way when she forgets I'm even coming.

"Typical Leo, so dramatic," she says, pouring wine into two glasses. "Don't be in a bad mood in front of Barry, darling."

I pinch the bridge of my nose. Shouldn't Barry be trying to impress *me*?

I follow her into the living room, where she collapses beside Barry on the couch, the hem of her skirt riding up past her knees.

His fingers graze her thigh, and I grimace.

"Tell us all about London!" Her eyes sparkle. "Have you been on the London Eye yet?"

"Not yet," I say. "But I love the South Bank. Megan and I hang out there a lot. It's got great markets and bars."

"I can't wait to visit you for a weekend. Barry, perhaps we could go for the weekend to visit Elly?"

"That would be lovely . . ." I trail off as she smiles at him coyly. He licks his lips and tickles her ear with his finger.

Dear God.

"I'm going for a walk," I mutter. I might as well not be here.

I leave the room to go get a fork to gouge my eyes

out.

Of course, I want Mum to be happy and find a partner, I just wish she wouldn't be so blatant about finding him directly in front of me.

Grabbing my coat, I slam the door behind me and walk with purpose to the green fields bordering the town.

Every time I visit Mum I feel on edge. Between the house-share and my bedroom in Wales being used for storage now, I feel a bit driftless. Someday I'll own a house of my own and then I'll call it *home*.

Until then, I'll indulge in online house porn.

There it is. The cottage I've lusted after for two decades. It lords over the valley like something straight from the pages of a fairy tale. The owners retained its original character with beams and exposed stone walls, but I know they have a hot tub in the garden.

When I was younger, they used to have loads of kids playing in the garden. Now the gardens are deserted, and the children are grown up and have moved away.

I sit on the grass, looking out over the peaceful countryside, and take my book out to read. My plan is to stay up here long enough for Mum to exhaust Barry. Hopefully he's not on Viagra.

19

Tristan

Nine hours later after dropping Elly off at Paddington station, I'm kicking a football around the backyard with Daniel. Exhausted is not a word I could apply; no I need a word much stronger. I would have had a better night's sleep if I'd lain down on the street and paid for a bulldozer to drive over me. I've had two espressos but no amount of stimulants will fix the dull pain in my lower back from sleeping on a tiny shit-quality bed.

Still, it was worth it. *She* was worth it.

"You look really old today," Daniel informs me.

Thanks, son.

"I have a secret to tell you," he says as he walks towards me. The match is finished, and it didn't take much for Daniel to win today. "I've got a girlfriend," he announces proudly.

"Oh yeah?" I raise my eyebrows. "Is this a girl from your class?" The kid looks like a catalogue model. No wonder he's doing well with the ladies at school.

"Uh-huh." He nods. "Talia."

Nice name. "How long has she been your girlfriend?"

His brow furrows in deep concentration. "About a week," he finally says as we walk into the kitchen. "I was hoping Miss Hargrove would be my girlfriend but she's a son of a bitch."

"Daniel." I stop him in his tracks. "We've been through this. You can't call people that, especially not your teaching assistant." I don't want another angry phone call from Mrs. Maguire, and she *is* a son of a bitch.

"I'm telling Talia tomorrow," he adds, matter-of-fact.

"Telling her what?"

He looks at me like I'm stupid. "Telling her she's my *girlfriend*."

Do I have to teach my son about rejection at seven? "Maybe ask her, buddy, you know, rather than inform her she's your girlfriend," I advise. "She might want a say in it."

"She holds my hand," he says, deadpan, and cuts me a glare that tells me I'm not qualified to give dating advice. "Yesterday, I gave her my juice."

That's a good start. "Maybe don't rush into commitment," I offer. "There's plenty of time for girlfriends in a decade. Just concentrate on being her friend now."

He looks up at me. "Like you and mum are best friends now?"

I force a smile. "Exactly like that."

His phone beeps in his pocket. It was a tough decision to buy it. It's ludicrous for a seven-year-old to have a phone, but it's the only way I have a direct line of contact, since Gemina is volatile as fuck.

"Who's messaging you, Daniel?" The phone is just for me to message him, he's too young to be talking to anyone else on it.

He takes it out of his pocket and reads it. "It's Mummy. She's waiting outside. Does that mean we can't have potato waffles?"

My chest tightens, and I fake a smile for my son's sake. What's she playing at? She should be messaging me, not Daniel, and she shouldn't be cutting into my visitation time.

I ruffle his hair. "We can still have potato waffles. Stay here, and I'll speak to your mum."

A big goofy smile plasters across his face. If only frozen potato waffles could solve all my problems.

Before I get a chance to go out, there's a knock on the door. I open the door and stare at the woman I loved for over a decade.

"Hi Tristan," she says in her soft American twang. It has been toned down from years of singing on the London stages. "How are you? You look tired."

"Gemina." I greet her, feeling my temperature rise. "You're not supposed to be here until 4. I have forty minutes left."

Her eyes search mine. "I hope you're looking after yourself," she replies, ignoring my complaint.

I wish she wouldn't do this. Pretend she cares.

Not when she destroyed me.

Twice.

"Change of plan," she says when I ignore her. "We're going to spend the night at the holiday home in Devon. We need to leave now. I'm sorry."

"You can't do this," I say gruffly. "When you agree on a time, you stick to it."

As I look down the driveway, I see the red Porsche that I bought for Gemina.

He's here. The man I would do a prison sentence over.

"So, he's driving my car now?" I snarl, trying to temper my anger.

I glance back to make sure Daniel is out of earshot.

She chews on her lips, studying me. "Tristan . . . you know things will have to change. We have to talk. We need to tell Daniel."

"No." Pain takes over my voice. "Don't do this to me," I beg in a strained whisper. "Don't you dare talk to Daniel without me. Please."

"This isn't going away." Her eyes flicker with wariness then she sighs, defeatedly. "Let's deal with this when I get back from Devon, okay?"

I change the subject. "You look good." I smile sadly.

Her eyes glaze over. She looks tired too.

"Thanks," she says awkwardly. "We have to go. I'm sorry. Daniel," she calls over my shoulder. "Get your things together."

He runs to the door. "But Dad promised me potato waffles."

"Not today, baby," she says. "Some other time."

He looks up at me, and my heart breaks.

"Sorry, son." I run my hand through his blond hair. "No potato waffles today. Next time, I promise. I'll see you on Thursday night, okay? You can tell me more about Talia. Aunty Charlie will want to hear about her too."

Daniel nods and runs into the living room to collect his trucks as I retrieve his Spiderman coat from the hallway.

I hunker down on my knees and bundle him up in my arms so I can give him a proper goodbye hug.

He wraps his arms around my neck. "Bye, Dad. I wish you were coming with us."

"Me too, buddy." I smile at him. "I'll see you in a few days." My voice is strained. I can't wait another seven days to see my kid. "Can we lock in Thursday night, Gemina?"

"Sure," she says, too breezily for my liking. Her flakiness is breaking my soul.

"Bye, kiddo." Watching them walk towards the car, I am filled with a sick sense of disappointment as I always am when I see my son leave. He shouldn't be living somewhere else, he should be living here in the house he grew up in and called home since he was born.

Daniel looks back at me and gives a little wave as Gemina takes his hand down the driveway.

I don't look at the driver of the Porsche. I can't.

I close the door to my empty townhouse. The silence is a sharp gloomy contrast to the sound of us laughing thirty minutes earlier. The laughter that reminds me of what my life used to be like.

***

"Tonight, we have a selection of Irish-influenced dishes, sir." The caterer opens my commercial-sized oven and points at the first dish. "Guinness braised pork topped with cabbage, green crema, and queso fresco. Next"—she points at the second dish—"corned beef tacos served with a creamy, spicy mustard sauce, and a simple cabbage carrot slaw."

She pulls out the second chrome wire shelf. "The main dish—slow-cooked lamb shank with a selection of three potato dishes."

The Irish theme is for my County Cork-born mother.

I inspect the dishes and nod my approval as the intercom buzzes.

"We'll let ourselves out discreetly, Mr. Kane." The caterer smiles at me as if we're sharing some big secret.

I'm not sure why, I'm very open about the fact I don't cook my own dinners. I often work twelve-hour days so the last thing I want to do is come home and spend an hour cooking. There's no chance of the Kane ladies thinking I cooked any of this.

I walk down the hall to greet my guests and open the door for Danny, my mum, and my two sisters, Charlie and Callie. Callie, my youngest sister, sports one of those rings that goes right through her nose like a bull ring. We all hug.

Mum kisses both cheeks, leaving lipstick smudges I'm sure, and marches in briskly, peering over my shoulder. I know what she's at . . . she's scouting to see if Natalia, my housekeeper, is here. Natalia keeps my house in a permanent state of clean, the fridge stocked, my suits dry-cleaned and pressed and the bed linen changed at least once a week. None of this sits well with my mum who thinks that letting a stranger in to do your washing is vulgar. As far as she is concerned, it's as bad as having a harem of women living in the house with me.

There are twenty years between the three Kane siblings. We joke that Charlie and Callie are accidents. In the seventies, Mum and Dad met in London when Mum was at nursing college and Dad was a labourer. They came from an era in Ireland when condoms were frowned upon, and the withdrawal method was the choice of contraception. None of us were planned, hence the age gaps. When I was fifteen, Dad decided he had enough of England and us, and skipped over the water to be with a woman from Kilkenny. A *harlot*, as my mother would say.

I spot Jack walking towards the house. Good timing. "Go into the bar area," I instruct the others. "I'll let Jack in."

Off my kitchen is a custom-designed cocktail bar, one of two in the house. The second is in the cinema room downstairs. I'd spent a few million buying the house and the same again on the renovation job.

"Mate." Jack grins as he approaches the door. He hands me a bottle of Scotch.

I spot the vintage and nod approvingly.

"You know I had to send my PA all over town because of your particular tastes?" He hands me his coat, and I lead him into the hallway. "She called five times in a panic. She said I can only find a twenty-five-year Glenfiddich vintage reserve. 'Is that sufficient, Jack?' I had to say, 'No, Julia. It must be at least a Glenfiddich 1975 or older.'"

I shrug. "I have good taste and know what I like."

We join the others in the bar area where Danny is serving up the drinks.

"Mrs. Kane, your favourite sherry." Danny hands my mum her tipple, beaming at her. Lickarse. He's even more attentive to her now he's dating Charlie. "Sweetheart, what do you want to drink?" he asks, kissing my sister on the forehead as she pops herself onto a barstool.

I resist the urge to snap at him. While I'm delighted that my best friend and sister have found happiness together, the big brother instinct sometimes takes over.

When I found out about their secret relationship, things were rough between Danny and me. I knew Danny when he was working his way through every beautiful woman in London. That's not what I wanted for my sister. It was a dark time when I thought I'd lost my closest friend, but Danny and

I hashed things out when I realised he was serious about Charlie. In fact, we all spent Christmas in Danny's holiday home in the Shetlands.

Still, they are a new couple and it's taking us all a while to adjust to the change in dynamics.

"Wine, please." Charlie smiles back at him adoringly. "This smells amazing, Tristan." Her eyes dance with mischief. "We hear you men had a lovely night out last week at the Regency."

Danny flinches.

For fuck's sake, he's a leaking tap now he's with my sister. Doesn't he understand bro code?

Mum looks up sharply. An Irish mammy can sniff out a story that's been kept from her.

"Ah, yes," Jack pipes up. "We met a lovely female lawyer that works for Tristan. Tristan knows her quite well, don't you?"

"How well?" Mum asks briskly.

I grimace. "Not well enough to send me up an aisle, if that's what you're asking." I take the canapés out of the warming oven.

Charlie eyes them suspiciously. "What are these? No surprises tonight, Tristan."

I grin. "Smoked Gammon Ham with mustard glaze."

She sucks in air. "Pig is out. Sorry, I just can't."

"I think you should write out menus for us," Jack says, taking three. "Do you have any of those pork pastry things that you had last time?"

I skewer him with a look. "No, Jack, you slept with my last caterer, remember?" I shoot an apologetic look at Mum.

His brow furrows as he thinks. "Oh, yes! That's unfortunate. If I knew I had to give up those pork pastries, I wouldn't have done it."

I lead them into the dining room, where the caterers have set the table according to the menu, and then I return to the kitchen to fetch the first course.

Danny follows me out. "You okay?"

"I saw Gemina earlier," I reply flatly, lifting the braised pork from the warming oven.

"And?"

"And she says she wants to talk. She suggested telling *Daniel*, for fuck's sake."

"She's right. About the talking at least. This isn't going away."

"Jesus, Danny, whose side are you on?"

Danny pours himself another Scotch. "Yours. Always yours. But I can't just tell you what you want to hear. We'll find a solution to this that doesn't involve murder." He swirls the liquid in his glass. "Enough about the past. What about the present?" His eyes twinkle. "You booked Asha's private room last night, didn't you? You know they had to cancel some Chinese billionaire's booking to squeeze you in. I reckon your boner cost us twenty grand."

"It was worth every penny." I hand him two plates of pork then crick my neck. "Although my back is killing me now."

"I'll assume by that comment she finally relented," he says dryly. "Can't keep up with a twenty-five-year-old?"

"No, can't sleep on planks of wood." I grimace. "Didn't sleep a wink. She lives in a noisy house-share with a million people. One of them even barged into the bedroom in the middle of the night."

The corner of his mouth quirks up. "Let me get this straight. You stayed at her place?"

"Had to," I grumble. "She refused to come back to mine."

"So, it's heating up then," he muses as we walk back through to the dining area.

"Heating up? It's so hot the Met Office will need to issue a weather warning. Everything about the woman is perfect."

"Nobody is perfect, Tristan. You learnt that lesson the hard way," he says in a low voice so the others don't hear.

We place starters down on the placemats and I pop open a bottle of champagne to toast us.

"What's new with you, Callie?" Jack throws me a lifeline and diverts attention from my love life.

My youngest sister shrugs.

"You're in your final year now, right? Remind me what degree you're doing?" Jack probes.

"History of Art," she tells him.

He nods. "What will you use that for?" he asks.

"Fuck all," Callie replies. "I just like the student lifestyle."

"Language, young lady!" Mum interjects, her face blanching.

"Maybe I'll do a second degree afterwards like

History of History." Callie sniggers, and I bite my lip. I'm paying her university fees.

Mum smacks her lips. "God above, give me patience. Over my dead body. You'll earn a living like everyone else. I didn't raise you to be lazy."

Callie groans. "If you don't stop nagging me, Mum, I'm going to drown myself in this soup."

Charlie darts a glance at me then turns to Callie. "Callie," she says, "you can't be a student forever. I'll help with your CV."

"Mr. O' Neil even offered her a job in the arts and crafts shop," Mum explains.

"I'm not working for your *boyfriend*," Callie moans.

"What?" I sit up alert as Charlie smirks at me like she knows something I don't. "Who is Mr. O' Neil?" I ask sharply.

"My companion," Mum announces.

"You have a boyfriend? What?"

"Don't be silly, I'm too old to have a boyfriend." Mum tuts. "He's my *companion*," she repeats. "Don't call him my boyfriend. People will talk."

"What people?" Charlie rolls her eyes. "Who are these people you are always worried about?"

I frown. "Who is this guy?"

"Don't give away any details, Mum, unless you want poor Mr. O' Neil subjected to criminal checks." Charlie laughs.

"Of course, I won't," I say, but that's exactly what I'm going to do. I make a mental note to get his details from Charlie later and to ask what the hell is the difference between a boyfriend and a companion. At least it must be innocent enough if she's still referring to him by his second name.

The conversation swings to Jack's new hotel project, and my mind drifts to my Elly. What's she doing right now? Is she enjoying dinner with her mum? Her home life seems unsettled. The father in me wants to mollycoddle her and to protect her. To give her emotional and financial stability. To invite her to my home, to this dinner with my family.

Pretending to listen to Mum, I retrieve my phone from my pocket under the table.

How is Wales? I message.

I see her typing then stop.

The birthday present I had planned for my mum didn't go as planned.

I frown. **Everything OK?**

She doesn't reply quickly.

I miss you this evening. Stay with me tomorrow night.

Two simple letters pop up on the screen. **OK**

Before I can stop myself, I tip my head back and smile unrestrainedly.

"See?" Mum says as I drift into the conversation again. "Tristan is delighted to give Callie a job at Madison Legal."

What?

20

Elly

After I exit the underground at Holland Park, I turn right onto a tree-lined street with huge Victorian townhouses hidden behind tall gates and high hedges. Megan and I stalked the address online and found out how much he paid for it. Actually, Megan stalked the address and made me guess. I went big at five million and she laughed and said you couldn't buy a ham sandwich with five million in that area. In fact, I needed to add on another fifteen million, which is what he paid for it seven years ago. It's loose change considering it's nestled in the exclusive W8 Kensington Palace, one of Britain's most expensive postcodes. Megan asked me to keep an eye out for Madonna.

Hold on a second . . . I recognise this street. The Uzbekistan Embassy beside Maria Garcia's residence stares down at me, and I shake my head. So he really *did* make an unnecessary round trip just to talk to me?

I turn the corner onto a private street. A burst

of giggles erupts in my belly as I walk past each tank of a house in turn. I can't believe he stayed the night in my house-share; no wonder he was so keen for us to stay in his house. The street is decorated with intimidating neighbourhood watch signs, and I begin to wonder if snipers are watching me. Driveways are lined with more luxury cars than the Grand Prix.

Number twelve—this is his. I gawk at the three-storey townhouse that screams of stinking rich.

Holy shit.

I flatten down my skirt. I'm wearing a black leather skirt, a loose woollen sweater that reveals a shoulder on one arm, and ankle boots. The target is 'effortless chic.' I've opted for minimal hairstyling and make-up after the epic contouring fail on the first date.

A petite brunette answers the imposing door.

"Oh," I say, confused. "I must have the wrong address."

"Elena?" she asks with an accent I can't quite place.

My heart rate kicks up a notch. Is this his mother? That doesn't sound like an Irish accent. I didn't have my glasses on at the hotel the morning of his mum's birthday.

Tristan comes to the door in socks and a torn T-shirt, and I try to ignore the way his muscles look underneath. His lips part in a grin.

"Hi." I shift awkwardly.

"You should have let me get you a car," he says as

I step into the high-ceilinged hallway. He takes my coat from my shoulders and leans down to kiss my neck. He's a full head taller than me so my eyes are parallel with a thick chest.

"Elly, this is Natalia."

Phew. Not his mother.

Natalia and I exchange pleasantries.

"Nice skirt." His eyes roam up and down my bare legs as if Natalia isn't in the hall. "I like leather."

My eyes widen. Does he have to look at me in such an overtly sexual way in front of Natalia? She could probably write a book on Tristan Kane's sex life.

"Whoa!" I exclaim, my eyes roaming the hallway. "Your house is the same style as the Uzbekistan Embassy! It's beautiful."

He shrugs sheepishly. "Nice, isn't it? It's the same architect that designed the Embassy." He turns to Natalia. "Do you want to head off?"

When she nods and leaves the hallway, I feel slightly relieved.

"My housekeeper and saviour," he explains.

"Thank God," I say. "I thought she was your mother."

He laughs and pulls me to him. "Don't say that to my sister Charlie if you meet her. She says the same. Also don't say it to my mother who sees Natalia as a threat."

My cheeks burn at the casual suggestion of meeting his family.

He holds me still in the hall for a minute, staring at me with a smouldering gaze that instantly gets me flustered. "I've missed you," he says after a beat.

"It's only been forty-eight hours," I reply breathily. *The longest forty-eight hours of my life.*

He wraps his strong arms around my waist. He leans down, his legs widening, and presses his body close, bringing his lips to mine. I feel his growing hardness between my legs and respond by pushing my tongue against his. Every kiss is so damn *sexual.* A kiss is never just a kiss with Tristan.

"I couldn't wait any longer for that," he says as he breaks the embrace.

My cheeks heat up even further.

"Priorities. I need to feed you first. Would you like a tour, Elly?"

"Yes, please." I nod. "I feel like I should be paying for the tour."

He laughs. "Come on, I'll show you the basement first." He takes my hand in his and leads me down the stairs. "It's a listed period home," he explains. "But I've spent years modernising it while retaining the Victorian period pieces like the fireplaces."

I follow him through all four floors in awe. "How many rooms are there? I could get lost here."

"Eight bedrooms, the living area, dining area, the study, gym, home cinema, and wine cellar." He counts in his head. "Fourteen? Oh, my office. And the bathrooms, of course."

I draw in a breath. The guy is so rich he's forgotten how many rooms are in his house.

"Would you like some wine?" he asks.

"Sounds lovely." I follow him into the kitchen.

The house is intimidating me. At my house, he was just a hot handsome guy. Here, there are constant reminders of how successful Tristan is. It's a kitchen designed for a Michelin chef team, and I have a feeling a few may have cooked here before.

An enclave in the kitchen leads to a bar area. "You must do a lot of entertaining here," I say. *Like every single woman in the online pictures*

"Sometimes," he replies nonchalantly. He hands me a glass of red. "This will go perfectly with dinner. Are you hungry? Natalia has made a beef bourguignon."

"Starving."

He takes two dishes out of a warming oven that could fit an entire cow, and I follow him into the dining area.

"Natalia can cook!" I say. I can tell just by the smell wafting through the dining room. I take a seat at the impeccably set table.

"I told her I was trying to impress a very special woman tonight," he replies, setting down the food. "It's gluten-free, dairy-free, and free of something else I can't remember. I did some research, and it said that would be better for Crohn's disease."

My face heats. I can't believe I disclosed my condition to him after a few glasses of wine. It's not exactly the sexiest revelation, is it?

"That is the sexiest and sweetest thing anyone has ever done for me," I say, and it might be true. My eyes linger on his face. Is he always this considerate? "It's a big house to live in all alone. Do you ever get lonely?"

"Daniel stays over at least once or twice a week."

I nod. "It must be tough not seeing him all the time. Would you like more kids?" I add tentatively.

"Maybe." His lips press in a tight line. "I never meant for this house to just be for me."

Perhaps a conversation for another day. "How was your afternoon with Daniel?"

The grin reaches his eyes as it always does when he is talking about Daniel. "Fantastic. But exhausting. I have you to blame for tiring me out."

You'll be just as tired tomorrow morning. "Is it easy co-parenting?"

His grin gives way to a pained expression. "Not for me. Gemina holds all the cards."

I wait for him to elaborate.

"I'm not Daniel's paternal father."

My eyes widen. I think about my hurtful comment at the drinks when I asked if his son looked like him. "I'm sorry . . ." I trail off, not knowing what to say. "Is that why you divorced?" I ask tentatively.

"Not completely." He exhales roughly. "I found out about two years ago. She told me it was a mistake so I tried to make it work for well over a year. We went to counselling. We continued living as a family. In the end we couldn't make it work."

Fear trickles through me as I hear the thick emotion he tries to mask. I'm only chipping the surface of this. I'm not sure if I want to know the truth.

Baby steps.

I change the subject. "This is delicious. I can't imagine eating meals of this quality every day. Eating in my house is stressful. It's a queue for the kitchen, then when you do gain entry, half your ingredients are gone."

His eyes crinkle. "I'm glad you approve, Elly."

"How am I ever going to cook you a meal?" I muse. "If this is the norm for you. When was the last time you were in a supermarket?"

He starts laughing then looks serious. "Shit." His brow furrows. "I can't remember." He has the grace to look a little embarrassed. "I have to be economical with my time. I spend at least twelve hours a day working, sometimes more."

"Why are you interested in me, Tristan?" I study him. "What do I bring to the table?" I'm not talking about beef.

He frowns. "Is this a serious question? You're intelligent, funny, and driven. You have a really mature head on you. In fact, Danny and Jack would say you are more mature than me." He chuckles.

Then something in the way he looks at me changes.

"You take my breath away. I'm so insanely attracted to you, Elly." His voice thickens with lust. "You know, I think about you every night."

I close my eyes briefly. The pain in his eyes from earlier is still haunting me.

"I think about you every night, too," I whisper. "When Frank the Shagger is at it, I close my eyes and think of you."

He laughs. "I'm not sure that's a compliment. I might have to buy you earmuffs." He nods to my empty plate. "I'm glad you enjoyed it, sweetheart. Natalia will be happy. Is your Crohn's okay?"

I frown. What a way to dampen the mood. Moving from his bad ex-wife to my bad bowel isn't how I planned the conversation to go. I need to move us to the next course. I push my chair back and slowly walk to his side of the table.

He leans back in his chair.

Keeping my gaze fixed on him, I peel my lacy thong down my legs, then step each leg out of it.

He leans back further in his chair, watching the show.

I lift my sweater over my head so that I'm standing only in my leather skirt and red lacy bra.

His thighs spread as a ridge forms in his jeans.

Without speaking, I step between his legs, unbutton his jean button clumsily, and then pull down his zipper. When I push down his boxers, his erection juts upwards, thick and ready.

"You want it?" he asks hoarsely. "Take it."

My knees drop to the floor between his thighs. I wrap my hands around the base of his shaft and push his cock deep into my mouth.

He groans and places his hand on the back of my head fisting handfuls of hair.

I yelp as he tugs too hard.

"Sorry," he says, watching me from above.

With both hands wrapped around him, I suck

him from the top to the base, thrusting him in and out of my mouth. I speed up, making him hit the back of my throat every time.

"Elly," he moans.

Before he can climax, I withdraw him from my mouth. He grunts in response. Tough, I'm in control now.

I rise from my knees and wrap my legs around his hips, lowering myself down so I can grind myself against his length. I'm going to come just from rubbing myself against him.

"Sit on it," he says, growling. "Stop teasing me."

I want to have the willpower to tease him longer, but I'm too horny to last. With a sharp movement, I impale myself down onto his erection, crying out as I forget his size.

That's the spot.

At this angle, I can force him deep. My thighs flex around his hips, and I move up and down, controlling the rhythm to my own enjoyment.

My fingers lock possessively around his square masculine jaw. I'll never get over how handsome his face is, it's why I can't make myself last. His gorgeous thick dark locks flop over his forehead and he stares up at me with such adoration, I whimper.

"I'm not going to last if you keep doing that," he says through clenched teeth, holding my hips with an iron fist.

"It's fine," I murmur. "I want to feel you come inside me." With every thrust, I slide further into oblivion. This man is going to be the undoing of me.

My chest presses against his, and I can't tell if his heartbeat or mine is racing or both.

My core clenches tighter each time I drive him into me, making his groans louder and more urgent. My body is in control now, not my head.

"You feel so good," he says, his voice thick and heavy as I ride him. His head jerks back in pleasure. The tempo of our breathing quickens together as I buck so hard I'm close to falling off him. He blows out a final hiss of breath and erupts inside me, holding my hips tight in place.

He stays inside me for a long time, both of us reluctant to move.

Finally, I lift myself off. "I'm going to clean up," I say, my voice hoarse.

I stumble to the master bathroom on shaky legs. I'm definitely taking a dip in that tub before work tomorrow. No wonder he smells like money. The soap is the type of soap they attach to the walls in luxury hotels so people don't steal it. I chuckle to myself.

This bathroom is every IBD sufferer's wet dream.

21

Tristan

My hand rests on Elly's lower back as I lead her across the golf clubhouse. I use any excuse to touch her these days. There's a not-so-subtle turn of heads from men as we traverse to the terrace, and I feel a flush of pride. *That's right, you can look all you want, but she's mine.*

I'm ashamed to admit that we have been inseparable since she first stayed with me last Sunday night. I don't usually lose my cool over a woman this quickly, and I certainly don't cancel on my friends, but this week I couldn't help myself. The only night we didn't see each other was when Daniel stayed.

Jack and Danny glance up from their seats, amusement flashing across both their faces. I shoot them a warning sign to be on their best behaviour.

"Elly, you remember Danny and Jack."

"Nice to see you again, Elly." Jack's eyes gleam.

I wrap my arm around her waist. Jack's a mate and would never overstep the boundary, but he's still a bloke. He would need to be gay to not be attracted to her.

He gives her a wolfish smile. "Sorry we ambushed your date the other night."

"I'm not sorry," I growl, pressing her body into mine.

Mischief sparkles in his eyes. He's not finished. "We didn't get to meet you properly at the Regency. Or that morning in the Rosemont. You ran off in such a hurry."

More like escorted off the premises.

A blush creeps over her. "That night was a series of unfortunate events."

"We've all had one or two of those nights." Danny laughs.

She wraps a curl of her hair around her finger and scuffs her toe into the ground. "Nice to meet you both under better circumstances."

I feel a twinge of annoyance as she eyes Danny nervously. Women always get star-struck over Walker, and Elly is clearly not immune to his brooding good looks.

Danny smiles warmly. "Don't believe everything you've heard about us."

I nudge Jack. "Move over so Elly can sit down."

He rises, offering her the seat. "I was just about to get some refreshments. Take a seat, Elly." She sits down opposite Danny, crossing her long shapely legs.

"What would you like to drink?" I ask her. "We never drink alcohol before a game but don't let that stop you."

She shrugs. "I'll have a beer."

Those big blue-green eyes stare up at me, and I resist the urge to climb over the sofa and take her in my arms. Instead, I lean down and kiss her forehead.

"So?" Jack's voice is loaded with questions as we walk to the bar.

"So what?"

He studies me, smirking. "So, you are so taken with this girl, you can't bear to be apart from her, and you bring her to golf? Even Danny hasn't invited Charlie here."

"Stop making it into a big deal," I say, irritated. "You and Danny are acting like a pair of children. Act your age."

"Touchy, Kane." He chuckles. "This is highly unusual. It's the first time I've seen you flapping over a woman since . . ."

I rake a hand through my hair. "Piss off. I'm not flapping," I snap at him. "I'm just so damn *horny* all the time. No woman has driven me this wild for days on end. I don't know how I'm gonna play on form today." I lower my voice. "Don't fuck this up for me. *Everything* is censored. Understand?"

He raises his hands in self-defence and laughs. "My lips are sealed. It's nice to see you happy, mate."

As Jack orders the drinks, I turn my head to the terrace to find her laughing loudly at something Danny says. What the fuck is he saying that's so funny? Why did I bring Elly to meet Danny and Jack again? Danny might be with my sister, but women still fall at his feet.

"Let's get back," I say as Jack watches the scene in amusement. We collect the drinks, three sparkling waters and a beer, and return to Danny and Elly.

"It's supposed to rain in a few hours. Come on, let's head out to the first tee," I say confidently, ready to showcase my skills to Elly.

I lift mine and Elly's golf bag. I've hired her clubs and accessories for the afternoon. At the side of the lawn, Danny grabs a four-person buggy and we climb in, Jack and Danny up front and Elly and me in back. Unfortunately for her, my legs take up most of the space. I lift her leg over mine.

"It's just a short journey to the first tee," I explain, draping my arm over her shoulder.

"Sure," she replies, sipping her beer.

Danny parks up.

"Walker, you're up first," I say as I take out golf clubs for Elly. "Since you lost last time, we'll give you a head start." I like to remind Danny when he's losing.

He lines his ball up on the tee, planting his feet in a wide stance. Minutes pass as he shuffles his feet, his jaw set in deep concentration. We'll be here all day with Danny playing.

His brow furrows as he finally connects the club with the ball. I'm the strongest golfer out of the three of us and, to my pleasure, it infuriates the hell out of Danny. If we were playing for cash, I'd make a fortune.

Our eyes follow the ball down the leafy, parkland course.

We chose the club because of its incredible views of the city skyline, which is why it has a year's waiting list for new members. That, and the fact that it costs a small fortune to join, meaning everyone is so wealthy that no one pays attention to us.

"Good range, Walker." I might have competition today.

"This is a difficult course rating," Jack mutters to me, out of Elly's earshot. "Isn't this a little harsh? Especially with the wind today."

"I don't think Elly is too bothered," I whisper, glancing over at her as she takes a large swig of beer.

Jack's up next. He lines his ball up, licking his lips with the same concentration as Danny. He's a sore loser also. It falls short ever so slightly of Danny's. He groans as Danny slaps him on the back.

"Elly, do you want to go next?" I ask.

She picks up a golf club and ambles over.

I line the ball up for her and come in behind her as she grasps the golf club. My hands grip her hips and pull her flush against me.

"Stand with your feet hip-width apart and bend your knees slightly," I explain.

"Like this?" She ever so slightly grinds against me.

"Yeah, that's on form." I stifle a groan as I momentarily forget we are in broad daylight in the middle of a golf course.

In my peripheral view, Jack and Danny exchange a glance, sniggering.

"Now lean forward at your hips and keep your weight evenly distributed on the centre of your feet."

She follows my instructions, thrusting her hips deeper into me. "Just like this?" She tilts her head, smiling up at me.

I swallow hard, feeling the blood rush south. "Yeah, just like that." This is the most sexualised game of golf I've ever had.

She makes a motion to swing, rubbing her buttocks harder against my growing excitement. Christ, we've got another eighteen holes to get through. If she keeps tormenting me like this, I'll be able to play golf with my dick instead of the golf club.

I exhale, breathing into her neck.

"Tristan." She stands up straight. "Can you move back, please? I think I'm fine by myself."

My ego is wounded as I take a step back, bemused. If she breaks someone's nose, it's her own problem.

There's a loud clang as the ball connects with her club. It flies through the air, slamming down past Jack's and Danny's, dangerously close to the hole. The three of us collectively freeze.

I suck in sharply.

"Fuck me," Danny splutters, eyes bulging out of his head. "That's a near perfect shot."

"Christ." Jack squints. "That's at least a birdie."

I stare at her dumbfounded. "You never said you could play golf. Don't tell me that's beginner's luck." I feel a strange sense of pride.

She looks at me pointedly. "You never asked. I didn't realise you guys were so competitive. I used to work on a golf course in Wales," she explains, swinging her club. "I just picked it up."

The three of us stare at her with fresh awe. *Damn*, the entire morning I have been ranting about how I've been playing for two decades. My confidence in winning this game is waning.

Her eyes light up. "It's your turn, Tristan. Did we agree on what the winner gets?" she adds, blinking innocently.

Jack lets out a loud laugh. "Oh my God, this really is the woman of your dreams, Kane."

***

We leave two hours early to get to Bronzefield prison. One, because crossing London is a nightmare and two, from experience I know how slow it is to get through the prison processing. Adi and Elly have accompanied me. Both Adi and I have been to prisons many times, including high security prisons, but this is clearly Elly's first visit, as she peers around it, wide-eyed. My lips twitch as she looks completely freaked when she's asked to stand still while the drug sniffer dog inspects her. To reassure her, I place my hand on her lower back, then drop it when I realise where I am.

Maria is waiting for us in a private visitor room. It's a far cry from the former Embassy that she was holed up in. She might be up for murder, but her husband owned a number of hotels and assets in her name making her a very rich woman.

She looks shockingly stunning for a prisoner. The woman takes care of what nature has blessed her with.

"How are you, Maria?" I pull out a chair for Elly then take a seat beside Maria.

"Shit," she snaps in her sexy Colombian accent. "When are you getting me out of this dump?"

"We're building a compelling case to bring to the Supreme Court. I'd just like to circle around a few things one more time."

She nods that she understands.

"We need your full disclosure, Maria," I say. "If all the facts aren't revealed up front, if some are missed, there is the potential that they could surface at a later stage and be used against you." I lean forward in my seat. "Remember you have our full confidentiality under your client privilege."

She crosses her legs, relaxing one leg on top of the other.

"We need to know all the facts, no matter how insignificant you may think they are. Us lawyers hate surprises." I smile, hoping it will reassure her. "You previously told us you never came into contact with any of the victims. Did your husband ever mention their names in front of you?"

"No."

"You never saw photographs, never heard phone recordings, heard any of their names in conversations?"

"No to all," she repeats sharply.

I nod. "So, the first time you were aware of any of the victims was two nights before your husband's death, is that correct?"

"Yes. Where is this going, Mr. Kane?"

I smile warmly. "The phone records will go back one year so we need to make sure that there's nothing that could bring your case into dispute."

Something flickers on her face. It's gone before I can process it.

Adi jumps in with further questioning, ironing out details on what happened in the two days leading up to her husband's death. Something is off. I wasn't joking when I said lawyers hate surprises. I'll speak to Adi later; we're going to have to check those phone records with a fine-tooth comb. If there's one thing that gets my blood boiling, it's someone tarnishing the Madison Legal brand.

22

Elly

I'm in deep trouble.

Any sense of self-preservation or rational thought has evacuated my body, and I've fallen for Tristan Kane *hard*. Since our golf outing two weeks ago, I've had so many orgasms I'm concerned my face will freeze in a permanent contortion. Sexologists will study me.

Then there were the heated visits to Maria Garcia in prison. Tristan was accompanying us less these days, but on the two trips he did join us, I felt like the others could tell I was fucking the boss just from my face. Especially since I *had* just fucked the boss a few hours before.

On the second visit, he sat beside me in the meeting room, and his thigh touched mine for the entire hour. At one point, his hand went under the table and skimmed over my thigh, and I nearly yelled. Focusing on what the team was asking Maria took all my strength. In contrast to Tristan, who was able to conduct a full client interview.

I told him off after that meeting. Even if he is a skilled multitasker, he cannot be so overtly sexual with me at work.

Megan was right about the lethal body, face and accent combination, but for me it was not just about physical attraction; it never had been. The guy has the sexiest mind. Never mind trainees, established lawyers with years of experience would kill to be shadowing Tristan Kane on a case.

I shouldn't have let things get so intense this quickly. The harder I fall, the more scared I am. I spent pretty much the entire two weeks holed up at his stately home being treated like a queen.

The cynic in me worries that it's just a matter of time before my Anne Boleyn-style fall from grace, since there are plenty of hot Jane Seymours vying to take my crown.

"Are you coming, Elly?" Amy asks, handing me a coffee.

I nod, and we step in line with Sophie and other lawyers from the Financial Services sector. Madison Legal's annual conference is being held at the Business Innovation Centre, one of the only venues in London with enough capacity to accommodate the UK offices. Crowds move forward into the auditorium.

"This place is huge!" I gasp as we enter the domed amphitheatre with cinema-style seating.

There's a loud hum of conversations as the 2000 Madison Legal UK employees cram into the theatre. A mixture of accents colour the room. People have flown in from the Scotland and Northern Ireland branches and other European satellite offices.

"Music events and theatre productions are held here as well as corporate events," Sophie explains as someone ushers us down an aisle to our seats, halfway down the auditorium.

"I forgot my glasses," I mutter. "This place is so big I won't be able to see." To see *him*.

"Don't worry," she says over the dull roar as we sit down. "The speakers will be on the big screen."

Tristan has to talk in front of all these people? I feel a pang of panic for him, which is silly because he barely mentioned the conference last night. He even polished off half a bottle of wine with me.

"Our Managing Partner and CEO Tristan Kane will now open the event," the Head of Events announces through the microphone.

Spotlights from above focus on the centre stage. Conversations peter out. Everyone is waiting for him.

The air in the room changes as he strolls onto the stage like a man who owns time, his tall, confident posture and smooth hand gestures showing no sign of nerves. When he reaches the podium, he gives the crowd a crooked smile, and everyone claps. Somehow, before he even speaks, he has total command of the room.

I sit on the edge of my seat, watching his projection on the big screen. The three tiers of seating surrounding the stage give all 2000 of us an exceptional view of him. He has so many eyes on him from all angles. How does he cope?

Is this the same man whose house I left this morning?

In his confident and controlled voice, he projects over every speaker, giving Churchill a run for his money. His crisp white shirt shows off his athletic figure. His sleeves are normally rolled up to his elbows, but today they are cuffed and tightened by cufflinks. I get a flashback of this morning when he was wearing nothing but his shirt, unbuttoned.

How lucky am I? There isn't a chance in hell that every woman in this room isn't dreaming about what he's like in bed.

I bite my lip to stifle a smile. I try to concentrate as he tells us about the top achievements of the company this year and the long-term strategic vision. Who knew that the financial forecast would be so arousing? The only thing I can focus on is that mouth enlarged on the screen. The mouth that spent twenty minutes between my legs last night, making me moan.

He pauses between sentences like he has all the time in the world. Every sentence is composed, eloquent, said with precision, and it's the hottest damn speech I've ever heard. I know he's accustomed to doing TedTalks. I watched a few of his talks that have over a million views last week, and I was ashamed of myself for not knowing who he was when we met in Mykonos.

Next up is the awards ceremony for the best talent. Lawyers wait their turn to receive awards and shake hands with him. Mara, the hot redhead who attended the intern welcome drinks, walks onstage. The men in the room visibly perk up as she is broadcast on the big screen. I feel a twinge of jealousy as the commenter lists her achievements for the year. She simmers towards Tristan, and he smiles broadly at her, whispering something inaudible to the audience.

Seeing his smouldering gaze on her, I wonder for the umpteenth time if I'm taking this too seriously. She's already an established lawyer and gorgeous as hell. What's he doing with me?

I don't see much of Tristan after the awards ceremony. We had a packed schedule of breakaway groups all afternoon tailored to the different industry sectors. I'm wrecked, moving from talk to talk, so I can't think what he must be like as the centre of attention all day.

After 6 p.m., one of the conference rooms becomes a bar.

Half the attendees have left, some to catch flights back to other parts of the UK, but hundreds of us are still packed into the conference area, accepting complimentary champagne and wine from circulating waiters. It's the whole point of why we turned up. With no dinner and free drinks, the drunk level in the room increases a notch.

I'm talking to Juan, a senior lawyer at Sophie's level.

"I work in Financial Services under Sophie," I say, nodding in her direction, hoping to include her in the conversation. Juan is easy on the eye but is a bit too intense. Unfortunately, Sophie is just out of reach. "I'm also shadowing on the Garcia case. It's an amazing learning experience."

As he steps into my personal space, I retreat subtly. We continue to play this game until he has me backed into a corner.

"Under Tristan Kane?" he asks with a gleam in his eye.

"Uh-huh."

"He must have a personal interest in that case," he muses. "Do you know what it is?" His eyes search my face for inside information.

I shake my head. "I'm just there to shadow and support."

Juan looks disappointed. "I'd love for us to go for a coffee some time," he drawls, placing his hand on my lower back. "I've spent four years in Financial Services. I can give you some guidance."

Now I'm in a dilemma. It should be perfectly routine for a senior lawyer to invite a trainee for coffee to discuss work at a work conference. It might even look unprofessional to turn him down. The ask is professional.

But I understand the language of flirt and a hand on your lower back translates as *I want you on your back.* I can tell by his look that he has no intention of remaining professional on our coffee date.

I smile, guarded. "Sure."

A waiter passes, and Juan lifts two more champagnes from the moving silver tray and puts down my empty flute.

"Oh, I'm not sure if I want another . . ." My voice trails off as I see Tristan and Mara deep in conversation on the other side of the room. The other two people are listening in on their conversation, but it is clear that the discussion is mostly between them. Unease washes over me. Tristan is focused solely on Mara. He smiles intently at her, and she leans forward so that he can hear what she is saying.

Mara talks the language of flirt as well. Her head tilts up towards him, eyes sparkling. Gentle nudges, open mouth, exposed neck, hair flicking, the woman could write the flirt manual. And why wouldn't she flirt? As far as everyone is concerned, he is single.

I turn back to Juan. His hand drops lower now, now a questionable line between lower back and upper ass.

"Actually, I will have another."

Juan hands me the champagne and I take a sip. He looks delighted in the sudden mood shift as I clink my flute with his.

His hand curls around my waist.

My phone vibrates in my bag. "One sec," I say, retrieving the phone. Terry flashes on the screen. My fake name for Tristan in case anyone saw his number at work.

"Excuse me," I say to Juan with fake regret.

"Hello?" I answer the phone and turn to face him. His phone is in his ear as he leans against the bar out of range of Mara's hearing. His face is taut.

"What the hell are you doing?"

I hear his voice as I lip-read him across the room while we stare at each other. "What?" Flinching, I move away from Juan so he doesn't hear the angry tone through the phone.

"Lover boy is very fucking over-familiar, Elly."

My cheeks flush with the heat of his sharp gaze. "So, it's okay for you to talk to a colleague but not for me?"

"Are you trying to make me jealous?" His voice is strained.

I narrow my eyes. "Don't be ridiculous. My life doesn't revolve around you, Tristan. You might be the boss, but you don't get to dictate who I talk to."

We glare at each other, silently.

Finally, he lets out a heavy sigh. "Make your excuses and meet me on the third floor. Take the stairs to your left and say you're going to the toilet."

The phone goes dead, and he returns to Mara and the two lawyers.

Moments later, he walks across the conference room, bypassing everyone trying to hijack him, and proceeds directly to the elevators. His eyes snap to mine with a flash of impatience.

"Excuse me, Juan," I say distractedly. "I'm going to the bathroom."

Juan nods, his disappointment evident. "I'll be here. In case we lose each other, I'll give you my number."

He puts his hand out to take my phone, and I hand it over. Out of the corner of my eye, I see

Tristan watching us from the elevator.

"There you go." Juan smiles and hands me my phone back with his contact information.

I'm more breathless than I should be when I reach the top step of the third floor. How chivalrous of Tristan to give me the stairs option while he takes the elevator.

I see him leaning against the wall beside the door. He opens it, beckoning me to follow him.

I enter with slight apprehension as I try to figure out whether he's angry, aroused or a bit of both. It's a dressing room for the conference speakers.

The door is barely shut before he turns to me, nostrils flaring.

"I don't like my employees touching you like that," he says, growling through his teeth, his chest rising and falling. He closes the distance between us. "Are you trying to tease me, Elly? Because you're doing a good job in pissing me off."

"I wasn't teasing you," I snap. "Juan asked me to go for a coffee. It's not my fault you employ handsy lawyers. Besides," I add indignantly, "I'm surprised you noticed. You were too wrapped up in Mara."

Furious, he takes another step forward. "So you thought you'd flirt with anyone that gives you attention? I'm not interested in women who play games."

"How dare you!" I spit, narrowing my eyes into angry slits. I've never seen Tristan like this before. He must be high on his own glory. For the second time since meeting him, I want to slap him.

I turn to leave, but two hands grab my hips from behind and press them against his thighs.

He's hard.

I freeze as he holds me in an iron grip. After what he said, I should protest, storm off, smack him . . . instead, I find myself pressing into him so my ass is hard against his arousal. As he lifts up my dress in one fluid motion, I feel him grow even harder.

I'm wearing a black thong to prevent visible lines. My bare buttocks rub against him, straining against his expensive cashmere suit pants. A low guttural growl erupts behind me, and he slaps one of my ass cheeks hard. I yelp at the sting.

"Do you want me to teach you who's boss here?" He breathes in my ear, sending a shiver from my ear the whole way down my body. *I like this role-play.*

"Two thousand of my employees here, and all I can think about is you," he murmurs as he guides me a few steps forward to the dresser table, then bends me over, so I have to catch my weight with my forearms on the tabletop.

Behind me, I hear him whipping off his belt and the zipper of his trousers being yanked down. He pulls my thong string to one side and uses the other hand to run his hardness up and down my dampening slit.

I let out an involuntary moan. "*Please.*" I want him to *own* me. My arousal has been simmering all day ever since he took control of the stage; now it's a pot ready to explode.

He lifts my hips and thrusts his cock deep into

me. Once he's in, he pushes me down onto the dresser, so I'm at a right angle, then he really gives it to me, his hips slapping against my thighs.

I practically convulse. This is angry sex, not tender. Crazed, urgent sex that makes me want to start an argument with him every day. As he pounds relentlessly, his hand curves around my hip and his thumb rubs circles on my clit.

"Ah!" I cry. The man can multitask.

He teases my clit faster with his fingers until my whole body is shaking.

I grip the dresser for control. "Tristan," I moan. "I can't take it. I'm going to—"

"That's right, Elly," he cuts in with a possessive growl. "You're mine."

"Tristan." I groan over and over as his fingers massage me relentlessly. With one final thrust he releases into me and shudders so hard, a glass falls from the dresser.

Holy shit.

My breathing is out of control. "I think I might be going into cardiac arrest."

Behind me, his touch becomes tender as he moves my hair to kiss my neck. I feel drops of his perspiration.

"You're mine too," I whisper, staring straight ahead.

He's silent for a moment while he adjusts my thong and smooths my dress down past my thighs. "I'm yours too," he repeats gently into my neck.

23

Tristan

I leave Danny and Jack playing the last few holes by themselves. Danny gets slower every time he tries to beat me. He can have this one; today I've got no time. I've been crawling in traffic for two hours across central London and the exhibition closes in twenty minutes.

Finally, my phone tells me I've reached the destination, a humble-looking library in South Tooting.

I coax the car into the parking space, feeling apprehensive. I have a surprise planned for Elly, and I'm not sure how she will react to it. I've arranged to meet her at Megan's art exhibition then we can drive to the surprise. I haven't seen enough of her this week.

I have some making up to do since I over-reacted at the all-staff event. I don't handle jealously well after my previous experiences.

It doesn't take long to find them in the library. They are the last stall of about twenty selling various crafts, paintings and soaps. Charlie would like this. The crowd looks like it's dying.

"Hi, ladies," I say as I approach the table. "I'm sorry I'm late, the traffic was horrendous." My mouth comes down on Elly's, restraining myself enough to kiss her like a gentleman in public.

Her breasts press against my chest as she breaks the kiss. I resist the urge to run my hands all over her body.

"You should have taken a chopper," she teases. "Better late than never."

"I sold a fucking painting!" Megan cuts in. "It's the first I've ever sold! A hundred quid! This time next year I'll be a millionaire." She grins, doing a little victory shuffle.

"That's amazing." I step back to take in her paintings, which are mainly landscapes. They're not bad at all, although some look a little rushed. "You're very talented, Megan."

"I know." She shrugs, making me chuckle.

"Have you been to all these places?" I ask, scanning the landscapes of Tibet, China and, I think, Peru.

She shakes her head. "Not all. Some are from pictures. You'll recognise these ones."

She points to a collection featuring white houses with blue domes in the signature Greek landscape.

"Beautiful." I smile. One in particular catches my eye. It's a girl sitting on a beach in a summer dress. Her long brown hair is flowing in the wind and the brush strokes have aptly captured her long, graceful neck and high cheekbones. "I love this one," I murmur.

"Thought you would." She smirks.

I cross my arms over my chest. "How much?"

Megan's eyes light up as her brain ticks over pound signs. She knows I'm not going to hustle with her in front of Elly. Let's hope she doesn't say a ridiculous figure like fifty thousand.

"Tristan," Elly starts, "you don't need to—"

"Elly, you ain't the seller, buyer or barter so stay out of it," Megan cuts in quickly, her eyes glinting.

I cock my head, waiting. "Well?"

She licks her lips, sizing me up. "Three thousand!" she shouts.

"Steady on, Pablo Picasso," Elly grumbles. "At least give him a realistic price."

Megan doesn't speak. She studies me, as I pretend to mull it over.

"Sold," I say simply.

"Yessssss!" She screams, making every stall holder turn to see what the commotion is. I laugh and stand back as she fist-pumps the air.

Elly stares between both of us, dazed. "Tristan, you don't have to do this. Megan! See sense. Three grand?"

"I want it." I shrug. "Besides, I don't want you hanging on anyone else's wall. I was thinking I could put you in the Madison Legal HQ reception?"

"Wha—"

"I'll remove the aquarium and put you there instead."

Elly opens her mouth to say something then closes it. She looks so shocked, I almost worry she is going to faint.

Elly

We drive north towards central London. I haven't seen enough of him since the conference last week as he had to visit the Hong Kong office for a few days. He asked me to go with him, but I'm not good at lying to pretend to my team that I coincidentally booked a last-minute Asia trip on the exact same dates as our CEO.

I've no idea where we are going. He says he has a surprise but is giving nothing away. I'm not sure I can handle any more surprises today after the painting purchase. Megan is bouncing in the backseat, ecstatic that the surprise, whatever it is, involves her too, and she gets to travel in a Porsche. So far, with three thousand more to her name, it's been a good day for Megan. What a hustle.

It's our first time in a sports car. Megan's and mine, obviously, not Tristan's. The guy collects cars like they are toys free with breakfast cereal. George usually drives him wherever he needs to go in his Aston Martin. He says he needs to take 'her' out to push the battery.

I call bullshit. I think he's peacocking.

In less than a mile, two other cars tried to race us despite loggerhead traffic, and a random bloke on the street clapped at Tristan. Almost every pedestrian gives the car a second glance—some curious, some hostile, some flirtatious—eager to know who owns it. I don't think he'll take it too kindly if I admit I'm a tad embarrassed.

"It's just off this street," Tristan says as he slows down to check the GPS.

Whatever *it* is.

We are on a main road bordering Battersea Park. He steps on the gas and accelerates down the street, the engine roaring.

"Do you need to go so fast?" I hiss.

He laughs. "Elly, we're only doing forty. I've got it on sport mode so you can feel the full effect."

Oh. I check the speed dial. He's right! Forty kilometres. It feels and sounds like eighty.

After a left turn, the car slows to a crawl. The man who stood up in front of 2000 people last week seems mildly flustered today.

"Brilliant," he says quietly. "He's here."

"Who's here?" I peer out the window. I'm so low to the ground in this sports car, my vision is impaired.

"You'll see," Tristan says, mischievously coaxing the sports car into a parking space.

A bloke stands on the street in full business attire with a waistcoat, tie and fancy shoes. It means only one thing on a Saturday, he's an estate agent. I wonder if he always dresses like this or if it's because he's meeting Tristan Kane.

I take ages to step out of the car for fear of

damaging '*her.*'

The young estate agent with the fancy shoes spots us and licks his lips. I'm starting to get a bad feeling. Surely Tristan hasn't bought an apartment near us because of my lousy bed?

Since that first night, I've been going to his house. Part of me is annoyed for making our relationship so one-sided. After all, why am I always travelling to see him? Then the other part of me thinks, how can I be so cruel to force anyone to stay overnight at my house where you can't sleep, eat or shag in peace?

Besides, I like his lush house. It feels like staying in a five-star hotel. But some nights when I've worked late, I've grumbled mildly about travelling to him too much. Surely . . . he hasn't bought this to stop me complaining?

"Mr. Kane." The young man runs forward to greet us and shakes Tristan's hand. "Such an honour." He turns to us. "And you must be Elly and Megan. I'm Dave."

"Don't ruin the surprise," Tristan says to Dave while smiling at me.

"Of course, sir, would you like us to start the tour?"

Tristan nods. "Lead the way."

We follow Dave across the street to a high-rise all-glass lavish apartment block, perhaps twenty storeys high. I'm not sure if it's offices or apartments. His dress shoes tap loudly on the marble floor as he leads us into the impressive lobby.

"Welcome to luxury living in Nine Elms." Dave

flashes his best sales smile as we approach the elevator. Almost like a robot, he says, "Amenities include a fully equipped spa with swimming pool, sauna and steam rooms, residents' lounge, rooftop bar and twenty-four-hour concierge."

Megan eyes me excitedly.

I shoot her a warning look. *No*.

I stay silent as we ascend.

Dave and Tristan converse politely about the building's architectural features.

"You've certainly done your research, Mr. Kane," Dave gushes.

"I'm familiar with most of the new builds in this area," Tristan replies dryly. "The Lexington Property Group owner is a good friend of mine. This is one of theirs." It's said matter-of-fact rather than bragging.

Dave salivates, smelling money.

As I stare sideways at Tristan, I attempt to decipher his unreadable expression.

"Here we are," Dave announces dramatically. "The *nineteenth* floor."

Dave leads us down the corridor to the door at the end. "It's the best one on the floor. You'll see why." He winks conspiratorially and flashes a white card across the door, like in hotels.

We step inside a brilliant white apartment with panoramic views overlooking the Thames. And I mean *everything* is white, the floor, the walls, the sofa, all the furnishings. Like a beautiful surgery waiting room with sleek, stylish Deco.

"Whoa!" Megan and I shout simultaneously.

"Welcome to the ultimate smart home," Dave declares, making exaggerated sweeping hand gestures. "Everything is sound-controlled or app-controlled based on your preference—heating, lighting, doors, air-con, even the underfloor heating."

He pauses for effect.

"There's a connected home sound system in all rooms, even the bathroom. Concealed speakers with voice control, *obviously*."

"That's good." Tristan nods approvingly. "Hopefully, it will understand the Welsh accent." He winks at me.

"Tristan," I start the second Dave is out of earshot, "are you moving in here? I don't understand why we're here."

"It's yours," he announces. "If you like it."

I blink wildly as my brain misfires. "Mine?"

"We'll take it!" Megan shrieks.

"I mean as a rental, not to own," he adds quickly. "There are three bedrooms, so you and Megan have a bedroom each plus a guest room when you want someone else to stay. It means your mum can visit."

Before I can react, Megan does a victory dance beside me.

"Thank you, Tristan!" she screams, flinging her arms around his neck.

"Megan and I can't afford this place," I say in a low, strained voice so Dave can't hear me.

"Don't worry, it's covered." He dismisses me in an authoritative tone like he's telling off an employee.

Maybe he is.

What?

"It's covered?" I repeat. "Cool it, Megan! We are not moving in here!"

She's bouncing around like a refuge dog who has found a new home. "Speak for yourself."

"Tristan," I say in a controlled tone as Dave's fancy shoes click out of the kitchen. "I don't know what you mean by '*covered*' but you're mistaken."

The light in Tristan's eyes dies. "Let's just finish the tour first. Just hear him out." His voice is hard.

I cross my arms across my chest as we follow Dave into the kitchen. I feel more uncomfortable by the minute. What is Tristan proposing exactly? That Megan and I live here rent-free? I'd be a gold digger.

"The smart fridge!" Dave gestures to the white fridge. "There are cameras inside that send pictures to your smartphone, allowing you to see what's inside your fridge from *anywhere*. So, when you're in the supermarket, just have a look inside the fridge, and you know what to top up. Simple!"

"Thank God we don't have it in our house." I shudder. "Only scientists would want to watch that video."

He opens the fridge, pointing to an appliance at the top. *There's more?*

"The food sniffer is your own electronic nose. It also connects to your smartphone and tells you how fresh your food items are."

The tour continues into the bathroom. "In Nine Elms luxury living, your bathroom is as smart as the rest of your home," Dave explains. "The showerhead has built-in Bluetooth speakers, motion-activated night lights *and* a smart toilet with automated flushing and built-in cleansing technology."

It's every IBD sufferer's wildest dream.

"This really is a first-world apartment," I marvel. "I'm wondering how I survived for so long."

"Why are there two toilets in the bathroom?" Megan asks. "In what situation would you need that? Is this for your IBD?"

I roll my eyes. "It's a *bidet.*"

"This is off the charts BDE," she says in a low voice. Thankfully, the acronym of Big Dick Energy washes over Tristan and Dave.

"Now for the bedrooms." Dave winks at Tristan conspiratorially, directing us into one of the bedrooms. It's white.

"We don't want the beds supplied," Tristan says firmly. "We'll secure our own."

"And will both ladies be staying in the apartment?" Dave asks.

"Yes," Megan and Tristan both say.

"That's the tour." Dave beams. "It speaks for itself, really. Do you require any other *apartments,* Mr. Kane?"

My eyes widen. Oh my God. Dave thinks we're part of a harem of Kane women holed up in various apartments across London.

"Not for the time being," Tristan replies.

What the hell does that mean? *Is* there a harem?

"Tristan." I smile politely for the sake of

Dave. "The apartment is lovely, certainly the most *intelligent* apartment I've ever been in, but Megan and I aren't looking right now."

"Don't be silly," he says, scoffing. "You can't stay in that house. See sense."

"See sense, Elly!" Megan yelps behind me. "For the love of God, see sense!"

My nostrils flare. "You're treating me like a child, Tristan. You can't railroad me into moving."

A muscle in his jaw ticks. "Let's not do this here," he grinds out. "Don't be rash, Elly."

"I'm not being rash," I say through equally gritted teeth. *"Daddy,"* I add with a growl. "You never consulted me on this before you sprung it on me. This is a huge deal."

"Is it the area?" he asks, bewildered. "I was considering putting you in one of my apartments that we rent out in Mayfair, but I thought Battersea would be better for your age group."

"Putting me . . . ? It's not the flat or the area, Tristan," I say with forced calm. "I'm not accepting free rent from you."

"Can you give us a minute?" Tristan says, turning to Dave. Dave nods and retreats into the kitchen.

"Elly!" Megan wails. "Don't be stupid. Take the goddamn flat. I'm sick of keeping all our baked goods in my bedroom."

My scowl deepens. "You want me to take this flat even though it would make me some sort of gold-digging freeloader? You would be a freeloader too, you know."

"Yes!" Megan claps her hands. "Stop being a moron. I don't want to live in our house-share. There are crumbs everywhere. No wonder we have mice. I think some of those crumbs are from the year it was built."

"It's Victorian." I roll my eyes. "And what happens if Tristan doesn't want to go out with me anymore? What if he goes off me? When we move, we move our way."

"Elly, you are being ridiculous," his gravelly voice cuts in.

"Stop antagonising me, Tristan!" I snap. "You do realise that Dave thinks you're a sugar daddy? He's looking at me like you've got women holed up all over the city."

His expression is stormy. "He thinks it now."

I try to calm myself down. "Look, this is really sweet of you, but I can't accept this. I'm not a charity case."

"I'd thought you would be happy with this place," Tristan says sullenly.

"I don't mean to sound ungrateful," I continue. "But you can't make decisions like this for me without consulting me. Bringing Megan along without asking me was unfair. Now look what'll I'll have to put up with." I nod to Megan standing mournfully beside the window, already grieving her loss. "Imagine what our colleagues would say."

"Excuse me?" Dave sneaks back in. "Will you be wanting the keys?"

"No," Tristan and I both say at the same time.

Dave looks devastated.

"I'll be in contact," Tristan says to Dave dully. "Let's go, ladies."

The elevator ride down is very different from the ride up. The longest elevator ride of my life. You could cut the awkwardness with a knife. Even Dave stands rigid in the corner, the sales fever sucked out of him by the wrath of Tristan, brooding in the other corner.

We walk out of the intelligent building and towards the car in silence, Tristan three strides ahead of Megan and me. I give her a warning look to be quiet.

Tristan jabs at the car fob opener, and the car beeps open. He gets into the car on the driver's side and slams the door shut. I don't know if the offer extends to Megan and I. Tentatively, I open the car door, and Megan crawls in the back.

Tristan turns on the ignition, it revs, but we don't move. Instead, he stares straight ahead. Megan and I sit in silence, glancing at each other in the front mirror. I still my breathing so as not to disturb him. Is he going to flip? Are we about to see the full wrath of Tristan Kane?

His steely eyes turn to me. "So, I fucked up, huh?"

"A little," I say. "It was a nice gesture but heavy-handed."

He exhales heavily. "Sorry."

"You made a mistake," I say softly. "Since when are you afraid of making mistakes?"

"When it comes to you, I am." His hand reaches

up to brush a strand of hair from my cheek.

"Tristan, if I have sex with you, can I stay?" Megan pipes up from the back seat.

24

Elly

Three missed calls from Mum instantly fills me with dread. Especially since it's three calls in the space of twenty minutes. No one calls repeatedly just for a chat. Definitely not my mum on a Friday night; at this time in the evening she should be down at The Wee Donkey, the life and soul of the party.

So I call her back, my heart starting to race. She answers on the first ring.

"Elly!" Something has happened. She's panicked.

"Yes, Mum?" I spring up from Tristan's sofa. "Is everything okay?"

Frowning, Tristan looks up from where he's reading the newspaper on the sofa.

"There's been a bit of trouble." Her voice is breaking and breathy.

"What trouble?" I gasp. Now my heart is hammering in my chest.

Concerned, Tristan stands up.

"Someone put a brick through the front window," she tells me.

"What?" My voice spikes upwards. "Why would someone do that?"

"Barry's son." She sniffs. "I called the police but I can't prove it was Barry's son."

"What did Barry say?" I ask bewildered. I knew bloody Barry was trouble. "Why on earth would his son do this?"

She hesitates. "Barry and his wife hadn't split up too long—"

"Mum, please tell me you weren't having an affair."

"No!" she says indignantly. "But the wife isn't happy about the separation. There's been a bit of talk in the village. You know what they're like."

I do. That's why I left.

"I'm coming home." I check my watch, my head full of fog. I usually know the train times but I can't think straight at the moment.

"No, love, don't be silly. It's fine. I'm fine."

"I'm coming," I say firmly. "It'll be close to midnight though. I gotta go. I'll text you."

We say goodbye and I hang up. Tristan watches me intently.

"Did you hear all of that?"

He nods. "Just about."

"I have to go to Wales tonight," I say, overwhelmed. One minute I'm going to spend the evening in Tristan's jacuzzi bath after a long work week, the next minute I'm heading to Wales to deal with a brick-firing lunatic. "If I hurry I can get an eight o'clock train."

"No need. I'll take you," he says.

I pull back to stare at him. "Tristan, that's so kind but you don't need to do that. Anyway, it's quicker to get the train than drive. I'll be fine," I reassure him.

"And it's much quicker to take a helicopter than the train," he counters, getting out his phone.

I stare blankly at him. "What?"

He doesn't look like he's joking.

"The helipad is thirty minutes from here. Then I can have you in Wales in under an hour," he states, tapping at his phone.

"Don't be silly. I can't get a *helicopter* to Wales. I'll get the train."

As I lift my phone to check train times, he grips my arm.

"I don't want you getting off a train at midnight alone," he replies, almost grumpy. "Look up somewhere for us to stay tonight while I notify air traffic control. I'll ask Danny and Charlie if they fancy a trip too."

I shake my head incredulously. So, he wasn't being facetious when he said he would get me a helicopter to Wales the night he stayed at my place. "Are you telling me you have a helicopter on *standby* for whenever you need it?"

"Yes," he says impatiently. "Now find us somewhere nice online nearby your mum's. We need to get going."

"But . . ." My protests trail off, he's already on the phone citing helicopter jargon.

An hour later, we arrive at the heliport in Chelsea Harbour. Danny and Charlie decided that an impromptu road trip, or specifically, *air trip*, to Wales was a fantastic idea. I'm a bit nervous to be meeting them, I've met Danny twice now and only saw Charlie from afar at the Rosemont. All in ludicrous situations and this one isn't any better.

A few helicopters circle and land as we arrive, and butterflies start swirling like rotor blades in my stomach. *Damn*, there's no toilets on a helicopter. What's a person with IBD supposed to do?

It's dark now, like, *really* dark. Do helicopter pilots have owl vision? I reassure myself that Tristan only hires the best in the business.

I'm not a nervous flyer per se, but that's on a commercial flight.

We walk across the helicopter parking lot and I try to calm myself down. I haven't been in a helicopter before.

"Hi, Elly," Charlie greets me with a big smile as Tristan and Danny head towards the reception. She looks like a female version of Tristan, which is a little freaky.

"Nice to meet you, Charlie," I say shyly. "I can't believe you guys agreed to come last minute. I wish I could show you around but I'm going to have to go over to my mum's and sort out a few things."

"Don't worry! We can entertain ourselves. I'm ashamed to say I've never been to Wales! Danny and I go to Scotland a lot." She leans in, excitedly. "And of course I wanted to meet *you*."

"Oh. So, you heard about me?"

"Only from Danny," she admits. "I haven't seen Tristan without Mum recently and he couldn't mention a girlfriend in front of Mum without being marched up the aisle." She glances over her shoulder to where Tristan and Danny are walking towards us. "He'll kill me for saying this but he seems quite taken with you from what Danny has told me. And Tristan has been in an unnaturally good mood these past few weeks. Do *not* tell him I said that."

"Bay four, ladies," Tristan calls out before I have time to bask in the news. We pick up our overnight bags and follow the guys.

"Will there be room for five of us?" I ask Charlie. Most of the helicopters seem to be four-seaters.

"No, just us four," she says. "Were you expecting someone else?"

"Uh, the pilot?"

Her eyes widen then she slaps a hand over her mouth. "Oh my God, he didn't tell you. Tristan's taking us. He's got his licence."

"What?" I squawk. "Are you taking the piss out of me?" No, he didn't bloody tell me that vital piece of information.

She shakes her head, laughing. "I wonder if this is all part of this plan to impress you. Although the two of them are so flippant about flying. Danny's got his licence for small aircraft. Tristan's training to get a small aircraft licence as well now."

Fuck.

The men stop outside the last helicopter in the bay.

"Tristan, you didn't tell me you were flying us." I swallow nervously.

His eyes crinkle in amusement. "I'm sorry, darling. I assumed you knew."

Bit of a leap there. "What do you need to do to get a helicopter licence?" I ask with a rigid smile.

"I thought you'd like to sit beside me." He opens the passenger door and returns me an easy grin. "Forty-five hours of flight training, including ten hours solo."

"Uh-huh." I wet my lips. He better have been top of the class. "How many solo hours have you done?"

"Ten hours and five minutes."

My lips thin into a painful line.

"He's messing with you." Danny chuckles. "You need to do over sixty hours to be able to fly at night."

"I'm not in the right frame of mind for wisecracks," I mutter as Tristan wraps his hands around my waist and lifts me up into the passenger seat.

The other three climb into their seats, clearly more relaxed than me, and the doors shut with an almighty bang. Danny even cracks open a beer.

"Would you like one, Elly?"

Hell, yeah. I take the beer gratefully. I could do with something stronger like a general anaesthesia but I'll settle.

He goes to pass a beer to Tristan and my mouth hangs open. "What? Seriously you can't—"

"I'm joking." Danny winks. "It's okay, Elly, you're in good hands."

"Don't tease her." Charlie scowls. "I was the same on my first trip with Danny." She pats my shoulder reassuringly.

Tristan leans over and tightens the seatbelt straps around me then buckles me in. "Have you been in a helicopter before?"

"No," I squeak.

"After this flight you'll never want to travel any other way," he says, fixing the headset on my ears. "You won't be able to hear me until I turn these on."

He fastens his seatbelt. I watch him flipping switches and other things with shiny lights in the cockpit. Holding my breath, I crush my knees into the window terrified I'll hit a gear stick or whatever the hell puts a helicopter into reverse.

The rotor blades start turning above us. I feel it in my stomach. It's so *loud.* We sound like we're going to explode. Tristan appears to be having a casual chat with someone through his headset but we don't move. The build-up is killing me. His Porsche does zero to ninety in nanoseconds and this thing will be on the ground all night trying to take off. There's no happy medium. Like sex with my ex, John.

Then finally, after what seems like decades, we lift off with a slight wobble and are airborne. The rotor blades are silenced as my noise-cancelling headset magically turns on.

Either that, or I'm dead and don't realise it.

I close my eyes and try to mentally push my

stomach back down my throat. It takes a good minute or two to overcome the unnerving feeling of weightlessness

"Open your eyes, sweetheart." The deep baritone feels like it's coming from the depths of my mind. A disembodied voice that can hear my thoughts.

I look over and he casts a smile in my direction.

"We are travelling at 1,000 feet above ground," his voice says in both my ears.

I let out the breath I was holding and take in the multicoloured London skyline with lights from the Shard and other monuments in the sky. It really is spectacular. I wish I had my camera with the good night vision with me.

"Enjoy the view, Elly." He sounds even deeper and sexier through the headset. I don't know if it's the adrenaline rush, or the fact my life is in his hands or the fact that he looks so damn sexy with his hand on that control but a sudden and severe bout of horniness hits. I must be ovulating.

"You know you sound like you're inside my head now." I let out a breath. "Can you hear all my dirty thoughts? You look so sexy flying this thing. Like a sexy Superman."

"We can all hear your dirty thoughts, Elly," Charlie's voice booms in my head.

I slap a hand to my mouth. Duh. "Sorry!" I say bashfully as Tristan flashes a smug grin at me.

We leave London behind, the sky grows darker and before I can finish my beer, Tristan informs us that we are landing in the designated heliport outside Cardiff. Maybe I could get used to this.

"We're taking this route because of air traffic control," Tristan explains.

I nod. Does he think I know if we are taking a wrong turn, for fuck's sake?

We land at a helipad ten miles from my village, which I never knew existed, because why would I?

I'm buzzing from the trip but also because I booked the cottage for the four of us to stay in. I couldn't believe it when I saw they had turned my favourite cottage into a holiday home.

I'll finally get to see what it looks like on the inside.

It's 10 p.m. before we arrive at the cottage. I message Mum to say I've arrived. The cottage is as picture perfect as I imagined with its exposed beams, big stone walls and cookstove in the middle of the living room. But I can't enjoy it until I sort out Mum's window and make sure she's okay. Maybe I'll even ask her to stay here. Then tomorrow, I'll think of a plan to appease Barry's brick-slinging son.

The four of us have chosen bedrooms as far away as possible from the other couple. After seeing pilot Tristan, my hormones are on overdrive. I'm eager for an early night.

"Let's go down to your mother's now." Tristan looks at me like he means business. "You won't be able to sleep otherwise."

"I can go myself," I protest.

He folds his arms across his chest. "In the dark?

Hell, no."

I guess I know who is boss this weekend.

We leave Charlie and Danny beside the fire and do the thirty-minute walk through the Welsh countryside to my village. It's dark and muddy and I'm relieved Tristan demanded he accompany me. I just wish it wasn't so dark so I could show Tristan the stunning Welsh landscape.

Mum flings her arms around my neck before I'm through the door.

"Mum," I say, hugging her as hard as I can, before turning her toward Tristan. "I got here as fast as I could."

"Miss Andric." Tristan takes her hand and brings it to his lips to *kiss* it. Lickarse.

"Oh, *hello*!" she swoons, her jaw hanging open slightly as she takes in Tristan's broad physique. He's wearing a blue woollen sweater that distractingly clings to his muscles and matches his eyes.

"This is Tristan, Mum," I say sheepishly.

Her eyes shine. She seems surprisingly relaxed for having a brick through her window. "What a pleasure! I hardly ever get to meet any of Elly's boyfriends."

Neither do I, Mum.

"The pleasure's all mine." He flashes her a signature Tristan Kane smile, and she giggles breathlessly. He's on his A game tonight. "I've heard so much about you."

Tristan is ushered into the 'good room' by Mum

who offers him tea, wine, whiskey, cakes and anything else she can find while I sort out a window fix. No wonder Tristan can't cook with so many women fussing over him.

He tries to arrange the window repair, but I insist. He also tries to pay but that was a firm no from me. I'm not a charity case.

Mum comes into the kitchen. "I'm glad you're happy, Elly. Tristan is so right for you. I always knew you would end up with a more mature man."

"I like him," I admit. "But it's early days so don't get too excited."

"He also thinks we look more like sisters," she says smugly.

My smile fades as I watch her breezily retrieve a pillbox from the cupboard. "Do you still need Valium, Mum? What did the doctor say?" I look at the half empty glass of wine pointedly. "You shouldn't be drinking wine with them."

She chews her lip. "Stop fussing! I just need a little pick-me-up after the Barry incident."

I frown. She's hiding something. She puts three of the pills in her mouth and swallows them with water.

"How many did the doctor say to take a day?"

She tsks. "I told you, stop fussing."

My eyes narrow. "Let me see them."

I put out my hand and she reluctantly hands over the pill bottle.

I study the bottle, confused. "It doesn't say how many to take." My eyes snap up to hers. "Where did you get these?"

She brushes off my question with a dismissive wave. "It's not like it's illegal," she says, sulking. "A friend of Collette's gave this batch to me. I'll pop into the doctors this week and get a new prescript—"

"You bought them from a random person?" *What the hell?* "You don't know what's in these, Mum! They're not necessarily safe. And Valium has to be prescribed by a doctor because it's so addictive."

I researched this as soon as I found out she was taking them. At least last time, the doctor had prescribed them. Now it seems she's self-medicating. "You need to stop taking these. Not unless you go back to the doctor, and he says you need them."

I put both hands on my hips in fight mode. She turns her back to me, pretending to need something from the fridge.

"Are you listening?" I ask crossly. "I'm not leaving these with you. What if something happens? I could never forgive myself."

With her back turned to me, her shoulders sag.

"Please stop taking these." My voice trembles. "If you need me to visit every weekend I will, whatever it takes, but you can't pick up drugs from random people. I'll be sick with worry."

My eyes tear up. "Mum!" I choke. "Look at me."

After a brief pause, she turns around, her lips pursed together. "Fine, sweetie. I'll go to the doc's and get a new prescription."

I nod and put the bottle in my pocket. "I'll take

these to the chemist and dispose of them properly."

I come back into the good room to find Tristan lying on the sofa with a glass of wine in his hand. His head dips back as his eyes close. Though he made helicopter flying look easy, he was concentrating on a million different lights and levers simultaneously, with the added pressure of playing God with our lives.

"Tristan," I say softly, thinking he is going to spill the wine.

Our eyes meet across the room and his face splits into the sexiest smile I've ever seen, as if I'm the best thing he's ever laid eyes on.

"I've sorted it," he says in a lazy tone. "Your mother gave me the number of the guy who threw the brick. He won't hassle her again."

"What?" I exclaim. "How?"

He gives a half shrug. "Easiest payout of my life. We have to go down to the local and pay his bar tab. Then he'll leave your mum alone."

I freeze in the middle of the room. "Seriously?"

When he smiles back, like it was no big deal, I burst into uncontrollable tears. I don't know whether they are happy or sad tears or maybe both. It's like a tap has been turned on. They run down my face so hard I can't see him, but I feel him scoop me up in his strong arms, burying my face in his chest. He doesn't ask why; he just holds me in his arms while my eyes soak his T-shirt.

And that's when I realise I'm hopelessly and utterly in love with Tristan Kane.

25

Tristan

"Are you watching me sleep, Miss Andric?" I fix her with a lazy squint and smile. She has an unruly mess of curls from sleep and my hands tangled in them last night, making her look dishevelled but stunning. Her breasts spill over my chest, intensifying the dull throb of my morning wood. Perfect. This is how I need to wake up every morning. I've been waking up to her most mornings since we returned from Wales a week ago.

She runs a finger down my chest to where the duvet has gathered around the V taper of my waist. "Guilty," she whispers. "Looking like an Adonis when you first wake up is not a small feat. Well done."

Bringing my mouth up to meet her sinfully beautiful one, I remember how amazing those swollen lips felt around me last night. I pull back, surprised. 'You've brushed your teeth?

She blushes. "I do it as soon as I wake up, then creep back into bed."

I chuckle as I study every line and feature of her face.

"What?" She smiles at me, confused.

"Nothing," I murmur. "It's just you take my breath away. Every morning, I wake up with you. I'm not sure I'll ever get used to this." My voice was hoarse with need and I wondered if I'd come on too strong. The last thing I wanted to do was scare her away.

It was true though. The mornings that I wake up with her are the mornings that my stomach isn't contorted with knots of stress.

Cheeks flushed, she stares at me, dazed, like my words come as a surprise. Can she not see how infatuated I am with her? "That's such a sweet thing to say."

I trail a palm down her jawline, her collarbone, her breasts and lower stomach, peeling the blankets off her as I do so. My fingers tease the delicate soft skin just above her clit.

She stares at me with those big blue eyes and pouty lips, mewling softly. Ready for me. Wanting me. Begging me.

Damn.

Her hips swivel, and she hoists a leg over mine, splaying herself open, on top of me. I tug aside the lace crotch of her panties and thrust two fingers inside her to find she's wet already. Probably because she's been rubbing against me all night, wearing nothing more than lacy underwear, getting us both worked up in our sleep.

Her lower stomach shudders in response as I

plunge my fingers in and out of her opening. Damn, she feels amazing. I watch her face contort and her breathing become jagged as she arches her back and really starts to ride my fingers, her muscles tightening around them. She whimpers as my thumb finds her clit and I rub it in small teasing circles. Hers is a beautiful face that I could spend hours watching.

My cock throbs with anticipation, waiting for its turn.

"Please," she moans. "*Please*, Tristan." A blush crawls up her neck, telling me she's close. I love it when she begs.

"Not yet, baby," I manage hoarsely. "I want to taste you." This morning I want to have her in the most intimate way a man can. I pull my fingers out of her wetness, and she groans.

She lets me pull her underwear down to her ankles. With small breathy pants, she wriggles out of them and pulls down the duvet so my cock springs free.

"You are so ready for me all the time, aren't you?" I murmur.

Taking her hips in my hands, I lift her up in the air so that she's straddling my waist. She squirms, attempting to level her entrance up with my cock but I lock her in a tight hold.

I smile wickedly. "You're going up, not down. I'm going to spread you wide on my face."

Her eyes pop wide. "I've never—" She stops when I push myself down and grab her legs so that she's straddling my chest.

"Higher," I say.

Elly tentatively inches forward so that her beautiful wet heat is directly above my face. With my hands around her thighs, I push her down on my face so that my tongue enters her.

From above, I hear her strangled cries as my tongue pushes in again and again.

"Oh my God!" She gasps, her hands shaking the bedpost.

My hands controlling the tempo, I grind her back and forward across my mouth, my tongue lashing against her clit each time. She squirms and writhes above me, letting out little grunts and moans that send me wild.

"Good girl," I grunt, thrusting my tongue relentlessly inside her like a man starving. Who needs morning coffee when I've got this to wake up to? "Relax, sweetheart. Let me give you what you want."

She's lost all the shyness that she had minutes ago and is now spreading her legs wider around me, squirming against my face. Her hips buck and jerk, telling me she's close.

I vaguely hear myself mumbling about how this is the best feeling in the world, how I've obsessed about her since I met her, how much I absolutely adore her and other truths I've never said out loud, my words spurred on by her pleasure.

I hear her loud cry as her thighs shudder and she comes hard against my tongue. Exhaling heavily,

Elly collapses on top of me, planting her entire body weight down on my face.

"Baby," I choke, struggling to breathe as she smothers me.

"Oops." She giggles, hoisting her hips up to release me.

Breathing deeply, I push her hips towards my aching cock. A gyrating Elly coming on my face has made me so wound up, I'm not patient enough to give her time to recover. I line my cock up against her drenched opening and slide it in. "Yes." I groan as her muscles clench my cock.

Her breasts bounce as she takes control of the tempo, rising up and down.

"That's it, baby," I say, my voice thick with lust as she drives my cock in and out of her in quick motions. I'm not going to last.

How can I when those big blue-green eyes stare down at me with undeniable adoration? All I can do is stare right back with the same intensity.

***

Pulling her into the shower, I take in every line, every curve of her body in the bright bathroom lights like I've just been given the gift of sight. She loves this shower. I don't blame her, I had a glimpse of the shower in her house, and she's better off washing with a bucket and hose. My shower, on the other hand, as she likes to tease me, is a *smart* shower. To her delight, I got Natalia to pick her up a robe, slippers and set of toiletries. Maybe it's my attempt to keep her here.

Under the water, she plays with the spray functions until she reaches the maximum pressure. "It's like a spa," she purrs as the soapy water forms waterfalls over her breasts. "You know I'm only using you for your bathroom."

"Fine. Whatever it takes."

"Can I stay in this shower forever?"

"Be my guest." I grin down at her, washing every inch of her body with meticulous detail.

"I can't." She groans, closing her eyes as the water runs down her face. "Daniel will be here in an hour. I'll get dressed and get out of your way."

"Stay, Elly." The words leap out of my mouth. Even as I say them, I'm conflicted.

Her eyes open and she rubs the water from her face. "What? Did Gemina cancel?"

"No, Daniel's still coming," I say slowly. "But I don't want you to go. It's fine, I'll introduce you as a friend. I'm allowed to have female friends."

I watch her reaction, surprised to find I'm nervous. She's twenty-five. She didn't sign up for this.

"Sure," she whispers, pressing her wet body against mine.

"Good," I reply, relief flooding me. In that moment, I realise just how much it means to me for her to stay.

"That still leaves us thirty minutes." I give her a

wolfish grin as my hands rove over her. "What can we do in that time?

***

"Relax." I slide my arm around her waist.

She chews on her lip. I've never seen her this nervous.

"It's fine," I repeat gently. "You're just one of Daddy's friends."

She raises a brow. "How many of Daddy's friends has he met?"

"Just platonic friends." I smirk. "None who sit on Daddy's face."

"Tristan!" she hisses, thumping my chest. "What if he doesn't like me? This is a big deal."

I kiss her forehead. "Why wouldn't he like you? If anything, I'll need to tell him to behave himself."

She chews on her nails, and I move her hand from her mouth. "Elly, we also have to consider informing HR soon."

"What?" she squawks, looking at me like I've just suggested we bathe in an acid bath. "Everyone will talk about me sleeping my way to the top. No, I can't handle that."

"It will be the minimum people required to know. I get that you want discretion, but we have to go public sometime."

"But what if it all ends?"

My face tightens. "And what if it doesn't end?"

She waves her hands at me. "Don't put both of

these things on me on the same day. I'm about to meet your son."

A car horn toots outside, and she jumps.

"We'll continue this later," I warn her and walk to the window. Daniel sees me from the car and gives me a lopsided grin. My throat constricts like it does every time I see him.

From the driver's seat, Gemina waves at me, and I give her a curt nod.

"I'll go outside and explain to him."

She nods, scuffing her toe into the ground. "I'll wait here. Send me a message if you need me to sneak out the back."

Sneak out the back door? I'm more worried about her running away of her own accord. I open the front door and walk towards the car with a big smile. Daniel takes out his fire engine-shaped backpack and skateboard from the seat.

I hunker down to be eye level with him as he runs into my arms. "Hey, buddy," I greet him as Gemina drives off. "I've got a friend visiting."

"Uncle Danny?" he asks excitedly.

"Not Uncle Danny. My friend, Elly." I take his hand and lead him into the house. "Are you okay with Elly spending the afternoon with us?"

He shrugs, not bothered.

Elly stands awkwardly beside the kitchen island as we enter.

"This is Elly, Daniel." I meet her eyes.

"Hi, Daniel." She gives him a formal smile like she's meeting a prince. "It's so lovely to meet you."

"Hello," he says politely. He turns to me. "She's a girl friend."

Elly's eyes widen in horror.

I study my son's reaction. So far, he doesn't seem upset. "Yes, Daniel," I confirm, something fluttering in my stomach. "She's a girl friend. *My* girlfriend."

He tilts his head to the side. "Like my girlfriend?"

I try to remember her name. "Talia?"

"No!" He scoffs. "Miss Hargrove. I told her yesterday."

Oh, Jesus, I'm going to get another angry phone call from the school.

He turns his attention to Elly. "Do you skateboard?"

"Love it," she responds without missing a beat. I arch a brow.

"Good." He approves. "I have my skateboard upstairs. Do you know any tricks?"

Her eyes widen at being caught by her lie.

"When were you last on a skateboard?" I ask casually.

"Quarter of a century ago, give or take," she mutters.

"Perhaps we'll eat before Elly shows you all her skateboarding tricks. Are you hungry, buddy? Elly is going to cook for us."

"Like Natalia? Are you here to help Daddy?" he asks uncertainly. His face scrunches up as if he's trying to remember something. "I know you. You were the lady on the boat."

Oh shit.

Her breath hitches sharply. "Uh . . ."

"That's right, Elly's a friend who likes boats too," I say smoothly. "Do you want to know what we're eating?"

Elly clears her throat. "A dish that I used to have a lot when I was a kid," she explains. She looks tense. "A traditional Croatian casserole."

"What that mean?" he shoots back.

"What does that mean," I correct him. "Do you know where Croatia is?"

His forehead furrows into a deep frown like I've asked him the cure for Aids. I reach for my phone. "Here, I'll show you."

"Yes!" He nods firmly. "Reema's from there. I went to her party."

I give him a blank look. I've met Reema's parents before and they are not Croatian. "Oh no," I say. "That's *Croydon*. Croatia is in South Central Europe." I show him on the map.

"Is that why you're so pretty?" he asks Elly, his expression serious. "Is everyone pretty in Croatia?" It sounds like my son has picked up a few tricks from me.

She laughs. "Thanks, Daniel. I'm half-Croatian but I'm Welsh, I was born in Wales. I'm not as pretty as your mum, though."

I clench my jaw. She has got to be joking.

He tilts his head, inspecting her. "You're prettier," he replies, matter-of-fact. The boy has got good taste, just like his father.

"Do you want to help cook, Daniel?" she asks. "We

can make a mess in your dad's kitchen."

I raise my eyebrows, and she smirks back.

"Okay," he agrees. "Should Daddy help as well?"

She looks between us. "Probably not. I'm not sure he knows how to operate half the devices in the kitchen. We'll give him some of the easier tasks."

I fire a napkin at her but take a seat at the breakfast bar. If she wants to go easy on me because I'm useless at cooking, that's fine with me. I'm not a man who's ashamed to admit his weaknesses.

She gets four saucepans and a frying pan on the go. "Damn," she mutters, then looks at me apologetically.

"I'm pretty sure he hears worse language in school," I say wryly. "In fact, he says worse things himself."

My phone buzzes. "I need to take this work call, Elly." I groan, rising from the stool.

She waves me away.

True to their word, my kitchen is a cooking tsunami when I come back. Daniel has food all down his top. "Daniel, go and get cleaned up. You're a mess."

He runs off to the bathroom. I grab Elly and pull her to me.

"Tristan," she hisses. "Your son is here! Don't touch me!"

I dip my head into her neck, my lips grazing her soft skin. I can't help myself. My hands creep down her backside when my phone buzzes again. I groan, my head still buried in her neck. "Sorry, sweetheart,

I'm going to have to get this again."

"It's fine," she murmurs, lacing her fingers with mine. "We have all the time in the world."

***

Forty minutes later, and my agitation is at a peak. The building surveyor drones on in great detail about the repairs to the restaurant as I barely listen. Asha's has received rave reviews, so Danny and I are opening a branch in Mayfair. I don't have the patience to do this right now, it's taking time away from Daniel.

A piercing scream makes my blood run cold. Elly. I drop the phone and sprint towards the kitchen, crashing into Elly running down the hallway.

"It's Daniel," she cries and my blood turns to ice. "Hurry, Tristan!"

"Where?" I bark back.

"Bathroom!"

I charge into the bathroom and see every parent's nightmare. My son sprawled across the floor; eyes closed. Is he breathing? Jesus, I can't tell.

I fall to my knees taking his head in my arms, stifling a cry. "Daniel!" I shake his head gently. "Wake up, baby!"

Elly bursts through the door, panting.

"Elly, the phone!"

"Here . . . oh, God, oh, oh, God."

I jab 999 with trembling hands.

"Emergency Services, which service do you

need?" the operator asks.

"Hi, I, uh, we n-need an a-ambulance," I stammer. "It's my son! He's unconscious!"

"What's your name, and where are you calling from?" they prompt. How can they sound so fucking calm? I half scream the details.

"Can you tell me what's happened, sir?"

"Christ, I don't know!" I bark. "Just send a fucking ambulance."

"Sir, I'll need you to calm down. Is your son breathing?"

"Um, yeah. Yes, but it's very weak!" I lean down to make sure that he is. His breath is barely there. "He's not responding to me."

"I've dispatched an ambulance to your address, sir," the operator explains with a continued calm. "Does your son have any underlying conditions, sir?"

"No, nothing." I close my eyes and summon a deep breath. "How long will it be?"

"Where are you, sir?"

"In the bathroom."

"Is there anything in the area that your son may have taken?"

"No, NO," I snap. "When will the ambulance be here?"

"It's two minutes away. Try to stay calm."

"Tristan," Elly whispers, grabbing my forearm with a shaking hand. I didn't even notice her standing over me. "Tristan" she repeats. "Oh my God," she sobs. "I th-think he got them from my bag.

I asked him to get my phone when we were cooking and he, he must . . ."

I snatch the empty pill bottle from her. "What?" I snarl. "What are these?"

"Valium." She gulps.

She recoils as I yell, "Valium! He's taken Valium."

"Can you determine how many he has taken?" the operator probes.

Fumbling, I check the bottle. "It says there were twenty pills in the bottle." I don't know, I can't think. Fear clenches my chest. "Please," I wail. "Please hurry."

"Ambulance is one minute away," she says in a soothing voice. "Are any of the pills on the floor?"

I scan the floor. "Um, some, four, maybe five."

There's a loud knocking on the front door. Elly runs out of the bathroom as I bundle Daniel in my arms and carry him to the hallway.

Three paramedics meet me with a stretcher. One of them feels his pulse while the other secures an oxygen mask around Daniel's neck.

"He'll be okay, won't he?" I ask in a strangled voice.

"We'll do our best, sir," says the one checking Daniel's pulse.

"Tristan, they're unprescribed," Elly whispers. "We can't be sure what's in them."

I stare at her as I take in her words. "You have to be joking."

"Where's the pill bottle, sir?" one of them asks as they carry him out in a stretcher. I hand it over.

"Who owns these pills?"

"They're my mother's," Elly sobs. "I brought them back from Wales. Tristan, I'm so sorry."

"Why would you do that, Elly?" I snap, nostrils flaring. "Why would you bring drugs into my house with my child here? Do you realise the damage you've done?"

She trembles. "We had a fight in Wales. I wanted to take them away from her, get rid of them . . . I wanted to—"

"Get out of my way, I don't have time for this." I push past her, grabbing my house keys. Daniel is all that matters right now.

Panic swells inside me as we climb into the ambulance. I grab his hand and pray.

26

Elly

There is nothing or no one more important to Tristan than his son. This isn't just a little lover's tiff like someone left the toilet seat up. The look on Tristan's face. It was like all his emotions for me had turned to anger in seconds.

The taxi jolts as the car in front fails to move with the green light. I fall forward in my seat.

The taxi driver flashes me a look of irritation. "Can you wear your seat belt, love?"

"Sorry," I say in a suffocated whisper, pulling the belt over me.

He watches me from his mirror, trying to figure out what's going on as I struggle to secure the belt with my shaking hands

It isn't just about whether Daniel will be okay. I'm ashamed to say my fears are about *me* as well. How will I live with the guilt? Tristan will never forgive me for this, I saw it in his face. I've crossed a line that I can't uncross. My recklessness put his son at risk. *His son.*

I've lost him.

Now, I fear *everything.* My one stupid careless mistake could mess up every aspect of my life. The taxi crawls along giving me the opportunity to spiral out of control. Can I lose my job over this? How can I continue to work at Madison anyway? Tristan won't allow it. Worse, is Tristan powerful enough to get me struck off, so I lose my right to practise as a lawyer? I've never seen this side of him, and I don't know what he's capable of.

What kid wants to swallow a bottle of Valium? Why the hell would you do that? I had them zipped in a side pocket, it's not like I added them to the meal. Part of me is angry at Daniel for what he did and I can *never* admit that to Tristan—if he ever speaks to me again that is. Some thoughts should stay private from the world.

My stomach contracts into a tight ball and I worry I'm going to throw up all over this taxicab as it starts and stops at lights and turns. I don't even know how I ended up in the taxi on the way to the hospital, almost as if I'm having an out-of-body experience.

This is all my fault.

Oh, what I would do to turn back time. All I had to do was drop the pills into the chemist. This morning, Tristan was telling me he wanted us to go public in our relationship, now I'm worried he's going to get me struck off the Roll of Solicitors

But Daniel was breathing. He'll be fine.

The alternative is unimaginable.

I didn't know how long I'd been gripping onto

the edge of the taxi, lost in my own world, until the driver's voice snapped me out of my daze. "You okay, love? The hospital is just over there."

I clear my throat to thank him. I fumble for my bank card to swipe the card machine. Usually, I curse at how much a taxi costs in central London, today I don't even notice the price.

As I pelt towards the hospital entrance, I check my phone for the millionth time. Nothing.

Inhaling that distinct hospital smell, I make my way to Emergency.

"Good afternoon," I say shrilly, twirling the loose strands of my hair nervously as the receptionist looks up from her computer. I'm breathing hard and I only ran a few metres.

She waits a moment before arching a brow for me to continue.

"Sorry, I'm here to see a young patient who's just come in with his father, Daniel Kane." My body spikes with adrenaline and the words come out in a rush.

"Yes, he came in fifteen minutes ago." She sounds bored as she turns back to her computer screen. "Only family members can see him right now. Are you family?"

"No."

"Take a seat for now and one of the family members should be out. We'll tell them you're waiting."

Oh *fuck.* I'm not sure I'm ready to see Tristan. I'm too scared. Surely one of the nurses can tell me how

Daniel is? "Can I just check how he is?"

"No, we don't disclose details of patients. Only the doctors or nurses can do that."

"Right," I mumble, nodding as there's nothing else I can do. "Thank you."

Finding a seat, I slump into it before checking my phone again. I turn it off and on, put it in aeroplane mode, and reset the Wi-Fi, all the things Megan tries when Damo ghosts her. I get it now, the agony of waiting for a text message.

No new messages.

In the waiting room, my doomsday brain decides it'll be the perfect time to think of every worst-case scenario. I'm a drug-pusher. What if Daniel doesn't make it through? Can I go down for manslaughter?

The internet claims most Valium overdoses only result in unconsciousness, and there have only been a handful of deaths. Please let the internet be right.

Except I can't even be sure what's in those pills.

Please let Daniel be okay—he has to be okay.

"Excuse me, my son, Daniel Kane?"

My head jerks upward at the sound of the soft panicked voice.

Shit. Tristan's ex-wife, Gemina. She looks pale and frantic and it's all my fault. She's prettier than I remember. Those cheekbones, no wonder she looked amazing in every photo I found online. *This* is what contouring is about. I bet she has a professional version of Megan working on her face every morning.

What will she say when she finds out it's my

fault? I hastily take a magazine and place it in front of my face. I don't know if she would recognise me, but I'm not taking any chances.

"I'll buzz you in now," I hear the receptionist say. "One of the nurses will greet you at the door."

Watching her stride in, I have no choice but to check my phone, again. I don't know how long I'm in this dazed state before a doctor walks out.

Quickly, I get on my feet. "Doctor, may I ask how Daniel Kane is doing?"

He takes a glance at me for a moment, giving his clipboard to the receptionist before turning to me. "Are you family?"

My face pales at his question. Classing myself as Tristan's girlfriend currently didn't count by any means. Am I still his girlfriend? Swallowing my nervousness, I stare up at him. "I'm the father's girlfriend."

"Unfortunately, I can't disclose the patient's status," he says apologetically. "I'll tell the father you're here."

Lowering my head, I return to my seat. Tristan already knows I'm here, he's read at least one of the messages.

I wait.

Visitors and hospital staff swing open the ward door each time, giving me false hope.

I wait some more.

And wait some more.

Finally, I see Tristan.

"Tristan!" I catapult towards him. "How's

Daniel?"

"He's in a stable condition," he mumbles, sounding utterly exhausted. "They pumped his stomach." Tristan's usual calm and collected demeanour has vanished, replaced by an almost robotic being. His hair is a mess, sticking up in all sorts of directions as he combs his fingers through it. "He'll be moved to a room for monitoring in a few hours before being released tomorrow."

"Oh, thank God," I say, finally feeling as if I can breathe again.

Daniel's going to be fine. Swallowing the large lump in my throat, I reach out for his hand only to have him take a step back. I feel it like a slap across the face. "Tristan, I'm so sorry, I—"

"I don't want to hear it right now," he grinds out coldly. "You should go." It's a demand not a suggestion.

"Please, Tristan," I protest, shaking my head. "I never meant for this to happen. They were tucked away in a side pocket. I'm so sorry that I didn't think when I asked him to—"

"It doesn't matter," he interjects, and I know it's taking everything in him to speak calmly in a public setting. "It doesn't matter anymore, Elly. Gemina is furious. My son overdosed in my care. On *unprescribed* drugs, Elly." He spits out the words.

"It'll b-be okay." I'm stuttering now, and people are staring. I have nothing sensible or logical to say. I don't know what Gemina will do so my reassurances are unfounded.

I trail off as he stares at me. I just want him to hold me, to tell me that it's all going to be fine but instead, his eyes are black. "I know that it was my fault for being careless, but . . . how . . . how could it not matter?"

"She's threatening to remove my visitation rights," he snarls, his voice ragged and hoarse. "Do you understand the severity of this? For me to lose access?"

Lips quivering, I try to talk. "I can explain to Gemina, I can fix—"

"You can't fix anything," he roars as he begins to lose control. "I'm going to potentially lose access to my son because you took drugs to my house."

"Tristan, please," I choke out, feeling tears streak my face. "If Daniel's safe it will be okay . . ."

He stares at me, his face paling.

"Taking Mum's pills was the dumbest idea I've ever had. I just wanted to get them out of the house. I was intending to dispose of them. I'm sorry, please, let's just—"

Our eyes lock, his filled with anger, mine soaked with tears.

"We can't see each other anymore."

"What?" I whisper.

His voice comes low and hard as a plethora of emotions flit across his face: fear, shock, confusion. But the one that cuts through me the most is his anger. "Neither of us had a prescription for those. My son overdosed on drugs that shouldn't have been in my possession. I'm a lawyer, Elly. I've enough experience of how these cases go," he says, his anger seeming to slowly disperse from his body. I would rather have him angry and berating me than dismissing me. "We're done. Go home."

"But—"

"I'll get you transitioned off the case if that's your concern," he continues, and it hurts even to think that right now, I even care about the job. It's the very last thing on my mind. "I said your career wouldn't be impacted by our relationship, and I'm a man of my word. Now go home."

"Please, Tristan." It's barely a whisper.

He shakes his head, saying two words so slowly that I know it's the nail on the coffin for us. "My. Son."

He doesn't wait to see if I leave. He turns and heads back into the ward, the door slamming shut.

I can't muster the strength to get back on the train yet. Finding a seat facing the wall, I let out large, unattractive grunts and sobs as I choke on my emotion. I'm ugly-crying so loudly the staff are either going to put me on a ventilator or kick me the hell out of the hospital.

A lady offers me a cup of tea. A nice cup of tea is the answer to every problem in Britain, isn't it? Slept with your boss? Nice cup of tea will sort that out. Accidently pushed drugs on your boyfriend's son? Add a biscuit or two with the tea. Dumped by the love of your life who happens to be your boss? Maybe brew a full pot.

"Yes, that would be lovely, thanks." I smile back at

the lady through wet tears, and she inhales sharply when she sees my face. I must look like *IT* the clown. I can tell by the waiting room folks that they think someone close to me has passed away. Nope, I've just been dumped.

"Elly," a female voice addresses me softly from behind. I turn to see Charlie, Tristan's sister.

"Charlie," I snivel and accept a tissue from her. "I didn't see you come in."

"He shouldn't have left you here crying." Her forehead creases into a deep frown. "This is so out of character for him. He's just really stressed about what might happen."

I blow my nose loudly. "I've never seen him this angry. At anyone, never mind me."

She sits down quickly beside me and wraps her arm around me. "Give him time. I've never seen him so unhinged. In fact, I don't think I've ever seen Tristan *cry.* He'll realise his anger is misplaced."

My jaw quivers. "It doesn't matter, though. He'll never forgive me if Gemina refuses visitation rights."

I can tell by her face she's worried about that too.

"How can she though?" I stare at her through tears. "Surely he has some rights? He brought up Daniel and his name is on the birth certificate, right?"

She frowns and doesn't speak for a long moment.

"It sounds like he hasn't told you the whole story yet. Elly, I can't . . ."

"It's fine," I sniffle. "I don't want you to feel

uncomfortable. Have you seen Daniel?"

"Yes." She nods. "I was just in. He's fine."

I blow my nose hard into the tissue and feel marginally better. "Thanks for checking on me. Why is it you always see me in compromising situations? Getting kicked out of hotel linen closets, and if I keep making a ruckus the way I am, I'm gonna get kicked out of this hospital too."

She chuckles and pulls me in for a hug. "I need to go in here, Elly. My mum's on the way, and on the warpath, so maybe you better hide. It'll all work out." She looks at me hopefully. "The main thing is that Daniel is safe. Tristan will calm down and think rationally again."

I force a smile. I'm not sure either of us believe that.

Just as Charlie is about to say goodbye, the door to the ward opens and Gemina strides out. I watch her approach a man in his fifties that has come into the hospital. I keep watching as they have a strained exchange of words.

"Who is that?" I ask Charlie.

Charlie grimaces.

"That's Daniel's birth father."

27

Tristan

I march through the restaurant ignoring the come-fuck-me looks I'm getting from the women to my right. Months ago, I would have flashed them my signature smile. The stunning redhead in the corner would have grabbed my attention and eventually made her way into my bed. Today, I have zero interest in seducing strangers.

I smile briefly at the hostess as she takes my coat. That's all I can manage these days.

Jack and Danny are already seated at the table, laughing at some private joke. They stop laughing abruptly when they see me, and their expressions become serious.

"Don't stop on my account," I mutter dryly, taking the third seat. "Just because my life is all shades of shit right now doesn't mean you two have to be miserable bastards as well."

"You look rough, mate," Danny says cautiously. "You need to look after yourself."

"Thanks." I slump into my seat. "I haven't slept in

five days."

Jack pushes a Scotch my way. "We thought you would need it."

"You thought right." I bring the glass to my lips and sink most of it in a few gulps. The burning sensation on my throat gives me mild relief.

They exchange looks.

"Don't fucking start," I growl at them, running my hand through my hair.

Jack puts his hands up in defence.

"Any news?" Danny asks tentatively. "Have you seen Daniel?"

"I've only seen him once," I say, doing my best to manage my tone. "Gemina's holding off access." I knock back the final dregs of my Scotch and nod to the bartender for the same again. "He's fine though," I say softly. "He's enjoying being the centre of attention and having time off school." I shake my head, letting out a bitter laugh. "I'm going to murder him when he's old enough to understand the drama he's caused. I thought I raised him to be smarter than that."

Danny laughs dryly. "Like you, he refuses to eat bread after its sell-by date. Yet he is curious enough to overdose on pills he found in a bag."

Jack smirks. "I'd rather take pills than eat some of the wacky canapés Tristan offers at parties." He cocks a brow. "Too early to joke?"

"Too early," I warn them. The bartender barely sets down my fresh Scotch and I lift it. "Gemina wants to see me this evening. A proposition, apparently."

"Do you have any idea what?" Jack asks.

I blow air into my cheeks. "Who the fuck knows, I'm sure nothing good for me."

We fall into silence as they exchange glances between them.

"Just ask," I snap.

"Have you spoken to Elly?" Jack asks.

"No." I scowl. "I haven't spoken to her in five days, not since the hospital."

"It was an accident," Danny says carefully. "You can't blame Elly. She didn't mean for this to happen."

I run both hands through my hair. "I'm furious with her," I snap. "It's my own damn fault for going out with a twenty-five-year-old. No sense of responsibility. Bringing unprescribed pills into my house with my son there."

Danny leans in. "You'll get through this but don't throw away something amazing. You haven't liked a woman like this in ten years. Not since . . ."

"Not since Gemina? Really? You're going there?" I glare at him and down the last of my Scotch. He'll understand when he has children what it's like to have a child in danger. The dull chest pain that has been plaguing me all week returns. My doctor tells me I'm stressed.

"I gotta go. I have to fix this. Whatever the hell Gemina wants from me, it's a yes."

***

Half an hour later, George pulls up outside Gemina's mansion. I'm used to collecting Daniel here. Often he runs straight out as soon as I pull up, and I don't have to get out of the car.

Not today, though. Today I would have to get out and grovel, kiss her feet, give her a blank chequebook or whatever the hell she wants me to do. Both of them. So if I have to play their game, that's what I'll do. The alternative is losing Daniel, and that simply isn't an option.

Taking a deep breath, I finally get out of the car and walk up the path to the house.

Gemina opens the door. She's wearing dark blue jeans with knee-high heeled boots, along with a loose, red wool sweater. Her long blond hair falls in waves over her shoulders. She looks like she's ready to go out, but then she always looks like that.

"Gemina."

"Tristan. I'm glad you came." She smiles but her eyes look red as if she's been crying.

"Is he here?" I ask curtly.

She shakes her head.

"Dad!"

I manage to crouch just in time as my son bursts through from the kitchen, a huge grin splitting his face. He throws himself into my arms. Once again, I feel the familiar jolt of pain at how much Daniel looks like his mother and nothing like me. Not that it alters how much I love him. Not in the slightest. "Daniel, Mummy needs you to go upstairs and play while she and Daddy talk."

"Only if I'm allowed a coffee." He pouts. "Mummy said I can't have coffee."

I look at him bewildered. "Why do you want coffee? You can have one tea on a special occasion. You know this." And if he thinks he's consuming anything without my consent for the next ten years, he's got another thing coming.

"I'm not a baby," he growls. "Can't you come up to my room and play for a while?"

"Not right now, buddy," I reluctantly tell him. I put my hands on my son's shoulders to look him in the face. "Mummy and I need to have a boring grown-up talk. I promise I'll be up to play as soon as we're done, okay? Then we both can have some frothy milk instead of coffee."

"You promise?"

"You bet. Why don't you go up and pick out what you want to play?"

"Okay!" Mollified, Daniel turns and runs up the stairs. I watch my son—and he is still my son, whatever any DNA test said—only turning back to my ex-wife once Daniel is out of sight.

"Can I get you a drink? Tea? Coffee? Scotch?"

"I'm fine."

"Come on." She leads me into the kitchen. "You drove all the way here. I have your favourite Scotch ready."

"George drove all the way here. Fine. Scotch then. With—"

"Two ice cubes." She smiles sadly. "You think I

don't remember?" Her hand brushes across the top of mine as I take a seat beside the kitchen island.

"What's the proposal, Gemina?" My nerves are shot.

Her back is turned to me. She says nothing for a moment as she pours. Slow deliberate movements. Finally, she turns to look directly at me, her eyes filled with tears.

"Hey," I say, closing the distance between us and taking her shoulders gently. "Daniel's fine, Gemina."

She lets out a loud sob and clutches my bicep. "Tristan. I've really fucked up. I've ruined everything. I'm so unhappy. Matias . . . I'm sorry, h-he's the biggest mistake of my life."

I flinch.

Matias.

The man I introduced her to. The man I invited into my home to help her career.

The man she had an affair with for four years. *Four years.*

He mentored my wife and fathered my child.

He stole my fucking life.

Her features contort with pain. "These past few weeks, I've realised . . ."

I stiffen. "What?"

"I want *you,* Tristan. I want *you.*"

I stare at her, speechless.

"I mean it." She clutches my forearm. "I love you. I realise I did some stupid things, and that I hurt you, but I want to try again. I miss you. I want us to be a real family again. You, me and Daniel."

"A family?"

"Yes. A family. A real one this time. I didn't realise before how much I took it all for granted. I was stupid. Daniel needs you, his real father. And I need you too."

I say nothing. Get back together with Gemina? Pretend the last two years never happened? I let out a bitter laugh. "I fell for that once before and look where it got me."

"I know, and I'm sorry . . ."

"Being a happy family didn't mean anything to you before."

"Yes, it did," she insists, "but you were always preoccupied with the firm. You worked late every night. I never got to see you. You stopped going to see my shows. I thought you fell out of love with me."

"I didn't." I swallow, slumping on the bar stool. "Not then."

I stare at her, bewildered. Sitting on the bar stool I'm eye level with her. More than anything, I want to laugh in her face. The idea of taking her back is ludicrous.

But to be a family again? To have Daniel back in my life full-time?

"Daniel and I can move back into the townhouse where we belong." She's going in for the kill now. "You designed that place for us. For us to be a family there."

The thought of waking up to Daniel every day is priceless. Even if he is a little bastard in the mornings.

“Matias wants your name removed from the birth certificate.”

I freeze. Is she blackmailing me?

"We could do it. I love you, Tristan. I may not have shown it well enough, but I see now how much I miss you." Her lips curl into that beautiful smile I had always found irresistible.

As her eyes lock on mine, she pulls her sweater over her head. Underneath, she’s wearing nothing but a deep-red bra. I can see right through to her nipples. *Damn.* The colour suits her pale skin perfectly, and it lifts her full breasts in just the right way. I recognise it. I remember buying it for her and fucking her repeatedly the first night she wore that lingerie set. She had to remember it was my favourite. Was she wearing the rest of it beneath those jeans?

I feel my body responding without my permission. We both know she’d once been able to bewitch me without even trying. And it’s not like she wasn’t still just as attractive as ever. It had always been part of her allure. Part of what made her the perfect wife. I'd revelled in being able to parade her on my arm. I would show her off at company gatherings and parties. Then later, when we were alone, we would discuss the way other women had glared at her, and other men had stared at her. It had turned us both on, knowing how much other people wanted her.

I was a fool.

I know exactly what she's doing. Perhaps she does want to reconcile, but I know now when she's manipulating me. She wants to make me unable to see past the promise of what would happen if I gave her what she wanted.

She steps forward. "I need you, Tristan," she whispers, reaching up to slide a hand around the back of my neck and pull my face to hers.

Maybe it's the alcohol but I feel my hands sliding around her waist without realising I had put them there. She grips my hair, and I don't stop her when she steps between my legs to press her body up to mine. My hands slide up her body, feeling the firm, soft skin. The feel of her, the smell of her, brings memories flooding back. Holidays spent never leaving the hotel suite. Times she had visited me working late in the office to slip under my desk to distract me. Getting home from the office to find her in a new lingerie set, begging for me to take her. How good she had made me feel over and over again.

She looks at me innocent and sweet, like she has the power to wipe out history. "We can be together," she whispers, grinding herself against me. "You can have me whenever and wherever you want."

I stare down at the woman I loved for over a decade, my brain misfiring.

I want her to make everything right again.

28

Elly

Heartbreak is not good for someone with bowel disease. You know that cliché of the gnawing feeling in your guts? Well, it applies literally to me. Even though I've no appetite, I'm sprinting to the bathroom every thirty minutes, you know, just in case. I can't figure out if the dull unease in my stomach is inflammation or just layers of unsettling emotion. It means that the toilet roll stash in my bedroom is diminishing faster than a supermarket in a pandemic. That's what getting dumped does to an IBD sufferer.

Apparently, the writer of *Alien* had Crohn's disease and based his infamous scene of the alien bursting out of his stomach on how he felt during a flare-up. I don't know if that's true but I couldn't have described it better myself.

All week, Sophie and Amy have been asking me if I'm okay. I don't know what I am. I'm just going through the motions of my job like a tinman. I've been walking around the office robotic, pale-faced, zombie-like. Doing everything with detached numbness. Hiding at my desk until it's time to leave for fear I'll bump into Tristan, although I never do because he would need to go out of his way to make that happen in an office this big. Mild polite conversation, barely passing as banter, is all I can manage. Even going to the canteen is soul-destroying because every damn menu option reminds me of him and his particular tastes.

Is this what grief feels like? I've never had someone close to me die before. The sorrow in my heart keeps me from sleeping, eating, talking, laughing—anything, really. It's just a constant wave of sadness washing over me, and I'm scared it will never cease.

What can I tell Sophie and Amy? I can't tell them the truth. *"Yes, I'm fine, I was sleeping with the CEO, but then I drugged his kid, so he dumped me and now I'm suffocating with sorrow and think I have broken-heart syndrome as well as irritable bowel disease."*

It's times like this when IBD comes in handy. You mention you feel poorly because of an irritable bowel, and it will kill *all* conversations. I had to tell them I had a bad cold as well to explain the sniffling symptoms. My eyes are constantly misting over, and my voice sounds tired and hoarse because I'm crying so much at night.

Only Megan knows the truth.

Right now, I feel like I won't recover, which I know is ridiculous because couples break up all the time, many after decades together. Tristan and I had just started out as a couple. But regardless, it's hit me hard. And it's only been seven days.

True to his word he's taken me off the Garcia case. At least he had the kindness to do it in a subtle way that didn't scream of 'you screwed the boss!' The story is that I'm needed in my current assignments. We're requiring less direct meetings with Maria these days so I knew my involvement would be petering off. I have one last meeting early next week and only Adi is attending so Tristan and I won't cross paths.

With me coming off the case, the only contact I've had with Tristan is a few short detached but polite messages to tell me that Daniel has recovered and is doing well. I've re-read the messages hundreds of times, trying to decipher his emotions from them. I even got Megan to dissect them. Does he miss me? Does he care for me at all? It's hard to tell from *'Daniel is recovering well, thank you.'* Every single one I follow up with "I'm sorry."

Nothing comes back.

I'm also dying to know, what did he do with the painting? Did he throw it out?

So here I am, outside his townhouse, fear and nerves swirling in my fragile gut. I have to talk to him face-to-face. I'll walk away with either closure or a second chance with him. Either of those options would be better than this horrible limbo.

I take a deep breath and rap on the knocker. I'm not sure if I'm hoping it's Natalia or Tristan.

My blood runs cold when I see who answers the

door.

Not Tristan. Not Natalia.

Gemina.

At first, she doesn't recognise me, then her eyes narrow in disgust. "You."

"I, uh," I stammer, completely taken aback. I had a speech prepared for Tristan, not Gemina.

"I don't recall arranging cleaning services," she says, eying me coolly. "And if I did, I wouldn't request you."

I'd be furious if I wasn't so devastated.

"Is Tristan here?" I ask, my voice trembling. Why did I think coming here was a good idea?

Her eyes narrow. "No, he isn't here, not that it's any of your business." Her eyes narrow. "You shouldn't be here."

"Have you moved in?" I choke out. I want to run away, but I need to know the whole truth.

She stares at me with a reserved intensity. "Yes. Daniel and I both live here, where we belong. Listen, I'm sorry that you got caught up in this but you need to stay away." The knife twists deeper with each word. "Stay away from me, stay away from my son and stay away from Tristan."

I get it, Gemina, you won. You were right, I was just a fling.

I turn on my heel and run down the driveway.

***

Two weeks ago, I would have been ecstatic to attend

the Madison Legal annual staff party. There has been a buzz around the office since I started. Even on my first day, people said "Oh, you started just weeks before the annual party, lucky you!"

Of course, the Madison Legal bash would be lavish and extravagant; Tristan Kane is notorious for his high standards of anything he puts his name on. Madison had rented out the Billingsgate Gold venue in East London and filled it with champagne, caviar and the same fire dancers from Venus Envy.

Now Friday night has arrived, and I'm forced to put on my big girl's smile, a party dress, a second attempt of contouring by Megan, and brave a night of Tristan Kane in the same room but so unreachable.

It's a great networking event, Sophie told us. A chance to rub shoulders with management and get noticed. Little did she know how many body parts of 'management' I had already rubbed.

If I didn't attend, then Sophie would know something was really wrong. Besides, I need to get back to normalcy sometime, right? It's been exactly two weeks since the incident with Daniel. I had to call in sick to work the next day after seeing Gemina at Tristan's townhouse. I said I wouldn't let this thing with Tristan affect my career. That's not me. Yet I called in sick to work because of a fling that went wrong with the boss. Talk about self-sabotaging my career before it's even started.

So here I am, braving it at the all-staff party, trying to claw back any dignity I have left. Sophie,

Amy, and I went for a quick drink in a bar next door; even Sophie said she gets nervous at these events and needs the courage.

We follow the crowds into the glamorous venue. This is no tired hotel conference centre with a sandwich buffet. Billingsgate Gold's triple-height ceilings make it uber decadent, but there are still enough discrete corners to understand why there's so much gossip about Madison Legal office romances. I gaze around the venue, taking in as much detail as quickly as I can. I won't rest until I know where he is so I can avoid him. I can hide amongst the throngs of people, just like in the office Tristan would have to go out of his way to find me.

"Are you alright?" Sophie peers at me. "Is it still you-know-what?" She makes eyes at my butt.

"Just cramps," I lie pathetically, taking the champagne she offers me.

I follow Sophie and Amy around for the next hour, my mind hollow as we mingle with other lawyers. I go through the motions of a typical office partygoer. I make tepid small talk with people I don't know, I dance a little to appease Sophie and Amy, and I avoid Juan, who is treating the event as a singles party.

I'm starting to think he hasn't turned up, until Sophie nudges me and I turn around to feel the heavy stare of Tristan. He is standing centre of attention, in a scrum of about ten lawyers. His jaw clenches as his gaze drops down to my dress. I'm wearing the blue flowing dress that Tristan bought as a surprise for me to wear tonight. I thought it would be a waste of a good dress if I didn't.

His eyes blaze. I recognise that expression. My skin prickles with a familiar awareness; a few weeks ago, I would have been excited by him watching me. It's irrelevant now.

"Soph," I say, breaking contact with Tristan. "I'm not feeling well. I'm going to head home."

She frowns, concern etched on her face as I struggle to keep the tears from falling. "Are you sure it's nothing more?"

Tristan is still staring at me.

I nod. "I'll be fine. I just need to go home." I give them both a hug good night and hurry to the cloakroom, then teeter down the stairs as fast as I can in heels. I just need to escape.

Pathetic. This is what pining over a man has turned me into. I thought I was stronger than that.

I'm a few steps away from the exit when I hear the low gravelly voice of my dreams and nightmares. "Elly."

Slowly I turn to face him. We stare at each other in silence for a few seconds. If I open my mouth, I might burst into tears.

Up close, he looks tired. "We need to talk." He runs a hand over his jaw. "Not here tonight. There's too many people. I have to go to the airport directly from here to fly to Hong Kong. I'm back in two days. I'll set something up for as soon as I'm back."

I look away, finding a sudden interest in the chandeliers. What does it matter?

"I'm not good with apologies," he says softly.

"It's fine, I get it," I say, my voice jerky. "He's your son. He takes priority."

"I was angry but I shouldn't have reacted the way I did. I thought I lost . . . everything," he says in a strained voice. "I'm sorry."

His chest rises and falls as he waits for me to respond.

"Mr. Kane!" a voice booms from the top of the stairs, and we look up to see some senior lawyers bolting down the stairs, ready to ambush the CEO.

I take my opportunity to escape. Exhaling sharply, I push the door open into the cool London night.

I should never have given him a second chance after Greece. The second time cut much deeper. But the second time will be the last time.

29

Elly

Now I understand what it means to be sick from stress. I've lost nearly two kilos in one week because I'm not eating. My IBD has flared up so severely that no matter how bland the food I eat, I'm still doubled up with stomach contractions. Eating is not worth the effort.

In general, I can deal with flare-ups, it's just part of life. You put your big girl pants on— literally —and make careful lifestyle decisions. But this is the motherfucker of all flare-ups, dictating all my decisions this week.

Which is why I'm standing on a packed bus that stops at every bloody red light and pedestrian crossing and hasn't advanced past walking speed.

I've never wanted a soak so much in my life. What I wouldn't do for that Tristan's smart bathroom with a million different spray settings. The water wouldn't relieve the cramps or pain but if I made it hot enough it would distract me for a while.

He messaged today while boarding a flight for

home. Apparently, we need to clear the air.
Could he be feeling guilty? The asshole's probably worried I'll have a hissy fit in the office.

I didn't respond. Fuck you, Tristan.

I know I was irresponsible. But at least it was a mistake. What he did to me was intentional, even if he didn't mean to hurt me. I was a rebound. *Everything* between us, every word, every look, every kiss, flushed away. It all meant nothing.

Today was my last meeting on the Garcia case. After travelling across London to the prison, I now have to do the same to get home.

I brace myself as the bus lurches forward again. I can't reach any of the bars. There must be a limit to the number of people on a bus but more and more people jam in until we are packed together tighter than two coats of paint.

The stomach contractions make me want to bend over but I'm trying my best to avoid spooning the woman in front of me. Unfortunately for me, the guy behind me doesn't appear to be burdened by such concerns. As he got in behind me, he pressed himself right up against me, smothering me in the stale smell of cigarettes. I take deep breaths and try to calm myself.

A violent wave of nausea rips through me. I don't know why I bothered leaving the house today. In fact, I don't know why I bothered leaving the bathroom.

Oh dear. This is not good.

Three more stops. I can make it.

I have three more stops.

No. I'm not going to make it. I have to get off this bus. *Now.*

"Excuse me, sorry, sorry, sorry." I push past disgruntled passengers. "Need to get off!" *Get out of my fucking way, I'm dying.*

After the longest minute of my life, the bus doors open and I limp out onto the street, doubled over.

I close my eyes and lean against the bus stop. The pain has never been this intense before. I'm scared now, really scared. What's happening?

Every organ seems to be malfunctioning. I'm nauseous, dizzy and sweating all at once.

My insides feel like they are exploding.

My heart is beating so fast my whole body is shaking.

I want to call Megan but I'm in too much pain to reach for my phone.

I hobble over to the door of the closest restaurant. It's an Indian restaurant, maybe. I'm too dizzy to read the writing above the door.

"Hi," I whimper to the guy staring at me with wide eyes. "Can I use your bathroom?"

The whole restaurant goes quiet.

I grab my stomach as another wave of excruciating cramps erupts, this one stronger than the last.

Megan, I need you. I fumble with the lock on my phone.

"What's wrong with her?" I hear a faint voice. I can't see the guy anymore, I'm doubled over.

"Is she overdosing?"

"Ambulance." I have just enough time to register the word. Then everything goes black.

30

Tristan

I arrive in Heathrow four hours later than expected, so it's 5 a.m. Hong Kong time and I haven't slept. Even flying first-class, the time zone difference messes me up for a few days.

When I turn on my phone, a strange number appears. I only answer anonymous numbers in case it's an emergency related to Daniel. I only give out my personal number to friends, family and school emergency contacts. My company phone is vetted by Ed, who filters out the unwanted calls, which is the majority of them.

So, when I see a strange number calling me, I answer it. "Hello?"

"Tristan?" a high-pitched Welsh lilt shrills. "It's Megan."

I instantly freeze. "What is it?" I ask sharply.

Heavy breaths are heard through the phone. "Elly's in hospital!" The rest is just a muffled noise with one word I can make out. Attack.

My heart stops. "What? Who attacked her?"

"Her IBD attacked her." Megan says breathlessly. "Frank and I are on our way to the hospital now."

"Megan, I don't understand. What?"

"She passed out," she stammers. I can hear traffic in the background. "It's bad, Tristan. This has never happened before. They took her away in an ambulance. A random restaurant called me from her phone."

"Is she awake?" I wrench my bag from the overhead locker with such force that nearby passengers give me filthy looks. I don't give a fuck. How bad is this? Can you die from Crohn's?

"I don't know." Her voice spikes upwards as she struggles to talk and walk. "I'm nearly there."

"What hospital?" I yell.

"St. George's, Tooting. Just round the corner from our house."

"See you there."

"Tristan?" she starts before I hang up. "I don't know if she would want me contacting you . . . it's just we don't know many people in London. I'm really scared."

"It's fine, Megan," I say in a softer tone. "You did the right thing. I'll be with you in about forty minutes. As quick as I can."

They haven't opened the plane doors yet and I'm starting to act like a caged rat. They need to hurry the fuck up.

I hang up and call George on speed-dial. "George, be ready at Arrivals. We need to go ASAP to Tooting hospital."

***

Elly

"Elly, I can't find a good vein on this arm. Let me try your hand." The nurse tilts my hand, running her fingers over the veins. She has tried so many, I look like a drug addict. Because I'm so dehydrated, the veins are impossible to stick a needle into. "Yeah, I'll give this one a shot."

"In the hand?" Megan whimpers from the side of the bed. "Oh Lord, I can't watch."

"You're not helping, Megan." I tilt my head away from the nurse and towards Megan. I can't watch either. The idea of a cannular in my hand makes me shiver, like someone scraping their nails across a blackboard.

The nurse lifts my hand because I don't have the strength to do it myself. The salt drip is working but not fast enough. I barely feel alive.

Everywhere I look there are cannulas hanging off me. They've inserted one to rehydrate me, another to take regular blood samples, and now they are sticking a third in me to administer a steroid drip. The steroid drip is to get my IBD flare-up under control.

The curtain rustles, and the doctor who spoke to me when I first came in pops his head around it. He's young and attractive but I can't look him in the eye.

Not since he performed an anal examination with his finger whilst making small talk. Not another finger-in-the-butt test, *please*. Neither my ass nor my ego can handle any more.

"How are you feeling, Elly?"

I shift in bed. "Bit better," I lie.

"I have your blood work back." He studies the chart in his hand then smiles sympathetically. "It's no wonder you are in so much pain. You have a severely inflamed colon. We'll get this under control but expect to be in here for at least four days. You need to receive steroid infusions until your blood work shows the inflammation is gone."

Four days? I need to finish the contract reviews Sophie has given me in three.

"I'll be back later to discuss more with you. Just rest up."

"Thanks, doctor," Megan purrs loudly as he closes the curtain.

I would roll my eyes if it didn't hurt. My head feels like I've been stuck in a desert for forty nights with no water.

"Elly, Tristan just messaged me back." Her eyes widen. "He's on his way. I'm sorry."

My chest tightens painfully.

No. He can't see me like this.

I contemplate making a run for it. Maybe Megan and Frank could wheel my bed into a different ward. Or the morgue.

I can't believe Megan called him. The last thing I need is for Tristan to check on me out of some misplaced guilt or obligation. Maybe he feels as if he has a duty of care as a boss or an ex-boyfriend. Or maybe he thinks I have no one else to turn to like some needy pathetic ex-girlfriend. It's humiliating.

I have tubes coming out of both my arms and my nose. My hair is greasy, my eyes are puffy, and I'm sweating from lying in this bed. I look hideous.

An inflamed colon isn't exactly a turn on, is it? If anything, it'll confirm to him that he made the right choice.

"It's okay," I whisper to Megan because it's not her fault. I don't blame her for panicking.

His visit is just another item to add to the anxiety list. My list is growing.

My Crohn's is officially out of control.

I'm as bloated as a Potbellied pig.

I'm stuffed full of steroids meaning by this time tomorrow I'll have a face the size and shape of a full moon.

It also means I'm stuck in hospital for four days and will miss my work deadlines.

My mum is taking unprescribed drugs that could be horse tranquilisers for all we know.

I accidently drugged my boyfriend's son.

Causing me to have no boyfriend.

There's a charge of ten pounds a day to watch TV from my hospital bed.

And last but not least, the massive gaping hole Tristan left in my heart after deciding I wasn't a good option after all.

I'm not sure what the priority order is.

I cry as I begin to lose control. Silent tears as I don't have the energy to blubber. I can't help this pity party.

I'm scared. I'm really fucking scared.

And stressed.

The nurse says don't stress; it will make my flare-up worse. Does she know how stressful it is trying not to stress?

Megan squeezes my hand.

I glance over to find her watching me worried. Frank is watching the football on the TV wasting my money.

"Elly," the nurse says gently as she peeps around the curtain. "You have another visitor."

My heart hammers in my chest. I'm not prepared for this. Not now, in hospital, when I'm at my lowest.

Tristan steps inside the curtain before I can protest.

Every part of me tenses.

"Elly." He stares at me, horrified. Like the devil has just materialised in front of him. I've never felt more unattractive in my entire life. He's in jeans and the T-shirt I first saw him in, in Mykonos, making my heart break a little bit more.

The stalled air I'd been holding expels from my lungs in a gargle.

I stare back, ashamed and broken hearted.

I *never* wanted him to see me like this. My red wine loose lips meant he knew about my IBD from the beginning, but I skirted over it and joked about it. I knew he didn't understand how bad it could get.

Not really. Most people don't. One guy I dated said it was too much information when I told him. When I had a flare-up, John simply ignored it. I stayed away and he let me.

Now Tristan can see it at its worst.

"You don't need to be here," I say, mortified. "I'm sorry Megan called. She just panicked. Its fine, you can leave now."

His jaw tenses as he scans my body taking in the various tubes and needles. "I do need to be here. I need to make sure you're okay, Elly."

I stare into his beautiful heartbreaking face. I hate how he has become the puppet master of my emotions.

Megan clears her throat as her and Frank exchange looks. "Do you want us to—"

"No," I cut in sharply. "Sorry about the inconvenience, Tristan, there was no need for you to come."

I focus on my cannula pretending to fix it. I can't meet his gaze, not when I know my eyes are so puffy I look like I've had a severe allergic reaction.

"Megan, Frank, can you give us some privacy please?" he asks.

"No need, stay," I say, begging Megan with my eyes.

Megan rises from her chair, tugging at Frank's arm. *Traitors.* "We'll be right outside." They close the curtain behind them, trapping me in the blue curtained stall with Tristan.

He takes a seat in the plastic chair that is way too

small for his frame. For a moment he just stares at me.

"Are you in pain?"

I stiffen. I don't need his pity. "I'm fine. I'm not your concern anymore."

"Right now, you are my only concern."

I stare back at him, angry and hurt. He has no right to say that to me. He made me trust him. He broke down my barriers when I wanted to keep them up. He told me I meant more. He let me fall in love with him. Then he went back to his real life. *Rich man's midlife crisis*, the movie.

His frown deepens. "What happened?"

"I passed out because I was so dehydrated and low in iron." I try to keep my voice steady. "Just a flare-up."

"A flare-up that landed you in the hospital," he murmurs. "We can get you private treatment. Madison healthcare will cover it. We'll sort this. Whatever it takes."

He reaches for my hand, but I snap it away.

I smile sadly at his ignorant optimism. "Money can't solve every problem, Tristan."

"Believe me I know that, Elly." He grips the steel railing of the bed tightly, making it shake. "When you get out, you'll come and live with me where I can look after you."

What?

My eyes snap up to his. "Is this a sick joke? You want me to stay with you and your ex-wife? Is this to do with some ridiculous guilt you have?"

He pulls back from me. “What?”

“I know you moved Gemina into the townhouse.”

“Did you call at my house?”

I stare at the TV, still showing the football, so he can’t see the fresh tears forming.

“Elly, Gemina and I are *not* back together.”

I let out an unattractive snort. “Bullshit. This whole time you string me along, telling me half the story. What was I? Rebound or a way to make her jealous?” My voice finally breaks.

“Neither,” he says forcefully. “You couldn’t be further from the truth. Look at me.” His hand takes mine and this time he doesn’t let me snap it away. “She wanted the house, and I gave it to her. I moved out and Daniel and Gemina moved in.”

I force my gaze back to his, blinking. “Gemina said . . .” What *did* Gemina say when I visited? I was too distraught to listen.

“It doesn’t matter what Gemina said. I’m telling you the truth. I’ll tell you the full story. Anything you want to know.”

“You’re not back with her?” My voice is so quiet I’m not sure I’ve asked the question out loud.

“No.”

“You’re single?”

“No.” He frowns. “I’m not single. I’m with you.” He takes a deep breath and scrubs his forehead with his hand. “But she did come on to me and I . . . nearly let it happen. My emotions were all over the place.”

I squeeze my eyes shut. I’m not sure why his words hurt so much since I already thought they were together, but having him say it out loud makes it ten times worse.

"I'm sorry," he says hoarsely. "It was a moment of poor judgement. Let me make it right."

"I knew getting involved with you would hurt me too much," I whimper.

"It doesn't have to."

"Did you sleep with her?"

"No," he says firmly. "Absolutely not. I came close to kissing her but stopped it. That's all. Let me wipe the slate clean. Even touching Gemina was a fuck-up. Blaming you for what happened with Daniel was a massive fuck-up. I couldn't see the wood from the trees. The fear of losing Daniel made me irrational. I'm sorry." Guilt flits across his face. "What happened with Daniel wasn't your fault, it was mine. I should have been watching my own son. I was hurt and lashed out at you. Forgive me, Elly. I don't handle stress related to my son well."

"I don't understand. I thought Daniel's real dad was a one-night stand." He stiffens when I say *real*. "But I saw him at the hospital."

His head drops, shoulders sagging. "I found out something a few weeks before you started at Madison. A couple years ago, I found out Daniel wasn't my son. I had come to terms with that—it didn't change anything. As long as Daniel's paternal dad was faceless, I could deal with it. I forgave her and for over a year I tried to save my marriage." He swallows hard. "But it wasn't just a one-night stand. Gemina lied. She had been having an affair on and off for four years with her mentor. The man I had introduced her to, to get her career moving. He's the birth father."

I stare at him for a long beat. No wonder he is so troubled about his son. "But now . . . she wants you back?"

"Apparently, yes. She doesn't know what she wants. That's Gemina. She said she's made a mistake. She wants us to be a family again. It's irrelevant. I love you."

My lips tremble hearing the words for the first time. These are the words I've longed to hear but . . . "Gemina will always have a hold over you. You won't choose me over Daniel and I don't expect you too."

"I'll figure it out. I can't be with Gemina just to see my son. Just like we will figure out how to handle your IBD. Together."

I bite by lip hard to stop my face from screwing up with tears.

A bell rings at reception meaning we have ten minutes left of visiting time.

"It's probably best that you . . ." I start.

He nods. "Can I visit you tomorrow?"

"No," I say in a hard whisper. "You don't get to waltz in and out of my life whenever you choose. I need time."

Looking flustered, Tristan rubs the back of his neck. As if for once he has no idea how to handle a situation. Even when Daniel overdosed, he panicked but remained in control. "I'll give you all the time in the world."

Silence fills the space.

"Where are you living?" I ask.

His lips twitch. "In one of Jack's smart apartments. Just until I buy somewhere else."

"How's that?"

"Things keep beeping in the kitchen. They're doing my head in. Less for Natalia to clean though so she's happy." He nods to my tray of compartmentalised dinner scraps. "How's the food?"

I let out a weak snort. "They ran out of horse tartare so I ended up going for the beef hotpot."

When he leans over to kiss my forehead I stiffen but don't pull away.

He leans so close to my ear, for a moment I think he's going to kiss it. "I love you, Elly. I fall a little more in love with you every day. Don't give up on us."

Rustling on the other side of the curtain snaps me out of my daze.

"I think they are wrapping up," I hear Megan whisper on the other side of the curtain.

Good," Frank mutters. "Because it's nearly into penalties."

31

Tristan

Elly was released from hospital this afternoon. Now she has the rest of the week off on sick leave. She's still requesting I give her space. I should be handed a medal for my restraint in not pounding down her door. It's killing me not being able to see her.

Instead, I spend my free time researching ways to control IBD. The responses range from prescribed drugs to healers, fortune tellers, and magic potions. She was right, there is no magic cure, no quick fix. This will take time. But it's time I'm willing to invest. Especially since this is all my fault.

At least she let me move her into one of Jack's apartments. It's near the hospital in Waterloo where she has been referred to as an outpatient. I know she must be bad if she's so fearful of being on public transport she swallowed her pride and let me relocate her. I fibbed and said Madison healthcare would cover it.

Megan needed no convincing to move into the penthouse apartment and I think Elly didn't have the strength to fight her.

Considering my thoughts are preoccupied with Elly, I'm mildly regretting agreeing to take Mum out for dinner this evening but it's already too late. George has picked her up from St. Albans and he's on his way to my apartment.

"Daniel," I call down the hallway. "Are you ready for dinner with Granny?"

"Almost," he shouts back from his bedroom. I walk down the hall and knock once on the door then push it open. He's naked except for a Superman cape around his shoulders. Bloody hell.

"That's not what I would call almost." I shake my head, stifling a laugh. I would let him get away with blue murder right now so long as I can see him. I had to beg Gemina. "Can you get dressed please into something sensible? She'll be here any minute now."

He pulls the cape off with a flourish and sets it over a pile of something colourful on the ground.

I frown, bending down to find a bag of sweets under it.

"Where did you get those?" I ask sharply. That's way too much sugar for him.

"I got them at the supermarket," he says in a small voice.

"I didn't buy them for you," I say, assessing the volume. He's allowed one maximum on a treat day. Gemina wouldn't buy him this much either. "Where did you get them?"

He bites his lip nervously and drops his head.

"Daniel," I say calmly. "Did you take these without asking me?"

He shrugs. "Got them in the supermarket."

I take a deep breath. "Did you walk out without paying for these?"

He looks back at me sullenly.

"Bloody hell," I mutter under my breath. I'm raising a criminal. This is how it all starts. One minute he's stealing sugary snacks, the next thing he's leading military coups. What am I doing wrong here? Is this normal for a seven-year-old?

"Didn't I teach you not to steal?" I run my hand over the back of my neck. "Do we need to have some more conversations about right and wrong? Tomorrow we're going to the supermarket, and you will explain what you've done. Then you'll pay this back from your pocket money. Granny will not be pleased."

His eyes widen. "Don't tell Granny Kane!" he cries, thrashing his arms about. I knew that would do the trick. Granny Kane is as scary as Mrs. Maguire.

"This is the second time you've stolen something." I come down to his level. Maybe we need to change counsellors. "You stole the pills from Elly's bag. I'm very disappointed in you."

"No, I didn't!" He stamps his foot in a ridiculous show of defence.

"And now you lie to me?" Now I'm really disappointed. "That's it, you're not going to Matt's birthday party on Saturday. You leave me with no choice if you can't tell the truth."

"That's not fair!" he wails, his face going red. His tiny hands ball into fists. "I didn't steal Elly's pills!

They were at Mum's house, so it wasn't stealing."

I stare at him, confused. "What do you mean you found them at Mum's house? They came from Elly's bag."

"No, they didn't." His bottom lip quivers at the injustice of being questioned over his actions. If I don't handle this carefully this will be a full-blown tantrum. "Mum said you would be upset if you knew and told me to say yes when anyone asked me if I got them from Elly's bag. I wanted to see why Mum liked them. Am I in trouble?"

The blood drains from my face.

"For stealing, yes," I say in a measured voice, putting my arm around his shoulders. "We shouldn't keep secrets from each other, do you understand? I'll explain that to your mother."

His lip stills and he nods.

"Now go put some clothes on. Granny is looking forward to seeing you."

I walk downstairs so Daniel can't see how angry I am as I process what he's said. So many thoughts race through my head. What the fuck? The pills were *Gemina's*? Is everyone on these bloody pills except for me? Is Gemina taking these pills while looking after our son? Sure, she's looked dazed and scatty recently, but she always looks like that.

The hairs on my neck rise. *She made my son lie to me.*

She's gone too far this time. The woman is going to ruin me.

There's a noise coming from the kitchen, an

incessant low beeping that I can't locate. For a second I wonder if it's my heart about to give in. The noise seems to be coming from between the fridge and the microwave. I open the fridge, the microwave, the cooker, fiddle with the smart water purifier, check the sensor trash can and turn off the coffee machine.

Nothing. What's the source? What's this thing that is intended to torture me?

"Jack!" I bellow to the roof even though he can't hear me.

Between my deceiving ex-wife, my criminal son, my girlfriend that never wants to see me again and this apartment with its smart gadgets talking to me, I've had better weeks.

Elly

I gaze out the window of the riverside apartment from my comfy armchair. We are in Waterloo, in the heart of central London, with a birds-eye view of the London Eye, Big Ben and the Houses of Parliament.

I feel as if I am living in a hotel.

There is a gym, swimming pool, sauna, steam room, spa and a communal roof terrace. If you asked me one year ago where I thought I would be living in London, I would have never imagined this place.

Megan hung one of her paintings in the hallway to see if anyone noticed. She hopes Jack Knight walks in, sees the painting, and decides he needs them all throughout the world. I can't fault her ambition.

It's a dream, but it's tainted.

We can't stay long-term, no matter how much Megan begs. The steroids are working and my inflammation is reducing so there is no reason for us not to move back into our house.

I'm making use of Madison's free counselling service. Since the flare-up I've been so anxious. Anxious for what could have happened and what could happen in the future. I had my first counselling session yesterday. I was so nervous I actually prepared answers to the questions I thought she would ask.

The speech went out the window with the first question. I can't even remember what it was. Her way of phrasing innocent questions seemed to pull the strongest of emotions from me. She had me crying within minutes. She didn't focus solely on my IBD either, she strayed into more dangerous territory like my relationship with my mum and what happened with Tristan.

But I came out feeling a little lighter and more optimistic and I'm trying to apply some of the techniques she has taught me for dealing with stressful situations.

I'm not good company anyway right now. Ironically besides the lack of housemates, I'm still not sleeping well. As I lie in bed, unwelcome visions of Gemina and Tristan flood my head. If I take him back, what happens the next time she threatens to take Daniel away? Will he sleep with her? She will always have a hold over him.

"There's another delivery," Megan calls as she comes through the front door. Poor Megan's mothering me like Florence Nightingale.

As I turn, I see an enormous bouquet of dark violet flowers.

She sniffs them. "They smell nice. What are they? Doesn't Tristan know that roses are sexy? These look like something I would put on my granny's grave."

I laugh. "They're the bearded iris, the national flower of Croatia."

Her mouth forms an O shape. "Sweet. There's a card. Here." She passes over the white envelope.

I tear it open, my heart in my mouth. It's in Croatian. It's pretty badly written with amusing typos but I get the gist.

Elly, it's taking all my willpower not to come across London and beg your forgiveness. It goes against my character to not go after what I care about most. But I want to give you the space that you need. I'm here, waiting, when you are ready. Tristan x

Something else is in the envelope. I stare down confused at the decorative wooden spoon then smile when I realise what it is. It's an old Welsh tradition to give your loved one a love-spoon as a token of your affection.

"He's really trying." Megan looks at me, hopeful. "He's hitting all the nationalities there. I mean it's soppy, but God loves a trier."

"He is that." I nod sadly. I'm just not sure he can give me what I need.

My phone vibrates loudly on the countertop. I look at the number lighting up the screen. "It's him."

"Stop!" Megan hisses. "Does he know we're talking about him? He just happens to call when I deliver the flowers to you? Is he *watching* us?" She flaps her arms in a panic. "These smart apartments are just a way to monitor us, like *Big Brother*!"

I roll my eyes. "Calm down, Megan. No one is watching us. And if they were, they'd soon get bored of watching us watching telly."

"Although if Jack Knight wants to watch me, I'm down with that." She lifts her top up flashing her breasts. "Hi, Jack! If you want a closer look, feel free to come over."

I roll my eyes. "I think everyone on the London Eye saw that."

We both stare down at the phone while it continues buzzing.

Her eyes go wide. "He's persistent."

Before I can stop her, she answers. "Tristan. Hi, she's here." She puts the phone on speaker and hands it over.

I narrow my eyes mouthing "What the hell" at her.

"Check your bag, Elly," Tristan's gravelly voice demands over the phone.

"What?"

"Check your bag," he repeats. "The side pocket where you stashed your mum's pills. Check it now."

I scan the living room for the bag, spotting it under a heap of Megan's bras on the sofa. In silence I fumble with the zipper and push my hand into the side pocket.

"Did you find it?" he demands.

I stare down at the full bottle of pills in my hand, confused. "But—"

"It wasn't your fault. I'm so sorry, Elly," he says gruffly. "Daniel admitted he took them from Gemina. He'd seen his mother taking them all the time and wanted to try them.

I fall back onto the sofa as Megan gasps beside me. It wasn't my fault. I didn't cause Daniel's overdose. Guilt lifts from my shoulders like a heavy weight.

"I love you, Elly."

My face screws up in tears as I hang up.

Megan watches me, wide-eyed. "What are you going to do?"

I look out at the iconic London skyline and know what I need. "I'm going home."

32

Elly

Almost a week passes, and it is the longest I've spent at home with Mum since before I started university. We needed this time together. She was distraught when she found out I was in hospital. When she visited, I realised how much I needed her and remembered the times when I was younger that she would look after me when I was in a flare-up.

It became evident to me that she cared about my life, she just didn't ask me questions because she didn't know what to ask. My visits became fleeting and I always had one eye on the clock checking the train. If I'm honest, I treated going home like a chore. So, the visits grew shorter and the conversations more superficial until the bond between us was so strained we simply didn't know each other as people anymore.

Today, we spent the afternoon at a spa setting up an online profile for her on a serious dating website and trawling through suitable candidates for dates.

I told her all about my job and life in London,

of the perils of living in a house-share and how expensive London is for a new grad. To my surprise, she thought my London life was high-flying and glam with parties every night.

We reviewed her Valium tapering-off schedule from the doctor and have planned something fun every two weeks as a milestone. We've arranged for her to visit me in London (God knows where I'll find a space for her to sleep) and we've booked flights to Croatia.

I spoke to Tristan on the phone once. He wanted to give me an update on the case. Turns out I was right that there was something off with Maria. She *did* know the girls that were trafficked. In fact she was an instrumental part of the operation and even took a cut of the profits. If there's one person you shouldn't withhold information from, it's your lawyer. And your anaesthesiologist. No good can come from either. Madison Legal withdrew from the case and Maria was sent on a flight back to Colombia where she stands trial for murder and now numerous counts of sex-trafficking. Some part of me takes satisfaction that I detected the anomalies in her statements.

Mum suggests walking the long way home from the bus stop. All afternoon, we meandered from hot room to cold room, steam room, ice room, mood shower, plunge pool . . . until we looked like two prunes. I had been steamed, rubbed and wrapped more times than a turkey getting prepped for dinner.

For the first time since the mother of all flare-ups, I feel ready to enter the real world again. Madison Legal insisted I take all the leave I need but I want to get back to normality. Besides, Megan complained that the apartment was smarter than her, and still thinks Jack Knight is spying on her.

I've had two more counselling sessions and it's slowly helping. I've slept better this week in Wales.

I'm surprised Mum suggested walking the long way home since it involves climbing up a savage hill.

"It's got a great view." She gasps for air as we ascend. "I needed some fresh air today."

I look at her dubiously. Usually I have to drag her up a hill kicking and screaming. Today she seems intent on going this way even if it gives her a collapsed lung.

The cottage comes into view, *my* cottage as I like to call it even though I've no claim on it. Now everything about it reminds me of the happy memories of that weekend with Tristan.

Which makes me sad.

I miss him. I miss everything about him. Old impulses die hard. Every night I still think about him before I go to sleep. Every day he sends me little messages in Greek, Croatian, Welsh, Gaelic, most of the time slightly wrong. Superficial messages asking me how my day was or if the weather's nice in Wales. Nothing further.

At least I no longer feel guilty about drugging his son.

We stop at the top of the hill just outside the

cottage so Mum can catch her breath. I lie down in the grass and close my eyes. I sleep so well in Wales. Gone are the London sirens, drunkards returning home, early bin men, constant traffic, shagging foxes and coughing, sneezing, grunting, snoring humans. I call it 'the sounds of London' CD. I could dose off.

"Elly."

I think I'm imagining it at first. Sometimes I hear his voice in my head.

But then a shadow looms over me and I smell that familiar scent that makes my heart hammer in my chest.

"Tristan?" I snap open my eyes in shock and headbutt him.

"Fuck," he hisses.

I'm too surprised to apologise. "What are you doing here?"

Mum has crept over to the cottage garden and is pretending to be fascinated by the daffodils.

He holds out a hand and I take it, stunned, as he lifts me to my feet.

He stares down at me with that deep blue gaze that has haunted my dreams every night since I met him. "I can't stay away any longer, Elly. It's killing me."

We stand frozen, staring at each other. My heart is in my throat. Only once have I seen him look this serious, and that was when Daniel overdosed.

"Just hear me out," he demands. "I know I have baggage. I work too many hours. I have a love life that is splattered all over the internet. I have a beautiful son who needs most of my time and an ex-wife who has my neck in a noose. You'll always worry that your career is tarnished with gossip. You could go out with that Chris bloke that works for Danny and not have all this shit. I get it."

"Who's Chris?" Mum chimes in.

I glare at her.

"But I promise no one will work harder to make you happy and love you more than me," he continues, his eyes fixed on mine. "Just give me another chance."

I swallow the hard lump on my throat. "When the incident with Daniel happened you just dropped me. You cut me out for days. I'm not sure I can handle the heartbreak again."

His face falls. "I made a mistake, Elly. Holding it against me forever doesn't help either of us."

"What do you want from me, Tristan?"

He takes both my hands in his and pulls me against his chest. "I want everything from you. And I want to give you everything if you'll have me."

"Why?" I ask sadly. "I see the women that throw themselves at you. The ones in the pictures. Most of them are a cross between Mother Teresa, a Victoria's Secret model and Einstein. Models. Fashion designers. Women at the top of their game." *And I bet none of them fall asleep on a loo some nights.*

He sighs heavily and squeezes my hands. "None of them are you. Think about our future, not my past."

"I'm a trainee who lives in a house-share who doesn't have her shit together. And gets randomly sick every now and then. How do I know you won't get sick of me?"

"Are you kidding?" His voice rumbles deep in his throat. "I didn't stand a chance from the moment you stepped in front of me in that godawful bar in Mykonos. I love everything about you. Your sense of adventure. How determined, intelligent and ambitious you are, your resilience. How you always find the best in situations. I love how you protect Megan and your mum and everyone else around you. I love your relentless wisecracks that take the piss out of me, worse than Jack even. I want to build a life with you if you'll let me. I want to be your guy when you need to get to Wales in under an hour. Or when you need to call in the heavies to get rid of brick-throwers."

He smiles, leaning closer. "And you talk dirty to me in multiple languages. Is that enough?"

I swallow hard. That's a good starter.

"Hold on a minute." I turn to Mum who is pretending not to hang on to every word. "You knew he was coming here, didn't you? It's the only reason you went up the hill."

"Guilty." She smiles. "And that's the last time I'm climbing that hill, so I expect you to take him back."

"So?" Tristan asks impatiently. "Do I need to get on my knees in the grass? Or shall I take you inside our new holiday home?"

I frown, confused. "What?"

He tilts his head in the direction of the cottage. "I bought it. I wanted this to be somewhere we could enjoy together."

My brain misfires. "You bought . . . the cottage?"

"Yes," he says simply. "I know how much you loved it."

I blink, speechless.

"You know I don't do things by half, Elly." He cups my face with his hands. "I've committed to having a holiday home near your mother. That has to count for something."

I'm gobsmacked. "How did you get the sale so quickly through the conveyancing?"

He chuckles. "*That's* what you are interested in? Typical lawyer, needing to know all the facts. If you must know, I had to expedite it through a lot of effort. Well? Will you give me another chance?"

My eyes mist over. "Yes, Tristan," I whisper as he pulls me flush to his body. Our tongues meet, and it's desperate and feverish and tender all at the same time.

Not because of the cottage. It's just bricks and mortar. I stare at the guy who sends me articles every day about suggestions on how to manage IBD.

A soft smile spreads across his face as he pulls back to meet my eyes. Then he pauses as if getting ready to speak. He's nervous. "Elly, I'd like to ask you . . ."

My eyes widen. *Oh fuck.* He's going to propose. I'm not ready for this. I love him but it's too soon.

". . . if I can cook you dinner?"

My eyes shoot to my hairline. "*You* are *cooking*?"

He smirks playfully. "Thought I'd try a stuffed leg of Welsh lamb."

Oh shit, I'm going to have to check the local takeaways, he'll never nail this.

I take his hand as he leads me down the lane to the cottage.

It seems I got tired of resisting Mr. Kane.

One week later

Tristan

For the first time in over a decade I work from home for an entire week, in Wales. I suspect my management team thinks I'm having some sort of breakdown since this is my first board meeting over the phone.

But nothing could tear me away from Elly right now. She had four counselling sessions but she's still fragile. I pinch the bridge of my nose as I try to focus on the board agenda but all I can see is a topless Elly floating in the jacuzzi. Her head is tilted back, her eyes are closed, and her arms are spread wide so that those beautiful breasts can be seen bobbing up and down. I have ten minutes before the meeting finishes and I can sink into the water and sink into her. My cock grows hard in anticipation.

"What's left on the agenda?" I ask impatiently. As

if Elly senses me watching her, her eyes flicker open and she gives me a shy sexy smile. My teeth latch on to my bottom lip in frustration.

"So we have the global all-staff conference in two months. We need to think about keynote speakers." Rebecca is talking way too slowly. "Tristan, do you have anyone in mind?"

Elly emerges from the jacuzzi dripping water all over the deck, showing off her shaven pink flesh. She looks so beautiful.

Mine.

Willing my dick to settle down, I answer Rebecca's question. "Happy for the events team to own sourcing candidates. I'll review the final set." My words catch in my throat. It's a shit response. No direction whatsoever.

Elly opens the patio door and walks purposefully towards me, leaving behind wet footprints.

I swallow hard as she comes right into my space and presses her wet chest against mine, smiling innocently up at me.

"Anything else?" I snap into my mic.

"So for the event we'll do breakout sessions . . ." one of my senior partners drones on about the all-staff event. I stare at Elly. What the hell is she playing at? Now? When I'm in the board meeting?

With one smooth pull, she removes my tracksuit bottoms and boxers. My jaw tightens. Good thing it's not a video call.

My cock juts out, oblivious to the work discussion I'm having with fifteen of my employees. Fuck, this woman will be the death of me. Here's hoping I don't have to make any decisions on this call.

Taking my hand, she slides two of my fingers deep into her. *Damn*, that feels good. So wet. So ready.

Although I'm trying to follow what the team is saying, my brain is losing the battle with my dick.

With her other hand she pushes me down so that I'm leaning against the table, grips my cock tightly and begins to stroke me. Long hard furious strokes like she is in a rush.

I let out a strangled growl.

"Tristan? Rebecca asks. "Did you say something?"

"Just something stuck in my throat."

Elly stifles a snigger and I give her a severe look. She continues to stroke my cock as if this were the most natural thing in the world to do to me right in the middle of a board meeting.

She releases my fingers from inside her. That's it, game over. She doesn't have the nerve to go further. Not my sensible Elly.

But she was luring me into a false sense of security.

She wraps one of her legs around my hip, and before I can react, she spreads herself open with her hands, lowering herself onto my throbbing cock.

A hiss escapes through my gritted teeth.

"Final agenda item," Simon, Head of Recruitment, says, oblivious to the fact I've got my cock buried deep in Elly. "The open managing partner position we need to fill ASAP to cover

Oceania. Tristan, we have candidates lined up ready for interview."

"Good," I grunt, as Elly rides my cock, controlling the tempo with her hips. I can't stop this even if I wanted to.

"Are you going to fly out to Sydney for the final interviews or do you want to do them remotely?" Simon asks.

"Yes," I groan in response, unable to complete a coherent sentence whilst Elly is riding me like a crazed cowgirl.

"Um, I'm not clear on which option, sir. Do you mean you are coming to Sydney?"

Elly clenches hard around me. I'm so close. I can't stop.

I close my eyes and grip the edge of the table with both hands like my life depends on it.

Fuck me.

"Yes. I'm . . . coming," I call out in a strangled voice as my whole body tenses and I explode hard inside of her in a final jerk.

I let out a ragged breath. "Are we done?" I bark.

"No further items for today," Rebecca says tentatively.

I hang up without saying goodbye. I'll have to apologise later and say I'm having a bad day.

"Elly." I stare at her, trying to steady my breathing. "Never mind *your* job, if I didn't own the company, you might get me fired."

She winks. "Just showing you who's boss."

EPILOGUE

One year later

Tristan

"Are you okay, Tristan? Your forehead seems sweaty."

No, I am not fucking okay. I'm far from okay. My nerves are shot to pieces and my heartbeat feels like it's in my head. I'm surprised Elly can't hear it through the headset. I won't tell that to Elly, no one wants to hear that their pilot is fraught with nerves. A Scotch would be good right about now but that's not the best solution operating a helicopter over central London.

Funny enough, I wasn't nervous the first time round doing this, which speaks volumes.

I take a deep breath and try to get a grip. I must breathe loudly into the mic because she looks over at me again, this time more warily.

Now, I'm making her nervous.

I have thirty minutes left on the route approved by air traffic control clearance. If Jack, Danny and Charlie aren't ready, I'll blow a fuse.

"I think we'll pass the golf course," she says innocently. "Danny and Jack might see us!"

I know we will and yes, they will.

We soar 800 metres over the city taking in the capital's iconic landmarks. The Shard. The Gherkin. The Walkie Talkie. They're just bricks and glass today, I can't focus on them.

I glance over at Elly who is scanning the scenery, oblivious to what's going on in my head.

She's perfect.

My heart tugs like it does every time I look at her. It's only been months, not years, but when you know, you know.

A few months back, we moved in together into a quaint little mews house in Notting Hill. Turns out I don't need a four-storey townhouse with a cinema room and two bars when I have my Elly with me every night. Megan's paintings hang in the hallway and are the first thing you see when you enter the house. It was a sweetener for taking her flatmate away from her. She only overcharged me three times the going rate this time, so I got off lightly. Jack let her keep the painting in the lobby of his Waterloo apartment block and he only had to pay double. I think she's got a bit of a crush.

Daniel stays with us three days a week now. We eventually reached a fragile peace treaty with Gemina a few months back and it was Elly I have to thank for that. She went for the strategy of killing her with kindness. Whilst they will never be best buddies, Elly's consistent checking in on her and inviting her to occasional lunches wore her down. In fact, for the first time in years I invited Gemina over for lunch at mine and all cutlery remained unbroken.

Daniel now has two dads and I've nearly come to terms with that. What matters most is his happiness, not mine, Gemina's or Matias's.

"We're coming up to the golf course now," I say with a lump in my throat. I fumble with the side compartment to find the box. This is it.

"Are they having some type of event at the clubhouse?" She squints down. "I can't see, I need my glasses."

For fuck's sake. I can't fly any lower.

"Oh!" she cries. "There's a massive sign on the ground! Like the banners you see flying behind planes."

Yes, except we are doing it the other way round.

"What does it say?" I ask, using one hand on the controls to hover above the golf course and the other balancing the black box on my thigh.

"Uh . . ." Her nose wrinkles as she tries to make it out. "Someone is proposing . . . it says, *Will you marry—*" She stops short. "Elly," she whispers into her headset. "Will you marry me, *Elly*."

That's my cue.

"Elly, this is my way of sweeping you off your feet." I try not to stutter my way through the words. "I love you. More than anyone I've ever loved before. I want to start a family with you." I pause and lift the ring box in my sweaty hand, snapping it open. "Elly

Andric, will you marry me?"

Her hands fly to her mouth then she lets out a loud screech that assaults my ears through the headset.

That's it, that's all she offers.

Is she going to answer the goddamn question?

Her mouth seems frozen in shock. *Shit*, is she going to say no?

I might crash the helicopter if she does, I don't think my poor heart can take it. Perhaps I didn't think this romantic proposal through.

"Elly?" I hold out the ring, waiting.

It's nowhere as ostentatious as the one I bought for Gemina. Elly and I don't need to speak in money to each other. With Elly's mother from Pašman, the island known as the green gem of Croatia, and my parents from the Emerald Isle, it felt right to get a green gemstone.

I need both hands to start turning soon so she needs to make up her mind. "Are you gonna just keep me hanging?"

Her eyes lock on mine as she chokes back tears. "Yes."

A single word has never sounded so good.

"Yes, I will marry you. Oh, come on, how can I say no to the irresistible Tristan Kane?"

Roughly one year later

Elly

"Elly, are you alright?" Megan asks, concerned.

I feel Mum's touch on my arm. "Relax, darling. Deep breaths. You'll get through this."

You would think they were coaching me to go into labour or surgery. Actually this is one of the happiest days of my life, I've been told. Or it will be in hindsight. Right now, I feel faint.

We are standing on the steps of St. Dominic's Church, a beautiful Gothic-style church in Dubrovnik, Croatia.

I take a few deep breaths. When I'm this nervous it could go one way or the other. An uncontrollable fit of giggles sometimes occurs. I can't walk down the aisle giggling. Tristan's mother would never forgive me. The alternative would be a joint wedding and funeral if I don't stop the heart palpitations.

"I'm fine," I say to myself more than the bridal party. Megan and my friend Sarah from school are my bridesmaids. Mum is giving me away. All of them look amazing—classy but understated, just how I wanted it. Megan and Sarah are in sleek royal blue dresses to their knees.

I'm wearing a simple flowing wedding dress. No outrageous gown, no bling, no rhinestones, no massive tent or the opposite—no tight dress that I can't move freely in. It's enough for me to walk these thirty-two steps to the top of the aisle without worrying about getting stuck in the aisle.

"You look so beautiful," Megan gushes and for a second I think she might cry. It might be the Buck's fizz we had for breakfast to calm the nerves.

I do look beautiful. From my head to my toes, my entire body has been professionally designed. The ostrich has been transformed into a Victoria Secret's model.

"Head up, bouquet low, belly sucked in, eye contact with the crowd," I mutter. Holding a bouquet isn't just grabbing it by the stem. Oh no. Apparently there is a correct angle for positioning your bouquet for optimal photos. "I'll be okay once I get this bit over."

"You mean the most important part of the whole day?" Megan sniggers. "The ceremony where you promise to stay with this man for life?

"The bloody walk," I squeak. "Right now, I'd prefer to walk over hot coals."

"Just focus on Tristan," Mum reassures me.

"Ready?" Father Murphy asks me. Father Murphy has flown over to marry us. Tristan's mother was delighted when she found out I was a Catholic. I think it's my main selling point.

No.

"As long as you have no secrets from this man, you'll be fine." He winks.

What the hell? What does that mean? Since when do priests wink? Is he talking about the copious volumes of premium bamboo rolls I've stolen from Madison Legal?

"Ready." I nod, taking my mum's arm. We've been practising to make sure our pacing matches.

Father Murphy opens the double doors to the chapel and the music starts. The music. The 'here comes the bride' music that sounds so surreal when you are the bride.

He walks up the aisle like it's just another day in the office, followed by Megan and Sarah.

Inside, all our friends and family are watching the bridal procession.

Now it's my turn. My final steps as an unmarried woman. Head up, check. Bouquet low, check. Belly sucked in, check. Keep it together, Elly.

Please God. This is your gaff. Do me a favour and make sure I don't fall.

I enter the church wearing ivory bridal shoes that do not feel worn-in.

There is a 180-degree turn of every head to look at me. I'm at risk of a full blown anxiety attack.

Then I see him.

Tristan.

He's wearing a traditional black tuxedo and his slightly wavy hair is slicked back.

When our eyes lock it's the most intense, intimate moment of my life.

He takes my breath away. Not only because of how handsome he looks, reminding me that I'm the luckiest woman on earth.

But because of the way he is looking at *me*.

Like I'm the only thing that matters to him. Like I am his whole world.

There are sixty people watching us, but it's just us.

I don't even notice myself gliding up the aisle; I've lost count of what step number I'm on now.

Emotion floods his face.

Keep it together, Elly.

Sophie and Carlie snap pictures to my right. They are beside some of my new colleagues from Carson Payne LLP. I finished my trainee contract with Madison Legal and now I'm a fully qualified lawyer. I convinced them to move me to the human rights division for the last leg of my training. Carson Payne LLP are smaller than Madison Legal but specialise in human rights, asylum and international protection immigration issues, which is exactly where I want to be. I thought I would never want to leave Madison Legal. It's funny how things change. I'll keep my maiden name professionally. The Kane brand can be a double-edged sword when people find out.

The Croatian side of my family are a few seats up. Tristan and I are going to spend our honeymoon travelling around Croatia stopping off at a gut retreat before we head back to London. That's how I'm so certain about this man. He knows all of me and he loves all of me.

Tristan's side of the chapel looks like a billionaire's convention. London's elite has descended upon Dubrovnik old town, mixed in with his Irish cousins who aren't wearing enough sun block.

Further up, Charlie is attempting to calm one of the twins down while her mother appeases the other. Danny is the best man on the altar beside Tristan. They found out they were having a baby a few months after Tristan and I got together, then they found out that it was two rather than one. Jack and Daniel are on the altar beside Tristan and Danny.

And before I know it, I've reached the altar. Mum lets go of my arm and Tristan takes my hand.

"Hi," my future husband says softly.

"Hi." My voice cracks.

"Are you ready to become Mrs. Kane?"

"*Táim réidh*, Mr Kane," I say in Irish.

I'm ready.

ABOUT THE AUTHOR

Rosa Lucas

Rosa writes steamy, contemporary romance novels with feisty heroines and sexy alpha heroes. She likes her characters to be relatable and flawed with real-world issues and insecurities but always have a happily-ever-after waiting for them.

Her favourites to write are billionaire alphas, age gap romances, workplace romances, enemies to lovers and romantic comedies.

Printed in Great Britain
by Amazon